BROTHERLY LOVE

Fury washed over Sabrina. "I'll do what I bloody well please, and if that includes kissing an old friend—a man I have a strictly brotherly affection for—that's what I'll damned well do."

"That's hardly how you kiss a brother."

"Oh, really? And I imagine with your vast expertise in such matters, you are an expert on how one kisses one's brother?"

Nicholas grabbed her shoulders and yanked her into his arms, her hands trapped flat against his chest. "I have a sister, remember? And this is how one should be kissed by a brother." He brushed his lips lightly over her forehead. A distinctly unfraternal thrill shivered through her. "Or this." He placed a soft kiss first on one cheek, then the other.

She glared up at him and pushed against the hard muscles of his chest. "Very well; now unhand me."

His black eyes gleamed. "I don't think the lesson is quite over yet. A brother should never kiss like this." He skimmed his lips lightly over her eyelids. "Or like this." He feathered kisses down the side of her neck. Her breath caught in her throat.

He stared down at her, his endless gaze drawing closer, melting her defiance, sapping her control. "And never . . ." he kissed the tip of her nose, "ever . . . " he nuzzled her ear, "should a brother kiss like this."

VICTORIA ALEXANDER

the Perfect Wife

LEISURE BOOKS **NEW YORK CITY**

This book is dedicated with love to Ann, Mary, and in memory of Rosemarie—mothers and heroines all.

A LEISURE BOOK®

February 2002

Published by

Dorchester Publishing Co., Inc.
276 Fifth Avenue
New York, NY 10001

ISBN 0-8439-4108-1

Printed in the United States of America.

Visit us on the web at www.dorchesterpub.com.

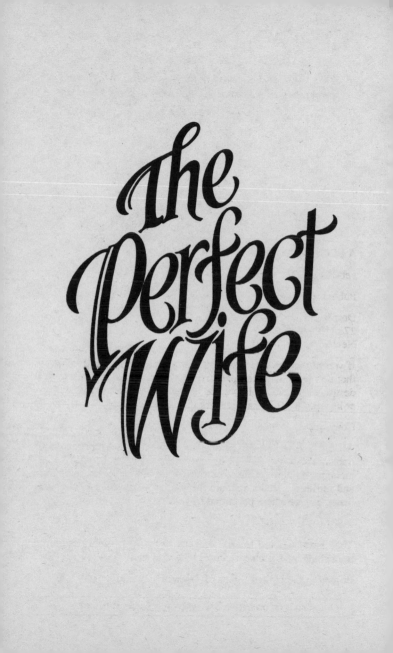

Prologue

1808

Awareness teased the corners of his mind. Damp, dank air weighed heavy on his skin. The salty, rotted scent of the sea assailed his nostrils. Dimly, the roar of the ocean and crash of the waves sounded. Distant . . . hollow. A steady drip splashed and echoed. All in the blackest black. Was this a dream? Or death?

He jerked his head and hot pain lanced through the back of his skull. A gasp escaped his lips, but the ache cleansed his mind. His senses sharpened. His disorientation vanished.

A wide scarf covered his eyes and face and his hands were bound behind his back, his feet tied at his ankles. He tested the bonds. There was only enough give to allow him to touch the rough wooden planks behind and beneath him. He sat propped upright, his head cradled by what he immediately assumed were crates of some type.

That made sense; much of a smuggler's contraband was transported by crate. And only a fool would fail to realize he had discovered the band of smugglers he'd searched for.

Victoria Alexander

Or rather, they had discovered him.

He remembered watching the illegal activity on the beach far below his vantage point on the rocky cliffs. Now that he had finally determined their methods and, more importantly, the location of their operations, he planned to return with reinforcements and catch them in the act. He cursed himself for coming alone, for the arrogance and stupidity that had brought him to this point. Judging by the pain in his head, he'd been spotted and rendered unconscious.

A low murmur of voices caught his attention and he strained to hear. The unmistakable lilt of a woman's voice tempered rough, heavy, male conversation. In spite of his precarious position, a spire of exhilaration shot through him. He had indeed found the band that had long eluded him and other agents of the Crown. Not as large as many smuggling rings, but clever and tenacious and, up to now, invulnerable. And they were led by a woman.

A woman.

Even after weeks of surveillance, of clandestine midnight meetings that brought little of worth, of dressing and living in disguise, he still could not quite believe it. In his world there were only two kinds of women: those meant to be charming ornaments and produce heirs, and those with the appropriate talents for enjoyable nocturnal entertainment. He had considerable experience with both. His pleasant, undemanding wife had obediently provided him with a son and then conveniently died. As for the other kind . . . well, they usually lived up to his expectations.

But this woman defied any of the categories he reserved for the fairer sex. Obviously, she was intelligent. The frustrating fox-and-hounds game he'd played, and lost, was proof of that. She also seemed to elicit the kind of loyalty monarchs expected and generals demanded. In spite of his best efforts, including the making of bribes and threats, not one soul in this rough, tiny seacoast village would give him so much as a morsel of information.

They called her Lady B, and most of what he had learned was more fancy than fact. Try as he might, he could not find a noblewoman in the area who might be the mysterious

8

lady. Grudgingly, he'd developed a certain amount of respect for her and her people. Times were hard and smuggling was an opportunity to put food on the table. Still and all, it was hardly legal. And demoralizing to the efforts to defeat the French as well. But this was a dangerous business, and he could not question her courage. He hoped she was not ruthless as well.

The voices grew louder but remained indistinct. He clenched his teeth in frustration. Whatever he could learn here would only help his pursuit of the smugglers. If he survived.

He sensed movement around him. Hushed voices brushed past. Activity seemed to increase. He tilted his head slightly, a mere fraction, in an effort to decipher the muttering.

"Milady," a low voice rumbled in his direction, "I think our friend has awakened."

"Hold your tongue, man." Another voice sounded impatiently. "We don't want him able to recognize us if he should come upon us later."

"And will there be a later?" he said in a loud, authoritative tone, with all the strength of a man who knew he had nothing to lose.

A ripple of female laughter echoed around him.

"There is always a later, my lord." The feminine voice was low, slightly husky.

It might have been the damp in the air, it might have been the way she always spoke, but he was stunned to note that the voice fired his blood and smart enough to realize it wasn't merely because he was finally in the presence of his quarry. His hunt for this woman had become an obsession. And now revelation struck him. In spite of the impropriety and absurdity of his sudden desire, he wanted nothing more than to take her as his own. Then, he would clap her in irons.

"I fear though . . ." A vague, spicy scent wafted around him. "There will be no later for us."

"Oh?" He arched an eyebrow under the blindfold.

"Alas, my lord." She sighed, a breathy, provocative sound. Her voice seemed to circle him. "You have made life far too difficult for our feeble efforts. Tonight is our final run."

A tentative touch lingered below his right ear. Cool, gentle fingers, light and teasing, traced the faint, silvered scar that ran the length of his neck. Typically, his high collars and cravats disguised the mark. But he was not wearing his usual attire. A delicious shiver ran through him at the unexpected contact.

"A badge of honor, my lord?"

"Merely a boyhood misadventure." He shrugged nonchalantly, struggling within himself to regain control of his heretofore unsuspected response to this woman. "Do not let yourself believe, even if you cease your activity, that I will stop attempting to apprehend you and your men."

She laughed again. "You are no fool, my lord. You have proved that full well in our little game these past weeks. And I am certain you have already realized, if we discontinue our operation, there is very little chance you will discover us. Ever."

She was right. If the smugglers disbanded, they would fade into the fabric of village life. They would disappear. Frustration swelled within him. She would disappear. His mission would fail. And failure was the one thing he could not allow.

"I warn you," he said, a growl in his voice, "I do not accept defeat easily."

"And I, my lord—" Her breath, fragrant with an intoxicating promise, caressed his face. "—do not accept defeat at all."

She paused, and he wondered at the tension between them. Wondered if she sensed it as well. He caught her breath once more upon his upturned face and, faintly, her lips brushed against his. He started, then involuntarily strained toward her. Her lips parted and her tongue teased the inner edge of his mouth. Desire pounded through his veins. His mind worked feverishly. What kind of woman kissed so boldly as this? Perhaps . . . it no longer mattered.

Her lips withdrew and disappointment surged through

him. Her presence still lingered on his face and her voice was soft.

"I regret more than ever, my lord, that there will be no later for us." She sighed. "Only now, only this moment."

Her voice turned brisk. "And we have much to finish this night. So, my charming prisoner, I will bid you *adieu.*"

"What do you—" In his last moment of consciousness before succumbing to the darkness brought by the crash of something on his head for the second time that night, he too regretted . . . there would be no later.

Chapter One

1818

"Bloody hell."

Sabrina Winfield muttered under her breath and glared with distaste at the offensive paperwork spread before her.

Absently, she drummed her fingers in a rhythmic tattoo on the well-worn, highly polished mahogany desk and scanned the papers littering the desktop once again, hoping to find something, anything, that would make a difference. Already she knew full well all hope was futile. The accounting sheets and investment reports painted a dismal picture.

"Damnation." She groaned and glanced quickly at the closed door to her library. It would not do to have the servants or, worse yet, her daughter hear her talking like a common woman of the streets. But in all her years of living the proper life expected of someone of her social status, she had never found anything quite as satisfying as a good curse. Privately, of course.

Sabrina returned her attention to the documents before her. She had enough funds left to live a respectable, if somewhat frugal life. Unfortunately, *frugal* was not a word she took to easily.

It was all that idiot Fitzgerald's fault. She should have known the little pig-faced man who slobbered all over her hand in lieu of a greeting would spell disaster. Why she had let him handle her financial affairs when his father died was beyond comprehension. Obviously a misplaced sense of loyalty.

The elder Fitzgerald was a man with a solid business head and a shrewd eye. He discreetly handled her affairs for nearly nine years before his inconvenient demise, and built her initial investment into a substantial, comfortable, and even excessive fortune. And, in spite of her gender, he listened to her suggestions and wishes and accepted her financial acumen. But in the short year since his death his fool of a son had whittled her funds down to the meager accounting now laid out before her.

A nagging voice at the back of her mind pointed out, perhaps, it was not entirely the junior Fitzgerald's fault. Oh, she'd taken a firm hand with her investments as usual at first, but her attention slackened. Reluctantly, she admitted she had not kept the close eye out she should have, distracted by her daughter's coming out season. A season on which she had squandered far more than was prudent.

Still, she thought stubbornly, it was money well spent. Belinda deserved the best. Besides, the gamble had paid off handsomely. Belinda was in love and wished to marry a charming young man from a well-respected family. He was heir to an impressive title, with a family fortune both immense and sound; Sabrina had made discreet inquiries just to make sure. She did not want her child's life ever to be threatened by the need for money and the lack of it. Not the way hers once was.

The marriage that would ensure her daughter's future was exactly what made her present financial difficulties so distressing. A wedding meant a dowry commensurate with Sabrina and her late husband's social position, a dowry worthy of the dowager Marchioness of Stanford. Hah! An impressive title, but that and half a crown would get her a hired carriage ride around the city and little else.

She had no idea how to raise the kind of funds necessary for an impressive dowry. There were very few acceptable ways for a woman to make money. Her own marriage would, of course, solve all her problems. Most, if not all, the women she knew married with wealth and rank in mind. Still, marrying strictly for monetary gain seemed somehow distasteful. She certainly hadn't married for money the first time. Life would have been much easier if she had. Her daughter would not marry for money either. Still, the presence of substantial wealth, while not a requirement, was most definitely a delightful bonus.

Sabrina sighed and pushed her chair away from the desk. There would be time enough to return to her vexing financial problems tomorrow. Time enough to deal with the panic threatening to rise within her. Tonight she and Belinda were to attend a soiree at her future son-in-law's. Both parents had already given permission for the match, even though it was yet to be formally announced. Sabrina expected tonight to finally meet his father.

The elusive Earl of Wyldewood was well known in government and diplomatic circles, but he had never crossed Sabrina's path and she admitted to a certain amount of curiosity about the man. Gossip told her he had a sizable reputation with women and was considered something of a rake. Sabrina refused to hold that against him. After all, her husband had been a well-known rake before their marriage, and everyone knew reformed rakes made the best husbands. She liked the son; surely she would like the father as well.

Rising to her feet, she cast one last disgusted glance at the pages littered over the desk. Sabrina shook her head in irritation and prayed all would work out. Her natural optimism rose and she smiled. All had certainly worked out the last time she'd faced a financial crisis this severe. But the solution she'd found those many years ago would not serve now. Realistically, she could not take up smuggling again.

Her reluctance had nothing to do with the illegality of the activity. It was not a question of morality or conscience. Sabrina was, above all, a realist. With the war over, and most goods flowing freely, there was no real call for smuggling.

A pity, really. Today there was simply no money in it.

Nicholas Harrington, Earl of Wyldewood, gazed around his ballroom with equal parts dismay and curiosity. He was usually more than comfortable in a social setting. But this was his own home, and the scale of preparation necessary for such an event seemed massive. Fortunately, he had the able assistance of his sister Wynne.

If he had a wife, surely he could relax, confident in his mate's ability to handle the social niceties. His sister had pointed out that fact with increasing frequency in the two years since the death of their father and Nicholas's inheritance of the title.

Reluctantly, he admitted she was right. The appropriate wife would be an asset if he continued his interest in government and politics. And should he ever wed again, he had no doubt his countess would be a polished hostess. It was a requirement of the position.

But Nicholas had no real desire to marry. He hadn't particularly wanted a wife the first time and was not anxious for his son to wed either. The boy was barely one and twenty, and there was plenty of time for marriage. But Erick insisted he was in love. And what could Nicholas say? He freely and proudly admitted he had never been touched by that particular emotion, so he could not quite understand. He was surprised, however, and touched, to discover the boy's ardor moved him more than he suspected possible. That, coupled with a vague sense of guilt for not having been present while his son had grown up, made him consent to the match.

Nicholas surveyed the rapidly filling ballroom. He had already met Erick's young lady and found her more than acceptable. Tonight he would meet the mother. Nicholas knew a great deal about the lady, thanks to the work of a discreet investigator paid a substantial sum to supply accurate information and keep his mouth sealed.

He spotted his son on the other side of the room, and an

15

involuntary smile creased his lips. Intelligent and honorable, Erick was a son a man could claim with pride. Nicholas regretted he deserved little credit for that. The boy had been raised by Wynne and his damnable grandfather. Although, he grudgingly admitted, the old man had done a good job.

Erick caught his gaze and raised a hand in greeting. He escorted two woman. The lithesome blonde on his right was his fiancée, Belinda, a lovely, ethereal creature. On his left was a somewhat shorter woman, blond as well and, even at a distance, extremely well proportioned. Nicholas wondered if this was perhaps a sister he was not aware of.

The trio drew closer, and Nicholas caught his breath. The lady was indeed a beauty. A bit older than Belinda, but startlingly lovely. A serene smile played across shapely, inviting lips. Her eyes flashed a rich emerald.

They stopped before him. She was small and came barely to his shoulder. In spite of her stature she seemed to almost shimmer with suppressed energy. He glanced away quickly. No one stared in their direction. The music played on. Conversations continued.

Amazing. Was he the only one who noticed the subtle power of her presence? Did he alone sense a change in the very air around them? Did excitement and mystery call out to him and no other?

Inevitably, his gaze was drawn back to hers, and he lost himself in the glittering green depths of her eyes. Depths that spoke of promises and passion and, at the moment . . . amusement.

"My lord." Her voice was low and husky, sensual and inviting. An unexpected shiver ran through him at the sound. "Have I done something to cause you to stare so intensely?"

He reached for her hand and brought it to his lips. His gaze never left hers, and his earlier sense of discomfort vanished. Confronted by a beautiful woman, he had no lack of confidence. In many circles he was considered an expert.

"Why no, my lady, I am simply struck with awe in the presence of such beauty."

She laughed, a delightful, honeyed sound that wrapped

around him and settled in his soul.

"Father," Erick said, "may I present Belinda's mother, Lady Winfield, the dowager Marchioness of Stanford."

Nicholas started. This magnificent creature was the lady he had investigated. His reports had mentioned she was considered a great beauty at her first season nearly twenty years ago, but nothing he read on paper could have prepared him for meeting her in the flesh. Cool, creamy, porcelain flesh. She wrinkled her nose at the word *dowager,* and he thought the gesture charming. Perhaps this marriage was not a mistake after all.

So this was Erick's father, Sabrina thought. He was far more handsome than she'd been told. Extremely tall, with hair and eyes nearly as black as the evening coat that stretched across broad, muscular shoulders. A flirtatious smile lingered over full, sensual lips. An aura of strength and · power surrounded him. Intriguing, beckoning, irresistible.

She gazed into his eyes. It was obvious he was taken with her. The realization gave her a certain amount of satisfaction. Even at the advanced age of six-and-thirty she could still turn a man's head. She couldn't resist angling her face slightly and deepening her smile, a gesture certain to reveal the dimple in her cheek.

"So, my lord, I gather we are to be family soon?"

"Family?" He appeared startled, then quickly recovered. "Oh yes, of course, family."

He glanced at his son and future daughter-in-law. "And what a charming family it shall be with two such lovely ladies as its newest members."

"Oh, Erick, look. Isn't that Anne Hartly?" Belinda nodded at a young woman across the room. "Mother, do you mind?"

"Of course not, darling. You two go along." She glanced demurely at Nicholas. "I feel I'm in very good hands."

The two young people headed toward their friends, and Sabrina's gaze followed. "They seem so very young."

"You are not so terribly old yourself," Nicholas said, a note of appreciation sounding in his voice.

17

Sabrina snapped her gaze back to his. "Age is such a relative thing, is it not? When I was their age I thought someone as old as I am now was ancient. Now they are grown, yet I see them as children. And I still feel as I did then. My emotions are no different now than they were in my first season."

Nicholas stared down at her. "I regret having missed that first season."

The intensity of his words gave Sabrina pause. Abruptly, she realized that without thinking, she'd dropped her well-practiced guard. It was indeed past time to return to the meaningless, flirtatious banter with which she was so skilled.

She lowered her gaze. "I fear, my lord, we are becoming far too serious for an event such as this." Sabrina flashed him her most polished smile. "And I, for one, refuse to be serious when I hear music. I would much prefer to dance."

Nicholas's smile echoed her own. "I can think of nothing I would rather do."

He took her in his arms and drew her onto the dance floor. A waltz played, and Sabrina noted how well, how easily, how naturally her body fit to his. His hand against her back, strong and sure, the muscles in his arm, solid beneath her touch. The heat of his body enveloped her in a heady haze of beckoning desire.

Whirling around the room, gazing into his eyes, she wondered at the immediate attraction between them. Something about this man, some indefinable quality threatened to break down her defenses and leave her vulnerable and unguarded. It was almost as if they weren't strangers. Almost as if destiny had taken a hand here. Almost as if it were magic.

Magic.

She'd found magic once before in the arms of her husband. Or what passed for magic then. When Jack Winfield swept her into his arms during that first season so long ago she'd lost herself in the passion and fire of a rake who had eyes only for her.

Magic.

She'd nearly found magic again, three times in the thirteen years since his death. Three men selected for the hint, the tinge, the trace of magic in their look and their touch and their smiles. While each in his turn vowed undying love and all had asked her to wed, true magic remained elusive, lingering just out of reach. She gently broke off each romance and somehow managed not to break their hearts as well. Sabrina matter-of-factly suspected all still harbored a secret hope for more.

Magic.

Now, in the arms of this man, the promise of something wonderful was powerful, almost tangible. Never had she known a pull this strong. Could he be the one to return the magic to her life? The one to finally cure her restless desires? The one to make her complete? She would settle for nothing less.

But what would he want in return? The unexpected query flashed through her mind, and she nearly stumbled in midturn.

His brows drew together in a concerned frown. "Is there a problem?"

"A simple misstep." She tossed him a reassuring smile. A man like this would expect—nay, *demand*—a woman to be the epitome of social correctness. To be placid and pliable. To yield and obey. A man like this would expect her to be exactly what she appeared to be, to live up to the lie she lived every day.

No. No matter the attraction, the spark, the simmering desire, it would not do to become involved with this man. She could not run the risk of allowing him to discover the woman carefully buried beneath the layers of acceptable behavior. A woman hidden for nearly a decade. She could not risk his disapproval.

He held her daughter's fate in his hands. With one word he could put an end to the marriage plans. That she could not, would not, allow. No, regardless of this compelling and unexpected attraction, Nicholas Harrington must remain no more than the father of her daughter's fiancé. No more, no less.

The music drifted to a close. Reluctantly but firmly, Sabrina stepped out of Nicholas's arms. She needed distance between them, physically and emotionally, and quickly. Already she'd allowed him to glimpse much more than he should.

She glanced up at him, the passion he aroused carefully concealed beneath a calm exterior, the serene mask again firmly in place. "We must speak in depth about the marriage arrangements at some point. Right now, I am certain you will want to see to your other guests, so I shall not detain you any longer."

She nodded politely and turned away, allowing him no time to respond. But she could not miss the puzzled look on his face and the way his dark eyes smoldered.

Sabrina refused to look back.

Accepting a glass of champagne from a passing footman, her hand trembled. Why did this stranger effect her so deeply? There was no logical reason for it. Sabrina shook herself mentally and headed for the room reserved for card playing. A relaxing game was an excellent idea. After all, tonight as usual, she'd had more than enough practice in the fine art of bluffing.

Nicholas eyed her hasty retreat and annoyance surged through him. Why on earth had the woman cut him like that? Had he done something to offend her? It had seemed as though she was enjoying their flirtation as much as he, at least initially.

Of course; he should have realized it sooner. His suggestive manner had obviously scared her. According to his investigators she was a quiet and reserved woman who ventured into society no more than necessary. Her name had been linked with several men through the years, but no hint of scandal, no improper gossip accompanied the talk. As best he could tell, she had lived a spotless life since returning to London after her husband's death.

A slow smile spread across his face. She was not merely beautiful but well-bred, reserved, even a touch shy. He pushed aside a vague sense of disappointment. Somehow, he'd instinctively expected more from her.

When his gaze first met hers, he swore he'd glimpsed a

spark, a spirit that stole his breath. But apparently his first impression was misleading, his original reaction in error.

He observed her elegant glide across the room, the graceful way she selected a glass. Nicholas narrowed his eyes thoughtfully. In spite of her relationships with men during her widowhood, and who could fault her for that, she was both discriminating and discreet; she might be exactly what he needed. A presentable partner to further his career. An attractive ornament to display on his arm. A perfect wife.

His smile widened to a grin. Such a countess would not inconvenience him at all. She would have little effect on his well-ordered life, his private pursuit of pleasure. And he had not forgotten his immediate attraction to her. Although, a distant voice in the back of his mind pointed out, this was not the kind of woman he usually desired. She was pleasant and pretty, but in spite of his initial reaction she had no real zest, no promise of excitement, no sense of impending adventure. How could his initial instinct be so wrong?

He ignored the tiny doubt. Ignored the questions and concerns that drifted through his mind. He turned to speak to newly arriving guests and firmly pushed away the nagging, nibbling voice.

A perfect wife . . . how frightfully dull.

A scant twenty minutes later Sabrina was immersed in a pleasurable and undemanding game of whist with three elderly lords. A good player, steady and unemotional, she never wagered a lot, and never more than she could afford to lose. In spite of that, or perhaps because of it, she typically left the table with more than she'd started.

The winnings were often fairly paltry. The real prizes were the bits and pieces of financial chatter, nuggets of investment strategy and tidbits of political gossip dropped by men who assumed she was uninterested or bored. Men who assumed her lovely, composed facade hid an equally vacant mind. Who assumed she neither cared for nor listened to their talk.

During these games Sabrina likened herself to a fine hunting hound, whose rapt attention was only captured when a red fox was in sight. There were very few red foxes here tonight. The conversation meandered aimlessly, the words drifting past her unheeded. Sabrina kept enough of her mind on the cards to play respectably, but allowed her thoughts to wander to a tall, powerful figure with piercing black eyes.

"Isn't that right, my dear?"

"Pardon me?" Sabrina's attention jerked back to the table, and Lord Eldridge at her right.

He cocked his bushy eyebrows in mild reproof. "I was commenting on the news of a proposed expedition to the Americas to search for Spanish treasure. Surely you've heard of it?"

"Of course." Sabrina vaguely remembered having read something about a hunt for sunken treasure in the West Indies, possibly a Spanish galleon wrecked centuries ago. It was not the kind of investment that would have caught her eye. Too speculative, too risky and far too expensive, without a guaranteed return.

"Well," Eldridge said, "I was just saying that one needn't go halfway around the globe to find treasure. No one ever did recover Napoleon's gold from that shipwreck off the coast of Egypt. Twenty years ago, now I think." His gaze searched her face curiously. "But of course, you'd know more of that than us, would you not?"

Sabrina frowned in puzzlement. "I'm afraid I have no idea what you're talking about."

"Nor do I, Eldridge." Lord Connelly cut in impatiently. "What are you trying to say?"

Eldridge sighed in obvious exasperation. "Very well. I can't believe you have all forgotten this story." He glared at the three sets of eyes staring at him expectantly.

"Get on with it, man." Lord Rowe said tersely. "We're waiting."

Eldridge huffed and grumbled something under his breath before leaning back in the attitude of a veteran storyteller with a good tale.

"It was, as I said before, twenty years ago, in 1798. Napoleon's troops were in Egypt. A ship set sail from France carrying gold for payroll and various other expenses. It

22

never made it, sunk by one of our own fine ships. According to the stories, officers on board managed to get the gold to land before the ship went down and hid it. Buried it, most likely. Probably planning to return later and claim it for themselves.''

He surveyed the trio with the air of a man who has an audience in the palm of his hand. "And you, my dear," he paused, lengthening the dramatic moment, "you know where it is."

"I?" Sabrina laughed. "How on earth would I know where French gold hidden in Egypt is?"

"Yes indeed, Eldridge." Connolly frowned. "How would Lady Stanford have that knowledge?"

"Because . . ." The gleam in Eldridge's eye matched the triumphant flourish in his voice. "Your husband won the information in a card game."

"Jack?" Sabrina stared. "When?"

"It was a few years before his death." Eldridge flushed, apparently abashed at the mention of her husband's demise. "If memory serves, the game took place at his club; my club as well, you know. Someone at his table wagered a letter he claimed contained detailed directions to the gold. I believe it was passed to him from a French sailor."

Eldridge paused and drew together his bushy brows thoughtfully. "Or maybe it was a French expatriate. At any rate, everyone thought it was a colossal joke." He glanced at the men around the table, as if sharing a male secret. "You know how things like this are. Stanford won the pot. Everyone assumed the letter was fake. Stanford even joked about it."

He turned toward Sabrina and frowned. "You did not know any of this, my dear?"

Sabrina shook her head. "I'm not sure. It sounds vaguely familiar, but . . ." She shrugged her shoulders in a gesture of helpless femininity. "I really don't know what ever became of this mysterious letter. And, although the idea of hidden gold is an intriguing one, it is too far-fetched to dwell on." She tossed the trio an engaging smile. "Now, my lords, shall we continue our game?"

The men settled back into play and Sabrina joined them with a show of modest enthusiasm. But her mind was far from the cards in her hand.

Directions to a fortune. The very thought triggered a rush through her veins such as she had never thought she'd feel again. The longing for adventure buried years ago raised its seductive head. The lure of excitement pulled her as strongly as any tide.

If indeed such a letter existed, it would be the answer to her financial problems. The quest alone would fill a need she hadn't realized until this moment still lingered within her.

In a split second Sabrina reached a decision: When she returned home she would find that letter if she had to take the house apart brick by brick. And when she found it, in spite of the difficulties, the problems, the obstacles, she would head for Egypt.

And she would permit absolutely nothing to stand in her way.

Chapter Two

Belinda fairly danced down the hall, her feet barely skimming the floor. It was an exceptional morning, following on the heels of a truly marvelous evening, spent with an absolutely wonderful man. Erick was all she had ever dreamed of, and she thanked the stars every day for a mother who allowed her to make her own choice of a husband instead of arranging a marriage for her.

Last night Erick's father said he would put the announcement of their engagement in the *Times* at the beginning of the week. Excitement thrilled through her at the thought. Soon it would be official for all the world to see.

Belinda approached her mother's door and knocked lightly. No response. She rapped again, louder and sharper this time. Still no reply. Gently, she pushed the door open.

The room stood in perfect order. Nothing was out of place. No discarded ball gown from last night lay strewn across a chair. No jewelry and baubles scattered carelessly over the dresser. No stockings or slips littered the floor. In an ordinary household that would have been to the credit of a lady's maid. But Belinda's mother tended to dismiss her maid as soon as she'd been helped out of whatever exquisite gown she'd selected for the evening. She claimed the immediate solitude well worth the inconvenience of waiting until morning for her room to be put in order.

Belinda took it all in with one swift glance. What disturbed her most was her mother's bed. It was turned down, as if ready for its occupant to retire for the evening. Exactly the way it had looked when she bid her mother good night. It hadn't been touched. Obviously, no one had slept between its sheets.

Where was her mother? And if she hadn't slept here last night, where *had* she slept? She'd seemed preoccupied at the party, but Belinda had disregarded that; her mother was typically reserved and quiet in public. Belinda frowned and hurried down the hall, passed the adjoining room, the chamber that was once her father's. She glanced absently at the open door and gasped, stopping dead in her tracks.

The room looked like the aftermath of a devastating windstorm. Every drawer was open, some completely pulled out of dressers and tossed carelessly on the floor. Clothes were heaped in haphazard mounds. The doors of the wardrobe hung open, its contents scattered throughout the room. Even the feather bed and mattress lay sprawled betwixt the bed and the floor.

What on earth was going on? Had they been robbed? Fear crept to the edges of Belinda's mind. She swallowed a rising sense of dread and sped through the hall, hitting the stairway nearly at a run, flying down the steps to pull up short at the closed door of her mother's library. She hesitated for a moment; this was, after all, her mother's private sanctuary. Belinda took a deep breath, squared her shoulders and, gripping the knob, firmly opened the door.

The sight here was little different than upstairs. The room looked as if a giant hand had picked it up, shaken it roughly and casually tossed it down. Half the library shelves stood empty. Books covered the carpet, escaping from careless piles to devour unsuspecting floor space. Papers littered the room, white punctuation marks liberally scattered over everything in their path.

Her mother sat perched on a desk amid the wreckage. She still wore the gown she'd had on the night before, now wrinkled and dusty. Belinda narrowed her eyes in puzzled concern and studied her mother, impatiently picking up a book. She flipped through the pages, then grabbed the offending volume by its spine and shook it viciously. Belinda couldn't quite catch the words her mother mumbled in obvious frustration before she tossed the volume behind her and selected another.

"Mother, what has happened here? What are you doing?"

Sabrina's gaze flew to her offspring's, surprise scrawled across her dust-smudged face. She wrinkled her nose in a habitual gesture that had broken more than one man but made no impact on her daughter.

"Spring cleaning?" she said.

Belinda sighed in annoyance. She was one of the few people who knew of her mother's rather unique sense of humor, her way of looking at the world around her. Usually, it was a quality Belinda appreciated, even if she found it somewhat puzzling. But not today.

"Mother, I want to know what you are doing. Why you have ripped apart two rooms." She eyed her mother sharply. "It is just two, isn't it?"

Sabrina arched an eyebrow, an amused smile on her lips. She hopped off the desk and brushed an errant cobweb from her ravaged gown. "Yes, my darling, it is just two. However, I cannot guarantee there will not be more."

"Why?" Belinda wailed, and asked for the third time, "What are you doing?"

Sabrina gestured vaguely at the room around her. "Looking for something that is apparently misplaced. Or well hidden," she added under her breath.

"Well, I certainly hope you find it before you pull the entire house down around our ears."

Sabrina's gaze shot to hers, and a sinking sensation in the pit of her stomach warned Belinda that she had just stepped over the bounds of mother-daughter behavior.

Her mother spoke in a voice quiet and controlled, and the

knot in her stomach tightened.

"Belinda, first of all, this is my home, and if I wish to pull it down around our ears, I shall do just that. Secondly, I am the parent here, not you, and I do not wish to be addressed as if the positions were reversed."

"Oh, Mother, I know and I'm truly sorry." Belinda's eyes filled with contrite tears. "It's just that when I saw the room upstairs and now this, and you hadn't slept in your bed and . . ."

"It's all right, darling." Sabrina crossed the room and put her arm around her child. Gently she steered Belinda toward the door. "And nothing to be concerned about. However, I think you should know that I may have to leave London for a while."

Belinda's mouth dropped open in shocked alarm. "What do you mean? Where are you going?"

"Oh, here and there. Visiting, seeing the sights, attending to a minor matter," Sabrina said, her manner vague and elusive, all the while continuing to edge Belinda to the door. "It really is nothing to worry about. In spite of appearances, your mother is quite capable of taking care of herself."

Mother and daughter stood toe-to-toe in the doorway. "You run along and don't let my activities concern you. You just concentrate on that charming young man and what a wonderful life you will have together." Sabrina drew back and gave Belinda the tiniest shove into the hall. "I am not quite finished here, so we shall continue this discussion later. Good morning."

The door shut gently but firmly, leaving Belinda gaping at its paneled face. For a moment she could do nothing but stare. Bewildered, she considered her mother's words. They simply didn't make sense.

Why would she leave London so abruptly, so mysteriously? It was not at all like her to be impulsive and secretive. Belinda knew her mother better than anyone, and while she realized there was far more to her than she revealed to most, she had never done anything like this before, tearing the house apart and announcing an unplanned departure. What had come over her?

Something was definitely amiss. Belinda glared at the library door, then turned and headed back upstairs for paper and pen. She had no intention of letting her mother take off for God knows where. Not if she could help it.

She snatched a delicate leaf of stationery from the lady's desk in her room and quickly penned a note. Belinda certainly could not stop her mother on her own, so she did the only thing she could under the circumstances.

She sent for Erick.

Sabrina rested her back on the closed door and pushed a stray lock of hair away from her face. She simply could not tell Belinda what she searched for or what she planned to do when she found it.

In the first place, the child had no inkling of their financial difficulties. And secondly, Sabrina had done an excellent job of raising Belinda to take her place in society, to assume her birthright as the daughter of a marquis. Brought up in the proper surroundings, given the proper education and training, with the expectation of assuming the proper position in life, Belinda would never understand how her mother could even consider searching for something so ludicrous as lost treasure.

Perhaps she had done too good a job. The child was beautiful and charming, with all the social graces, but she didn't seem to have much of an imagination. The reckless streak inherent in both her mother and father appeared to have bypassed Belinda completely. Realistically, as a concerned and loving parent, that was all for the good, but occasionally it would have been nice to have a daughter with whom one could share one's more outrageous, even scandalous, dreams. However, there was little she could do about it now.

Sabrina stepped away from the door and surveyed the library. Even when Jack was alive it had been her own private place. He thought of it simply as the kind of room a man of his position ought to have. But from the first Sabrina loved it. Loved the dark wood shelves reaching heavenward, flanking the floor-to-ceiling bowed window. Loved the gray marble mantelpiece and the deep red of the walls. Loved the snug warmth and comfort that seemed to surround and soothe her whenever she stood amid its confines. Even the scent of books and leather and wisdom called to her.

And Sabrina was grateful to have it. Jack inherited the town house years before their marriage, and on his death she discovered it was virtually the only thing he owned free and clear.

The letter had to be here, if indeed he had saved and hidden it. This, and Jack's bedchamber, were the only rooms that had not been redecorated in the last decade. The letter would have been found years ago if it had been secreted anywhere else in the house.

If it isn't all a joke, an annoying voice in the back of her mind chimed rudely. Sabrina ignored the thought. Jack never quite grew up, never quite accepted the responsibilities of adulthood and, real or a hoax, the mere idea of a lost treasure would have appealed to him. She was certain he would have kept the letter, if only for the spirit of the quest.

But where? She clenched her hands in frustration. This willy-nilly search would get her nowhere. She had to take this logically, rationally and methodically. Assess the possibilities and proceed one step at a time.

Sabrina drew a calming breath and turned toward the wall to her left. Paintings covered the crimson surface; Winfield family portraits, landscapes, still lifes, most of them with only sentimental value. Could the letter be hidden behind one of them? Not a far-fetched possibility, but probably not quite clever enough to suit Jack's sense of humor. And none of the paintings touched on the theme of treasure or gold or even Egypt.

She turned to face the bookshelves, now half empty, their contents lying scattered on the floor. So far, her search here had been futile. Was there a volume still untouched that held his secret? Was a clue concealed in the gold-scripted title on its spine?

The fireplace dominated the third wall, its simple, classic lines revealing no obvious hiding place. Her gaze strayed upward to the portrait of Jack centered over the mantel. His bright blue eyes danced in his strong face, the unruly quality of his golden blond hair captured by the artist. The slight, amused smile playing forever on his lips.

"Jack." She sighed. "Why couldn't you have made this easy for me? God knows nothing else was easy after you died."

Sabrina shook her head and smiled back at the painting. There had been a time when she couldn't smile at the thought of her husband. When she raged and screamed until her voice grew hoarse at his lack of foresight in leaving her practically penniless. Sabrina had come to grips with those feelings years ago, and if she never quite forgave him, with the passage of time she at least understood him a little better. She gazed at the portrait. Could the letter be hidden behind his painting? Concealed behind his cocky smile, his laughing eyes?

So far she had Jack's portrait, the other paintings and the remainder of the books left to search. And there was still the furniture. Her cozy library held only the desk and its chair, plus a worn wing chair near the fireplace and her chaise longue. She studied the pieces with a critical eye. All looked their age and should have been replaced years ago. But they were as much a part of this room as the bookshelves and mantel.

Her gaze lingered on the couch, which beckoned seductively. Weariness slammed into her. It wouldn't hurt to lie down for a few moments. She'd been up all night, and if her head wasn't clear, she'd never find that bloody letter.

Sabrina sank into the tufted comfort. Through the years her form had left its impression in the worn, scarlet upholstery, and the chaise conformed to her curves like a velvet caress. Her eyes drifted closed.

She'd thought about Jack more in the last few hours than she had in a long time. Now, she remembered how he had bought her this piece. The couch was one of the few gifts from him she hadn't had to sell after his death. Even her jewelry had had to go.

Sabrina hovered somewhere between awareness and oblivion and the years rolled away. She remembered how Jack presented her with the couch and ceremoniously declared the library her own personal kingdom. She snuggled deeper. Memories wafted through her mind. He said, when she reclined on it, she reminded him of Cleopatra. She smiled to herself, and coherent thought drifted farther away.

Jack always said that on the chaise she looked like a queen . . . like the queen of the Nile . . .

The queen of the Nile.

She bolted off the chaise, immediately alert, exhaustion forgotten. Sabrina stared at the unsuspecting couch. Could it be? Was it possible?

Swiftly, she ran her hands along the serpentine lines and the curled head, down its velvet length, around to the carved feet. She poked in each seam, every tufted crevice. She prodded and probed every point where clawed wooden feet joined the frame. She perused every surface, examined every inch.

Nothing.

Sabrina stepped back and narrowed her eyes in concentration, studying the puzzle. So far there was no indication of any disturbance, no mended tears in the fabric, nothing out of the ordinary. Perhaps if she turned it over and examined the underside . . .

The couch proved far heavier than Sabrina expected. Several minutes of pushing, lifting and tugging left her breathless, but finally the chaise flipped over on its side. One more shove and it toppled onto its back, looking for all the world like a wounded beast begging for mercy.

Sabrina laughed aloud in triumph. Quickly, she examined the underside. A coarse fabric tacked securely at the frame covered the bottom. Thoroughly, she studied every stitched section and every point where wood met material. Just as on the other side, here, too, nothing appeared touched. Jack was no upholsterer, no seamstress. Surely if he had hidden something here it would be apparent. Her momentary sense of triumph vanished, replaced by a surge of disappointment.

"Bloody hell." She gazed with disgust at the innocent chaise. Like a spark amid dry tinder, anger flared in her veins. She glared at the portrait over the fireplace.

"It isn't fair, Jack. I really need that gold. I need it for your daughter and I need it for myself. Damn you, Jack, why does it have to be so bloody hard?''

The smile on his lips lingered unchanged. Frustrated and furious, Sabrina drew back a slippered foot and let it fly. Flesh and bone connected with wood. Pain speared up her leg.

''Yow!'' She clutched her throbbing foot, plopped down on the floor and massaged her aching appendage. ''This is really quite absurd.''

She scowled at the offending couch leg, gasped and stared in stunned disbelief.

Her kick had dislodged the leg from the frame, and it tilted at a slight angle. She leapt up, ignoring the pain in her foot. Gripping the carved wood in both hands, and throwing all her weight behind it, she pushed with every ounce of her strength.

For a long moment nothing happened. Abruptly, the leg gave way. Sabrina sprawled forward on the back of the couch, it's claw foot clutched in her hand.

She tumbled to the floor. Apprehension and excitement battled within her. Carefully, she turned the leg over in her hands to view the hollow end where it had been affixed to the frame. Cautiously, she slid two fingers in the narrow space. The inside did not have the rough feel of wood. Rather it seemed smooth. Smooth, like paper. Her heart hammered in her chest and she forced herself to remain calm. She gently withdrew her fingers and gingerly inched out a rolled leaf of vellum.

Sabrina tossed the leg aside and set the page on the floor. Her hands trembled with the anticipation raging through her. Slowly, she smoothed the curled sheet open. She could scarcely believe her eyes. It was definitely a letter. Definitely old, yellowed with age.

And it was in French.

Chapter Three

"She is not acting at all like herself. She spent all night tearing half the house apart, looking for God knows what, and now she says she's leaving London. Erick, I'm extremely worried."

Belinda paced back and forth in her mother's front salon, Erick's gaze appreciatively following her every move. She was indeed a diamond of the first water, a reigning beauty of the current season. And she was his.

"Have you tried talking to her?" he asked, his mind far busier contemplating the graceful way her hips swayed and the ivory bosom discreetly hidden beneath the day gown than her words.

"Of course I have." Belinda turned concern-clouded sapphire eyes toward him. "I have no idea what she is up to, and she simply refuses to talk to me." She heaved a heartfelt sigh. "Mother treats me like a child still in the schoolroom."

"But what a lovely child," he said under his breath. His gaze lingered on her seductive curves, full and luscious and ripe.

The Perfect Wife

Erick dreamed of the moment he would have the right to explore those curves in detail, to caress the pouting breasts and allow his lips to linger over the recesses of her delectable body. To claim her and teach her and make her in every way his own. So far they had shared but a few kisses, each less chaste than the last, each giving a promise of growing passion hidden beneath her well-guarded innocence. Even now the warm scent of her, an intoxicating blend of perfume and femininity, wafted around him, arousing and tantalizing.

"Erick!" Impatience rang in her voice. "Are you listening to me?" Her eyes flashed blue fire and he wondered what they would flash in the throes of passion.

"Of course." He shepherded his wandering thoughts. "Yes, of course I'm listening. Where is your mother now?"

"In her room. I believe she finally went to sleep late this morning. When she retired to her chamber I think . . ." Belinda's eyes were wide with disbelief, "she was singing!"

He pulled his brows together in a thoughtful frown. "Singing? From what you've said I gather that is not her normal behavior?" She nodded. "Could she be ill, do you think?"

Belinda scoffed. "I doubt it. Neither is she insane, nor is she stupid. I know her far better than anyone. She has always been something of a private person. But she has never acted especially impulsive or heedless of propriety before." She gazed up into Erick's eyes, and instinctively his arms curled around her, drawing her close. A cry caught in her voice. "Oh, Erick, what am I to do?"

This bewitching woman wanted to know what he thought. She turned to him to solve her problem. Erick believed that was as it should be, but, even so, his chest swelled with masculine pride. He would take care of it for her. He would show her he could handle anything.

"If she will not talk to you, perhaps she will speak to someone closer her own age." He smiled into her worried gaze. "If you wish, I could ask my father to have a chat with her. He is well versed in diplomacy. Surely he can determine what is amiss."

She returned his smile with a sigh of relief. "That would be wonderful."

He bent his head, and his lips met hers in a gentle kiss, meant, quite honorably, only to provide comfort. Her breath teased his and spurred his unquenched need. Her lips opened beneath his increasing pressure and his tongue tentatively traced the full, pouting curve of her mouth. She sighed, and her body melted against his. Erick knew he would withdraw momentarily, stifling his desire, marshalling his control, but for now he lost himself in the still forbidden taste of her.

Belinda's eyes closed, and she marveled in the new and unique sensation of his lips on hers. His exploring tongue triggered a wave of odd but delightful shivers starting deep within her core and vibrating outward. A vague desire for something more floated through her, and her body molded itself closer to his. What that something more was, she had no idea.

Locked in his embrace, at this moment all thought of her mother's behavior vanished, obscured beneath a haze of mysterious and elusive desire.

Sabrina tugged on the bellpull by her bed and impatiently awaited the arrival of her butler. She'd slept soundly after translating the letter and was now eager to set her plans in motion. The directions to the gold were both concise and clever. It was no wonder the treasure had never been located. It did bother her that she had only the second page of the missive, and she wondered if there was anything of importance on the first page, anything that would bear on her search. But she waved the thought away. This was all she had, and it would have to do.

Right now, though, she faced a more immediate challenge: Simply getting to Egypt would cost a frightful amount of money. She was by no means destitute, but neither did she have the extra funds such an expedition would require. As much as she hated to do it, as much as the thought distressed her, she would have to sell her jewels.

Sabrina sat down before her dressing table and pulled open the bottom left drawer. A large Italian marquetry box filled the space. She tugged it out and hefted its substantial weight onto the table. With a reverent touch, she opened the lid.

Now this was treasure. She'd bought and paid for every piece herself. Selected every bauble with care. Delighted in every sparkling ruby and every glowing emerald. For the second time in her life Sabrina would have to sell her jewels to ensure survival for herself and her daughter. The sheer panic of those long-ago days lingered in the back of her mind. But now, as then, she squared her shoulders and stifled the fear. The marchioness of Stanford was made of sterner stuff.

Sabrina pulled out strand after glittering strand. Perfectly matched pearls. Diamonds flashing rainbow fire. Sapphires the deep, soulful blue of true love. It was not a particularly extensive collection, but the quality was impeccable.

A discreet knock sounded at the door.

"Come in," she said absently.

"You rang for me, milady?"

Sabrina turned at the familiar voice. "Yes, Wills, please come in and close the door."

Wills complied and stood waiting in an attitude of dutiful expectancy. She eyed him thoughtfully for a moment. No doubt he would not like what she was about to say.

"Wills," her words came slowly and deliberately, "I fear I shall have to leave town for a while." She hesitated, watching warily for any reaction to cross his controlled, expressionless face. "It may be a very long while."

Not a sign, not a quiver, not a twitch broke his solid, country-breed visage. "Smuggling again, milady?"

"Wills!" The shock in her voice failed to hide the smile in her words. "You know those days are long behind me. Besides . . ." She shrugged, and the smile escaped to dance on her lips. "There's no money to be made smuggling these days."

She quirked an eyebrow and nodded toward the door. Wills immediately stepped to it and turned the key in the lock in unspoken understanding. He was the only one in London who knew of her nefarious past. A footman in her great-aunt's house in those days, he had also served as her second-in-command, as her guardian and her confidant. In many ways he still did.

When she'd moved to London she'd brought Wills along, elevating him to the position of butler. He ran her house, made sure her home and her life functioned smoothly. And, at least once a month, the bonds of mistress and servant vanished, and two longtime comrades shared a drink together.

Sabrina moved to her wardrobe and rummaged in the farthest corner for a brandy decanter and glasses. Belinda would be scandalized if she ever learned of this highly improper ritual. Her daughter would never understand that while Wills's birth dictated his station in life, his actions had earned Sabrina's respect and friendship.

She poured a glass, passed it to him, then gestured for him to sit in one of two chairs before the fireplace. Sabrina filled her own glass and settled herself in the remaining chair.

Wills spoke first. "If not smuggling, then what is this unexpected departure about?" It always amazed Sabrina how the years vanished whenever she and Wills relaxed together like this. The confident, capable, imperious butler fell away, and in his stead sat the courageous older man, ever watchful of his young mistress's safety, eager for adventure in his own right.

Sabrina took a deep pull of the pungent liquor and savored the burn cascading down her throat. "Treasure. Gold. Hidden for twenty years and just waiting for the right person to come along." She toasted him with a jaunty gesture. "And that person is me. But . . ." She sighed. "I can't go without money."

She rose and strode to the jewels on the dresser. Regretfully, she tossed them all back in their chest. Silently, Sabrina bid them farewell, then closed the lid with a decisive snap.

She turned to Wills and raised her chin in resignation. "I want you to sell these. It must be done quickly, but try to get a good price for them."

Sabrina cast a mournful glance at the box and handed it to Wills. She sank back in her chair and took another sip of the amber liquid. "I know that surely it's sinful to love things, inanimate objects, the way I love these jewels, but . . . even if I burn in hell for it, I do truly love them."

Wills quickly tossed back a deep swallow of brandy, though not quite quickly enough to mask a choked chuckle.

"Very well." She laughed. "I know I sound absurd, but I had to sell all the jewels Jack gave me. And these I bought myself. With money I earned."

Wills cocked an eyebrow at her words.

"Earned by smuggling, I admit," she said, irritated by his unspoken admonishment, "but earned all the same." She threw one last wistful gaze at the box. "It hardly matters, I suppose. I probably would have had to sell them sooner or later anyway."

Concern creased Wills's face. "Money problems, milady?"

She nodded, wrinkling her nose. "A bit. Oh, we have enough to live on, but there's no money for anything extra. And nothing for a dowry." She leaned forward eagerly. "That's why I have to go after this gold, Wills. It's my only hope."

His eyes narrowed in interest. "Would you be needing any help on this quest?"

Surely the gleam in his eye must match her own. "Life has been fairly dull for us these past ten years, hasn't it?"

He shrugged in simple acknowledgment.

"I can't think of anyone I'd rather have with me, but . . ." She paused and took a deep breath. "I need you here. To keep the house running, to keep an eye on Belinda."

Disappointment flashed across his face and he frowned. "I don't believe it's wise for you to undertake such a venture alone."

"I don't seem to have a great deal of choice," she said impatiently. "It's not as if I can put a notice in the *Times* saying: *'Marchioness seeks companion for treasure-hunting. Previous experience in smuggling or other similar ventures preferred but not required.'* There is no one I can turn to for help with this. And no one I would particularly trust.''

Wills swirled the brandy in his glass. The light flashed off the golden surface, and he studied the liquid for a long moment. Finally, his gaze caught hers.

"There is one," he said quietly.

"One? Who do you—'' Sabrina jerked upright. The meaning of Wills's comment struck her with an almost physical force. Of course; it was perfect. Her spirit leapt. She had not thought of that. Of him. The only real flaw in her plan so far was the difficulty of an unprotected woman traveling alone. This would solve that problem plus answer her need for transportation. Wills's idea was more than likely impossible to execute, but not bad; not bad at all.

"Do you think he'd be willing to help me? It has been a very long time, after all. I have not seen or spoken to him in ten years.''

Wills leaned forward and locked his gaze with hers. "I believe he'd do anything just for the pleasure of your company.'' Heat flushed up her face and he grinned at her discomfort. "The pleasure of your company and a sizable fortune.''

Sabrina ignored the comment and thought for a moment. "I really have no idea where he is. He could be in America or anywhere else in the world. Have you had any contact with him in recent years?''

Wills shrugged. "I still have a few old friends here and there. I'm not completely out of touch. I'll check the docks and try to discover whether he's in England.'' He tossed back the last of his drink and shot her a warning glare. "If we find him, I'll have no objections to this treasure hunt of yours. If we can't, we'll have to think of another way. I won't let you go off by yourself.'' He gave a sharp nod and quickly pulled himself to his feet, once again the ideal butler.

He picked up the jewel box. "I shall take care of this at once.'' He crossed the room, turned the key and left, closing the door quietly behind him.

Sabrina stared at the glass in her hand. Wills's threat didn't bother her. She'd do exactly as she pleased. He knew she wasn't stupid and would not make foolish mistakes. No, he was merely concerned about her safety, an old habit she honestly appreciated.

But he was right: It would all be so much easier with a partner, especially the right partner. A man with whom she could drop her prim and proper facade. A man who recognized that intelligence and courage were not strictly male qualities. A man who expected nothing more from her than the free spirit she had once been, and now, perhaps, would be again. The idea triggered a rush of excitement in her blood that rivaled even the lure of a fortune in gold.

She was more than willing to share the treasure. According to her translation, it was worth at least a half million pounds. More than enough for two.

Oh, yes, a partner would be the perfect answer. If, of course, she could find him.

Nicholas leaned back against the tufted velvet seat of his carriage and wondered for the hundredth time what on earth Lady Stanford could possibly be up to. When his son asked him last night to have a talk with her, it seemed a minor request. Nicholas looked forward to seeing her again, especially since he was more and more convinced she would make an acceptable, even exceptional wife. But the more he pondered her unusual behavior, the more he wondered if indeed she was quite what she appeared to be.

What did he really know about her anyway? Certainly her widowed years here in London had been quiet and discreet. Before then, of course, was a different story. A story familiar to most in the ton.

She and Jack Winfield had run off to Gretna Green a scant week after her come-out. Nicholas believed she was seventeen at the time. Their six-year marriage was fraught with wild living and the flouting of convention. Gossip branded the marquess and marchioness of Stanford outrageous and extravagant. No one was surprised when Stanford died in a carriage accident during an extremely high-stakes race.

The ton generally agreed that her husband's death had changed Sabrina. She'd apparently mourned deeply, secluding herself in the country for a full three years. She and her daughter eventually returned to London, but she did not resume her reckless, fast-paced life, living instead in relative quiet.

Nicholas's carriage pulled up to her town house, and he jumped down. He cast a critical eye on the structure, then blessed it with a nod of approval. It was as acceptable and proper as he'd been led to expect, pleasant enough in a fashionable neighborhood, nothing out of the ordinary.

He climbed the steps and rapped sharply on the door. Within seconds it opened, and a tall, powerfully built man towered before him. A spark of surprise flickered in the man's eyes so briefly, Nicholas assumed he was mistaken.

"May I help you, milord?" The man's deferential tones at once marked him as a servant, no doubt a butler.

"Yes. I'm here to see Lady Stanford."

"And whom shall I say is calling?"

"Lord Wyldewood."

The butler ushered him into the house and escorted him to a small salon. "I shall inform milady you're here."

"Thank you."

The butler nodded and left the room, closing the door firmly behind him.

Odd. The man certainly did not look like a servant. He was built more in the style of a dock worker than a household retainer. Oh, his manner could not be faulted, and his apparel was impeccable, but there was something about him ... Nicholas frowned in puzzled concentration. Somehow, he suspected there was more to this butler than his composed expression would have one believe. Nicholas tried to dismiss the thought, but it nagged at him. The man was simply not the sort of servant he envisioned the serene, reserved Lady Stanford to have.

Wills did his job well. Sabrina's jewels fetched more than enough to finance her quest. And even better, he'd found her old partner as well, or at least her partner's ship. It was set to sail this afternoon, and she was determined to be on it.

Sabrina's small, serviceable portmanteau lay open on her bed. She would not be accompanied by servants and planned to travel as light and as fast as possible. She ran a hand lovingly over the two pairs of breeches and several loose men's shirts already folded in the case. Beside them lay a pair of men's leather boots, butter soft and well worn. Even the look of them gave a promise of adventure, and delicious anticipation shivered through her.

The clothing had been stored untouched for nearly a decade and remained serviceable. She intended to wear men's clothing as much as possible on this trip, for safety and for comfort. As for servants, she would hire what she needed in Egypt.

Sabrina tossed a few day dresses into the case, some undergarments and, as an afterthought, grabbed a shimmering, emerald evening gown from the wardrobe. Extremely daring and the height of fashion, it was her favorite, and brought out the sparkle in her eyes. She couldn't foresee the need for such a dress on this trip; still, it would do no harm to take it along.

Sabrina snapped the case closed and moved to her dressing table. Her gaze skimmed the note she had written to her incompetent solicitor, advising him that Wills would be in full control of the family accounts and her other assets. On impulse, she reached for a pen and scribbled a brief postscript. She selected some of the money from the sale of her jewels, wrapped it in the note and sealed the now bulky packet. The rest of the money she divided between her reticule and hidden pockets she tied beneath the skirt of her dress.

Eager to get underway, Sabrina pulled open her door to find Wills's poised to knock.

"Excellent timing, Wills; my bag is ready. If you would take it downstairs . . ." Sabrina handed him the note for her solicitor. "And give this to that idiot Fitzgerald, and be certain he understands you have complete authority over my finances while I'm away."

Wills lifted an eyebrow. "No message for Lady Belinda?"

Sabrina folded her arms stubbornly and stared at the floor. "We have already said our good-byes." She glanced at Wills. "No doubt she is still weeping in her room?"

Wills nodded. There was no reproach on his face, no censure, no accusation. Even so, a wave of guilt passed through Sabrina.

"She simply could not understand. Everything I've done since her father's death I've done for her. My activities before we returned to London and literally how I've lived my life since have been for her. God knows, I had quite a reputation to live down, and I did it." She glared at him. "And this is for her as well."

"Are you certain?" His quiet tone emphasized the query.

"Oh, I admit, the very idea of this quest has fired the blood in my veins. I feel alive for the first time in years." Sabrina stared defiantly. "But yes, this is for her."

"As you say, milady," Wills said in his perfect butler voice. Sabrina simply hated it when he used that tone with her. She turned and grabbed her reticule.

"You have a guest waiting in the front salon." Wills nodded politely. "Lord Wyldewood."

Sabrina groaned.

"Bloody hell."

Chapter Four

"Lord Wyldewood, how charming of you to call." Sabrina sailed into the room with an outstretched hand and a serene smile that hid the impatience churning within her.

Wyldewood took her hand in his and carried it to his lips. "Lady Stanford."

His lips brushed the back of her hand and his ebony gaze bored into hers. A thrill shot threw her at the look and the touch. What was it about this man that attracted her so? That he could have such an immediate and unwanted effect on her senses disturbed her. And the way his gaze captured hers all the while his lips caressed her hand had an annoying, practiced feel to it that indicated that he did it not only well but often.

She firmly pushed the intruding emotions away and withdrew from his unsettling grasp.

"It is a pleasure to see you again, and so soon, but I must admit I am at a loss as to the purpose of your visit." Sabrina tossed him a pleasant smile, all the while praying he would be both brief and to the point.

"My son asked me to speak with you. I believe at the

request of your daughter.'' Wyldewood surveyed the room casually. "May we be seated?"

"Of course." Sabrina directed him to a chair and then perched on the edge of a brocade sofa. A surreptitious glance at the ormolu clock on the mantel showed she still had time, but not much. This little chat really needed to proceed at a much more than leisurely pace. "I assume they wanted us to discuss the wedding?"

Wyldewood cleared his throat and, for the briefest moment, the self-assured diplomat appeared oddly ill at ease. "Actually, it's about your travel plans."

"My travel plans?"

"Yes. Um, Belinda is very concerned about an unexpected trip you seem to be considering, and she and Erick requested that I speak to you about it."

Sabrina's serene expression never faltered, never betrayed the seething irritation that grew with every word he spoke. "It is extremely kind of you to assist my daughter like this. And it's such a relief to know her future father-in-law will be there when she needs him. However, my plans are personal, relating to private business, and I am not at liberty to discuss them." Sabrina stood, prompting Wyldewood to rise to his feet. "So, I'm afraid your purpose in coming, while thoughtful, is unnecessary."

She beamed up at him, hoping to disarm him with her talk of privacy. Indeed, what well-bred Englishman would dare intrude in a private matter?

"Lady Stanford," Wyldewood's dark brows drew together in a forbidding frown, "if you were a man I would not dream of pushing this matter any farther, but as you are a lady, and one without benefit of male guidance, I feel it is my duty to pursue this."

Sabrina struggled to keep her smile plastered firmly on her face. Struggled not to clench her teeth and ball her fists in tight little knots. Struggled not to tell this pompous, arrogant, sanctimonious ass exactly what he could do with his male guidance.

He bestowed upon her what could only be called a condescending smirk. "As your daughter is about to marry my son, I consider that you as well are becoming a member of my family. And as the head of the family, I'm afraid I simply cannot permit you to depart London with only your vague assertion that your purpose is private.''

His words did not completely shatter her self-control. Sabrina was well used to restraint, well used to dealing with the inherent arrogance of the male of the species and well used to doing just as she wished. She had hidden her emotions behind a composed facade for years, polishing that skill to a high gloss finish. A finish Wyldewood's comments had marred with only a small nick, the merest scratch, a tiny crack, nothing Sabrina could not handle. She drew a deep breath.

''Lord Wyldewood, while I am truly grateful for your consideration, you must understand, I have been without my late husband for thirteen years. In that time, I have lived an independent life without benefit of . . . what was the term you used? Oh, yes—male guidance.'' She flashed him yet another practiced smile. ''And even you must admit, I have succeeded in handling my affairs quite successfully. So, while your concern is appreciated, it is also misplaced.''

She took his elbow and escorted him toward the door. ''I fear my time is extremely limited today. I am set to sail within the hour, so—''

''No!'' Wyldewood interrupted, halting their forward progress, and glared at her with annoyance. ''I am afraid you do not understand. I have no intention of allowing you to sail with or without an appropriate explanation.''

''Really?'' Sabrina stared at him pleasantly. ''I believe you have very little choice in the matter.''

A myriad of expressions played across his face, and Sabrina's irritation turned to smug satisfaction. He had no legitimate control over her actions, no legal rights, and his moral obligation was vague to say the least. Whether he liked it or not, there was nothing he could do to stop her.

''In that case . . .'' his dark eyes smoldered and a trickle of delicious fear shivered through Sabrina, ''. . . I shall simply have to accompany you.''

''What?'' Sabrina blurted. ''I hardly think—I can't believe—'' What on earth was he proposing? She couldn't possibly take him along. It simply would not work. This trip would take months. Months of being together every day, on board ship and in the desert. Could she possibly be around him day after day without revealing her true self, her real feelings? More to the point, could she resist the unexpected temptation this man presented?

Her eyes widened with the impact of the questions hurtling through her head and she stared. Wyldewood looked for all the world like a fox who'd successfully raided the hen house, confident, satisfied and, God help her, triumphant. Few people knew Sabrina well enough to know this was not a wise attitude for him to adopt, guaranteed to inflame her anger, charge her spirit and increase her determination.

She composed herself, tossed him her sweetest look and savored the indecision and doubt that flickered across his face in response. "Very well, then. It's time to leave." She nodded and stepped briskly toward the door, leaving him to trail in her wake.

"Wait!" he called, in a voice well used to issuing commands, a voice used to being obeyed without question.

Sabrina paused and tossed him a glance over her shoulder. "Is there a problem?"

"A problem? Of course there's a problem! I cannot be expected to go traipsing off on some ill-advised voyage without a moment's notice!"

Sabrina turned and favored him with the same patient look she would give a cranky child. "Lord Wyldewood, I do not expect you to go anywhere at all. I do not expect you to accompany me on this trip or anywhere else. I expect you to climb back into your carriage and return to your comfortable home. I further expect you to tell my daughter—and your son, for that matter—that I am a responsible adult, fully capable of handling my own affairs. And lastly, I expect you to understand that regardless of who marries whom, I shall be a member of your family by the tenuous bonds of marriage only.''

She took a deep breath and stared him straight in his

bottomless eyes. "And to me that means you have absolutely no right to tell me what I may and may not do." She nodded pleasantly and stepped into the foyer. Wills stood with her traveling case in hand.

"Very well," Wyldewood said calmly, one step behind her. She turned and gazed up at him. A fist knotted deep in her stomach at the gleam in his eye and the expression on his face. It was the look of a man who had just accepted a challenge. A look, God help her, of a man confident of victory.

"I believe we should be off if we are to sail on time."

Sabrina refused to show her dismay, struggling to maintain a pleasant, aloof expression. Especially when she noted Wills's still holding the portmanteau and realized the men's clothes she'd waited so long to wear again would have to wait much, much longer.

"Wills, please give my bag to Lord Wyldewood. He will be accompanying me." Wills's lips quirked at the corners and amusement flashed through his eyes so swiftly, Sabrina alone noticed. Her back to Wyldewood, she shot the butler a quick scowl. "Take care of everything while I'm gone. I shall post a letter to Belinda as soon as possible."

It was not the good-bye she'd imagined, but with this intruder along, it was the best she could do.

"Wills." Sabrina nodded at her old friend and breezed out the door with an air of confidence, determined not to let Wyldewood's presence effect her quest.

"Wills," Wyldewood echoed, and followed close behind. He assisted her into his town carriage and directed his driver to the docks.

Wyldewood settled in next to Sabrina, and she glanced at his firm, strong profile. His face gave no indications of his thoughts. Was he irritated? Annoyed? At least inconvenienced? She certainly hoped so. It would serve him right. She was definitely irritated, annoyed and inconvenienced enough for the both of them. This was not the adventure she'd envisioned, Sabrina thought with a mental huff, and leaned back in the cushioned seat.

The carriage rolled forward, and Sabrina gazed at the upstairs window of Belinda's room. Her daughter stood behind the glass, holding back the curtains. Sabrina lifted a hand in farewell. Without acknowledgment, the figure at the window let the curtains fall back into place. A lance of pain pierced Sabrina, and she blinked back the tears that sprang to her eyes. She thrust the ache and accompanying guilt away and resolved not to dwell on thoughts of Belinda. She was, after all, doing this for her daughter, to ensure her future.

Wasn't she?

What was this woman up to? Nicholas wondered, studying her lovely face. Her expression was serene now, but he hadn't missed the anguish that touched her lovely features when she'd looked at her daughter's window. What was so important it would take this woman away from the child who obviously meant so much to her? Envy stabbed through him, followed by momentary remorse. What would it be like to care for one's child that much?

Of course he was fond of Erick, even loved him in the reserved way a proper parent should. He simply hadn't been around him much. Hadn't watched him grow up, and, if the truth were told, didn't know his son at all. More and more these days, Nicholas was surprised to note, he regretted that. Regretted that the only reason he and Erick got along better than he and his own father had was because they were practically strangers.

Still, Erick was a good son. Nicholas could leave his affairs in his heir's hands with confidence and made a mental note to send word to Erick as to his unexpected journey the moment they reached the docks. In the two years since Nicholas's return to England, the boy had given him no cause for concern. He'd selected a more than acceptable bride. He hadn't really inconvenienced him at all. Erick treated him with respect and never asked for anything in return.

Except this. This request to talk to Lady Stanford. And look where it had brought him. Off on a voyage to who knows where with a glorious woman who obviously had far more spirit to her than he had first imagined. He wondered if his initial impression was correct, after all. If indeed there was far more to her than she let on. Nicholas smiled to himself and settled deeper in the carriage seat. There would be time enough to find out. Time enough to ferret out the secrets of the future countess of Wyldewood.

He would have to remember to thank Erick for this intriguing opportunity. Even though he was really doing all this for his son, to make up for the past.

Wasn't he?

Sabrina swept up the gangplank well in advance of Lord Wyldewood. During the ride to the docks she'd decided she would be pleasant and polite to him, but no more. Neither would she tell him their eventual destination nor the ultimate purpose of the trip. The decision brought her a small measure of satisfaction. If he wanted answers, let him figure them out.

She glanced over her shoulder. Wyldewood was still engaged in conversation with his carriage driver, no doubt giving the poor man the benefit of all that male guidance. The phrase still grated in her mind. At least his extended discussion gave her the chance she needed to board the ship before he did.

"Lady Bree!"

Sabrina whirled about at the enthusiastic cry.

"Simon!" She clasped the American's hands in hers. Tall and robust, in spite of the gray mingling with the sun streaks in his light auburn hair, the seaman's eyes sparkled in greeting.

"Welcome to the *Lady B.*"

"Simon, how wonderful! I was very much afraid, after all these years, there would be no one I knew in the crew." She cocked her head and surveyed him critically. "And still as handsome as ever, I see."

Simon MacGregor threw his head back and laughed. "It's good to see you've not changed. Not your saucy tongue nor your pretty face. It's good to see you, lass."

Sabrina narrowed her eyes in teasing speculation. "The last time I saw you, you were going to give up the sea and go home to your wife and all those children; in Maine, I believe. You were going to become a fisherman."

51

The big man shrugged, his eyes twinkling. "By the time I got around to it, the young 'uns were nearly grown. And the wife decided she liked being married to me a whole lot more when I weren't around than when I was. Seeing her a couple of times a year seems to make both of us a sight happier than being together all the time."

She laughed and shook her head. "You really haven't changed." Her gaze skimmed the rest of the ship and the crew. She craned her neck to see around him. "Is Matt here?"

"The capt'n had business to see to in Paris. We're to pick him up in a few weeks in Marseilles."

"Oh, dear." She drew her brows togther in disappointment and dismay.

"But don't you worry none. He'd be more than happy to know you were on board. He always said, if you ever had need of it, you could consider this ship your own."

"Mine?"

"In a manner of speaking." Simon grinned. "The capt'n's talked of you a lot through the years. Always said he'd see you again someday."

Simon leaned low, his words soft against her ear. "He named this ship the *Lady B,* you know."

"I noticed," she said wryly.

"It's an honor." His gruff tone chastised her.

"I know that, and I am truly honored, but . . ." She glanced behind her. Wyldewood was still on the dock, now talking to a member of the ship's crew. She didn't have much time. Sabrina nodded toward the wharf. "I have someone traveling with me."

Simon's eye's widened in surprise. "I didn't hear you'd gotten yourself a new husband." A distressed frown drew his sandy brows together. "Wills should have mentioned that to me when we arranged your passage. I daresay the capt'n won't be none too pleased about this. Ah, well, nothing to be done about it, I suppose."

"Simon, I am not married," she said sharply. Shock colored his face, and she could clearly read his thoughts. "Don't you even think that, Simon. Lord Wyldewood is accompanying me through no fault of my own. Believe me, I didn't want the man along, but I appear to be trapped for the time being. Is there a cabin you can put him in?''

Simon directed his words to her, but his thoughtful gaze lingered on Wyldewood, standing on the dock. ''We've got several passenger cabins. The capt'n was thinking of making this ship strictly for the transport of people. There's room for him.''

He studied Wyldewood for a long, silent second. ''Do you want me to throw him overboard once we get to sea?''

''Good Lord no!'' Sabrina cried. She glanced at Wyldewood and grinned. ''At least not right away.''

Simon offered her a broad smile in return. ''But I gather it would be acceptable if we made his voyage a wee bit uncomfortable. He's a tall, broad man, and I've a cabin that will suit him—if he's not too particular about standing upright.''

Sabrina laughed. ''It sounds perfect. Simon, the way I feel about that gentleman right now, making his life uncomfortable is more than acceptable, it's positively delightful!''

Wyldewood strode up the gangplank. Sabrina realized she still hadn't warned Simon. ''He knows nothing about my past and he mustn't find out. And if I am somewhat more reserved than I used to be, especially around him, please don't comment on it.''

Simon eyed her quizzically but said nothing. She would have some explaining to do to Simon and, later, to his captain. She wondered how long it would be before Wyldewood too insisted on explanations. He drew nearer, and Sabrina sighed in resignation.

Perhaps it would be easier to have him thrown overboard after all.

Nicholas's gaze scanned the ship and settled on Lady Stanford, earnestly talking to a hardy sailor. The woman was an enigma. He'd learned the eventual destination of the ship was Alexandria. What kind of business could she possibly have in Egypt?

''Welcome aboard, my lord.'' The big man greeted him,

a hint of sarcasm in his tone. Nicholas narrowed his eyes slightly. Good Lord! The man was American! He glanced upward at the main mast and tightened the muscles of his jaw at the sight of the flag fluttering in the breeze. The whole damn ship was American! That woman had condemned him to weeks aboard an American ship, surrounded day and night by bloody Americans. Nicholas liked Americans only slightly more than he liked the French. And he was not fond of the French.

Nicholas gritted his teeth and forced his diplomatic skills to the surface. It would not do to alienate the crew. He already suspected he would have a difficult enough time with Lady Stanford. Nicholas bestowed what he thought was a pleasant enough smile on the ruddy sailor. "Good day. Magnificent ship." He nodded his approval.

"Aye, the *Lady B*'s as fine a craft as you'll ever see." The seaman's pride in his vessel was obvious.

"Interesting name," Nicholas said thoughtfully, a vague familiarity nagging at the back of his mind. "Is she named for anyone in particular?"

The mate's eyes crinkled at the corners and he smirked in an oddly satisfied way. Nicholas glanced at Lady Stanford. Was that a glimmer of alarm that flashed through her eyes? No, surely not. Her unruffled gaze caught his and she smiled vacantly. He must have been mistaken. He seemed to be mistaken about Lady Stanford more often than not.

The American crossed his arms, his gaze flickering over Nicholas in an assessing and damned impertinent manner. Nicholas struggled to keep his expression friendly and interested.

"The ship's named for someone near and dear to the captain's heart," the sailor said. "A wonderful woman she was, like a sister to him. Brave and loyal and true, with a spirit and fire you don't see often in the fairer sex." He sighed dramatically. "But she's gone now. Cut down in the prime of life. It was a waste and a shame."

The story caught Nicholas's curiosity in spite of himself. "How did she die?"

"Oh no, sir." The big man shook his head regretfully.

"She didn't die. Might have been better all around if she had. No, she was scarce more than a girl when the weight of the world settled on her shoulders. Poor lass couldn't take it." He paused to let the full impact of his words sink in and rolled his eyes heavenward. "She joined a convent, she did. Became a nun. Sister B's what they call her now."

He shrugged in an exaggerated gesture of disbelief. "And the woman weren't even Catholic."

A strangled gasp came from the direction of Lady Stanford, and Nicholas turned toward her. Her face flushed crimson and she struggled to catch her breath between fits of coughing. Nicholas lunged toward her and clasped her arms.

"Lady Stanford, are you quite all right?" His anxious gaze searched her face. A few errant tears coursed down her cheeks.

"I'm fine," she choked. "Just very moved."

Nicholas stared sharply at her expression of complete innocence. If he didn't know better, he would think the woman was on the verge of losing a battle with unbridled laughter. Was there something humorous about that story he hadn't understood? It was a little odd, but he saw nothing of humor in it.

Lady Stanford glanced pointedly at his hands, still gripping her arms. "Thank you for your concern, but I really am quite recovered." Nicholas's gaze followed hers, and reluctantly, he released her. "I should like to go to my cabin now, Simon, if I may?"

"Of course, ma'am." The sailor's eyes twinkled at Lady Stanford, and Nicholas could have sworn a silent message passed between them.

Lady Stanford nodded in Nicholas's direction. "Lord Wyldewood, I have never taken well to sea travel, so I do not expect to see much of you on this voyage, at least for a while."

"Oh?" Nicholas quirked an eyebrow. "Somehow, that surprises me. I had the distinct impression from the manner in which you came on board that you are very much at home on a ship."

She laughed lightly. "Well, my lord, impressions can be

deceiving. You should not place such stock in them.'' She turned and took Simon's arm, and the couple stepped quickly down the deck.

"Perhaps you're right,'' he said to himself. "Impressions can be deceiving. But make no mistake, my lovely lady, I shall find out what you're up to.'' He stared after her thoughtfully. "And . . . what you're hiding.''

Chapter Five

"Egypt!" Belinda gasped. "There's nothing but sand and pyramids and mummies in Egypt! Why in the world would she be going to Egypt?"

She glared at Erick as if this were somehow his fault. He lounged on the sofa in the front salon and shrugged nonchalantly. "I have no idea, and apparently neither does Father. The message I received from him said simply that she had boarded a ship bound for Alexandria and he was accompanying her."

"What! He's going with her!" Shock widened her sapphire eyes. "Without a chaperone? Without even a servant? It's scandalous! It will absolutely destroy her reputation! She'll be the talk of every gossip in the ton!"

Belinda's voice rose and Erick eyed her cautiously. "Darling, I think your fears on that score are groundless. My father is an honorable man and he is with her only for her protection."

"Hah!" She threw him a scathing glance. "I've heard the talk about your father. He has a sterling reputation when

57

it comes to diplomatic matters, but he's equally well known as a womanizer and a rake!"

"Belinda!" Shock rang in Erick's voice. "I daresay—"

"Don't you 'daresay' me, Erick," she snapped. "You know as well as I do that his conquests at the courts of Europe were not restricted to treaties and government alliances. He was not what I, or anyone else for that matter, would consider discreet. And since his return to England he's already well known for his exploits with women." Outrage sparked in her voice. "And respectable is not a term I would apply to many of them!"

"Enough!" Erick leapt to his feet, drawing himself up in his best imposing manner. "I will not have my father slandered like this!"

"Slandered!" she sputtered. "I hardly think the truth could be considered slander!"

The two glared at each other for a long, tense moment. Anger and confusion battled in Erick. He had no idea how they'd gotten to this point. He understood her concern over her mother, but to suggest his father would take advantage of her was ridiculous. Belinda was far too overset to view the situation calmly. Why, she even had him up at arms, and all he wanted to do right now was wring her lovely neck. He would never hit a woman, of course. Still, Belinda could drive a rational man to completely irrational acts.

Within moments, the icy sparks in her eyes dissolved and her expression turned contrite. "Oh, Erick, I'm so sorry." She flew across the room and into his arms. Her supple form melted into his, and they sank back upon the sofa. His anger disappeared, banished by her intoxicating scent and the warmth of her body next to his.

He gathered her near and she sighed, snuggling closer. The touch of her breasts against his chest quickened his blood and he groaned to himself, all thoughts of her mother and his father forgotten.

"I did not mean to offend you, truly I didn't." She tilted her angelic face up toward his, her eyes misted by tears, her lips full and inviting. "I am so very worried."

"I know, darling." Just one kiss, he thought, simply to

calm her. His lips brushed hers and he marveled at the pliant softness of her mouth, the way her lips opened slightly and the heady feel of her breath joined with his. Obviously, she needed more comfort than one insignificant kiss could provide. As her fiancé, it was his responsibility—nay, his duty—to help her as much as possible. A duty he was more than willing to sacrifice himself for.

He feathered kisses along the line of her jaw until she moaned softly. Her head fell back, and he noted with satisfaction the dreamy look in her eyes.

It was ever so hard to concentrate when he kissed her, Belinda thought, but nice; very, very nice. He found a sensitive spot just below her ear and she gasped. She had no idea anything could feel quite so delicious. Lightly, he ran his lips down her neck, and her muscles dissolved in a warm puddle of trembling excitement. She sagged against him, an odd yearning for more building within her.

"After all," he murmured between kisses, "it's not as if we can do anything at this point." This point, he thought, this magnificent, bewitching point. Deftly brushing away her sleeve, he exposed one perfect shoulder. He teased the satin skin with teeth and tongue and then his mouth drifted lower toward breasts now heaving with newfound arousal and innocent desire. His tongue traced the neckline of her bodice and her skin quivered beneath his touch. His words whispered against the swell of her breast. "It's not as if we could go after them."

The temptation of the valley between her breasts beckoned and enticed. His tongue tasted her heated flesh, and she shuddered. Aching need surged in his veins. Any determination not to allow their passion to triumph over them ebbed away. They were to be married, at any rate. What harm could there be in a few passionate kisses, a few intimate caresses, a mere moment of shared arousal?

"Erick," she said softly. Vaguely, he noted that her breathing had slowed to nearly normal. He raised his head reluctantly and gazed into her eyes. A slight frown creased her forehead and a thoughtful expression graced her face. Erick stared in disbelief. His desire vanished, as if hit by an icy splash of water. Here he was, in the midst of a rather successful seduction, and the blasted chit wasn't even paying attention!

She stared up at him. "Why can't we?"

"Why can't we what?" She might have dampened his ardor, but it would still take him a few moments to get his mind off the temptations she'd been so close to offering and he'd been more than willing to sample.

"Go to Egypt, of course." She scrambled off the sofa and paced the room. Excitement built in her voice. "It's perfect, Erick. With us along, your father can't possibly take advantage of my mother."

Erick shook his head, still wondering how she could shift from the throes of passion to exhibit enthusiasm for something altogether different so quickly and easily. God knows he couldn't. He sighed in irritation, frustration sharpening the edges of his words. "I think you've forgotten a number of things."

He stood to face her and ticked off the items on his fingers. "Number one, she did not go with my father; he is accompanying her for her own protection. As a favor to me, I might add. Number two, your mother has some kind of mysterious business in Egypt, and from what she has or has not said to both you and my father, I don't believe she would welcome us along. Number three, they have already left. There's no guarantee we could catch up with them."

"And finally . . ." With a flourish, he presented his trump card. "We have the same problem our parents do: no chaperone. The whole idea is absurd."

"Piffle," Belinda said with a wave of her hand.

"Piffle?"

"Piffle." She nodded firmly. "Not one of your objections holds water." She cast him a triumphant smile, then echoed his earlier gesture, counting her reasons off on her fingers. "Your Aunt Wynne can be our chaperone. I daresay the poor old dear would love a trip like this. She doesn't seem to get out much. And if you go to the docks today, you can probably find out what route their ship was taking. With any luck we can take a ship with a faster or more direct route.

Finally, regardless of what my mother does or does not want, she is behaving so oddly, I think it is in her best interest for us to act."

"You mean interfere," he said wryly.

"Perhaps." She shrugged. "All I know is that my mother is normally a reserved, reasonable woman who never does anything the least bit impulsive or ill advised."

Erick drew his brows together in a thoughtful frown. "I have been wondering about all this. You can not remember her behaving like this before?"

"Never." Belinda shook her head in a blizzard of golden curls. "Although . . ."

"Yes?"

She hesitated, gathering distant, faded memories. "I was five when my father died and we went to live with a great-aunt of mother's. Somewhere north, I think, fairly close to the sea. We stayed for about three years. Mother would disappear for days at a time. Looking back, I assumed she was simply trying to deal with my father's death in her own way." Her eyes narrowed thoughtfully. "I was far too young to pay it any mind then and really haven't thought much about it since. And she hasn't behaved in any way unusual since we've lived in London."

"Well, there's probably nothing to it, then."

"Probably," she echoed. "So . . ."

"So?" He quirked an eyebrow at her.

"So, you talk to your aunt and then find us a ship." She grasped his arm and pulled him toward the door. "I'll begin packing."

He groaned. "Belinda . . ."

Her eyes sparkled with anticipation and she laughed. "We haven't any time to spare, so off with you." Belinda reached up and brushed his lips with hers, and for a moment the light in her eyes teased and tantalized him.

She practically pushed him out the door, and he paused for breath on the top step. He was not enthused at the idea of an ocean voyage that would very probably take months. Erick stalked toward his carriage in an indignant huff, wondering how he had gotten himself into this, and better yet, how he could get out of it. He would much rather stay in London, especially with Belinda's mother away. Allthough . . . the revelation thundered through his mind and pulled him up short.

This trip would allow him to spend a considerable amount of time with Belinda. Aunt or no aunt, there would very likely be time alone. Alone, with the subtle rocking of a ship, warm ocean breezes, the magnificent Mediterranean moon and nowhere to run. Add Belinda to that scene, and it was not an unappealing vision. In fact, it painted quite a promising picture. And even if they failed, even if they never caught up to their parents, would that really be so terrible? Erick grinned and strode toward his carriage, now eager to set his fiancée's plan in motion.

Absurd or not, there were interesting possibilities in her proposal. Possibilities and a great deal of potential.

Wynnefred Harrington paused before the gilt-framed mirror in the foyer and impatiently tucked a stray tendril of chestnut hair into place. Unruly curls struggled to escape their haphazard captivity high on the back of her head. Large, dark eyes returned her critical stare behind gold-rimmed glasses. It was really quite an attractive face, even pretty. Fat lot of good it did her, she thought wryly. Wynne shrugged and turned from the mirror. She had far too many things to do today to waste time wondering about what might have been.

Still—she leaned against the chest centered below the mirror—it was a topic that occupied her mind more and more frequently these days. At two-and-thirty she was firmly on the shelf. It wasn't that she'd never had the opportunity to marry; There'd been offers through the years. In her first seasons there were young men enamoured of her obvious charms, and later there were those more prone to appreciate her fortune than her face. But none had ever measured up to Father's standards, or, for that matter, her own.

She had never met a man who came close to the mythical heroes, legendary leaders and knights in shining armor she devoured in the books she kept constantly close at hand.

The Perfect Wife

Wynne was a genuine bluestocking and knew a certain amount of self-satisfaction in the derogatory title. She lived complete and happy lives in the stories and tales that filled her free time, exploring the world with adventures and travels and the latest scientific marvels.

Even without a home and family of her own, her life was exceedingly full. Besides her books, she'd been companion to her father, run his household with an efficient hand, acted as his hostess and, in addition, helped raise her nephew. And if the years had flown by unnoticed, so be it.

Now, Wynne's mind was filled with what she thought of as her own personal story. A story she had yet to write. A story she had yet to live. With Father dead two years now, and Erick about to marry, Wynne saw no reason why she should not do exactly as she wished with her life. If Nicholas needed someone to run his home, he could bloody well find a wife. Wynne had never complained about putting her father's and her nephew's needs first, but now it was her turn. Just as soon as she had Erick safely married, she would pack her bags and set off to see the world. See for herself all the places she'd only read about. Maybe Italy and Greece one year, and China the next. Perhaps she'd even visit America. A dreamy smile drifted across her lips, and images of exotic places and unknown lands teased her mind.

The crash of the front door rudely pulled her from her reverie and the voice of her nephew planted her feet firmly back in reality.

"Aunt Wynne . . ." Erick rushed to her side, clasped her hand and raised it to his lips. Wynne sighed to herself. As a child, he used to offer her some of his secret cache of sweets to get her to do what he wanted. With maturity came new techniques, but Wynne could still read Erick's intentions as well as any of her books.

She drew back her hand and studied him with a knowing gaze. "Don't bam me, Erick. What do you want?"

"What? Why, Aunt Wynne . . ." Erick's eyes opened wide with feigned innocence. "You wound me to the quick."

"Nonsense." Wynne sniffed. "I've known you all your

life and I certainly know when you are trying to wheedle something out of me. Now, what do you want?''

Erick took a deep breath. ''It's about the wedding. I'm afraid it has to be delayed.'' Wynne's heart sank. Her elusive freedom slipped farther away.

''Belinda's mother has taken off on a somewhat mysterious and ill-advised voyage to Egypt, and Father has followed her.'' He paused, as if to gauge her reaction.

Wynne simply raised an eyebrow, but her composed expression belied the rush of questions whirling through her mind. Nicholas had actually gone out of his way to go after a woman? Put himself to some trouble for a mere female? As far as she'd ever been able to see, her brother had no use for women except as managers of his household or fetching playthings to be toyed with and then disguarded. Disrupting his well-ordered life was unheard of.

During his long years of service to the Crown it had not been unusual for Nicholas to take off without a moment's notice. Then he was involved in diplomatic missions, ferreting out smugglers and, Wynne long suspected, even spying. But this was different. This was not for king and country. This was for a woman.

''Go on.'' She nodded for Erick to continue.

''Well . . .'' He hesitated, with that uncertain look on his face that always told her he was summoning up his nerve. His words exploded in a quick rush. ''Belinda wants us to go after them. But we can't go without a chaperone. So it would be of great assistance to us if you would agree to come along.'' He stared at her with a hopeful look.

Egypt? The mystical, magical land of the pharaohs? A thrill swept through her veins. This was her chance! Her first step toward a new life of her own. And who knew? Maybe she wouldn't come back. In her role of chaperone she could ensure Erick's marriage and her obligations would be at an end.

Her voice betrayed none of her mounting excitement. ''You say this is Belinda's idea?''

Erick grimaced. ''She doesn't seem to feel her mother's virtue is safe in Father's hands.''

"Wise girl," Wynne said under her breath. "Well, if we are to undertake such a venture, we have no time to lose. There are dozens of preparations to be made."

"You'll go?" Surprise flooded his face.

"Of course." Wynne nodded. She grinned to herself at his stunned expression. No doubt the boy was shocked that his competent, efficient, reliable Aunt Wynne would agree to uproot herself completely and head to the ends of the earth. The poor child had no idea of the dreams and desires of Wynnefred Harrington—dreams and desires she could see beckoning just over the horizon.

Lord Benjamin Melville impatiently thrust his coat at a footman and scanned the club lounge for his companions. He spotted the duo in their usual corner near the fireplace and hurried toward them, pausing only to place a drink order with a waiter. Bursting with the need to reveal the latest *on-dit,* he nonetheless restrained himself, now that the moment of release was at hand. Melville settled into a chair and savored the anticipation of imparting information to which he alone was privy.

Sir Reginald Chatsworth and Lord Patrick Norcross barely acknowledged his presence, resuming their lackluster debate on the relative merits of the horseflesh currently available at Tattersall's, and whether the absence of quality was inversely proportional to the outrageous prices required.

Melville surveyed his friends with a practiced eye, wondering, as he often did, how a group so dissimilar in temperament could be quite so compatible. The trio was of a like age and shared a common heritage and breeding. They were, to his way of thinking, a shining example of the best of English manhood. Still, Chatsworth was a talkative, amicable sort of fellow, where Norcross had a disturbing tendency to brood and frequently submitted to bouts of melancholy. As for Melville, he thought of himself as the best of the bunch: attractive, witty and generally not given to overexcitement. Except where the occasion warranted, and this was just such a time.

The companions shared one other thing that bound them

together, one factor that through the years had variously prompted rivalry, triggered resentment and, ultimately, a common sympathy. A bond that frequently filled their conversations with enthusiastic speculation, glimmers of hope and lengthy debate: Each had loved and lost the enchanting Lady Sabrina Winfield.

"She's gone off, you know," Melville blurted, his secret bolting toward freedom like a cornered rabbit desperate for the sanctuary of a hedgerow.

Norcross and Chatsworth turned to him at the interruption, satisfying Melville that he now had, if not their rapt attention, at least their mild interest.

Norcross raised a dark brow in a manner Melville found annoyingly superior. "She who?" he said idly, as if the answer were of no real concern, and the only purpose to his question was to cater to Melville's obvious excitement.

"Lady Stanford. Sabrina." Melville leaned back in his chair and smirked at the curiosity now evident on the faces of the two men before him. "She's gone off and . . ." he paused and took a swallow of the fine Irish whiskey in his glass, savoring the taste of the liquor not nearly as much as the expressions of his friends, ". . . she's not alone."

"What on earth are you babbling about, Melville?" Chatsworth snapped. "What do you mean?" He repeated Melville's words in a snide mimicry of his friend. " 'She's gone off and she's not alone.' Explain yourself."

Even Chatsworth's biting manner could not diminish Melville's pleasure at telling his tale. He considered just how long he could continue to delay without evoking real anger from his companions.

"Get on with it, man," Norcross added impatiently.

"Very well." Melville directed his gaze first at one, then the other. "Sabrina has left London on a voyage to Egypt. No one seems to know why exactly. Apparently, quite at the last minute I understand, she was joined by . . ." he hesitated, to allow his next words the impact they deserved, ". . . Lord Wyldewood."

"Wyldewood!" Norcross gasped.

"Good Lord," Chatsworth groaned. "Not Wyldewood.

Why did it have to be Wyldewood? I can't believe she would prefer him to one of us.''

"He is an attractive sort," Norcross muttered, "and rich as Croesus."

"We're rich!" Chatsworth sputtered.

"It does appear she has finally made her choice," Melville said morosely. In the excitement of possessing this exclusive information he had failed to realize, until now, that this bit of gossip shattered his dream of one day claiming Sabrina as his own.

The trio sank into a heavy silence, each man pondering lost desires, cursing the fickleness of fate and questioning, not for the first time, the inexplicable and wholly irrational mind of a woman.

Norcross swirled the amber liquid in his glass and stared at the whirlpool thoughtfully. "Why did you say Wyldewood joined her at the last minute?"

Melville shrugged. "I learned all this from my valet, who got it from servants from either Wyldewood's or Sabrina's household. You understand." The others nodded, knowing all too well the vast network of servants of the ton, who spread news, accurate and inaccurate, with a speed far surpassing the finest racehorse. "While Sabrina packed for the trip, Wyldewood did not. I hear his man prepared a valise for him without prior warning, and a servant barely managed to get it to the ship before he sailed. Word was also sent to his soliciter to procure letters of credit at the last possible moment. It's obvious he did not plan to accompany her."

Melville sighed dramatically. "It sounds very much as if they were overcome with romantic passion and sailed off together to exotic, foreign lands."

Norcross stared, an expression of amazement on his face. "I cannot believe you could say something that completely idiotic." He shook his head disparagingly at Melville's indignant expression. "Don't bother to deny it. For as long as I've known you, you have jumped to completely inaccurate, although I might add highly inventive, conclusions. I don't view this situation the same way at all."

He leaned toward them, and the others drew nearer. "I'm

not convinced Sabrina has made a choice. If they were planning to go off together, why wouldn't he already have a bag prepared? Why this last-minute haste? And why the secrecy? They are both of age. No one, beyond us, would censure them. Although . . ." he said wryly, ". . . more than a few would question both her taste and wisdom for becoming involved with a rake of his stature."

"So, you feel Sabrina did not wish to take Wyldewood along? That perhaps she is an unwilling companion?" Chatsworth asked. Norcross nodded firmly. Chatsworth considered his words carefully. "This puts a different light on the entire incident."

"Do you think she needs assistance?" Melville's tone displayed a hopeful eagerness. "That she is in need of rescue, perhaps?"

"Perhaps."

It was odd to think of Sabrina as needing help. All three had, at one time or another, been allowed an intriguing glimpse at the fire that lay hidden beneath the woman's serene exterior. Never more than a peek, a mere suggestion, the barest hint, and each man desperately wanted more. It was a continual topic of discussion among them and the reason why each had continued his pursuit, even in the face of her pleasant but firm rejection.

"If she is not with Wyldewood of her own accord," Chatsworth said slowly, "then I propose we follow her. After all, regardless of whether she has turned me—and all of us, for that matter—down in the past, we still regard her highly. And it's unconscionable to abandon her to the likes of Wyldewood."

Norcross gaped in disbelief. "Follow her to Egypt? It's preposterous!"

"Why?" Melville demanded. "I think it's a bloody good idea. It just might be exactly what she needs to open her eyes. To make her see that I—" he glanced apologetically at his companions, "I mean that one of us is the right man for her. We'll go after them and we'll rescue her!"

"Like blasted knights in tarnished armor," Norcross muttered sarcastically.

"No, like daring heroes," Chatsworth added, saluting with his glass.

The others joined in the toast. "To heroes," they chorused.

All settled into their own thoughts, of the woman, of the quest, of the triumph. All but one. He stared at his friends over the rim of his glass. Fools. They obviously saw this as a romantic quest for the woman of their dreams. He would have preferred following Sabrina on his own, but any overt discouragement on his part would very likely arouse suspicion. Their presence would make his plans difficult but not impossible.

He alone suspected the true reason for Sabrina's abrupt departure for Egypt. He alone knew the eminently high stakes involved. He chuckled to himself. He would be the one to return to London, victorious in a game that had nothing to do with affairs of the heart.

And he would return . . . alone.

Chapter Six

"He's got me trapped down here like a bloody rat in a cage!" Sabrina stormed, pacing the width of the spacious captain's cabin, arms folded across her chest. The hanging lanterns flickered in time with the rhythm of her movement. She turned and glared at Simon. "Every time I try to go on deck he's right there, difficult to ignore, impossible to avoid. But if I have to spend one more day, another hour, even a single, solitary moment more in this cabin, I shall go stark, raving mad!"

"It doesn't look to me as if he's the one keeping you here, lass," Simon observed mildly. "It looks more to me as if this is your own doing."

"My own doing?" She sniffed. "Hardly. I didn't ask him to come along. I don't want him here. He's sure to ruin everything."

Simon leaned back in his chair and studied her through narrowed eyes. "I still don't see why you refuse to be around him. Hard to believe the woman I once knew is frightened of anything." His eyes twinkled. "Especially of one, lone man."

The Perfect Wife

"Of course I'm scared. And you known full well, I have good reason." She strode to the table, lifted a mug and held it out to him. Obligingly, he poured a healthy draught of the captain's own, private brandy. It was her second of the evening. Sabrina drew a quick swallow, the pungent liquor searing her throat, matching her mood. She slapped the cup back on to the table.

"I've spent the last ten years of my life trying to live down the reputation Jack and I had when he was alive. A reputation, I might add, that was extremely well earned. We lived what could only be termed a very fast life. Oh, not completely scandalous, mind you—we did not totally disregard convention—but close enough. I've worked hard to overcome the memory of our behavior. And I've succeeded admirably." Her voice carried a note of satisfaction.

"I've lived a relatively sedate life, well within the bounds of acceptable behavior, even tottering at times on the edges of outright boredom, to ensure that my reputation would not be held against my daughter. To guarantee that she shall take the place in society due her. I'll not see that destroyed now. Not by any man, and especially not by Wyldewood."

Simon shook his head in a wry manner, amusement dancing in his eyes. "And you fear Wyldewood will see through that oh-so-proper Lady Stanford image you've built."

"You're bloody right about that." Sabrina sighed and sank into a chair. "He's not stupid. All I need is for him to discover that not only have I directed my own financial affairs, something no respectable woman would do, but I'm a retired smuggler as well, and it's all over." She picked up the mug and took another long, deep swallow. Her voice was grim. "He'd surely refuse permission for his son to marry Belinda. The entire story would come out. She would be ruined. I cannot allow that."

"I think perhaps you've misjudged the man."

An unladylike snort of disbelief was her only response.

"While you've been sulking down here these past weeks," he ignored the scathing glare she aimed at him, "I've been getting to know the man a bit. He ain't half bad, for a high-and-mighty English lord."

71

"You hate the English," she said under her breath, sipping her drink, the brandy now warm . . . soothing.

He grinned. "You're English."

"That's different," she said, her manner lofty and smug.

"All's I know is, the man's given up his fancy clothes, dresses more like one of us now. And he's pitched in to help when needs be." Simon shrugged. "I'm thinking if you give him half a chance, you might be able to reconcile your differences. Hell, you might like him."

"Like him? Hah! I'd sooner throw him to the sharks."

Simon quirked an eyebrow. "I think any time there's as many sparks b'tween a man and a woman as there are with you and him, feeding him to the fish is the last thing you'd be wanting to do with him."

Sabrina stared at the mug in her hand and refused to meet Simon's gaze. He smiled ruefully. Despite her words, she really hadn't changed. Even after all these years, he could still read her with ease. He'd suspected there was more to her refusal to be near Wyldewood than she'd let on. Suspected it the first time he'd seen the two of them together. Knew it for certain when she avoided the man like the plague and snapped at anyone who even mentioned his name. It took these last weeks of self-imposed solitude, not to mention tonight's plentiful helping of brandy, to get her to admit, if only to herself, the one problem she hadn't mentioned might well be her biggest.

"You're going to be with him on this ship for a long time yet, lass," he said gently. "You've got to be deciding what you really want out of all this." He stood and ambled toward the door. "And how you aim to get it."

Simon closed the door softly behind him. He chuckled to himself and wondered what his captain would make of this development. He grinned with anticipation. He could hardly wait till they picked up the captain. Then you'd see sparks, all right, and life aboard this ship would be anything but dull.

Sabrina vaguely noted his departure. Her unfocused gaze at her cup never wavered. What did she want?

She wanted the gold. She wanted to secure her daughter's

The Perfect Wife

future. She wanted to get out of this blasted cabin.

And somewhere, deep inside, she wanted . . . Wyldewood.

No! Ruthlessly, she crushed the traitorous thought. This damned attraction she had for the earl was nothing but a momentary inconvenience, a minor distraction, a blasted nuisance.

Sabrina rose, mug in hand, and resumed her pacing. She'd been in this cabin for—what? Weeks? Months? Forever? Time had lost all meaning. She'd already had more than enough time to study and examine and memorize the letter and the maps Wills had thoughtfully tucked into her bag. More than enough time to read every book in the captain's cabin. And more than enough time for her thoughts to dwell increasingly on Wyldewood.

The memory of their dance together intruded itself at the most inconvenient moments. Just when the monotony of her existence threatened to turn her disdain for him into something more akin to sheer loathing, she'd remember the power of his body against hers, the searing heat of his hand and the bottomless, black eyes that held unspoken promises, untold passion.

Sabrina pondered the strength of his pull for her. It was as if they'd known each other before, in another place perhaps, another time. Almost as if fate had taken a hand. She'd never before experienced this kind of overwhelming compulsion toward a man. Even with Jack, it was all so different. He'd quite swept her off her feet in a mad rush of fun and frolic; Jack's experienced touch would make any green girl straight out of the schoolroom fall blindly, recklessly in love. Still, as intense as that emotion had been, it could not compare to the immediate, compelling desire that struck Sabrina with her first look in Wyldewood's eyes.

She wondered what her life might have been like if she'd married someone like Wyldewood. If she'd met him before she met Jack. She never would have had to worry about money, or discovery or rebuilding a reputaion. He'd be a husband you could depend on. It was an intriguing thought. How very different it all would be if she'd married someone like Wyldewood.

She swirled the brandy in her mug, mesmerized by the amber liquid glimmering in the lantern light. Sabrina sighed deeply and faced the truth: The crush of a girl was nothing next to the desires of a woman. It would be increasingly difficult to be near the man without revealing far more of herself than she wished.

And that was the oddest thing of all. Ever since she'd found the letter, the serene, reserved personality she'd wrapped around herself for a decade like a cloak of invulnerability had eroded. Slowly . . . inevitably. It somehow no longer suited. It was as if the hands on the clock had turned backwards. More and more, the daring and defiant woman she once was crept upon her, invading her thoughts, stealing her soul. She yearned to say and do exactly what she wanted and damn the consequences. Sabrina resented not permitting herself to do just that. Resented Wyldewood. Only his presence held her back.

Well, no more. Fueled by the liquor and her own frustrations, she turned and slammed the mug back on the table, burnished gold droplets sloshing over its rim. She'd bloody well had enough. She was the one who belonged here, not him. And she'd be damned if she'd let him keep her an unwilling prisoner for one more minute. Sabrina took a deep breath, resolved to maintain her control no matter what, and headed for the quarterdeck.

It was almost a disappointment to find him nowhere in sight. Gradually, muscles tensed in expectation of a confrontation relaxed, and she leaned on the taff rail. The sea at night was a special, mystical world of its own. The moonlight danced off the midnight waves; the stars glittered in the velvet sky. The breeze lifted her hair and tendrils danced around her face in a soothing welcome. Irritation slipped away. Serenity and peace flowed into her soul. It had been so very long since she'd stood on the deck of a ship. Too long since she'd breathed the heady scent of the sea. There was nothing she loved more than the sea.

Every childhood summer had been spent in the quiet coastal village where her great-aunt retired for the season. She'd grown up playing with the children of fishermen and shopkeepers, free of the restrictions that fettered most children of titled families. Sometimes Sabrina wondered whether her great-aunt meant for the orphaned child thrust upon her to be deliberately exposed to those beyond her own privileged world, or if she simply didn't care how Sabrina filled her days. Whatever the reason, she was grateful for the carefree, independent years of her youth, which taught her lessons that, eventually, served her well.

The ship rolled beneath her feet. She threw her head back and nearly laughed aloud with the sheer joy of freedom the water always gave her. This was where she belonged. Never was she as alive as when she was near the sea.

"I see you've overcome your discomfort with sea voyages." An amused and all too familiar voice sounded behind her.

"It was a mere trifle, my lord." She shrugged lightly. She'd spewed that nonsense about not taking well to sea travel in the first place simply to avoid him. And the moment the words were out of her mouth she knew he knew it was a lie. An incredible, overwhelming, earth-stopping lie.

Now, in his presence at last, she was somewhat surprised that her reserves of self-control had not deserted her. Was it experience built up over a decade or merely the brandy? Sabrina kept her gaze turned toward sea and sky merged into endless black, satisfied that she was, as always, the perfect Lady Stanford.

"Nicholas," he murmured.

"I would think it presumptuous to address you by your Christian name."

"We are to be family, after all." A hint of laughter caressed his words. She sensed him behind her, near enough to touch. Sensed his strength, his power. Still, she didn't turn. It was far easier to play this game without gazing into eyes as dark as night and far more dangerous. This game of verbal cat-and-mouse. She'd played before with any number of men, and she played the game well. He was no different than any other. With every word, her confidence grew.

"Very well." She sighed, as if acquiescence pained her. "Although I hardly think it proper."

"Proper?" His laughter echoed on the breeze; rich and mellow, it shivered through her blood. "I daresay it's too late to worry about that now. We have, after all, abandoned London for parts unknown. Without chaperones, without even servants. I fear it's far past time to consider propriety, especially when it comes to a point as minor as how we address one another."

Try as she might, Sabrina could not prevent a laugh from bubbling through her lips. "Touché." She turned and rested her back against the rail. "Nicholas and Sabrina it shall be, then."

The pale glow of the moon and the few lanterns on deck cast an indifferent light, but she could well discern his striking face towering above her. Now by his side, she noted that the man was far taller than she'd remembered.

"Still," she said, a teasing lilt in her voice, "I should think a man like you would be very concerned with propriety."

He lifted a questioning brow. "A man like me?"

"A man well versed in diplomacy. A peer. Now, I gather, becoming involved in Parliament and politics. I should think you of all people would be highly concerned with the appearance of things."

Nicholas grinned ruefully. "I suspect you're right; at least public appearances."

She laughed in thorough enjoyment of the lighthearted banter. "And privately?"

"Privately?"

"You are nearly as well known for your private . . . shall we say, intrigues, as your public accomplishments. Is your reputation with the fairer sex well earned?"

A warning note sounded in the back of her mind; she navigated dangerous waters here. But somehow the lure of this duel of words was far too strong to resist.

"Well earned?" He laughed again. "What an intriguing question. I suspect most men would prefer to believe their reputations when it comes to matters of the heart are well earned. But, of course, you of all people should know how easily reputations are made and broken among the ton."

"And why is that?"

"Well," he paused, as if weighing the effect of his words, "you and Stanford had quite a reputation yourselves."

"It's hardly the same . . . Nicholas. Granted, our activities did not strictly adhere to society's rules, but our minor adventures did not include amorous dalliances." She tossed him a sly smile. "As I said, it's not the same at all. And it was a very long time ago."

"Indeed." He studied her for a brief moment. "Have you changed so very much?"

"More than I can say," she said softly. Her words drifted off on the breeze and silence lay between them. Sabrina realized how very close he stood. Too close. Did she only imagine the seductive warmth of his body drawing her near? Was it his heartbeat that thundered in her ears? Was it her own?

His eyes reflected the moonlight and glittered, intense, dangerous . . . exciting. She noted vaguely that his hair had grown a bit during the voyage and now curled beneath his ears. Sabrina resisted the impulse to reach up and pull a silky strand through her fingers. Her gaze caught his, and the lightness of the moment vanished, replaced by a tension stretched taut between them.

"Why are you here?" she whispered.

He shrugged, the answer obvious. "Erick asked me to speak to you about this voyage. It was to no avail. You issued that ridiculous challenge and . . ." He shook his head sharply and stared into her eyes. "Why am I here? I don't really know."

He stepped nearer. "All I know is that from the moment we met you intrigued me. Captivating me one second, cutting me directly the next. I came to believe the fascinating woman of whom I caught a momentary glimpse was a passing illusion, a mere mirage. And the lady well known throughout society for her reserve to be the true woman. I believed that calm, proper personage would make an appropriate countess."

"Countess!" Sabrina gasped, shocked at the implication of his statement. "Marriage? To me?"

He placed a finger over her lips, quieting her words. A shiver of anticipation shot through her. His arms encircled her waist and he drew her close, an unresisting puppet pulled by an invisible string.

Nicholas brushed a stray tendril of hair away from her face and gently cupped her chin. "But when you defied me, stood up to me, virtually challenged me to accompany you, that's when I began to wonder if the lovely Lady Stanford was indeed the proper, somewhat dull paragon of virtue my investigators had prepared me for. I would wed the lady." The intensity of his gaze held her speechless. "I wish to know the woman."

"I scarcely think—"

His lips crushed hers, silencing her protest, stealing her will. Desire suppressed since the moment they met exploded within her. She clung to him, powerless to fight the urgency of her need for his touch. Greedily, her lips parted and greeted his exploring tongue. Welcoming. Inviting. Demanding. He tasted of limitless passion and raw power. Sensations she'd long forgotten, or perhaps never knew, surged through her, and she strained her body toward his.

He splayed his hands across the width of her back and drew her tightly against him. Full breasts pressed into his chest, pebbled nipples hard and arousing. Her brandy-scented breath mixed and mingled with his own, and he thought liquor had never tasted so good. He groaned and pulled his lips from hers. Her head fell back and he trailed kisses the length of her neck, his lips settling in the warm hollow of her throat.

She raised her head and ran her fingers through the thick, silken threads of his hair. Drawing her hands down to frame his face, she guided his lips back to hers. Sabrina wanted—no, *needed*—to devour him, to be devoured in return. Dimly, she realized, this passion on the deck would soon not be enough.

Jack had taught her many things about the pleasures that could be experienced between a man and a woman. And not since his death had she wanted to share such intimacies with a man. But even Jack had not elicited this immediate reaction, this insistent desire.

Nicholas nibbled her shoulder. A skillful hand caressed her breast through the thin fabric of her gown. She trembled beneath his fingers, yearning for more. What would he think when this paragon of virtue took him to her bed? This proper, somewhat dull paragon of virtue.

". . . the proper, somewhat dull paragon of virtue my investigators had prepared me for."

Investigators?

He'd had her investigated?

Fear of discovery mingled with indignation and passion extinguished like a wave upon a flame. Frantically, she cast her mind over their conversation, searching for any hint, any clue that he had uncovered her past. Surely if he knew, there would have been some indication. The fear diminished, leaving only a growing outrage. She'd had far too much of far too many arrogant men through the years to let yet another think he could do as he wished simply by virtue of his gender.

Nicholas continued his exploration, concentrating on a point where graceful neck met creamy shoulder, a point he'd learned long ago was particularly arousing for most women.

"Nicholas . . ."

"Hmmm?" The warm flesh beneath his lips seemed subtly cooler.

"Why did you have me investigated?"

The chill in her voice penetrated his haze of arousal and he drew back, perplexed. Her eyes gleamed in the moonlight.

"I see nothing unusual in it. My son is to marry your daughter, after all. Naturally, I would be concerned about the girl and her family."

Sabrina untangled herself from his arms and stepped back. "And just what did your inquiries tell you about my daughter and myself?"

He stared, trying to make out her expression in the dim light. "Nothing out of the ordinary, I assure you. You have lived a relatively conservative life since your husband's death, retiring to the country after his demise for a more than respectable period of mourning. You are well received, although not overly involved socially. There have been a number of offers for your hand through the years, but the names of only three men have appeared in the betting book at White's as serious contenders for your affection. And you appear well suited financially. Hardly earth-shattering revelations. As to your marriage . . .'' He shrugged. ''I had no need of an investigation for that. The activities you and Stanford engaged in are well known; bordering, I might add, on the level of legend.''

Indignation overrode relief at his words. He knew nothing of significance. She ignored the annoying thought that she had also made inquiries about him. Were his actions so very different from her own? He only did what he had to to protect his son, much as she had to protect her daughter. Was it the investigation itself or his conclusions that angered her? His words throbbed in her head.

Dull, boring paragon of virtue.

''Did my daughter live up to your expectations for a wife for your son?'' A seed of an idea took root in the back of her mind.

He nodded. ''Of course.''

Sabrina stepped to the rail and stared out over the sea. The idea burst into full blossom. Absurd. Ridiculous. Disasterous. An irrevocable mistake.

''And I gather I too lived up to your standards?''

''Well, yes, I—''

She whirled to face him. ''Just what are your qualifications?''

''My qualifications?'' Confusion colored his words.

''Your requirements?''

''My requirements? I'm afraid I don't quite understand.''

''For the position,'' she snapped. ''For a countess. For your wife?''

''My wife!'' he sputtered. His reply was cautious. ''Why, the same as any other man in my position, I would imagine. I need an accomplished hostess, capable of managing my household. I would prefer a woman of passing intelligence, one not difficult to look at, as well. And, naturally, someone with a spotless reputation and impeccable breeding."

Nicholas winced and Sabrina noted the expression with satisfaction. Even he could see how arrogant and selfish his admission was. It would serve him right if she took him up on his proposition.

Dull, boring paragon of virtue.

"I see." Her voice rang controlled and calm. Far too calm. A fist clenched in the pit of his stomach. She paused, as if in thought. "You did not mention love or even affection, so I presume you want a relationship that allows you to continue to live your private life as you wish. With whomever you wish. You seem to be seeking a strictly public relationship, one for the sake of appearances only. A marriage of convenience."

"I hadn't quite thought of it that way," he said wryly.

"Perhaps you should. And according to your investigations, with the exception of my somewhat scandalous marriage, I meet your qualifications?"

"Why, yes, but—"

"It sounds as though you've forgotten." Cool surprise sounded in her voice. "Very well, then. I am not used to lauding my own accomplishments, but they are extensive. I have run my own household for many years and I am a polished hostess, well versed in the social niceties. I speak French quite well and know a smattering of Spanish and an equal amount of Italian. My mother's family can trace its heritage back to King Richard." Starlight flashed in her eyes and the chill in her voice grew even colder. "Men have dedicated poetry to my obvious charms, and my reputation is—how did you so graciously put it?—oh, yes, I am a dull and boring paragon of virtue. I think I more than live up to your standards. Don't you agree?"

Nicholas thought himself an intelligent man, but not until Sabrina nearly spit the words at him did he realize that this was not going at all well. It was certainly not the conversation he had envisioned when he took her in his arms.

"Of course, Sabrina, however—"

"Very well then." She squared her shoulders and addressed him in a tone worthy of royalty. "I accept your proposal."

He stared, shocked. "I wasn't aware I had extended a proposal."

She shrugged. "Call it what you will. You said you would wed the lady. And whatever else I have heard about you, I have also heard you are a man of honor. A man of your word."

He pulled his brows together in a considering frown. "I cannot believe you would agree to such an arrangement. A marriage of convenience, as you put it?"

"Under certain terms and conditions." Sabrina nodded.

He bit back the chuckle rising to his lips. Whatever else this woman might be, his investigators had it all wrong. She was definitely not dull and boring. He wondered what else they'd gotten wrong. "Just what are these terms and conditions?"

She crossed her arms and paced to and fro before him, her face and form growing crisp, then indistinct in the shadows and the moonlight.

"First of all, you must not withdraw your permission for Belinda and Erick to wed, regardless of what happens between us."

"Agreed."

"Secondly, all property and wealth I bring to this marriage remains under my control. I would like papers drawn up to that effect. I will not forfeit my financial independence."

He pondered the idea briefly. While it was not unknown for a wife to have her own resources, it was extremely unusual. However, he certainly did not need her money and could well afford to be generous. If this demand kept her amused, so be it. "Very well."

"We will be equal partners in any business venture in which we are jointly engaged in."

"Business ventures?" He narrowed his eyes in suspicion. "What type of business ventures?"

She stopped her pacing and tossed him a wary look. "It doesn't signify at the moment. I simply need your word."

"You have it." He grinned. "Anything else?"

"Yes." Sabrina stepped forward and gazed up at him. The glittering heavens reflected in her eyes, and he had to stop himself from reaching for her.

She drew a steady breath. "Since this is to be a marriage of convenience only and privately we shall continue to live our separate lives, and since you already have an heir, I will expect you to respect my privacy."

"Respect your privacy?" he blurted, stunned. "Do you mean to say you will be my wife but you will not share my bed?"

"That's exactly what I mean," she said earnestly. "I shall be everything you want in a countess. I shall be the perfect wife. But I shall not share any man's bed with other women, and I shall not give my favors to a man I do not love."

She stepped back. "I suspect you would never wish the public spectacle of a divorce; therefore, if we do not suit, we can have the marriage annulled, or we can do what so many do and live completely apart from one another. If these terms are unacceptable to you . . ." Sabrina tilted her head in a questioning manner. "Well, Nicholas, what's it to be?"

He stared, the silence growing between them. He had thought she'd be the appropriate wife for his purposes the evening they first met. But now he wanted more. Much, much more. The light of the moon cast a shimmering halo about her hair, caressing her finely carved features, her classically sculpted form. She was a vision in the misty magic of the black and silver shades of the night. He could only remember one other time in his life when his desire for a woman had been this overpowering. Irrational, instinctual and, ultimately, undeniable. He would take her as his wife, terms, conditions and all.

"I have a condition of my own," he said softly. "If we decide we do not suit, it must be a joint decision. We must agree to separate."

"Is that all?"

The moonlight reflected the surprise on her face. Nicholas smiled to himself. Obviously, she did not think he'd accept her outrageous proposition. He nodded.

"Then as acting captain of this vessel, Simon can marry us. Is tomorrow acceptable?"

"More than acceptable." He pulled her into his arms.

"Nicholas," she gasped, "I hardly think this is an auspicious start to a marriage of convenience."

"We are not yet wed," he murmured, "and at the moment I find this wonderfully convenient." He pressed his lips to hers.

The pressure of his touch stole her breath and sapped her will. She struggled to fight a sea of powerful sensations, flooding her veins, throbbing through her blood. How would she resist him? If he could do this to her with a mere kiss . . . she shuddered with anticipation and ignored the distant warning in the back of her mind; it was not to be.

He held her close, plundering her lips with his own. Instinctively, he sensed her surrender, knew the moment of her defeat. Satisfied, he released her. Lifting her chin with a gentle touch, he gazed into eyes aglow with the power of his passion.

"Until tomorrow."

It took but a moment. Nicholas noted Sabrina gathering her wits about her. Noted her transformation into the cool, collected Lady Stanford. She was good, his bride-to-be, very good.

"Tomorrow." She nodded politely, turned and walked into the darkness. He rested his back against the rail and watched her disappear into the night. Her scent lingered in the air, vaguely spicy, hinting of a long-forgotten memory. A smile grew on his lips and he considered the unexpected benefits of taking a wife.

Nicholas, Earl of Wyldewood, was a man of honor, and he would abide by their bargain, abide by their terms.

All, of course, except one.

Chapter Seven

"Have you lost your mind? This is the most harebrained scheme I've ever had the misfortune to hear! What's got into you, lass?" Simon glared at her.

"I think it's an excellent idea," Sabrina said defensively.

"Excellent idea!" he roared. "Just last night you stood in this very same cabin and told me, in no uncertain terms, mind you, how his mere presence was ruining everything. How you'd be just as happy to see him feeding fish at the bottom of the sea. Now you want to marry the man!"

"I simply changed my mind." She sniffed haughtily. "Besides, marrying Wyldewood solves all my problems."

"Oh?" He raised a sandy brow in a sarcastic gesture. "And how, pray tell, does your getting yourself leg-shackled to a man you scarcely know and can't stand to boot solve anything?"

"I presented him with a list of terms and he agreed to them. For one thing, he promised he would not withdraw his permission for Belinda to marry his son." She crossed her arms over her chest. "Her future is now assured."

"And?"

"And, he's agreed to be equal partners with me in any business venture."

"By business venture do you mean this French gold you're going after?"

"Exactly." She nodded.

He narrowed his eyes and studied her. "Did you tell him about the gold?"

"Good Lord no! I wouldn't hazard to guess what he'll say about that. But sooner or later he is bound to find out, and this way I've secured his promise and assured my share."

"Seems to me, if you're married to the man, there's no need to pay him a dowry so's your daughter can marry his son. So there's no need to go looking for this gold."

"No, Simon." She shook her head vehemently. "I won't be dependent on any man financially ever again."

"But marriage, lass," he said softly, catching her gaze with his. "When I first met you, you were newly widowed. If I recall, you were almost as relieved to be free as you were sorrowful at your husband's death."

"Simon! That's not true!" she said sharply, denying the feelings it had taken her years to accept. "You make it sound as if I was glad Jack died. I never wanted him dead." She sank into a chair, laying her head on the back rest, and gazed unseeing at the low rafters above. "I just wanted him . . . to grow up. Life with Jack was one unending entertainment. A magnificent, midnight masked ball. Fast and exciting and full of adventure. But even the best of parties grow wearying after a time.

"I was so very tired at the end. Tired of living far beyond our means and always pretending not to know how deeply in debt we were. Always pretending tomorrow would never come." Sabrina closed her eyes for a moment, memories of her marriage, memories of Jack, crowding her mind. Setting them aside, she firmly closed the door to the past.

"However," her tone turned brisk, "that was a very long time ago. And this marriage shall be far different."

"I can't believe the man would agree to these so-called

terms of yours," Simon grumbled. "And I still don't see why you need to wed him."

"I'm heading to a rather primitive place," she said in her loftiest manner. "A lady alone. Unprotected. Sometimes a woman simply needs the protection of a man's name, if nothing else."

"Hah!" He snorted. "That smells worse than a crock of week-old fish. I've watched you bully a rowdy bunch of smugglers, as well as throw your weight around on a ship loaded with salty sailors. Hell, I taught you myself how to handle a knife. I've yet to see you need a man for protection from anything."

"You've never seen me scared either!"

"What the hell does that mean?"

"We've both agreed the bloody man has a brain. He's already had me investigated. No," she shook her head in response to Simon's questioning look, "he doesn't know. And he had the arrogance to inform me he had already selected me as the perfect countess for him."

She rose and paced the room. "With the marriage of our children and his interest in acquiring the perfect wife I fear, eventually, he will learn the truth." She turned a pleading gaze to Simon. "Don't you see? As his wife, I'll not only have the protection of his name but the power of his title and position and wealth. He will have to do all that is necessary to make sure I'm never exposed." She shrugged. "The public scandal would ruin him, and I suspect Wyldewood is a highly ambitious man."

"Still, I don't . . ." He stopped and stared at her sharply. She grew uncomfortable under his scrutiny. Abruptly, his eyes widened. "You lost your temper didn't you, lass? That's it! That explains it all! Whatever did he say to put such a bee in your bonnet?"

"He called me dull and boring," she muttered, refusing to meet his eyes.

"Ain't that exactly what you've been wanting folks to think these past years?"

"Yes. No. Oh, I don't know." She plopped back in the chair and wrinkled her nose. "I've lived an extremely respectable life, never revealing my feelings and never losing control. But lately I feel different. I feel more like the smuggler than the lady. And when he called me dull and boring and''— she tossed him an incredulous look— ''a paragon of virtue as well, something simply snapped.''

''So you'll marry the man to teach him a lesson?'' Simon snorted. ''That's daft, lass, downright stupid.''

''Tell me something I haven't already told myself. I know this is nothing short of idiotic.'' Sabrina hesitated, wondering just how much she should tell Simon, then tossed caution aside and plunged ahead. ''It won't be at all bad, really. It's simply a marriage of convenience. I'll have to keep up public appearances during the Season and when Parliament's in session, and various and sundry other things, but I expect we shall live completely separate lives eventually.''

''Oh?'' His eyebrow soared heavenward again. ''And what if children come of this marriage o' convenience of yours?''

''Simon!'' She laughed. ''There won't be any children. We're not going to . . .'' Her face flushed with heat and she winced at the look in his eye.

''Good Lord, woman! You're telling me you're taking the man's name, but you're denying him his marital rights? Is that another one o' your terms?''

''Well, he agreed to it. And he's an honorable man, a man of his word.''

Simon shook his head, disbelief evident on his face. ''No man is that honorable and all men have their limits, lass. I hope you haven't pushed Wyldewood too far.''

Sabrina couldn't tell him that particular condition would be as hard for her as it would be for Nicholas. But she'd come to grips with her desire for him, recognizing it as lust, pure and simple. She wanted nothing more than the touch of his hands, his lips, his skin next to hers. Wanted to explore his hard, heated body. Wanted fire to surge through her veins and burn in her heart. She wanted magic. Magic. Love.

Not the girlish crush she'd had with Jack, but something real, tangible. She'd resisted plenty of opportunities through the years to succumb to enticing pleasures of the flesh. But love had always evaded her. With her marriage to Nicholas, she realized, perhaps it always would.

She meant every word she'd said to him. If he wanted to continue his rakish ways, she would not protest, but she would not share any man with other women. And she would not give herself to any man without magic, without love. She would not give in to her desire at the risk of losing her self-control. Losing her soul.

Sabrina grinned. "I hope he hasn't pushed me too far."

Simon groaned and headed for the door, shaking his head. "I don't know what the capt'n's going to say about all this."

"Good Lord, Matt! I hadn't even thought about that."

Simon pulled open the door. "Well, you'd damned well better think about it. It's less than a week till we dock in Marseilles. He'll not be happy to find you married, by me no less, and to a blasted English lord. Won't be happy at all." He shook his head and stepped through the door, closing it behind him.

"Bloody hell." Sabrina threw herself down on the bed. Matt could be a problem. Not only would she have to spring her partnership proposal on him about the gold, but inform him there would now be a third partner and, *oh, yes, Matt dear, did I mention that our new partner is my husband?*

She groaned and rolled over on her back. Staring at the ceiling, the odd turn her life had taken struck her, and she couldn't suppress the hysterical laughter building inside. This was not quite the adventure she'd envisioned when she started out.

But it was definitely an adventure nonetheless.

The ceremony was simple, as befitting the circumstances. Simon performed with a grace Sabrina had not expected. She stood by Nicholas's side, on his left, nearest his heart. They exchanged vows on the forward deck, their promises drifting away with the wind.

Sabrina had thought to wear her emerald gown, going so far as to pull it out of her bag and struggle into it, a difficult task without a maid. It was not only a favorite, but flattering as well, turning her hair a richer gold, heightening the creamy color of her skin, highlighting the green of her eyes. In spite of its wrinkled condition, the effect pleased her.

Until her gaze caught on the breeches and men's linen she'd so lovingly packed. It was an outrageous thought. A scandalous idea. Definitely not dull and boring.

Nicholas never said a word when his bride appeared in men's clothing, complete with knee-high, butter-soft boots. He merely smiled pleasantly. His composure was nearly her undoing, but years of practice came to her aid. Even as he tipped her head back and placed a chaste kiss lightly on her lips, signaling she was no longer Lady Winfield, Marchioness of Stanford, but now Sabrina Harrington, the Countess of Wyldewood, she remained to all eyes calm, cool, controlled.

The crew insisted on celebrating the match. Someone pulled out a fiddle, another man a flute, and Sabrina danced with every sailor on board. There was no danger in this; this was no endless sea voyage with men too long denied the company of women. They had already put in at several ports and would stop at many more before the journey's end. Only when she danced in Nicholas's arms did her facade of serenity threaten to crack. Only when she gazed into his black eyes and wondered at the amusement lingering in their depths. Only when the nearness of his body warmed her own did she fear the results of her actions.

It was late before Sabrina returned to her cabin. Exhausted, she sank onto the bed and relaxed, the tension of the day flowing out of her. She hadn't the strength left to perform the simple task of changing into her night rail. Maybe if she just lay here for a moment. Perhaps two.

The door to the cabin burst open and a small valise sailed into the room. Sabrina shot to her feet.

"What in the—"

"Good evening, my dear." Nicholas grinned in the doorway. "Or should I say, my dear wife?"

She gasped. "What do you think you're doing here?"

He strode into the room and kicked the door closed behind him. "It's my wedding night. I couldn't bear to spend it anywhere else."

"But we—we're not—you're not . . ." Sabrina sputtered.

He shrugged. "Appearances, my pet. Appearances are everything."

He ignored the scathing glare she threw at him and casually surveyed her quarters. "Very comfortable. Far nicer than my previous accommodations." He quirked a brow. "And here I can actually stand upright."

Sabrina had the good grace to blush.

His eyes narrowed slightly. "I wondered if you'd had a hand in that. No matter; I'm here now, and here I shall stay."

"Oh, no, you won't. This is my cabin." She folded her arms over her chest and nodded impatiently toward the door. "Now get out."

He shook his head and laughed. "I'm afraid, my dear, you don't quite seem to understand." Nicholas swaggered past her to the berth. He sank upon it and stretched out, cradling his head on his laced fingers. "I have no intention of leaving. This is no longer your cabin. Now it is our cabin." He gestured lazily with one strong hand. "Our cabin, our table, our chairs, our bed. And a surprisingly spacious berth it is too." He patted the bed beside him. "Join me?"

Sabrina clenched her teeth. "I believe you are forgetting the terms of our arrangement."

"Ah, yes." He sighed tolerantly. "The terms. I really have been meaning to discuss those with you. I suspect a little clarification is in order."

"What do you mean, clarification? I thought it all perfectly clear."

"Nothing is perfect, my dear. Now, about those conditions . . . The first is the marriage of my son and your daughter. I see no difficulties there."

Sabrina released a breath she wasn't aware she'd been holding. "And the rest?"

He pulled his dark brows together in a curious frown. "My, you are impatient. Hardly what one would expect from the cool, collected Lady Stanford. Of course, you are the Countess of Wyldewood now, and that shall, no doubt, mean changes. Still,'' he shook his head in a mock serious manner, "one would not imagine those changes, particularly changes in personality, to come so soon after the ceremony. It's extremely puzzling.''

She stared in amazement. Nicholas lay on the bed, looking for all the world as if he belonged there. Resembling nothing quite so much as a lazy lion, surveying his pride. That was all very well and good for a lioness, but for Sabrina, his behavior irritated and annoyed and frustrated.

"What do you want?'' she snarled.

A slow smile of smug satisfaction spread across his face. Good Lord, the man was baiting her! Attempting to discover just how far he could go until she lost her temper. Well, she damned well wouldn't let him succeed.

She drew in a deep breath. "Forgive me. It's been a long day.'' She seated herself in a nearby chair with all the grace she could muster and gathered her wits about her. It appeared she would need them. "As I was saying, the other terms?''

They were at eye level now. Even from across the room she could see him studying her, could see the glitter of amusement in his eye.

"I must admit to some confusion. Let's see if I understand this correctly. I am to support you in the manner and style appropriate to my wife, to a countess of no little social standing. In return, you maintain control and ownership of all your assets, wealth, property and so on. Is that accurate?''

She squirmed uncomfortably. "You make it sound very unfair and quite selfish.''

"Isn't it?'' He raised an innocent brow.

"Hardly.'' Sabrina forced herself to remain calm. "I merely want to ensure my financial security.''

"You mean in the event I turn out to be a scoundrel and a gambler, as well as a rake?'' His eyes gleamed in the lantern light. "It is hardly a flattering portrait.''

Heat flushed Sabrina's face. "It was not meant as a personal affront."

"Nonetheless, when one's bride admits to requiring safeguards against the possible flaws of a new husband, one cannot help but wonder what their future holds." He paused for a long moment and added thoughtfully, "Or what occurred in the past."

She threw him a sharp glare. Absolutely no one knew how little money Jack had left her, and Sabrina wanted to be certain no one ever would. As many faults as Jack had, indiscretion when it came to his financial instability was not among them. She'd worked hard to quietly pay off all his creditors and make good his debts.

"And the next term?" she asked, her voice cool, hoping to steer him away from the question of finances.

"Ah, that one is intriguing. That is the business ventures condition."

"Yes?"

"I have mulled it over in my mind, trying to ascertain just what kind of business a reputable woman such as yourself might be engaged in. I have come up with a number of amusing, although highly unlikely possibilities. I suspect it would not be beneficial to our future relationship to reveal them now." He tossed her a boyish grin and she stifled a childish urge to stick out her tongue.

"Do go on."

"I have reached the inevitable conclusion that the first so-called business venture you, or rather I suppose I should say *we,* are involved in must have something to do with this jaunt to Egypt." He paused. "We are headed to Egypt, are we not?"

She nodded. It was only her own irritation that had kept her from telling him their destination in the first place. She realized as soon as they boarded the ship that he would discover where they were going. His knowledge came as no surprise.

"Now, I said to myself," he mused, gazing upward, "why would someone like the lovely Lady Stanford travel to Egypt? Alone. Suddenly and without notice. Why would she refuse to tell anyone, including her own child, where she was going and why?" He caught her gaze with his. "It is indeed mysterious."

"And did you solve this mystery?"

Nicholas studied her face intently. "Not yet. I shall, you know. At some point. Unless you choose to reveal the answer to me first. After all," his dark gaze deepened, "we are now man and wife."

Her breath caught in her throat. Even from across the room, his gaze bored into hers. Beckoning. Magnetic. Irresistible. A yearning ache fluttered deep in her core, and she wrenched her gaze away with a nearly physical effort. Sabrina's fists clenched in her lap, so tight her nails dug into her palms. The pain cleared her mind, and the expression she turned back to Nicholas was unruffled, belying the explosive emotions he triggered within her.

"No doubt you will discover the purpose of our journey soon enough. I see no urgent need to explain it all to you now." She leaned back and surveyed his relaxed demeanor with a measure of satisfaction. At least on this subject she had the upper hand. "So if we have sufficiently cleared up your concerns . . ." she cast him a pleasant smile and gestured with a tilt of her head toward the door, "get out."

Laughter danced in his eyes. He settled himself deeper in the berth. "Ah, but we have not discussed the final term of our arrangement."

"I would think that condition, above all others, would be easily understood."

"I simply want to be absolutely certain."

"I appreciate that."

"After all, I would hate to violate any of your rules and regulations. Are these standard with a marriage of convenience, do you think?"

Sabrina struggled to keep her composed smile from blossoming into a genuine grin. "I really have no idea."

"Neither have I." He sighed, as if the issue was of paramount importance. "I have never been in a marriage of convenience before. And I'm not at all sure if convenience is the proper word for it. So far nothing about it has struck me as at all convenient. In fact, I can see where some of it will be a damned nuisance.''

Sabrina wasn't sure if she wanted to laugh out loud or throw the nearest object at his head. The man was actually joking with her, breaking down her resistance, toppling her defenses. Startled, she realized she enjoyed this verbal fencing. Realized, as well, how Nicholas had earned his reputation with the ladies. The pompous, arrogant earl of Wyldewood was positively charming.

The grin tugged at the corners of her mouth. ''Nuisance or not, you agreed.''

He shrugged as best he could in his prone position. ''And that brings us back yet again to that last term. Now, what was it I agreed to? Oh, yes; you said you would not share your bed with any man you did not love.''

She nodded, wondering where this would lead.

''Very well, then.'' Nicholas swung his legs to the floor, bounded to his feet and in two long strides stood before her. He knelt before her feet and clasped her hands in his. ''I love you. I have always loved you. I shall always love you.''

''What?'' She tried to snatch her hand away. ''You can't be serious!''

''Oh, but I am, my dear. Need I prove my love to you?'' he asked dramatically. ''Since the moment we met I have lived only to be in your presence. Your hair is spun of purest gold; your eyes rival the most brilliant—''

''Nicholas!'' She laughed and pushed him away. ''That has the sound of a well-rehearsed play. How many times have you told some poor, unsuspecting woman you loved her?''

He stood and grinned down at her. ''This year or ever?''

Laughter bubbled through her lips. ''You are a rake!''

''At your service.'' He bowed with a sweeping gesture. ''Do with me as you please.''

''What I please is for you to stop this foolishness and leave so I that I may retire for the evening.''

He shook his head firmly. ''I fear you were not listening to me. I am not going anywhere. I am staying right here. In this room. With my wife.''

Victoria Alexander

The light moment they'd shared vanished abruptly. Sabrina leapt to her feet and glared up at Nicholas. "You gave your word. You promised to respect my privacy!"

"And so I shall. If you would like to change into whatever the thoroughly proper Lady Stanford wears to bed, I shall be more than happy to close my eyes. Although," his gaze flicked over her man's clothing, "I can't imagine anything would be as fetching as the attire you donned today."

"I most certainly will not change my clothes with you here," she snapped.

"That is entirely your decision. I find I am in agreement with you on one point. It has indeed been a long day, and I too would like to retire." Nicholas grinned down at her. "And since I have no such compulsion about privacy, consider this a warning. I do not find clothing especially comfortable to sleep in. Therefore, I sleep without any. I am going to prepare for bed now. You may do as you wish."

Incredulous, Sabrina glared at him. Surely the man did not intend to fully disrobe right here in front of her? In a swift gesture, Nicholas pulled his shirt over his head, revealing broad, hard shoulders and a firm, muscled chest. His skin was surprisingly dark, and she remembered that Simon had told her he'd been working with the crew, obviously without a shirt. Dark, crisp hair curled across his chest and drifted seductively down his flat stomach to disappear beneath his unmentionables.

She swallowed convulsively. Just how far would he go? Sabrina had not seen a man unclothed since her husband. But even she realized Nicholas was an outstanding example of the male animal. Tall and broad, he towered above her, filling the space in the now tiny cabin. She wanted to reach out and lightly run her hand over solid muscle sheathed in velvet skin. Wanted to absorb the heat of his body with her own. Wanted to . . .

"Sabrina."

His amused voice jerked her gaze to his face. She drew a deep breath and composed herself. "Yes?"

He leaned down and whispered in her ear, "I am now going to remove the remainder of my clothing."

She sighed and surrendered. "You really are going to stay here, aren't you?"

"Yes, my dear, I really am." Lightly, he kissed the tip of her nose.

"Very well." She strode to the bed and gathered a woolen blanket in her arms. Moving to a chair, she plopped herself down, wrapped the blanket around her and flipped her feet onto the seat of a second chair. She clasped her hands together in her lap and smiled pleasantly. "Then proceed."

For the first time that night he appeared uneasy. "Are you certain?"

Satisfaction spread through Sabrina as she realized the way to win this man's game was to turn the tables on him. Accept his challenges and repay him in kind. "Oh, absolutely. It's not as if you were the one who insisted on privacy."

His eyes narrowed suspiciously. "And you are going to remain seated? There?" She nodded. "It is not precisely what I expected from a woman with your reputation."

She widened her eyes in as innocent an expression as she could manage. "Why, Nicholas, I am truly sorry I am not living up to your standards of dull and boring. I shall try much, much harder to be the paragon of virtue you married."

She snuggled deeper into the chair and let her eyes drift closed. "I shall not share a bed with you, but I will share my accommodations. I shall be more than happy to sleep right here tonight."

"Delightful," he grumbled.

Eyes closed, she listened to him move about the cabin. The temptation to peek grew too strong, and she opened one cautious eye. He stood by the wall, his back to her. She caught only the briefest glimpse before he snuffed the lantern, plunging the room into night. The bed creaked and rustled under his weight.

Sabrina smiled smugly and closed her eyes once again. The chair was exceedingly uncomfortable, but a poor night's sleep was little enough price to pay to beat Nicholas at his own game.

She drifted off to sleep cloaked in a firm sense of satisfaction and dreamt of a laughing man with deep black eyes and the body of a Greek statue.

A tall, powerful Greek statue without even the benefit of a strategically placed fig leaf.

Chapter Eight

"Glorious day, don't you think?"

Sabrina didn't so much as flutter an eyelash in response. She leaned forward over the rail and stared out at the sea.

Nicholas suppressed a smile and tried again. "I find nothing is quite so refreshing as sleeping on board ship. It must be the sea air. Did you sleep well, my dear?"

Sabrina favored him with the barest of glances, flicking her gaze over him in a disdainful manner, then turned back to resume her perusal of a blinding blue sky and glittering azure waves. He grinned to himself. There was no doubt she had slept poorly in the uncomfortable chair. Throughout the night he'd heard several heartfelt sighs and a few low, incoherent comments. He really should have insisted that she take the bed.

A twinge of guilt tweaked briefly at his conscience. It was not his fault she chose to sleep where she did. In spite of the terms of their marriage agreement, he was perfectly amenable to sharing the berth. As to exactly what that implied, he would not force himself upon her, although, if truth were told, it was his legal right. But that step he would leave up to her, confident that she would come to him eventually.

No doubt it would take time. The woman was stubborn. Stubborn and clever and, very probably, courageous. His determination strengthened to peel away the layers obscuring what he sensed, what he hoped, what he wanted, was a fiery, passionate spirit.

He rested one arm on the rail and blatantly studied her profile. Strands of gold-washed hair drifted in the breeze, softly framing her delicate features. The masculine attire molded to her body, the linen shirt clinging to beguiling curves and fetching valleys. Her breeches outlined long, shapely legs and round, yielding buttocks. Never had male clothing looked so attractive, so enticing, so delicious. He hoped he would not have to wait too long.

Nicholas was not at all used to waiting for the favors of a woman. Typically, women he cast his eye upon were all too willing to enthusiastically submit to his every wish and desire, with little effort on his part. Oh, certainly, it required the murmuring of a few choice romantic phrases. Never having been in love, he did not think it particularly ill-advised to use the declaration of that emotion in his amorous conquests. He nearly chuckled aloud at the thought. It certainly hadn't worked with Sabrina. No matter; eventually he would determine just what would work. He wanted her and he would have her. It was as simple as that. He always got what he wanted, and he did not accept defeat well.

"What are you staring at?" Sabrina glowered at him.

Nicholas cast her his most polished smile. "You, my lovely wife. A vision of grace and beauty."

She stared, utter disbelief scrawled across her face. "I'm a vision, all right, but hardly one of grace and beauty. I have barely slept. My eyes feel thick and scratchy. My head aches, and turning my neck more than a fraction is extremely painful. Vision? Hah." She turned back to the sea, muttering under her breath, "I feel like bloody hell."

Did she say . . . no, surely he was mistaken. He thought for a moment, then stepped behind her, placing his hands lightly on her neck.

She jerked away and glared. "What do you think you're doing?"

"Since your discomfort is my fault, indirectly at any rate, the least I can do is make amends. Here." Grabbing her shoulders, he turned her around. He replaced his hands on each side of her neck and gently massaged. "Does this feel at all better?"

Better? she thought. It feels bloody marvelous. She groaned aloud. "Good Lord, yes. It's exquisite." Her head fell forward and his hands traveled down the slope of her neck to her shoulders. Stiffened muscles dissolved under strong, sure fingers. A thought drifted through her mind: What else could those nimble fingers do? She sighed. "Wherever did you learn to do this? Some foreign country?"

He laughed softly. "It's amazing the little things I've picked up on my travels. But this comes from the experience of trying to ease the aches and pains one has after going a few rounds with a fighter the likes of Gentleman Jackson. I frequent his rooms in London."

Relaxation flowed from his soothing fingers, and Sabrina thought surely she could stand here under his ministering touch forever.

"So you enjoy boxing," she said absently. "Tell me, do you have any other interests—besides women, I mean. It strikes me I know far less about you than you do about me."

"Perhaps. Although it appears much of my information about you was in error. What exactly do you know about me?"

"Oh, this and that. Public knowledge, mostly. I have heard you are highly thought of in government circles and expected to make a mark in Parliament. I know your wealth is both impressive and solid."

"Is that public knowledge as well?"

"Not at all." She closed her eyes, lulled by his skillful touch. "I had inquiries made."

His hands stilled on her shoulders. "You inquired about me?"

"Um-hum."

He gripped her shoulders and spun her around. Sabrina blinked rapidly in astonishment. His voice was stern, but amusement lit his eyes. "Let me get this straight. You had inquiries made about me, yet you were angered that I had you investigated?"

"That's different," she huffed.

"Hardly." He laughed. "But it's of no consequence. It simply puts us on an equal footing. I prefer everything out in the open. I value honesty highly, particularly between men and women."

"Of course," she said faintly. "So do I." She paused, considering his words. "Honesty. As in telling a woman you love her for your own purposes?"

He grinned roguishly and threw her words back at her. "That's different."

"I see." She returned his grin. "So all really *is* fair in love and war."

"Precisely."

Sabrina merely shook her head. The more time she spent with Nicholas, the more the man worked his way past her defenses. He was every bit as charming as his reputation attested, and far more amusing than she'd expected. She noted with surprise that she actually liked the man.

She had not counted on that when she plunged unthinking into this marriage. But since she was tied to him now, perhaps forever, liking him might well be for the best. Still, would that affection be the first step toward love? Loving Nicholas would only spell disaster. She had no doubt a man who used words of love so easily was a man for whom they meant nothing.

No, she would allow herself to like him, even to enjoy his easy wit and flirtatious banter, but she would not permit herself to love him. That was no way to conduct a marriage of convenience.

And there was still that awkward question of honesty. There was much about herself, past and present, she hid from him. Much she determined to keep hidden forever. What would his reaction be to her secrets?

* * *

By the time the sun set Sabrina could barely keep her eyes open. She and Nicholas had spent a pleasant enough day, occupied in idle conversation, with no treacherous subjects broached. He seemed to enjoy her company and, slowly, she relaxed in his presence, buoyed by the realization that she could indeed drop her guard somewhat without undue risk.

With every hour spent together, more of her true self emerged. Her conversation grew increasingly daring, and she sensed no censure, no disapproval from him. Relief accompanied the realization that Nicholas found her not simply attractive, but interesting and enjoyable as well. She knew of many marriages based on far less.

Sabrina returned to the cabin well before her new husband and wondered what this second night of wedded bliss would bring. She cast a disgusted glance at the chair. tonight she wished to sleep, not spend hours restlessly searching for comfort. He could spend the night in the bloody chair if he chose; tonight the bed was hers.

Stripping off her clothes, she threw them atop a low chest, washed herself with the water from the pitcher and pulled a nightrail from her portmanteau. She tossed the sheer linen garment over her head and let it drift down her body, delighting in the caress of the lightweight fabric. Sabrina, never one for high-necked, flannel sleepwear, much preferred the decadent luxury of linen and lace.

The nightrail was far more provocative and revealing than she would have wished under the circumstances. But it could not be helped. If she had suspected she would be in the position of sharing her quarters with a man the likes of Nicholas, perhaps she could have found a bit of flannel, for protection, if for no other reason. Her arms reached skyward and she indulged in a long, luxurious stretch.

"Now that is a fetching sight to welcome a man." Nicholas stood in the doorway, a grin of appreciation on his face. "I daresay marriage definitely has its benefits."

"Nicholas." She sighed, fighting the impulse to cover herself. "Did no one ever teach you to knock before entering a lady's chamber?"

103

The grin widened. "I can't say I remember ever having had complaints before."

"Well, you have one now." She kept her voice brisk and businesslike in an effort not to betray the fluttering deep within her triggered by his presence. It was a disturbingly intimate scene. The tall, broad-shouldered man in the doorway, his dark eyes aglow in the lantern light, and she, dressed in apparel now suddenly seductive and alluring.

Sabrina drew a deep breath. "I assume you insist on sleeping here again tonight?"

"I can think of no place I'd rather be." He closed the door firmly and stepped toward her.

"What are you doing?" she snapped, nerves taut.

Nicholas halted and lifted a questioning brow. "I was merely going to sit down to remove my boots. Is that permissible?"

"Of course. I simply . . ." She shook her head in a futile attempt to clear her mind of unwanted images of his nude, bronzed body. Odd; she hadn't been troubled by last night's glimpse of him before now. But somehow, in the close confines of the cabin, with barely a whisper of linen concealing her and an undeniable glint of desire in his eyes . . . "I must be very weary," she finished lamely.

"No doubt," he murmured. His gaze wandered over her, intimate and caressing. She wanted to run, to hide. She wanted to stay. Everywhere his glance touched grew hot, singed with a fire she'd never known. Her nipples tightened, and she feared he would see the evidence of her arousal beneath the sheer fabric of her gown. Would see it and then . . . Heat flushed her face and an ache throbbed deep within her. The very room seemed to pulse and reverberate with the slow simmer of suppressed passion.

The cabin was hot. Very hot. Why had she not noticed it before? It was increasingly difficult to breathe, and she unconsciously fanned her face with her hand. His gaze caught hers and she froze. Love or no love, would it be so very wrong to take what she wanted? What might well be inevitable? He was, after all, her husband.

"Nicholas, I . . ." She stepped toward him.

"Sabrina." Her name was little more than a sigh on his lips, his voice an odd mix of warning and desire.

He pulled her into his arms, and eagerly she met his lips with her own. Current arced between them, and the sizzling sensation radiated through her. His tongue plundered and pillaged and she countered his demands with her own, teasing, insistent. He smelled of sea and sun. And Sabrina realized a kiss alone would soon not be enough.

Nicholas wrenched his lips free in an urgent need to taste more of this intoxicating creature. His mouth trailed eagerly down the slope of her neck to where delicate lace framed firm, full breasts. She threw her head back and moaned softly, and he nudged the gown down. The exposed nipple, ripe and tight, beckoned. He groaned and gently pulled it into his mouth. With tongue and teeth he toyed and teased until her breath came in short gasps and her body molded against his.

He ran his hand along one shapely leg to the firm, succulent curve of her derriere. Slowly, he gathered the fine material until his searching fingers found bare flesh. She shuddered beneath his touch, and he drew his hand up along her leg to the curve of her hip. His fingers trailed across her flat stomach, lower to the guardian nest of silken curls. His hand cupped her, his fingers exploring the delicate folds of flesh, now heavy and damp with desire.

"Nicholas," she moaned. Her thoughts no longer lucid, she focused only on his touch. His arousal pushed hard against her through the fabric of his clothes and hers, determined and demanding. Her body yearned for more, for the press of his flesh, naked and searing against hers. She was his and that was what she wanted. All she wanted.

He knew the moment she surrendered. Knew the instant she was his for the taking. Satisfaction surged in his veins and he ground his lips against hers, savoring the sweet taste of triumph. The eagerness of her response drowned him in heady anticipation of their coupling.

". . . I shall not give my favors to a man I do not love."

Her words, her ridiculous terms, rang in the back of his mind. He ignored the glimmer of guilt, the merest whisper

105

of shame that nibbled at the fringe of his conscience. This was not an innocent virgin straight from the schoolroom; she wanted him as much as he wanted her. As if to prove his point, Sabrina clung to him, her tongue invading his mouth, her body straining for contact with his.

Would she regret this? Would she hate him for losing control? Would he hate himself?

"I have also heard you are a man of honor. A man of your word."

Nicholas groaned to himself. He *was* a man of his word; perhaps not as scrupulous in his dealings with women as in other areas, but a man of honor nonetheless. The damned woman probably trusted him. God knows, she'd very likely needed the guidance of a man long before now. He could not disappoint her.

With a strength of will he never dreamed he possessed, Nicholas smoothed her gown back over her hips and pulled his lips from hers, cursing the poor timing of a long-sleeping conscience. He struggled for control.

"I believe I'll sleep on deck tonight." Turning quickly, he headed for the door. He yanked it open and glanced back, nearly losing his determination to leave.

Sabrina stood motionless in the center of the cabin. The lantern light glowed through the translucent fabric of her nightrail. Her hair and gown were in disarray; her lips were swollen and bruised, her face flushed. Emerald eyes stared, wide with shock, glazed with passion. He ached to return to her.

Nicholas drew a steadying breath. "You may indeed have the bed." He nodded curtly and stepped outside, closing the door sharply behind him.

Sabrina stared at the closed door, stunned by his abrupt departure. Why did he leave? What had she done?

Never had desire overtaken her like this. Never had she wanted a man with such sheer uncontrolled urgency before. She'd not been with a man since Jack's death, but even he never triggered this kind of stark, overwhelming passion.

Weak and shaken by unfulfilled need, she clenched her hands at her sides. After thirteen long years she'd found a man who ignited flames of desire with an intensity she'd never dreamed possible. Nicholas. Her husband.

Frustration surged, quickly replaced by a mounting anger flaring within her. Was this some kind of vicious joke? Was he merely trying to prove a point? Prove he could overcome her principles and reservations and expressed wishes and have her any time he chose? Bloody hell, he nearly had. Her defenses had crumbled under little more than the smoldering look in his eye.

She hugged herself tightly and stalked the length of the cabin. How could she have been such a fool? He was very likely up on deck right now, chuckling to himself over his victory. Why he had chosen to halt when he did made no sense, but it was more than likely part of his plan. Obviously he didn't really want her. The growing enjoyment they'd known in each other's company was quite probably a sham, all designed to embarrass her. To put her in her proper place. She meant no more to him than any number of countless women who had come before. No more than a common street slut.

She jerked up her head and glared at the berth. To think she was ready, and far more than willing, to give herself to him. To trap herself irrevocably in this ludicrous marriage. Well, he'd had his chance. There would not be another.

Sabrina threw herself on the bed and yanked the coverlet close around her. The beat of her heart drummed in her ears. She pulled the blanket over her head and squeezed her eyes tight.

Tight. To snuff out the memory of his taste, his touch.

Tight. To quell the need still aching within her.

Tight. To vanquish the pain.

His knuckles whitened with the intensity of his grip on the railing. Blindly, Nicholas stared into the night. He struggled to compose himself, battled to return his breathing to normal, to quell his racing pulse. And trembled with the effort.

Never in his life had he left a woman when success was within reach. Never had he refused what was freely and easily offered. Never had conscience interfered in his pursuit of pleasure.

What on earth had come over him? Why did taking Sabrina to his—to their—bed seem not merely dishonorable but somehow wrong? It was what he wanted. All he wanted. Wasn't it?

No! The insight hit him with the impact of a fist to the belly. He wanted more from her. More than a moment of mindless passion. He wanted . . . what?

Love?

Nicholas thrust the thought away, but like an annoying insect it returned to harry and harass, refusing to be ignored, insisting on attention. Love; what an odd idea. He had never been touched by love and didn't quite believe the emotion actually existed. Would he even recognize it?

The thought settled in his mind. Perhaps it explained a number of questions plaguing him: his peculiar behavior when it came to Sabrina, and the conflicting emotions now churning inside him. It could explain why her kiss brought a shock of recognition so strong he nearly reeled with the blow. Explain why physical satisfaction alone was no longer enough, why the thought that she would despise him was nearly more than he could bear.

Ridiculous. If he was fool enough to fall in love, surely it would not be with a woman even remotely like Sabrina. Oh, she was beautiful and, God knows, burned with a passion he had only suspected before, but the woman was stubborn and far more intelligent than any woman had a right to be. She'd already proved to be more than a match for him in battles of wit. No, common sense dictated he would fall in love with someone complacent and yielding. A woman who acquiesced to his demands and respected his authority.

Love was not the answer. There had to be another reason why he'd stopped when he could have brought her so eagerly to his bed. Why he'd abruptly taken her concerns and her wishes to heart. Why he'd cared about what she wanted and what she thought.

He stood alone on the dark deck, with only his frustration

and confusion and misery to bear him company. If indeed this was love, he wanted no part of it.

It would be a very long night.

Sabrina would not have dreamt it possible, but she slept even worse in the berth than she had in the chair, tossing and turning much of the night. She vowed to avoid and ignore Nicholas, but the moment she came on deck he was there.

"Sabrina," he began, "about last night..." His dark eyes radiated caution and concern, and she hardened her heart against his words. He had played her for a fool and she would not soon forget.

"I do not wish to discuss last night," she said coldly. "I would prefer to forget the entire incident." She turned away and directed her attention toward the sea.

"I'd like to explain."

"I don't believe an explanation is necessary." She shrugged. "I think it's all perfectly clear."

"Is it?" He grabbed her arm and twisted her around to face him. "Then perhaps you would be so kind as to explain it to me."

She glared at him, her resolve to pretend last night had never happened wavering under her swelling anger. She clenched her teeth in one last effort to remain calm. "Let go of me."

"Not until you tell me what you meant." Amber flames sparked in his eyes.

"Very well." She wrenched her arm out of his grasp and winced at the momentary pain. "You wanted to show me I was no different than any other woman when it came to succumbing to your infamous charms. To humiliate and embarrass me. To put me firmly in my place. It was not necessary to actually complete the seduction to prove your point."

"That's what you believe?" he asked, his voice incredulous. Stark disbelief shone on his face. "You honestly think I would do that to you?"

"Yes, I do." She shot him a look of defiance, daring him to deny her charge.

"Why, Sabrina? What possible reason would I have to want to humiliate you?"

"Reason?" She hadn't thought of that. Hadn't thought beyond her own anger and hurt to look for a logical motive for his actions. "I don't know," she snapped.

"Well, know this." His gaze burned into hers, and a morsel of unease and doubt tweaked her conscience. Could she have made a mistake?

"I have wanted you since the moment we met. Wanted the proper and serene Lady Stanford. But not nearly as much as I want the fiery, unpredictable, stubborn, infuriating Sabrina Harrington, my wife, if you recall that minor detail." He clasped her shoulders in an iron grip. "But, fool that I am, for the first time in my entire life I placed a woman's wishes above my own desires. Granted, I should not have let things get to the point they did, but, ultimately, I left. I upheld the idiotic terms of this so-called marriage. Preserved the privacy you value so highly."

Sabrina stared up at him, mesmerized by the vehemence of his words and the fury in his eyes.

"And for that you dare to accuse me of the vilest of acts." He released her abruptly. She opened her mouth to speak but could not find the words. Her anger fled in the face of his righteous indignation.

He flung her a withering glare. "Furthermore, I resent your use of the word *seduction*. It seems to me there was a considerable amount of seducing on both sides."

"You are blaming me for this?" Anger reignited in her blood. "I'm not the one with the flirtatious manner. I'm not the one who casts assessing glances that make me feel as if I were not clothed. And I certainly did not insist on sharing a cabin with you."

"No, but we shall continue to share that cabin," he shot back. "In the interest of public appearances, I will not have this crew believing we are anything but blissfully wed."

"I doubt if it will come as much of a surprise if you do not lower your voice," she hissed.

He drew a deep breath in a visible effort at self-control. His voice rang calm and cold. "You may, however, feel free to relax your guard. There shall not be a repeat of last night. I will respect your wishes, your terms."

"Fine," she snapped.

Nicholas tunneled a hand through his dark hair in a weary gesture. "I will agree with you on one other point, as well. I too would prefer to forget the entire incident. I did not sleep at all last night and I think it's best if we put this behind us."

"You didn't sleep? What a shame, Nicholas." She smiled smugly and turned to the sea. "I myself slept extremely well."

Throughout the day Sabrina remained cautious and careful around Nicholas, as if treading on eggshells. The companionship they'd shared before last night was now strained, and tension marked their time together. By nightfall they'd declared an uneasy truce.

Again, that night Sabrina was the first in their cabin. She changed quickly and climbed into the berth. Nicholas actually knocked before entering, and she could not help but regret, if for only a moment, their marriage terms and his inopportune remembrance of them last night. He was cordial and polite, even somewhat pleasant, but nothing of the notorious rake appeared however briefly. He lived up to his promise to the letter, and Sabrina was more than satisfied with his behavior. Still, she could not help but wonder why that satisfaction was not quite as sweet as it should have been.

They bid each other good night and Nicholas took up her previous position in the chair. Dim moonlight danced in the many-paned window at the bow end of the cabin and silhouetted his shadowy figure across the room. She was sharply aware of his every movement, every breath, every sigh.

The ship creaked and moaned through the night, an unsteady pulse that surged in her blood and toyed with her mind. The sea cradled the vessel, rocking and lulling its passengers in the seductive, age-old rhythms of life itself. The slap of waves against wood echoed and throbbed.

And no one slept.

Chapter Nine

The docks at Marseilles buzzed and hummed with an intensity well worthy of a thriving seaport. Sailors and other various and unique forms of life swarmed and scurried. Carts and wagons, heavy with cargo, lumbered along, mindless of the bustling throng. Crates were stacked high here and there in unsteady caricatures of medieval castles. Voices in a dozen different languages assailed Nicholas's ears, the smells borne of men and fish and God only knows what, assaulted his nostrils. Still, he savored the pleasurable feel of firm footing and solid ground.

Oh, he'd always enjoyed being on the sea. He'd even considered going to sea as a lad, a frivolous and unthinkable idea for the sole heir to a substantial fortune and significant title. But as agreeable as life on board ship was, it was still nice to have the earth back beneath his feet.

He ducked and dodged the lively goings-on and headed toward the town center. Sabrina had asked him to post a letter to Belinda, and he had obligingly consented. He tried to be as amenable to her as temperament allowed, in a valiant attempt to ease the strain between them. They treated

Victoria Alexander

each other with the caution of natural enemies forced together against their will.

He strode through the docks and considered the matter.
Something had to be done. Nicholas had no desire to continue with this icy barrier between them. He missed the
charm and the challenge of her companionship. A polite,
formal tolerance of each other was not at all what he wanted
from her, though he'd yet to answer the question of just
what he did want.

Perhaps the ship's captain could help shed light on the
matter. He was expected to join his crew here. Simon said
this Captain Madison was a very old friend of Sabrina's,
practically a member of the family. Nicholas held a picture
in his mind of a grizzled, old sea dog, something of a pa-
ternal figure. If the man had known her for long, he could,
no doubt, provide some insight into her character. Nicholas
could certainly use all the help he could get.

He expected help from another quarter, as well, and had
his own letter to post, in addition to the letter to Belinda.
This missive was to his solicitor in London, directing the
man to hire a decent investigator and not another idiot. Nicholas was now firmly convinced that the explanation behind
one of Sabrina's marriage conditions lay in her past. Why
on earth would a woman who'd always had social position
and wealth concern herself with financial independence?
Whatever the answer, it remained well hidden. The easiest,
although not always the most reliable, information was simple ton gossip. But neither he nor the original incompetent
he'd hired to look into her background had come up with
even the slightest indication of monetary difficulties.

Nicholas worked his way down the docks, deep in his
own thoughts. An ornately outfitted town carriage drew his
attention, and he slowed his steps. The elegant vehicle was
distinctly out of place in the seamy atmosphere, and he wondered as to its purpose.

The carriage door flew open and a man about Nicholas's
height and build bounded out with a fluid, athletic grace.
Impeccably attired, his fair hair contrasted with his darkened
skin, indisputable evidence of long hours of work under a

hot sun. A feminine bejeweled hand extended from the carriage's open door. The man clasped the hand in his, lifted it to his lips and expertly flipped it over, placing a single kiss in the palm. Nicholas grinned at the well-rehearsed and, very likely, quite effective bit of gallantry. The subject of his scrutiny firmly closed the carriage door and turned, his gaze catching Nicholas's. The man shrugged and winked, and Nicholas nodded in acknowledgment, an instinctive recognition between men who share a common bond: the pursuit and enjoyment of women. The stranger swaggered off, and Nicholas continued on his way, unable to suppress an appreciative chuckle.

Nicholas disposed of his errands swiftly and returned to the docks. He was still a good distance from the ship when he spotted Sabrina's figure on the deck. She'd not left the ship while they were in port, for once agreeing with him that unless she wanted to change out of her man's clothing and into proper attire, as well as taking several sailors as escort, her safety would be in jeopardy in this colorful but disreputable place.

She glanced in his direction and waved eagerly. In spite of their differences, was she now glad of his return? Odd, how the pace of his feet and the race of his heart picked up whenever she came into sight. He raised his hand in response.

"Bree!" a voice rang out from somewhere nearer the ship.

Bree?

Nicholas slowed, perplexed, and spotted a broad shouldered man taking the gangplank in long, easy strides. From the back, the cut of his clothes, the jaunty spring in his step, seemed familiar.

Sabrina raced down the deck. Nicholas quickened his steps, an uneasy apprehension urging him forward. The stranger reached Sabrina and at once she was in his arms. He lifted her off her feet and swung her around, golden, unbound hair flying free. Even at a distance the delight in her laughter was unmistakable. Stunned, he watched the man wrap her in his arms and plant his lips firmly on hers.

115

Nicholas strode up the gangplank in time to see the end of what appeared to be a distinctly passionate kiss. Anger swelled within him. Who was this man and why did he kiss Sabrina in such an intimate manner? Sabrina. *His wife!* He gritted his teeth, his hands tightened into fists, and he willed himself to remain calm.

"An acquaintance of yours, I presume?" His voice was cold and hard.

Sabrina and the stranger broke apart and turned to face him. Good Lord! It was the man from the carriage. He grinned at Nicholas and kept one arm possessively around Sabrina, in a manner that did nothing to quell Nicholas's simmering rage.

"You! Who are you?" Nicholas demanded.

"I should ask you the same question," the fair-haired man drawled, his tone insolent. "Since this is my ship you're on."

"Your ship?" Nicholas said in confusion.

"Nicholas, may I present Captain Matthew Madison," Sabrina cut in, a challenging gleam in her eye.

Nicholas stared, shocked at the introduction. This was no fatherly figure, no wise, aged man of the sea. This was a rogue, a rake, probably a scoundrel.

"Matt, this is Nicholas Harrington, Earl of Wyldewood."

Madison shrugged. "All right, that's his name. What's he doing here?"

"I'm her husband," Nicholas spit the words through clenched teeth.

"Husband?" Madison's eyes widened in surprise, and he turned to Sabrina. "Is that true?"

Sabrina wrinkled her nose. "More or less."

"More or less?" Madison raised a puzzled brow. "What the hell does that mean?"

"It means nothing," Nicholas said sharply. "And I will thank you to take your hands off my wife."

Madison hesitated, hugged her quickly and then removed his arm from around Sabrina's waist. She cast Nicholas a disdainful glare and turned to Madison.

"We really must talk. It's been a very long time and there

are—'' she waved her hands in a vague gesture, ''—well, matters we need to discuss. I'm sure you have some questions.''

''Oh, I definitely have questions.''

She turned a scathing look on Nicholas. ''I'm going to my cabin now. Alone.'' She pivoted and stalked off.

Nicholas stared after her. Madison wasn't the only one with questions. But Nicholas was damned if she would leave his questions hanging. He wanted answers and he wanted them now.

Madison chuckled beside him. ''She's really something, isn't she?''

In his younger days Nicholas had been in numerous tight spots, circumstances in which his life hung by a thread. He hadn't seen military service during the war but had served in other ways. All the attributes that had once made him an extremely dangerous man, a man who fought for and expected—no, *demanded*—success, now surged within him.

He cast a cold, calm, deadly glance at Madison and made certain his voice matched his eyes. ''Touch her again and I'll kill you.''

Nicholas nodded curtly and strode off after Sabrina.

Sabrina slammed the door to her cabin and paced the room. Nicholas had no right, absolutely no right, to treat her like a piece of property; his property. She deeply resented his telling Matt about their marriage. Sabrina would have told him soon enough in her own way. And Nicholas had been so bloody cold and nasty about it all.

Certainly he had come upon them at an inopportune moment, but it had been no more than the greeting of two old friends after the separation of a decade. Still . . . Sabrina drew up short, stopped by a sudden insight. Nicholas didn't know that. He'd never met Matt and had no inkling as to their past relationship. All Nicholas knew was what he saw: his wife kissing a dashing and extremely attractive stranger in what could possibly be called an enthusiastic manner.

He was jealous! Sabrina grinned at the revelation. Of course, that was it. What a lovely idea. If he was jealous, he must care about her, if only a little. The thought warmed her. She was tired of being at odds with him and wanted the friendship that had been growing between them back. Beyond that . . . well, she was no longer sure whether she wanted strict adherence to all the terms of their marriage.

The door flew open in a thundering crash and Nicholas stormed into the room.

"We are going to talk!" His voice rang with suppressed rage, and fury sparked in his eyes. He slammed the door behind him and moved toward her.

Instinctively, she took a step backward. "Very well. Talk."

"Who is he?" Nicholas grated through clenched teeth.

"Matt?" she asked innocently.

"Of course Madison. Who else are we talking about?"

There was no doubt in her mind now. He was definitely jealous. This was glorious. Sabrina could barely keep the grin off her face.

She widened her eyes and smiled sweetly. "Why, Matt's the captain of the ship, of course."

Nicholas glared. "You know perfectly well that's not what I meant. And don't give me that insipid look. You and I both know you're not stupid; that's simply part of the ridiculous act I suspect you've put on for years. The serene, dull, boring Lady Stanford certainly doesn't exist now, if she ever did."

Sabrina stared, shocked into silence. Had she so let down her guard with this man that he could see right through her? Had the freedom of the voyage and the adventure of the quest broken down all the walls and barriers she had so thoroughly built? Or was ten years simply long enough, or too long, to hide? She drew a deep breath.

"Very well." She clasped her hands in front of her and gazed straight into his eyes. "What do you want to know?"

Nicholas's eyes narrowed suspiciously at her compliant response. "How do you know Madison? What does he mean to you?"

"Years ago we were involved in . . . oh, a sort of business proposition. You could consider us partners."

His brows drew together in a puzzled frown. "Business proposition? What kind of—" understanding broke on his face, "—is that why we're here? This current so-called business venture we're involved in now? Is he a part of it?"

She shrugged. "Hopefully."

"And your previous venture; what sort of business was that?"

"Oh, shipping, trade, that sort of thing." Sabrina deliberately kept her manner vague. How in the world did one describe smuggling, anyway, without it sounding like . . . well . . . smuggling?

Nicholas cast her a thoughtful glance and seemed to consider his next words carefully. His voice was quiet and intense. "How close a partner was he?"

Sabrina's throat tightened. "Are you asking if we were lovers?"

Nicholas nodded. She stilled the impulse to reach out and touch the tension in the air. It would be so easy to let him believe what he wished. It would very likely serve him right.

"I've always loved Matt," she said slowly. The muscles in his jaw tightened. "I've always thought of him as I would a brother."

"A brother?" Nicholas said, disbelief on his face.

Sabrina nodded firmly. "A brother."

"That was no brotherly embrace!"

She could scarcely believe her ears. "You are complaining about an insignificant greeting? I haven't seen Matt in years."

"I don't care if it's been a lifetime; I think complaints are well warranted when I find you in the arms of someone like Madison."

"What do you mean 'someone like Madison'?"

A lofty note sounded in his voice. "From what I've seen the man has no scruples when it comes to women."

"Well, you would certainly recognize that attribute when you see it!" she shot back.

Nicholas ignored the well-placed jab. "As to the behavior I witnessed from you today, I will not allow it."

She fought to keep her mouth from dropping open in

amazement. Jealousy or no jealousy, this was too much. "You will not allow it? I scarcely think you have much to say about it, since under the terms of our marriage it was my distinct impression that you planned on continuing the little dalliances you are so well known for. And if you have that right, I certainly assume I do, as well."

"Well, you don't," he snapped.

Fury washed over her. "I'll do what I bloody well please, and if that includes kissing an old friend—a man I have a strictly brotherly affection for—that's what I'll damned well do."

"That's hardly how you kiss a brother."

"Oh, really?" Sarcasm dripped from her words. "And I imagine with your vast expertise in such matters, you are an expert on how one kisses one's brother?"

Nicholas grabbed her shoulders and yanked her into his arms, her hands trapped flat against his chest. "I have a sister, remember? And this is how one should be kissed by a brother." He brushed his lips lightly over her forehead. A distinctly unfraternal thrill shivered through her. "Or this." He placed a soft kiss first on one cheek, then the other.

She glared up at him and pushed against the hard muscles of his chest. "Very well; now unhand me."

His black eyes gleamed. "I don't think the lesson is quite over yet. A brother should never kiss like this." He skimmed his lips lightly over her eyelids. "Or like this." He feathered kisses down the side of her neck. Her breath caught in her throat. Anger ebbed away under the onslaught of his touch.

He stared down at her, his endless gaze drawing her closer, melting her defiance, sapping her control. "And never . . ." he kissed the tip of her nose, "ever . . ." he nuzzled her ear, "should a brother kiss like this."

His mouth descended on hers, firm yet gentle. She lost herself in the spiraling sensations brought on by the mere touch of his lips. Desire rose unbidden within her, and she clutched his shirt convulsively. Her knees weakened and she clung to him. He stole her breath, her will, her soul.

He pulled away, his expression set and hard. She stared

back, past caring that he would surely see her passion mirrored in her eyes.

"Now that you know what not to do with a brother, see that it never happens again. Especially with Madison." He released her, strode toward the door and turned back. "I forbid it."

Her desire turned to disdain. "I told you, I'll do what I please. You have absolutely no right—"

"Ah, but I do, my dear." He opened the door and smiled pleasantly. A heavy knot weighed in her stomach. "I am, after all, your husband. I have every right in the world." He stepped through the door and snapped it closed behind him.

Sabrina stared, fury welling through her. What an insufferable, arrogant, self-righteous, condescending ass! She wanted to scream at the top of her lungs, to rage uncontrollably. Not in years had this urge to do something, anything, just to release the frustration inside, assaulted her like this. If he walked back in at that moment, so help her, she'd be hard pressed not to tear him apart with her bare hands.

A sharp knock sounded at the door and it swung open. He was back. Without thinking, she turned, grabbed a heavy mug off the table and hurled it with all her might. It shattered above the door, bits of pottery flying in a furious rain.

Matt leaned against the doorframe, arms folded across his chest, amusement dancing in his azure eyes. "And here I thought you were glad to see me."

"Matt, good Lord, I'm sorry." She brushed her hair back from her face. "I thought it was him."

"The husband?" He raised an inquisitive brow. Sabrina grimaced in acknowledgment. "I see. We have a lot to talk about, don't we?"

"Very probably." She sighed.

He closed the cabin door and stepped to the chest that stored his best brandy. Matt pulled out the bottle, eyed it thoughtfully, and cast her a questioning glance. "Was it good?"

She moved next to him, picked up a mug and held it toward him. "Delightful."

Obligingly, he filled the cup. "Why did you marry him?" he asked, his voice quiet.

Sabrina shrugged helplessly. "I'm not really sure. It seemed like a very clever idea at the time."

"Simon told me you got angry, and the next thing he knew, there was a wedding."

She took a deep swallow, the sting of the brandy biting and hot. "Something like that."

"You could have married me, you know. You always seemed to be mad at me." He grinned a lopsided smile that had melted more than one woman's heart.

"Matt!" She laughed. "I have certainly missed you." She stepped to the table and set down her mug.

He came up behind her and wrapped his arms around her. Sabrina rested her head against his broad, powerful chest. It was somehow comforting to stand here, close and secure. She had missed him.

"Do you remember the last time we saw each other?"

"Of course." Her mind wandered back beyond the years to a time when intrigue filled her days and adventure charged her nights. She could still recall the delightfully sinful excitement of danger. "It was the night of our final run. That annoying government agent was making life too difficult, and we had to bash him on the head to get him out of the way."

Odd, she hadn't thought of him for a long time. For years the man whose face she'd never seen had filled her fantasies. In her dreams she relived the memory of her impulsive kiss. He was the second man she'd ever kissed, and when she thought about it later she wasn't certain what had prompted the rash action. She hadn't told Matt about the kiss then and wouldn't tell him now.

"I remember, when all was completed, that we walked on the beach before you sailed."

"I wanted you to come with me," he reminded her.

"Matt, I had a child to raise and a life to build." She laughed softly. "We wouldn't have suited. You'd have been off chasing lightskirts in every port. And I would have had to cut your heart out."

"But I loved you, Bree," he said mournfully.

She laughed again. "If I remember correctly, we settled that."

"Remind me," he growled, resting his chin on her head.

"I said we were too good friends to be lovers. I told you, you were the brother I never had. And then you kissed me. And . . ."

He sighed. "It was just like kissing my sister."

Sabrina smiled at the thought of her discussion with Nicholas over the proper and improper ways for a brother to kiss a sister. Matt's kiss was pleasant enough, but it never took her breath away or turned her knees to mush and her heart to fire. Not like that bloody man she'd married.

Matt stepped back and turned her around. His gaze searched her face. "Does he make you happy? Do you love him?"

"Love?" Sabrina scoffed and pulled away. She retrieved her mug and took a sip. "Love has nothing to do with it. This is strictly a marriage of convenience."

"A marriage of convenience?" Matt snorted. "What in the hell is that?"

"Bloody difficult, actually."

"It shouldn't be." He picked up his own cup and drew a deep swallow. "I've seen the way the man looks at you— like a shark sizing up a minnow." He nodded toward her. "I know that look. The man wants you. He even threatened to kill me if I so much as touched you."

"Truly?" Sabrina couldn't suppress a smug smile. "How rude of him."

Matt threw her a skeptical glance. "Somehow, I don't think the thought of my death at the hands of your husband has you quite as torn up as I would have hoped you'd be." Surprise washed across his face. "You really do care for him, don't you?"

"I don't know how I feel about Nicholas right now," she snapped. "And I really don't want to talk about him."

Matt shrugged. "I'm more than happy to oblige on that score. I can think of a lot of things I'd rather discuss than your husband." He strode to a chair and sat down, swinging his legs up to rest them on a second chair nearby. He leaned back until he tottered precariously on two wooden legs. "So let's talk gold instead."

Sabrina swept his feet off the chair with a wave of her hand and Matt thumped to the floor. She sank into the now vacant seat. "What has Simon told you?"

"Not much. Something about gold hidden in Egypt by the French."

She leaned forward eagerly. "It's a fortune, Matt. At least a half million. Left there for twenty years. Waiting . . . for us."

"I can't say it's not an interesting story, but why are you after this gold? The last time I saw you, you'd amassed quite a sizable fortune for yourself." He narrowed his eyes and studied her face. "Are you broke, Bree?"

"Not exactly," she hedged. "I've simply had some financial reversals. A problem with the management of my investments. And with Belinda about to be wed and the need for a respectable dowry, well . . ." She glared at him defiantly. "I need the money, that's all. And what about you? I can't believe you couldn't use a few additional funds."

"I don't know." He shrugged. "Money doesn't seem as important as it once was. The *Lady B*'s just one of a half-dozen ships I own now. So you see, I've done pretty well for myself. Of course . . ." he flashed her a grin, "making my fortune in legal and respectable ways isn't nearly as much fun as when there's a little larceny involved."

Sabrina's heart sank. The search for the gold was a speculative and possibly dangerous quest. If Matt really didn't need the money, there would be no reason for him to help her. And without Matt she wasn't at all sure how she'd handle Nicholas.

"Very well," she said slowly. "I understand why you don't want to be a part of this. Still, I do appreciate your—"

"Hold on there, Bree." Matt leaned toward her and grabbed her hands. "I never said I wouldn't do it. It's just that the money itself doesn't mean a lot. But life these days has been resoundingly dull, and what you're proposing sounds a great deal more exciting than anything that's crossed my path lately." His eyes twinkled. "Besides, you really didn't think I'd pass up the chance to work with my old partner again, did you?"

Relieved, Sabrina returned his grin and quelled the impulse to throw her arms around him. Matt's agreement left only one man to convince, and she wasn't at all sure how to handle that. At this point she didn't even know when she would spring her treasure hunt on Nicholas. But with every passing day the ship drew closer to Egypt, closer to the treasure, closer to telling her husband at least one of her secrets.

"But tell me something else, Bree. You've got this rich husband now. Why are you still worried about money?"

She removed her hands from his grasp and leaned back in the chair. "Matt, you remember when we met I was struggling to turn a miserable army of villagers and fishermen into something resembling a competent smuggling operation." He nodded. "You know, Jack left me with practically nothing. Only my jewels, the London house and quite a few debts."

She gazed across the room at a distant spot and a far-ago time. "All my life I always thought someone would be around to take care of me. Actually expected it. First there was my great-aunt, after my parents died. And even though she packed me off to school eventually, she still paid the bills. Then there was Jack, who didn't feel a mere woman should be involved in matters of finance. While I long suspected our pockets were nearly empty, he would not discuss it or even admit it to me. And he did seem to manage to handle everything.

"When he died I returned to my great-aunt's, fully expecting to be taken care of once again. She lived about a day's ride from the village where you and I met. There I was, a young, virtually penniless widow with a small child, and one day I overheard the servants talking about what a great strain on the household our presence was. I don't know if they knew I was listening or not. Regardless, the entire discussion brought home to me how dependent I was.

"Odd I had never thought of it before, and perhaps if I

had, I would not have considered it a problem. I daresay most women don't. But somehow, listening to those hard-working people and knowing I contributed nothing—was practically worthless, in fact—filled me with shame and a certain amount of self-pity. After all,'' she laughed softly, ''there are few ways for a respectable female from a good family with a good name to provide for herself.''

She took a deep pull from her mug and stared directly into Matt's eyes. ''The pity became determination to help myself. I vowed right then never to have to depend on anyone ever again to provide for me. And so far . . .'' she raised her mug in a toast, ''I haven't.''

He pulled his brows together in a thoughtful frown. ''Why haven't you told me this before?''

She arched a brow. ''When, Matt? When we first met and you were highly suspicious of a titled Englishwoman proposing to help smuggle goods into her country? Later, when I occasionally sailed with you? My dear friend, the question of why I was doing what I did never came up.'' She tossed him a wry smile. ''And you never asked.''

He toyed with the mug of brandy before him and refused to meet her gaze. ''I do understand now, of course, but are you sure it wouldn't be much simpler, and safer, for me just to give you the money you need? Strictly a loan, of course.''

''Matt . . .'' She laughed, and his startled gaze met hers. ''I fear you haven't been listening. I have to do this myself, just as I had to do it before. I don't want your money. But I needed your help then, and I daresay I shall need it now. Besides . . .'' Sabrina tossed him a cocky grin, ''if you think your respectable life has been boring, I can't begin to tell you what mine has been like. I've been sedate and serene, always minding my manners and doing what's proper. I've been so well behaved my dear husband even refers to me as dull and boring.''

The moment the words passed her lips Sabrina realized what she'd said, and her eyes widened in horror. She had her own personal code of honor and, despite her problems with Nicholas, it dictated that there were some things that should stay strictly between husband and wife.

Matt's face split in an ear-to-ear grin. "He doesn't know you very well yet, does he?"

"I suspect he's beginning to."

Matt flicked his gaze over her. "And what does he say about those quite fetching but definitely improper clothes you've been wearing?"

"You know, it's extremely odd," Sabrina mused. "I fully expected him to demand I change at once, yet he hasn't offered much more than an occasional compliment."

Matt raised a questioning brow but said nothing.

"At any rate," she bounded to her feet and twirled around the cabin, "it feels absolutely delightful to wear these again."

He grinned at her antics. "Before you get too involved in enjoying your bit of forbidden freedom, suppose we talk about this gold business, shall we? It seems to me Egypt is a mighty big place."

Sabrina whirled to a stop and grabbed the table to keep her balance. The childish gesture was just what she needed to restore her excitement about the search for the gold, the adventure awaiting them.

"Oh, I doubt if it will be too difficult." She breezed over to her portmanteau and kneeled before it. Flipping open the case, she dug beneath the layers of clothes. Triumphantly, she pulled out the letter and waved it before him. "You see, Matt, we have a map."

Crossing to his side, she slapped the letter on the table. "Look at this. It's all in here, every detail, every direction."

He glanced at the paper before him and frowned. "It's in French."

"Of course it's in French. It was written by one of the officers who hid the gold." She narrowed her eyes in suspicion. "Can't you read this? I thought your mother was French."

"Of course I can read it," he said loftily. "I'm just a little rusty, that's all. Besides, I've always been able to get my point across without having to depend on writing it down." He favored her with a wicked grin. "Especially in French. I've always found even the most innocent comment sounds so much more ... intimate when it's spoken in French.''

"Matt! Would you kindly try to remain serious and keep your mind on the matter at hand.''

"All right.'' He sighed in resignation. "But I can think of a number of things we could be doing together that would be far more interesting than studying an old letter.''

"Interesting perhaps, Matt,'' she murmured, ignoring the suggestion behind his comments, her gaze scanning the page before her, her mind firmly centered on the scrawled handwriting, "but not nearly so profitable.''

Still standing, she bent low over the letter, her head next to Matt's. The two studied the words long and carefully, one occasionally drawing the other's attention to a particular point. Matt concurred with Sabrina's conclusion as to the approximate location of the gold. The ship creaked around them, the noise a constant blurry background, complimenting their conversation. She no longer paid notice to even the loudest squeaks. After several moments she straightened up and stretched. Matt glanced up at her.

"You say you don't know where the first page of this is?''

"I have no idea. This is all I found.''

"Well,'' he said slowly, "looking at this, I don't think we need it.'' He grinned. "I think we've got ourselves real good directions to a king's ransom in gold.''

Sabrina laughed with delight. "Matt, I haven't been so excited in years. A fortune in gold, just think of it!''

A wry voice sounded from the doorway.

"I find, my dear, I can think of little else.''

Chapter Ten

"Don't you ever knock?" Sabrina snapped.

Nicholas smiled grimly from the doorway. "I thought we had thoroughly discussed that. Remember, this is my cabin."

"Yes, I know." She shot him a scathing glare. "Your cabin, your table, your chairs, your bed—"

"My wife." His icy tone shivered through her, but he directed his smoldering gaze at Matt. Matt leaned back in his chair, his attitude issuing a casual challenge.

"I think we are all well aware of that relationship," she said sharply.

"Excellent. I feared you had forgotten it." He raked his angry gaze over her. "Would you care to explain why you are here with Madison? Alone?"

Sabrina glared, exasperated and more than a little annoyed. Surely the man couldn't believe there was anything improper in her being alone with Matt? She had given him absolutely no reason to distrust her. And jealousy was no longer an acceptable excuse for his maddening and insulting suspicions.

"No, I would not care to explain. I do not believe an explanation is necessary." She nodded toward Matt. "I believe I made my relationship with Matt perfectly clear earlier."

"Oh?" Matt tossed her a knowing grin. "What did you tell him?"

Sabrina drew her brows together in an irritated frown and cast him a quelling glance. She turned to Nicholas. "I told you exactly how I feel about him. Therefore, there is no reason for you to storm in here like an avenging angel or a—"

"Betrayed husband?" Matt asked innocently.

Nicholas's anger was almost palpable. Fury sparked in his eyes. Sabrina had never seen him this irate, and she sensed he was hard pressed to contain himself. His voice came as hard as the set of his jaw, and a trickle of foreboding lodged in her midsection. "Yes, my dear, you have more than explained your feelings for this man. However, I am not aware of his feelings for you. Furthermore, I suspect he is not to be trusted when it comes to such matters."

Sabrina's gaze shot from Nicholas to Matt. He couldn't possibly take Nicholas's insults seriously, could he? Matt lounged in his chair.

"That sounds suspiciously as if you're accusing me of being lacking in honor." His indolent drawl belied the steely glint in his eye. Sabrina's apprehension grew with every word.

Nicholas raised a scornful brow. "I must say, you surprise me. I didn't expect you to be perceptive enough to comprehend my meaning."

"Nicholas!" His comments appalled her. In spite of their longtime affection, she feared Matt would not allow this insult to pass. The knot in her stomach tightened. Friend or not, Matt could be a very dangerous man.

Matt unfolded his long frame from the chair and rose to his feet, his nonchalant manner in stark contrast to his eyes, dark and stormy and dangerous.

"I will explain this to you once, Wyldewood." Matt's voice came surprisingly calm, cool, controlled. Hope of diffusing the rapidly escalating confrontation flickered within Sabrina. "Bree and I have known each other for many years. At one time we enjoyed a business relationship. We share a certain amount of affection. I care for her as if—"

"Yes, yes, I know," Nicholas interrupted impatiently. "As if she were your sister."

"Exactly." Matt nodded firmly.

Nicholas snorted with derision. "That should give Sabrina scant comfort, considering you could not properly care for your own sister."

Confusion colored Matt's face. "My sister?"

"His sister?" Sabrina echoed.

"Yes, his sister!" Nicholas snapped, glaring at them as if they had both lost their minds. Sabrina and Matt exchanged puzzled glances.

"What sister would that be?" Matt asked cautiously.

"The one who was cut down in the prime of life. The one who couldn't cope with all the problems she had to face. The one Simon told us about."

"Simon?" Matt was obviously still baffled by Nicholas's words.

Sabrina's bewilderment equaled Matt's. What on earth was Nicholas talking about?

"He told us everything." Frustration at their blatant incomprehension sounded in Nicholas's words. "About your sister!" he yelled in exasperation. "The one who became a nun!"

Realization struck Sabrina. Nicholas's rantings dealt with that ridiculous story Simon had fabricated about the name of the ship.

"What nun?" Matt's forehead furrowed in bewilderment.

"The nun," Sabrina jumped in. "Your sister, the nun."

Matt had the look of a man struggling to decipher an unintelligible code. "What sister?"

"The one who became a nun," Nicholas roared.

"The one you named the *Lady B* for!" Sabrina said, her voice sharp with rising panic.

"The *Lady B?*" Matt floundered for understanding. "But I named the *Lady B* for—"

"For your sister," Sabrina cut in desperately, her gaze trapping his, praying he could somehow understand her silent plea.

"Bree, I . . ." Matt stared straight into her eyes. His widened slightly as he finally grasped the full meaning of the conversation. ". . . named the ship for my sister, of course." He turned to Nicholas and shrugged. "It's been such a long time, and we were never really close."

Nicholas's eyes narrowed suspiciously. "I had the impression you were extremely close."

"Well, yes." Matt shook his head. "We were close once, but . . . then we weren't." He laughed awkwardly and cast a withering glance at Sabrina. "When she had her, um, problems we drifted apart. She would never accept anyone's help, you see. Stubborn little wench."

Sabrina clenched her teeth against an angry retort. "I'm sure she had her reasons."

Matt sighed in resignation. "Just pride and sheer mulishness. The woman never did know what was best for her. Especially when it came to men. Always made the wrong choices and found herself stuck in extremely difficult circumstances."

"Very likely nothing she could not handle," Sabrina snapped.

"What are you two talking about?" Nicholas exploded. "Nun or no nun, I don't give a damn about your sister! Sabrina is my only concern. And whether you think of her as a sister, or whether you think of her as a blasted nun, I want you to stay away from her!"

"Nicholas, you can't tell me what to do," Sabrina protested, resisting the impulse to stamp her foot for emphasis.

"Oh, yes, I can!"

She shot him an angry glare. "No one has told me what to do for thirteen bloody years! If you think you of all people are going to start telling me now what I may or may not do, how I shall and shall not conduct myself, you are in for a rude awakening." She whirled to face Matt. "Tell him, Matt. Tell him he cannot order me around like a servant. Tell him he cannot run my life."

"Bree . . ." Matt looked down at her with an apologetic expression. "Annoying as it may well be, the man is your husband and has certain rights."

Nicholas smirked triumphantly. It was all Sabrina could do to still the urge to smack him, and Matt too. Surrounded by people who insisted on informing her of her husband's rights, she was bloody tired of hearing it.

"Although," Matt's gaze shifted from Sabrina to her husband, his voice quiet, "he certainly has no such rights when it comes to telling me what to do."

Nicholas quirked an eyebrow in an obvious challenge, his voice as measured as Matt's. "You shall stay away from her, Madison."

"I will do as I please. This is my ship, and Bree is a very dear friend."

"And there you have it." Nicholas's hooded eyes and icy tones stilled Sabrina's heart. "She is not my friend at all; she is my wife. As such, I will not look favorably upon a repetition of the cozy scene I witnessed here."

Matt crossed his arms over his chest. "It seems to me you're demanding quite a lot in the name of husbandly rights. Particularly for someone who has yet to establish his claim on that title."

"Explain yourself, Madison," Nicholas said coldly.

Matt shrugged idly. "It is my understanding that there has yet to be a wedding night."

Only the creaking of the ship's timbers cut through the stark silence that fell like a blow. Tension in the cabin lay thick and stifling, and Sabrina gasped for breath. The two men traded icy glares from across the cabin, each sizing up the mettle of the other, judging strengths and talents, weaknesses and faults. Any attempt on Sabrina's part to avoid a direct confrontation now seemed effort wasted. Nicholas's hands clenched into fists and relaxed so quickly, Sabrina thought she was mistaken.

Nicholas's black eyes gleamed. "I believe you have pushed me too far, Madison. Although, I must say, I expected nothing better from . . . an American. In my experience Americans are coarse, crude and ill-bred." He fairly spat the words, and Sabrina groaned to herself.

Matt registered little outward reaction to the insult. Only the throb of an angry vein in his neck gave any hint that he was as enraged as Nicholas. "Well, at least when an American marries, the wife in question knows she's been good and truly wed."

"Matt!" Sabrina erupted, shocked by the innuendo. "That is quite enough! As for you," she turned to Nicholas, "he doesn't like Englishmen any better than you like Americans. So both of you, halt this ridiculous arguing at once."

Sabrina glared at first one and then the other. Both were too stubborn and too irate to pay her any mind. She feared the inevitable outcome of their rage.

"I must demand satisfaction, you know," Nicholas said, his manner cool and formal.

"I expected no less," Matt replied, his voice equally controlled.

Sabrina stared at the two in disbelief. It was almost as if, having exchanged their challenges, rational thought returned. Both were calm and composed. Only the light in their eyes revealed their true feelings. It was an eager light that told her they were actually looking forward to their battle. It made absolutely no sense at all.

"I hope you both understand, there shall not be a duel of any kind." She crossed her arms over her chest and glared. "I shall not permit it."

Surprise reflected on the faces of both men, and she wondered if they'd forgotten her presence.

"Tell your wife she cannot tell you what to do, Wyldewood."

"Sabrina, this is none of your affair."

"Of course it's my affair," she snapped.

Nicholas raised a dark brow. "You've known her far longer than I have. Has she always intruded where she did not belong?"

"Always," Matt confirmed.

"Would you cease discussing me as if I was not here!" Sabrina demanded. "I will not have you killing each other!"

Nicholas smiled indulgently. "Oh, I daresay we would

not both be killed. Typically, one is left standing."

Matt nodded sagely. "That is the usual outcome." He turned to Nicholas. "Since it was your demand for satisfaction I assume I may choose weapons?"

Nicholas shrugged his acknowledgment.

"In deference to Bree," Matt inclined his head in her direction, "I won't kill you. But I'd like nothing better than to beat you to a pulp with my bare hands."

Nicholas's eyes gleamed darkly in contrast to his pleasant smile. "And I have an abiding desire to batter you senseless."

"Shall we go up on deck?" Matt strode to the door and swung it open.

"By all means." Nicholas marched through the exit, Matt one step behind him. Sabrina stared openmouthed in the center of the cabin. By their manner, one would have thought they were off to an outing in the country.

"Bloody hell," she muttered and scrambled after them.

Moments later the two were stripping off their shirts on the main deck. The crew had gathered in a loose circle around them.

This can't be happening, Sabrina thought, gripped by a tight hand of panic. She wanted neither of these men hurt. Sabrina spotted Simon, wagering with several sailors on the outcome of the match. She caught his gaze and scowled; he too appeared excited by the promise of the fight.

"Can't you do something?" she insisted.

Genuine surprise shone on Simon's face. "Why in the name of all that's holy would I want to do that, lass? This will do them both a world of good, and provide a bit of entertainment for the men, as well. You may have missed it, but this has been brewing since the moment those two met."

"That was scarely an hour ago! I can't believe this much animosity has built up in so short a time."

"Perhaps you've forgotten their meeting?" Simon bent low and spoke softly in her ear. "When his lordship there first saw the captain he was giving you a greeting no husband wants to see his wife getting from another man."

"I explained that to Nicholas."

Simon raised a shaggy brow. "And he understood?"

"Well, no," she hedged, "not quite." She gestured toward the men still preparing for their encounter. "But I still don't see the need for all this."

"That's 'cause you're not a man, lass." Simon nodded wisely.

She stared at him in amazement. "If that's the way men's minds work, then I count myself lucky." Fear for the harm Nicholas and Matt could do to each other vanished with her words, replaced by an irritating sense of frustration.

"Well, if none of you men are going to do something about this, I am," she muttered, pushing her way through the circle.

Nicholas and Matt stood in the center, feet squared, ready to do battle. Sabrina glared at them both. "Are you two determined to go through with this?"

Nicholas's grim smile did not reach his eyes. "I am."

Matt nodded. "Looking forward to it, in fact."

Sabrina wondered if she shouldn't simply beat them both herself and be done with it. Annoyance rapidly turned to anger and she thought she was enraged enough to do just that. Sheer stupidity always incensed her, nearly as much as did arrogance. Here she was face-to-face with both. She drew a deep breath and forced herself to remain calm. For just a moment the serene Lady Stanford returned.

"Very well." She bestowed a tranquil smile on them and looked around curiously. "Where, then, would you propose I sit? To get the best view, of course."

Nicholas narrowed his eyes. "You plan on watching?"

Even Matt appeared uncomfortable. "It's really not suitable for a woman, Bree."

"Nonetheless," she said airily, "I have no intention of leaving." She spotted a water barrel and perched comfortably on the edge. Like a queen granting her favors upon a knight before a tournament, she gestured for them to begin. "Whenever you are ready, gentlemen."

Nicholas cast her one last considering glance and, as if

The Perfect Wife

dismissing her from his thoughts, turned his attention to his opponent.

The men circled each other warily. They were well matched, these two, of an equal height and breadth. Gladiators cut from the same mold, forged in the same fire. If not for Nicholas's dark hair and eyes and Matt's fair coloring, Sabrina thought they could have passed for brothers. And, she had to admit, their bared, muscular chests were not at all unpleasant to gaze upon; perhaps a shade unsettling, but definitely not unpleasant.

The similarities did not end with physical attributes. Both certainly had the same unyielding nature and arrogant attitude. She had adjusted to Matt's personality years ago and remembered fondly how annoying he'd been when they'd first met. She wondered if, in time, she would adapt as well to Nicholas's temperament.

And, of course, there was the easy manner they had with women. Sabrina couldn't suppress a fair amount of amusement at Matt's conquests, but the same could not be said of Nicholas. More and more his reputation as a rake grated on her mind. Was it all true, or mere exaggeration? How many women had known the touch of his lips? The caress of his hands? The singe of his heat?

"You surprise me." Matt's lips curled upward in a menacing smile, his voice deceptively mild. "I half expected you to beg off, to hide behind your wife's skirts."

Nicholas laughed. "Perhaps you have failed to notice, but my wife prefers not to wear skirts." His steely gaze narrowed. "And I hide behind no one. You shall regret your—"

Matt's fist smashed into Nicholas's lips before the words were out of his mouth. Sabrina winced inwardly but refused to allow anything other than an amused smile on her face. Nicholas's eyes registered surprise at the force of the blow and he hesitated, only to catch a second in his midsection. The sickening thud reverberated in Sabrina's stomach but barely budged Nicholas.

Matt failed to follow up, stepping back momentarily. He too wore an expression of incredulity. The power of his strike would have felled another man.

Nicholas recovered quickly, feinted a right hand and, instead, placed a sharp jab to the chin, stunning Matt briefly. Matt recoiled but countered. Both came together, toe to toe, in a wild blur of punches. Obviously, neither's estimate of the other had been entirely accurate. They were far better matched than even Sabrina had imagined.

But she had never imagined the brutality of the scene. Perhaps it would have been better if she'd foregone this particular form of masculine entertainment after all. Too many years of proper behavior stretched between her and rough-hewn men like this; she'd forgotten how savage even the best of them could be.

She was the only one not savoring the combat. There was no doubt of the crew's enjoyment. Cheers and jeers rang out over the whoosh of breath forcibly expelled and the nauseating sound of flesh crunching on bone.

Sabrina gritted her teeth and forced herself to watch the gruesome contest. She would not give either man the satisfaction of learning she could not face a simple fistfight, barbaric though it might be.

She maintained her pleasant smile and fought to hold on to her air of mild amusement, all the while fear for their safety grew within her. Neither man gained the advantage. Each absorbed the impact of punishing knuckles and returned swing for swing, stroke for stroke. Blood dripped from the corner of Matt's mouth. A gash opened over Nicholas's eye, and crimson drops flew at every punch. Both men, bloodied and battered, fought on, neither able to claim victory, neither willing to accept defeat.

Sabrina's stomach churned at the appalling sight. Would neither give up? What would happen if one were a clear victor over the other? Would their animosity grow? Or worse, what if neither won?

She wanted this ended and she wanted it ended now. Nicholas could barely stand, and Matt was no better. It was a struggle now less of skill and strength than of endurance and will. Each stubbornly continued to jab and thrust, their blows lacking force but just as punishing on the embattled bodies as when they'd begun.

They came together in a macabre dance and hung on each other as if one hoped to steal the might of his opponent or gain a momentary respite, only to push apart and go on. She could not, and would not, allow the two men who meant the most to her in all the world to continue this senseless brawl.

Sabrina's calculating gaze passed over the excited faces of the crew. She would get no help there. Even Simon was deeply immersed in the struggle of the exhausted combatants, although she appreciated the way he rooted equally for both his captain and Nicholas. At least he wasn't counting his winnings yet.

She narrowed her eyes and considered the possibilities. Simply declaring a finish to the match would never work. They would no doubt ignore her.

Typically, one is left standing.

That was it! If one fell, the contest would end. How to achieve that particular circumstance remained a problem. It was not as if she could bowl one of them over herself. Or could she?

Nicholas stumbled at Matt's last blow, and opportunity seized Sabrina. Deftly thrusting out her foot, she caught Nicholas's ankle, and he crashed backwards to the deck. For one terrified moment her heart stopped and her breath caught in her throat. Stunned, she pulled her gaze from Nicholas's still form. To a man, the crew stared awestruck at the sight of the fallen warrior, anointed with blood and sweat. Only Simon caught her gaze. He shook his head in a disgusted manner at her interference and strode to Nicholas's side. Sabrina reached her husband first and knelt beside him.

"Is he . . . ?" she whispered, unable to say the words aloud.

"He ain't dead," Simon said. "But he'll wish he was when he wakes up. His head will pound worse than a smithy's hammer on his anvil. I wouldn't want to be him." He stared straight in her eyes. "Nor the one responsible neither."

She returned his glare with one of her own. "This is not my fault." Sabrina sprang to her feet.

Matt still stood where he had when he struck the last blow, dazed and not altogether steady. Sabrina advanced with as much menace as she could muster, setting aside the fact that she was the one who essentially felled Nicholas. Fury surged through her.

Matt swayed on his feet at her approach. "Bree, I—"

"Don't you dare attempt to make excuses for this uncivilized and totally unacceptable display of masculine stupidity," she snapped.

Matt flinched at her tone and tried again. "Bree, I—"

"And don't you 'Bree' me either, Matthew Madison." Anger overwhelmed all other thoughts. They could have killed each other. Nicholas could have . . . fear gripped her at the thought of how very easily she could have lost him. And somewhere, beyond her rage, she acknowledged, and accepted, that she very much did not want to lose him. Not now, not ever. "If he is seriously injured, I will hold you fully at fault. I should beat you myself for this."

Sabrina splayed her hands against his hard chest and shoved with all her strength, a futile gesture under ordinary circumstances. Like a huge tree, strong and hard in appearance but with roots rotted and weak, he tottered backwards and sprawled on the deck, astonishment and pain washing over his face.

Hands on her hips, Sabrina glared at the fallen figure. "It's no more than you deserve, Matt. I am sorely disappointed in you."

He groaned and closed his eyes.

Simon stepped to his side. "Capt'n?"

"Is she still there?" he said in a weary voice.

"Still here." Simon nodded.

"I'm not moving until she leaves," Matt said in a dignified manner. Or at least with all the dignity a man lying prone on the deck of his own ship could summon. "Go away, Bree. Let me die in peace."

"Hah!" She snorted. "Death is too good for you." She turned to where Nicholas lay. He was gone. Panic rose within her.

"Simon," she clutched his arm, "what's happened? Where is Nicholas?"

"Don't worry yourself, lass. I had the men carry him down to your cabin and put him to bed. He'll be good as new."

She sighed with relief.

"Eventually." Simon smiled with the rueful look of a man well versed in the aftermath of physical conflicts.

Abruptly, a new misgiving gripped her. Casting Simon a troubled look, she spoke softly. She did not want Matt, lying at their feet, to hear her concern. "Do you think anyone else . . . um . . . noticed . . ."

"I don't think so." Simon shook his head. "I think I was the only one who saw what you did. No one else was lookin' at their feet." He eyed her sternly. "You had no right, lass, no right at all."

She stared at him in astonishment. "I had every right. The rest of you were all bound and determined to let them bash each other senseless." She sniffed and folded her arms across her chest. "Somebody had to stop it."

"Well, you better hope neither of 'em find out you're the one who ended their fight, or they'll be hell to pay. From both of 'em." He nodded sagely. "Go take care of your husband. You'll want to check his ribs, make sure none of the bones are broken." He shrugged and chuckled. "I've seen a lot of fights in my day, and this was a good one. But neither your Nicholas nor my capt'n will be worth much for the next few days. Now, off with you." Matt groaned, and Simon bent to minister to him.

Sabrina wrinkled her nose and turned toward her cabin and her unconscious husband. She paused by the railing and gazed out over the sea. Calm and tranquil, the water barely rippled, in stark contrast to her own chaotic emotions.

At least she didn't have to worry about Simon telling Nicholas or Matt her role in their little battle. She sighed and brushed her hair away from her face. The one thing she didn't need at this moment was yet another secret to keep. She already had more than enough of those.

Sabrina stared moodily at the sea. Nothing on this entire

voyage had gone as expected. She couldn't help but wonder, what on earth could happen next?

What on earth could happen next? Belinda wondered, propping her elbow on the rail and her chin in her hand. She gazed with annoyance at the placid sea. This voyage had been one minor, irritating crisis after another. It was not at all what she had imagined or, for that matter, hoped for.

When the idea had struck her of following her mother there had been more behind the suggestion than concern for her mother's safety. Of course, Belinda was legitimately worried that her mother's virtue lay in the hands of a notable rake. But beyond that, the notion of a sea voyage to an exotic land like Egypt had intrigued and excited her. It had seemed such an adventure. She'd never suspected she had a daring streak, and assumed it to be a legacy from her father. Her mother was far too proper for adventure. Or, at least, she used to be.

And then there was Erick. Belinda expected there would be the opportunity for them to learn more of each other while they sought their wayward parents. She hoped to spend her time by his side and in his arms, exploring the shivering heat he unleashed with his kisses. She particularly wanted to again experience the odd, aching tension that came with his touch. Belinda brushed away the distinct possibility of impropriety in her desires. After all, she and Erick were to be wed.

But reality was a far cry from her expectations. Erick had spent half the voyage doubled over the side of the ship, losing whatever vestiges of food he'd managed to keep on a turbulent stomach. The rest of the time he remained secluded in his cabin, groaning with a severe case of mal de mer.

She'd tried her hand at tending to him, but he was not an easy patient, preferring to be left alone. And she was not a compassionate nurse; rather, she was put off by the somewhat disgusting aspects of his illness. She herself suffered no adverse effects from the voyage and had little patience for those who did. No, it was not at all as she'd envisioned.

Erick's aunt was not as she'd envisioned either. The woman was indeed a bluestocking, and had apparently read everything there was to read about everything. Wynne was pleasant enough, with a sharp wit and an engaging laugh, but she was also more than willing to share her knowledge with anyone foolish enough to inquire. It was not at all an endearing trait, particularly to the captain of the vessel. Wynne had an annoying habit of attempting to tell the experienced sailor how a proper ship should be run, knowledge gained from her books. More than once, Belinda had overheard the mutterings of the crew. Wynne would be lucky if they did not simply toss her overboard.

Belinda sighed and shook her head. At least the ship traveled at a good clip. With luck, they should reach Alexandria well before their parents. As to what happened then, she shrugged, well, she'd wait and see. She had already come to one rather startling conclusion during the journey.

Her beloved, proper, serene mother was not at all as she'd appeared.

And, perhaps, never had been.

It was a beautiful day. The sunlight danced off the azure waves with the grace and charm of a corps de ballet. But he was in no mood to appreciate the scene before him. He leaned on the rail, straining forward as if to urge the ship on by sheer force of will alone. It was imperative that he arrive in Egypt before Sabrina and Wyldewood. His plans would be much more difficult otherwise.

At least his companions had given him a respite from their constant company. The fools were ensconced in the captain's cabin, engaged in games of chance. He did not have funds to spare in such idle pursuits and had little use for those who did. As much as he resented it, they did serve a purpose. The two had paid virtually all the expenses for this expedition, in the manner of wealthy men who do not think to question the fiscal capabilities of others and simply assume all will work out eventually.

He had always hidden his financial difficulties well. Even those who, when asked, would say they knew him best, never suspected his pockets were all but empty. For years he had concealed the true state of his depleted fortune. Once he had nearly acquired the means to remedy the situation, but the opportunity had slipped through his hands through no fault of his own.

He did not seek revenge. He simply wanted his due. If he had to kill the lovely Lady Stanford and whoever else sought to stop him, so be it. He would let nothing stand in the way of possessing Sabrina's gold. His gold.

He smiled slowly. It was indeed a beautiful day.

Chapter Eleven

Sabrina flinched at the sight of the battered body on the berth. The sailors who carried Nicholas to the cabin had removed his clothing, tossing it in a bloody heap on the floor. Only a light blanket covered his nude form.

Fearful of what she might find, Sabrina took a deep breath and folded back the coverlet, exposing his bronzed body. The rise and fall of his chest was even and steady, a good sign. Angry, scuffed, reddened skin confronted her, not yet showing the shades of blue and purple bruising that would come. But there were no breaks in the skin, no bloody gashes with white bones protruding. She released her pent-up breath with relief and gratitude.

Sabrina ran her fingers lightly along his ribs, searching for any abnormality, any indication of serious damage. Nothing. The flesh beneath her hand was warm but not feverish. Her touch drifted to his stomach and lingered. She reminded herself that this was an examination of necessity, nothing more.

Still, she could not help but marvel at the hard, muscled planes of his chest. Seemingly of their own accord, her hands stroked upward, her fingers tunneling through the mat of rough, dark hair. His heartbeat pulsed against her fingers.

What would it be like to be crushed against that chest? To feel his heartbeat next to hers? To have her own naked breasts flattened against his solid form? Her heart thudded at the thought, and longing throbbed within her. She wanted that intimacy and more.

A groan broke from his lips and she jerked her hands away, as if burned by the contact with his skin, or her own scorching desire. Irritated and shaken by her unthinking reaction, she glared at her unconscious husband.

"Bloody hell, Nicholas, you've gone and done it now." She dipped a rag into a basin of water and dabbed at his battered face. "You've made me love you."

Exasperation colored her words, but her hand was gentle as she sponged off the last traces of dried clay-brown blood. "I did not ask for this. It makes it all so much more difficult." A cut marred his handsome face above his right eye; the skin on his left cheek was puffed and bruised. Sabrina winced at his obvious pain and her tone softened. "It simply isn't done, you know. I don't believe I know of one wife in the ton who loves her husband."

Sabrina sighed and considered her confession. She had never known an emotion quite like this. Not with Jack. Not with anyone. She'd never even dreamed of a passion this powerful. A passion that had her willing to ignore a painful reality: Nicholas was not the kind of man who would return her love. He used the word itself like an inexpensive seasoning, with a generous sprinkling to spice and flavor a dish and no thought given to the food itself. Perhaps her love alone would be sufficient. Perhaps not. There would be time enough to deal with the consequences of her feelings later.

She gazed at him and wondered why he had not yet come to his senses. Simon said he would recover, unless there was a serious injury they had not noted. Smoothing his hair away from his face, she narrowed her eyes thoughtfully. He was no more badly beaten than Matt, yet he remained unconscious. Unless . . .

Sabrina eased her fingers under his head and carefully felt

the back of his skull. Within moments she found what she feared: a huge knot at the back of his head. The injury came not from the fight but from the fall—the fall she had precipitated.

Guilt swept through her and she stared helplessly at the silent figure. "Good Lord, Nicholas. I am so very sorry. I would not have you hurt for the world. You have to recover." She lowered her voice to an urgent whisper. "There is much yet to be settled between the two of us. I shall not allow you to leave me with so much unresolved. This is fair warning, husband; I shall run you to ground through the end of eternity if you do not return to me."

Impulsively, she leaned over him and lightly pressed her lips to his. It was not enough to satisfy her yearning to possess him, and be possessed in return. But it would do for now.

She dipped the rag in the water, wrung out rust-colored water and stroked his brow, keeping up a constant stream of chatter, a narrative that leapt aimlessly, detailing her thoughts and dreams and desires, her history and their future.

Day slipped into night and to day again, and Sabrina remained by his side. Simon checked on them both occasionally and agreed with Sabrina; the lump on Nicholas's head was very likely the reason he had not awakened. She slept little, bathing his face and his body and murmuring words of encouragement, of frustration, of concern and of love.

All the while knowing he could not hear a word. All the while hoping, perhaps, he might, somehow, understand.

Awareness teased the corners of his mind. Damp, dank air weighed heavy on his skin. The salty, rotted scent of the sea assailed his nostrils. Dimly, the roar of the ocean and the crash of the waves sounded. Distant . . . hollow. A steady drip splashed and echoed. All in the blackest black. Was this a dream? Or death?

Nicholas struggled to fight his way back from the darkness, swimming against a sea of oblivion. *He jerked his head, and hot pain lanced through the back of his skull.*

147

Pain. Familiar yet obscure. It pummeled his head and throbbed through his body.

He battled to open his eyes and failed. Was he too weak? Or did a blindfold shroud his sight? Voices drifted around him, only one penetrating the shadows of his mind.

The feminine voice was low, slightly husky. It might have been the damp in the air, it might have been the way she always spoke, but he was stunned to note that the voice fired his blood. In spite of the impropriety and absurdity of his sudden desire, he wanted nothing more than to take her as his own.

Wanted whom? Who was this woman he longed for, ached for? Confusing images assailed his mind. Thoughts and memories jumbled together in an indistinguishable kaleidoscope of meaningless emotions and desires, colored by time, shaded by pain.

Gentle fingers stroked his chest. *Cool, gentle fingers, light and teasing . . .* Fresh cloths soothed his face. *A tentative touch lingered . . .* He sighed at the press of warm lips against his mouth. *A delicious shiver ran through him at the unexpected contact.* Yet there was nothing to ease the burning frustration filling every unguarded crevice of his being.

She paused, and he wondered at the tension between them. Wondered if she felt it as well. He again caught her breath upon his upturned face and her lips brushed against his in a faint caress. He started slightly, then involuntarily strained toward her. Her lips parted and her tongue teased the inner edge of his mouth. Desire pounded through his veins. His mind worked feverishly. What kind of woman kissed so boldly as this? Perhaps . . . it no longer mattered.

What no longer mattered? Futility swamped him. Why couldn't he remember? It was so very important. Who was she?

Sabrina. The name appeared like a buoy bobbing to the surface of his soul. Bree. She was . . . what? *A vague, spicy scent wafted around him.* Her scent, a memory from today? From yesterday . . . from forever?

His wife; that was it, she was his wife. Fragments of memory emerged. Not the passive, insipid child-wife of his

148

youth; this was a woman to savor, to cherish, even to love. He had won her, hadn't he? Or at least claimed her. His most impressive triumph, or was it . . . his greatest failure? He did not know.

Sabrina . . . Bree . . . Lady B. The names, the impressions and emotions, the scents and sounds from now and from the dim recollections of a decade past scurried and scrambled in his muddled mind. Dreams and fantasy mingled with remembrance and reality, a haunting puzzle with questions he could not comprehend and answers that lingered just beyond reach.

He sank back into blackness, his exhausted mind succumbing to the needs of his body for healing sleep. A thought nagged at the back of his consciousness, elusive and vague. He battled to grasp it, knowing instinctively that it would provide the key he searched for, and the solution to mysteries he had long ago put aside.

And it would give him peace.

Nicholas pulled his eyes open with a strength born only of determination. His vision blurred and sharpened and his gaze flicked over a beamed ceiling. Where was he? He drew his brows together in an effort to recall and tried to sit up.

Sharp pain ricocheted around his head and radiated through his body. He gasped and sank back on the bed, closing his eyes against the pain.

"Welcome back," a low, sensual voice greeted him. Her voice. Sabrina's.

He opened his eyes cautiously, avoiding the slightest movement. Her face seemed to hover above him.

"Where am I?" He croaked the words, his throat parched and thick.

"You are exactly where you belong right now, in bed." A concerned frown furrowed her brow. "In your cabin. On the ship. Do you remember?"

The ship? Of course. The details remained indistinct, but he definitely recalled fisticuffs with that arrogant American.

"How do you feel?"

"Bloody awful." His head throbbed and pulsed, his muscles ached. Even breathing hurt. If he fared this poorly, surely Madison must be dead. "How is Madison?"

"Nearly as bad off as you." Her dry tone left no doubt as to her opinion of the entire incident. "Not that you both don't deserve it."

Nicholas drew his brows together, struggling to remember. Gradually, the fog in his mind lifted. The fight on the deck . . . the final blow . . . the fall. "I would have beaten him senseless if I hadn't tripped."

"Yes . . . well, you did trip, and that's the end of it." Her brisk manner signaled a close to that particular topic. Pity. He was extremely interested in knowing just how his skills compared to Madison's, but, apparently, that was not information to be gleaned from Sabrina.

Only concern and sympathy shone in her eyes. "You are terribly weak, you know, Nicholas. You've been unconscious for more than a day. You really need to eat or at least drink something. Do you feel up to that?"

His throat rasped, and hunger gnawed at his stomach; food and drink could only help. "I think so." He sighed. "As long as I don't have to move."

"Excellent." She beamed at him and stepped to the door. "Stay put and rest. You need it. I'll be back in just a moment." The door closed gently behind her.

Flat on his back, he stared at the ceiling. Tentatively, Nicholas flexed and relaxed his muscles, one at a time, in his arms, legs, hands and feet. Aside from an overall ache, he seemed relatively fit. With slow, studied movements, he pushed himself upright to a sitting position. The throb in his head did not diminish, but it did not increase either.

He had not experienced pain like this in . . . how long? A decade perhaps? Not since the last time he'd received a blow on the head that rendered him unconscious. Not since he had awakened alone on a deserted beach near a remote English village, the smugglers he sought long gone. There was something important about that recollection. Something he needed to . . .

"What are you doing?" Sabrina's voice cracked from the doorway. He jerked his head toward her, and agonizing pain fired flashes of light across his vision. Nicholas doubled over, catching his head in his hands, as if the pressure of his fingers would alleviate his suffering.

"Please, if you have any compassion in your soul at all, if only for children and small animals, take pity on me and do not raise your voice." Even his whispered words took their toll in pain. "My head feels as if I have consumed barrels of whiskey single-handed." He moaned. "And not very good whiskey, either."

She marched to the table and set down a tray. Stepping to his side, she thrust several pillows behind him for support. "I can't say you haven't earned it." Sabrina retrieved the tray and returned to the berth, settling on the edge of his bed. The tray balanced precariously between them.

He eyed the mug and accompanying bowl of steaming liquid through the gaps between his fingers. "What is that?"

"It's just broth." An amused smile quirked the corners of her mouth. "You needn't be so suspicious. I'm not going to poison you."

"You'd be a rich widow if you did." Nicholas uncovered his face and glared at the innocent soup.

"You're right." Her eyes widened, as if considering his suggestion. "I hadn't thought of that. What a cunning idea."

"Sabrina." He caught himself. The twinkle in her eye gave her away. "I am in no mood to be teased," he grumbled.

"What a shame," she said lightly, her manner annoyingly pleasant and brisk. "Now, will you eat this yourself or shall I feed you like a child?"

He relaxed against the pillows and gazed at her. She appeared weary. Abruptly, he realized that she must have been by his side the entire time he slept and probably had had little sleep herself. She looked fragile, ethereally vulnerable and infinitely appealing. An odd urge to protect and care for her surged through him.

His gaze trapped hers and lingered. The moment lengthened, becoming intense and weighted without warning. Her smile faltered. His breath caught in his throat. Deep in the emerald waters of her eyes, her soul simmered, calling to him. Somewhere, in their clear, shining recesses, inevitable passion beckoned. The urge to protect shifted, changed, evolved into a need more imperative and insistent and inescapable.

The ache in his head eased and he smiled slowly. "Feed me," he said.

Heat flushed up her face and she dropped her gaze to the tray beside her. Flustered, she battled to compose herself. This was absurd. Could she only express her newfound feelings when he lay silent and unconscious and there was no fear of his response? Why did his eyes, dark, devastating and brimming with danger, seem to search out her secrets and peer into her soul?

She drew a deep breath and picked up the spoon. Her hand trembled, and she steadied it through the sheer strength of her will. Dipping it in the broth, she brought the spoon to his mouth. His lips did not part and her surprised gaze flew to his.

His eyes smoldered and burned, and she struggled not to spill the spoonful of soup. "Open your mouth," she said, her voice quiet and firm, belying her inner turmoil.

"With pleasure."

She pushed the spoon into his mouth and he took the broth, his gaze never leaving her face. A second spoonful followed the first. The soup in the bowl steadily decreased. A tension inside her coiled tighter with his every sip. She avoided looking into his eyes, but it was impossible to feed him without staring at his lips.

Full and sensual, they did not merely accept the spooned offering, they welcomed it, enfolded it, caressed it. Mesmerized, she could well remember those lips on hers, recollect the sensation of his kisses trailing down her neck, recall the sense of urgency when he took her breast in his mouth. . . .

"I'm finished."

"What?" She jerked her gaze from his lips and glanced at the empty bowl. How could she not have noticed? "I can fetch you more, or something else, if you'd like."

"I should very much prefer something else." Intensity

edged the soft tone of his words.

Delicious fear shivered through her. She squared her shoulders, lifted her chin and directed him a challenging gaze. "What do you want?"

He stretched a long arm over the tray and cupped her chin in his hand. Gently, he pulled her toward him until their lips barely touched, soft and evocative, more a whisper than a kiss. He brushed his lips over hers, to and fro, delicate strokes, hot and silken.

Her eyes closed and her lips parted and a sigh whispered through them. She leaned nearer, the yearning inside her demanding more than this teasing, this hint, this mere suggestion of what would come.

Abruptly, Nicholas drew back. His gaze searched hers. "Sabrina, I want to make certain . . ." A question hovered deep in his smoldering eyes. "That is, if you . . ." Confusion played across his face. With an insight born of her heightened emotions, she realized he wanted only to make sure this was her desire as well as his. This man who was so well known for taking what he wanted from women was obviously concerned about her feelings. It was definitely out of character and absolutely delightful.

Joy surged through her, and she wanted to throw her head back and laugh with exhilaration. Surely, somewhere in the vast reaches of his heart he truly cared about her. And if he could care about her, then one day he could love her.

"If you are wondering about violating one of the terms of this marriage . . ." She shrugged and cast him an inviting glance. "I have discovered I find privacy highly overrated."

He stared for a moment, as if he didn't grasp the meaning of her words. Then, like a spark bursting to flame, understanding broke on his face. With one powerful arm, he swept the tray to the floor in a clash of metal and broken pottery. With the other, he pulled her into his embrace, dragging her forward, across his body, until she lay flat upon him, her heaving breasts pressed hard against his naked chest. The thin coverlet came only to his waist, and his hard arousal nudged her through the layers of blanket and her own clothing.

Sabrina gasped and stared into his eyes. "What about your head? Doesn't it hurt?"

He grinned. "I believe it has been replaced by a more persistent ache." He bent his lips to her neck and nuzzled the sensitive flesh. "An ache, I suspect, that can be most pleasurably attended to."

With wild abandon, she threw her arms around his neck and he clasped her tight to him. Their lips met, violent and exacting. Passion erupted in full force, demanding, insistent, greedy.

His tongue invaded her mouth to plunder and pillage. She responded in kind, not a submissive defense but a counter battle with her own weapons, her own commands, her own objectives. Her fingers twined through his hair. His lips crushed hers, intent on defeat, requiring surrender.

He nudged her back until she sat upon him, her legs straddling his. Impatiently, he pulled the man's shirt she wore out of her breeches and pushed it upward, his hands sliding over flesh taut with need. His searching fingers reached the underside of her breasts and she moaned aloud, her head falling back. He cupped the tender mounds with a gentleness that belied the raging hunger arcing between them and teased the pebbled nipples with his thumbs.

"Nicholas!" She gasped for breath and her head lolled on her neck. In one quick movement he twisted up to sit facing her. Swiftly, he jerked her shirt over her head, freeing her breasts to his gaze and his touch. His hands encircled them and he lavished attention first on one and then the other, teasing with his lips, his tongue, his teeth until she thought she would surely lose her mind from this exquisite torture.

He turned without warning, holding her close, shifting his weight and abruptly she no longer sat atop him but lay beneath. Gazing up, she read her own wonder and passion and yearning mirrored in his stormy black eyes. She tunneled her fingers through his thick, dark hair and drew his mouth back to hers, losing herself in a sea of erotic promise.

His hands, his mouth, his tongue sought out every part of her, drifting from lips to breasts and lower, ever lower. He trailed his touch over the flat of her stomach and beyond, slipping his hand between her legs and the secret heat still hidden by her breeches. He cupped the mound at the joining of her legs and fingered the point of her yearning, throbbing beneath the fabric.

Nicholas's hand moved to the waist of her breeches, and he dipped his fingers beneath the material, stretched tight across her stomach. He fumbled with the laces and she strained against him, desperate for the scorching feel of his skin against hers. She gripped his shoulders and strained for his touch, the tension inside her coiling tighter and tighter.

He groaned against her neck. "Sabrina."

"Oh God, Nicholas, please." Yearning throbbed through her. Why didn't he take her now? Why did he continue this sweet, intense torment?

"Sabrina."

"Nicholas." She nearly wept with desire, the ache for him, threatening to overwhelm every thought but one searing truth.

"I can't get the bloody thing untied."

"What?" His words barely penetrated the haze of her arousal.

"It's these damn breeches." He ran an impatient hand through his hair and glared. "I've never tried to untie someone else's breeches before, and I'm afraid I've gotten them in a knot."

She propped herself on her elbows and looked down. The laces crossing her stomach were indeed tangled and knotted. She gazed up at him in amazement. "Get them undone, Nicholas. Now."

"What am I supposed to do?"

She stared at him in disbelief. "I don't care what you do. Chew them off for all I care. Just get the bloody things off."

He bent to examine the problem. His nearness alone was enough to set Sabrina trembling. He shook his head. "Sabrina, I don't know . . ."

She widened her eyes in alarm. "Nicholas, I have come to a number of realizations about you and I in the last day. About what I want and what I need, about concessions and compromise. This is not merely a moment of mindless passion." She gripped his arm. "I do not give myself freely. I have had opportunity, but I have not lain with a man . . ." Her gaze dropped, the intimacy of what she was about to reveal astounding her. She drew a deep breath and turned her eyes to his. ". . . in thirteen years." Insistence rang in her voice. "Now get these bloody breeches off me."

The enormity of her confession seemed to stun him. A resolute gleam appeared in his eye. "I have an idea." He pushed her flat back on the berth and rolled over her, his feet nimbly hitting the floor by the side of the bed. In three long strides he crossed the room to his valise and fumbled inside the bag.

In spite of her frustration, she noted with awe the power of his nude form. His bronze skin glowed. His legs stretched long and lean. The muscles in his back rippled with his efforts and Sabrina's desire rose once again. She clenched her fists and closed her eyes only to open them abruptly when he grabbed her elbow and jerked her, with one strong hand, to her feet.

"This is your last chance." His black eyes glittered with promise and passion. "Do you trust me?"

Did she trust him? She wanted him. Needed him. But trust? She did not trust him with her secrets. Could she trust him with her heart? She lied. "With my life."

He laughed. She had not fooled him, he did not believe her words any more than she did. Nicholas pulled her tight against him, her naked breasts rubbing against the rough hair on his chest. In his other hand he displayed a long, sharp dagger, plain in appearance, obviously more for utility than display.

Sabrina gasped. "Nicholas, you're not—you wouldn't." The expression on his face said he would, without hesitation. "Wait. You don't understand. I have saved these breeches for years. I have only two pair."

"Excellent; then you will not miss these." His voice growled, deep and sensuous.

"But I—" His descending lips cut off her objections. He stole her very breath and she sagged against him. He could do what he wished with her breeches, or anything else for that matter.

The dull edge of the knife lay hard against her stomach, and she flinched. The laces popped with release at the smooth slice of the knife. It took Nicholas less than a moment to slice the confining strings, and he slid the breeches down the long length of her hips to fall unresisting at her feet.

She splayed her hands across his back and clung to him, her bare body pressed to his. His manhood throbbed against her, hard and powerful, and she drew a sharp breath. He scooped her up in his arms and carried her to the berth. With a gentle motion, he laid her on the bed.

She was all that he'd dreamed, all that he'd ever desired. Her breasts rose firm and full, nipples rosy and erect, her tiny waist flaring to seductive hips. Golden curls protected the portal to her pleasure. Nicholas had been with beautiful women before, and he wasn't sure how, but this was different. This was not an insignificant coupling, it was . . . more.

She stared at him provocatively, her eyes half closed and glazed with desire. He groaned and lay down beside her, wanting nothing more than to take her. Now. Hard and swift. But it had been so long since she'd known a man's desire. And he wanted this to be more than mating. He would pleasure her until she reached newfound heights of ecstasy and only then satisfy himself. With slow, lingering caresses he would draw out her passion, preparing her for their joining. Yes, he would take his time—even if it killed him.

His lips claimed hers and his control dissolved beneath the fury of her response. He stroked her supple body and she writhed at his experienced touch, his own desire spiraling ever higher. Her heated flesh seemed to singe his very soul, and he gasped with the urgency to possess and devour her.

Like an adventurer in an undiscovered land, he searched and explored her hidden secrets until his fingers reached the gate of tangled curls and slipped past to the valley beyond. He dipped into the fragile folds of flesh, wet with welcome,

157

quivering with need, and gently caressed the delicate bud of her womanhood.

She gasped with surprise and pleasure, and he bent his head to take her nipple in his mouth. Teeth and tongue echoed the stroke of his fingers, and she whimpered with the exquisite sensations coursing through her. Her hands clasped his head convulsively and she pulled his lips to hers.

"Take me, Nicholas. Take me now, husband."

He hesitated; then he poised above her, his manhood insistent, demanding, not to be denied. Slowly, he slid into her throbbing heat, deeper and deeper until he was fully submerged in the trembling fire within her. He drew back, prolonging the maddening anticipation, then plunged again and again, his thrusts growing harder, faster.

Her hips rose to meet his and they moved together in a rhythm beyond time, beyond truth. She called his name over and over in a frenzy of sizzling pleasure and selfish possession. He murmured words of wonder and magic and awe against her scorching skin. She was at once his master and his slave. He was conqueror and conquered. As one, the forces that joined them drove them upward to a desperate pinnacle, fierce and intense, where their very souls merged.

With one powerful thrust he drove deep within her. Sabrina cried out, the taut coil inside her exploding in waves of quaking ecstasy. Nicholas shuddered convulsively against her, his body clasped to hers, her name a breath on his lips. "Sabrina . . . Bree."

They collapsed together, spent.

Victorious.

Chapter Twelve

The laughter built deep within her. Sabrina buried her head in the crook of his neck and battled the irresistible urge to giggle. She bit her lip, suppressed laughter shaking her from head to toe.

"Sabrina?" Nicholas's arms tightened around her, a note of distress sounding in his voice. "Are you all right?"

"Fine, really quite fine." Her choked words muffled against his neck.

"Sabrina?" Nicholas pulled away, concern clouding his stormy eyes, and studied her intently. "Do you regret what has passed between us?"

"Regret?" She stared at him with amazement. Worry pulled his brows together. A dark bruise cast a roguish shadow on one cheekbone. The healing cut above his eye slashed a line of emphasis to his frown. He appeared so troubled, so anxious, so apprehensive, in such stark contrast to her own feelings, it was almost comical. Regrets? Hardly.

The laughter she'd successfully stifled now triumphed over her, bubbling to the surface and erupting in an explosion of mirth. Nicholas stared, dumbfounded. The expressions chasing each other across his face simply added to her amusement. Concern, followed by confusion, nipped at the heels of astonishment, trailed, finally, by mild annoyance.

He raised an eyebrow. "You know, my dear, a lesser man would take your reaction to our lovemaking as something other than complimentary." Nicholas's wry comment only served to trigger another wave of laughter.

"Oh, Nicholas, I'm sorry." Her glee belied her apology. "It's just that . . . well, I simply feel so wonderfully delicious."

"Delicious?" A slow grin spread across his face. "I hadn't quite thought of it that way, but *delicious* may well be an accurate description." His eyes twinkled and he brushed his lips lightly across her forehead. "Yes, indeed, *delicious* is definitely the right word for it."

He lay on his side, propped on one elbow. She gazed up and tossed him a teasing smile. "So, am I still a prim and proper paragon of virtue?"

He threw back his head and laughed, a deep, rich sound that shivered through her blood. "You have assuredly provided new meaning for that phase." His expression grew serious and he idly traced the line of her jaw with a long, bronzed figure. "Why did you do it, Sabrina?"

"Do what?" she asked, startled by the unexpected question.

"Hide yourself. Live virtually disguised all these years."

She stared at him cautiously. "Whatever do you mean?"

He shrugged, his fingers continuing their exploration, now trailing down the curve of her throat. "I mean, you have given the world the impression of a quiet, reserved woman. Quite sedate and extremely proper." His bottomless eyes seemed to search her soul. "You are not at all what I had been led to expect. And ever since we began this escapade your every word, every act, has convinced me your life in London was a sham. Why did you hide this daring, delightful woman I have finally had the good fortune to discover?"

She dropped her gaze from his and stared at a distant point far beyond the walls of the cabin. Her love for him dictated honesty, at least to a point. They would very likely

Join the Historical Romance Book Club and GET 4 FREE* BOOKS NOW!

A $23.96 Value!

Yes! I want to subscribe to the Historical Romance Book Club.

Please send me my **4 FREE* BOOKS.** I have enclosed $2.00 for shipping/handling. Each month I'll receive the four newest Historical Romance selections to preview for 10 days. If I decide to keep them, I will pay the Special Members Only discounted price of just $4.24 each, a total of $16.96, plus $2.00 shipping/handling ($19.50 US in Canada). This is a **SAVINGS OF AT LEAST $5.00** off the bookstore price. There is no minimum number of books I must buy, and I may cancel the program at any time. In any case, the **4 FREE* BOOKS** are mine to keep.

*In Canada, add $5.00 shipping/handling per order for the first shipment. For all future shipments to Canada, the cost of membership is $19.50 US, which includes shipping and handling. (All payments must be made in US dollars.)

NAME: _____

ADDRESS: _____

CITY: _____ **STATE:** _____

COUNTRY: _____ **ZIP:** _____

TELEPHONE: _____

E-MAIL: _____

SIGNATURE: _____

If under 18, Parent or Guardian must sign. Terms, prices, and conditions subject to change. Subscription subject to acceptance. Dorchester Publishing reserves the right to reject any order or cancel any subscription.

spend the rest of their lives together, and that was no longer a distressing idea. There was much about her past she would never tell, but equally as much he now deserved to know.

Sabrina caught his gaze with hers. "It was for Belinda. When we returned to London after Jack's death I knew I could not continue the reckless life I'd led before. The ton would probably accept me, but what would happen to my daughter when she was old enough to take her place in society? She would always be faced with a mother branded as fast and unconventional and God knows what." She shook her head. "I could not allow that. I could not allow my child to pay for my sins, petty though they might be."

She sighed. "So, I buried myself in propriety, going about in society no more than was necessary. Letting my presence be known without undue attention."

His fingers now drifted lightly down the valley between her breasts, and she quivered at his touch.

"So, you existed rather than lived."

She wrinkled her nose. "You make it sound awful. It wasn't quite that bad. It's not as if I was an absolute recluse. And besides, I had . . . other interests to keep myself occupied. But all in all, it has been rather—"

"Dull and boring." He leaned over and kissed her on the tip of her nose. "I promise, I shall not allow your life ever to be boring again."

She wrapped her arms around his neck. "And how, dear husband, do you propose to prevent that?"

He pulled her close. "I am willing to spend a very long time trying to devise ever more interesting and intriguing activities to deter tedium from creeping into your life." His lips met hers with a passion that sealed his promise and stole her breath. Her lips parted under his and she accepted his tongue eagerly. Desire rose again between them.

He pulled his mouth away and feathered kisses down the side of her throat. Excitement and urgent need coiled within her. She nibbled on the lobe of his ear and ran her tongue lightly down the curve of his neck, along a thin, almost imperceptible, silvered scar. It was obviously a very old injury. Such a serious wound surely would once have threatened his life.

"Nicholas, how did you come by this scar on your neck?"

His efforts at surveying the sensitive points of her body had progressed to her shoulders. His words mumbled against her flesh, tender with heightened awareness. "It's nothing. A trifle. A mere boyhood mishap."

Merely a boyhood misadventure.

She gasped with sudden understanding. Good Lord! Nicholas was the government agent she'd outsmarted all those long years ago! She had married the only man who held a real threat to her continued safety. The very man who'd haunted her dreams and filled her fantasies now warmed her bed.

The irony of it all threatened to overwhelm her. But it explained so much. Her immediate attraction to him. The vague familiarity of his voice, his scent, his kiss. Perhaps fate meant them to be together. And, thwarted once, now gave them a second chance.

His lips reached her breast and he drew the hardened bud into his mouth; his tongue teased and tormented. Apprehension battled with desire and lost. Her discovery and what it meant for the future faded under the onslaught of his touch. Time enough to dwell on this new development later. She could not sustain rational thought under the firestorm of sensation besieging her.

Sabrina abandoned herself to the erotic bliss of Nicholas's skillful touch and joined him without reserve. Lost in the oblivion of passion, her final thought was a simple acknowledgment: everything between her and this man, after all these years, could truly be attributed to magic.

Sabrina snuggled close by his side, Nicholas lay in the lethargic haze of passion well spent. One arm curled around his sleeping wife, the other folded behind his head. He gazed unseeing at the rough beams above him, suspecting the least astute of observers would call his grin idiotic. His lips quirked upward, held aloft by a delightful sense of peace and harmony.

Never had lovemaking effected him quite this way before. Oh, assuredly, he often ended a passionate encounter both exhilarated and exhausted. But this overwhelming sensation of well-being and contentment was an altogether new experience, an experience of which he doubted he would ever tire.

She sighed and shifted, and he drew her closer. He never imagined the serene creature he had dispassionately selected as the perfect wife would ultimately steal his heart. But she had swept into his life and his soul with the unrelenting inevitability of time itself. And Nicholas could no longer avoid the obvious.

For better or worse, Nicholas Harrington, Earl of Wyldewood, was finally, deeply and irrevocably in love. His doubt about the very existence of the emotion had dissipated, replaced by an inner warmth he had never known. Not the searing heat of passion, but something far more intense, somehow deeper, richer, more lasting. Odd, that love had come to him now, when he was far past the susceptible days of youth. He chuckled wryly. At least a man of his years and experience was intelligent enough to recognize the unique and fragile emotion and mature enough to cherish it.

He gazed at his wife and marveled at whatever quirk of fate brought them together. Her fair hair glistened in the late afternoon light like strands of gold, and he idly stroked it away from her face. He had assumed when they wed that she believed this avowed marriage of convenience would be much the same as many fashionable matches. They would go their separate ways, together only when the dictates of social pressures demanded it. But even then, he had wanted more from her. Now he would never let her go, and he hoped she would not want to leave.

Sabrina was obviously exhausted, but Nicholas was far too restless for sleep. A fair amount of soreness still persisted in his muscles, but the ache in his head had virtually disappeared. Only the fear of disturbing his slumbering wife stopped him from rising from the berth. He sighed and firmly closed his eyes, accepting his not unpleasant confinement, willing himself to sleep.

Fragments of elusive dreams drifted through his mind. Snippets of conversation, memories, fears . . . desire lingered just beyond reach. He struggled to rein in the meandering recollections, to make sense of the disjointed bits, the aimless pieces. It was something about the past. About yesterday? No, farther away than that. Something about the sea, a woman, the *Lady B* . . .

Nicholas's eyes shot open, and only his arm around Sabrina kept him from bolting upright. *Lady B*. The smuggler he had tried, and failed, to capture a decade ago. That was the name of this ship. The ship belonging to that bloody American. How could he have been such an idiot not to have made the connection before now?

Excitement surged through his veins, and he forced himself to stay calm, to examine this intriguing revelation with rational precision. Obviously the memories of that past incident had surfaced because of the blow to his head, a blow not unlike the one that had felled him ten years earlier.

He remembered waking up on a deserted beach, knowing before he opened his eyes that there would be no evidence of the smugglers he sought. He staggered to his feet and winced at the painful pounding in his head. Nicholas was at once grateful to be alive and livid at the failure of his mission. To this day his defeat plagued him. No particular blame was placed in the Home Office. Although he had not captured the band, he had at least halted their activities. But his inability to succeed in his quest had cast a black mark in his own mind, on his own private record. A record that before and after was composed primarily of success and triumph.

And his defeat was at the hands of a woman: the mysterious Lady B. He had combed the village with a corps of experienced men, thoroughly searched the countryside, all to no avail. Not only did no one admit knowledge of her, not a single soul so much as blinked at the mention of her name. Eventually, the futility of the effort forced him to concede, but he had forgotten neither the failure nor the woman.

Long after the details faded into vague impressions of the past, she haunted his dreams. For years she'd emerge from the mists of his memory with her voice, her touch, her kiss, renewing a raging desire for a woman he'd never known. The same unyielding need that surged within him now for Sabrina.

Abruptly, the similarities between his wife and the mysterious Lady B struck him. Both evidenced a courage and an independence he had not previously encountered in a woman. Both displayed far more intelligence than other women of his acquaintance. And both spurred his passion and fired his blood. How strange. Their attributes were the opposite of what he would consider acceptable in a woman, but in these two, those very qualities drew him toward them with an irresistible pull.

He shifted in the berth, tightened his arm around his wife and considered the matter. While it was very likely his presence on this particular ship was a mere coincidence, he no longer doubted there was a link between this vessel and his past nemesis. An unerring instinct deep in his gut confirmed the fact. It was more than probable that Madison knew the lady. The ship was allegedly named for Madison's sister, but with every word spoken on this trip that story grew more and more suspect.

Could Madison have worked with the smugglers? The man carried a certain arrogant, freewheeling, lawless air about him that bespoke disdain for government and authority. Madison could well have used his ships—this ship, perhaps—to supply the goods from France for smuggling into England.

Nicholas gritted his teeth. A driving determination built within him to find the truth. Not that there was any official action he could take; Madison was neither on English soil nor was he a subject of the Crown. But Madison could lead him to Lady B. And then what?

The question reverberated in his mind, and he examined his feelings carefully. Surprised, he noted that his long-held desire for the unknown woman no longer existed, supplanted, or perhaps merged, with the more immediate passion for his wife. And he realized Sabrina was the only woman he wanted in his life, now and forever.

Still, the need to answer the questions that had tormented him for a decade remained. If he could discover the identity of Lady B, he could redeem himself. Oh, not in the eyes of his one-time superiors—a ten-year-old smuggling case hardly still held the interest of the Crown—but in his own. Beyond that, perhaps, it no longer mattered.

It would not be easy to solicit information from Madison. Nicholas smiled slowly. But it would be exceedingly enjoyable. The life of an earl was not nearly as fascinating as his previous activities as agent, spy and diplomat. Playing cat-and-mouse with Madison would allow him to resurrect skills he had expected never to use again. The captain was very likely a challenging subject. Nicholas chuckled. He thoroughly enjoyed challenges.

Sabrina could tell him about Madison's background. He wondered briefly about this business partnership she'd once had with the American, then dismissed it from his mind. No doubt it was a trifling matter. Surely Sabrina had no knowledge of Madison's illicit activities.

He gazed down at her, and emotion swelled within him. The instinct he had trusted throughout his life now told him, regardless of circumstances, that Sabrina would never engage in anything against the law.

Sabrina stretched, a languid, luxurious indulgence. A smile of satisfaction creased her lips before her eyes fluttered open. The morning sun poured into the cabin, gilding everyday objects with a touch of gold, a hint of magic.

She sat up and glanced at the place beside her on the berth. The imprint of Nicholas's warm, wondrous body remained, but he was gone. His absence did not alarm her. Nothing could diminish the euphoria of yesterday afternoon and last night.

The door to the cabin swung open and Nicholas filled the doorway, holding a steaming mug of coffee in each hand.

Her gaze lingered on his strong, bronzed hands, and the pit of her stomach tingled at the knowledge of the pleasure they produced.

"Good morning." He grinned and strode into the room.

"Good morning." Her gaze met his and fell. She clutched the bedclothes to her naked breasts, abruptly shy in his presence.

He sat on the edge of the bed and offered her a mug. "I understand you prefer coffee to tea."

She nodded and accepted the drink. "Thank you."

Sabrina drew a deep swallow of the bitter brew, and her gaze returned to his over the rim of the cup. Amusement glittered in the depths of his black eyes. She held the coverlet clasped to her in one hand, the mug in the other.

His gaze traveled over her, approving and seductive. Heat rose in her face. "I daresay I should dress."

"Why? I find your attire, or lack of it, most charming." He leaned forward and kissed the tip of her nose. A tremor of excitement shivered through her. "Perhaps I should join you."

She stared at the desire that replaced the humor in his eyes. Her discomfort vanished at his look. Arousal curled deep inside. She was more than ready to invite him back beneath the covers.

"So, I gather there has finally been a consummation of this so-called marriage of convenience."

The intrusive voice rudely jerked their attention away from each other. Matt stood in the open doorway, signs of his fight with Nicholas faint but still evident on his roguish face.

"What do you want, Madison?" A growl underlaid Nicholas's words.

"What do I want?" Madison strolled into the cabin, pulled a chair to the side of the berth and settled into it. "Well, let me see. I have always wanted Bree."

"Matt." Sabrina shot him an impatient glare. "You have not. You're simply saying that to cause trouble. It will not work."

Matt rolled his eyes heavenward in the attitude of a rejected suitor. "You wound me, Bree."

Nicholas's eyes narrowed. "Once again, Madison, what do you want?"

Matt glanced pointedly at Sabrina. She pulled the shield of bedclothes tighter to her chest. "Obviously she has made her choice."

"There was not a choice to be made," she said.

Matt ignored her interruption. "But we're still partners, aren't we?"

Sabrina shot a quick glance at Nicholas and sighed. "Of course we are. Nothing has changed."

"Nothing?" Matt raised a brow.

"Nothing," Sabrina said firmly.

"Oh, I wouldn't say nothing." Nicholas displayed a satisfied grin.

Sabrina directed him a quelling glance. "Nothing regarding our partnership. Matt, we're still in this together."

"What about him? What about your husband? What part does he play in all of this?"

Nicholas's gaze caught her own. "Yes, my dear, what about your husband?"

Sabrina looked from one man to the other and back. When she'd started this venture there had been no husband to worry about; she and Matt would share in the treasure. Now, however, there was Nicholas to consider. Somehow, she doubted he'd leap wholeheartedly into her adventure. On the other hand, she didn't seem to have a great many options to choose from in the matter, and there was more than enough gold to go around.

She drew a deep breath. "Nicholas, naturally, will also be a partner."

A flicker of disappointment flashed in his eyes, but Matt shrugged, as if he had anticipated her answer. Nicholas's grin widened; he was so smug, she thought surely it would rekindle the antagonism between the two men. Perhaps a partnership would ease their distaste for each other. Or, more likely, they'd simply kill one another. And if Nicholas ever learned the truth about the nefarious past she and Matt shared . . .

"All right." Matt displayed a nonchalant expression. "But if you're going to let the damnable man be part of this, he should know it all. You'd better tell him what he's letting himself in for."

"Yes, my love, I'd say it's past time you told me what this voyage is all about."

"Very well." Sabrina handed her mug to Nicholas, settled back against the pillows and surveyed the men before her. She'd anticipated and dreaded this moment since they'd boarded the ship. For all his scandalous ways with women, Nicholas was well known as a high stickler. He was not one to flaunt rules and violate regulations, and definitely not the kind of man to run off willy-nilly searching for lost treasure. He never could have carved out the reputation he had in government circles otherwise.

She drew a deep breath. "Years ago, my husband, Jack—"

"Your first husband," Nicholas said. An undefinable expression briefly shadowed his features.

Sabrina tipped her head in acknowledgment. "Yes, of course, my first husband. Jack was quite a gambler. He loved games of chance in whatever form. You knew it was a foolish wager that cost his life?"

Nicholas nodded.

"It seems that during a fairly typical card game he won a rather unusual letter. The letter detailed directions for finding gold lost in Egypt twenty years ago. The gold was supposed to go to Napoleon to finance his Egyptian campaign. Instead, the ship carrying the treasure sank and the gold was hidden." She shrugged.

"The gold was never found. From what I've been told, when Jack won the letter everyone around the table took it as something of a joke. On him. The other players laughed that he had won a good story but an essentially worthless piece of paper. Jack apparently went along with the jest, but he must have taken it seriously. He hid the letter where only I could find it. Recently I did." She paused to gauge his reaction. "And that's why we're here."

Sabrina eyed Nicholas intently. Throughout her explanation, his expression had remained impassive; neither excitement nor disdain crossed his face. He could easily call off this entire escapade. As her husband, he had that right. Was she still willing to defy his wishes? She hoped he would abide by the condition of their marriage to share, or at least support, her business ventures. Still, they had already broken one term of their marriage agreement; would he hesitate to break another? She clutched the coverlet, absently twisting the bedclothes.

"Where is this letter?" Nicholas asked finally. His voice betrayed nothing. Sabrina could not read his thoughts, and apprehension thudded in her chest.

"I'll get it." She swung a naked leg from beneath the bedclothes.

Nicholas glared. "Sabrina!"

Matt smirked. "Bree."

She cast them both an impatient glare, frustration with the situation sharpening her words more than was necessary. "For God's sake, I was not about to leap out of bed naked. Nicholas, please give me some credit for intelligence. And, Matt, I have not given you a glimpse of anything up to this point and I am not about to start now. Honestly, sometimes men can be the stupidest creatures."

She deftly wrapped herself in the coverlet without revealing so much as a flash of bare skin and rose to her feet. An appreciative grin stretched across Matt's face. Nicholas's dark brows pulled together in a disgruntled and possessive manner.

Sabrina dismissed the thought that she surely resembled an Egyptian mummy in her wrapping, toddled across the room and flipped open her portmanteau. She pawed through the clothes inside and found the yellowed, aged sheet of velum. Crossing to Nicholas, she silently offered him the letter.

His reserved gaze swept over her from head to foot. "Don't you think this discussion would be best continued if you were dressed?"

She refused to allow his disapproving scowl to intimidate her and stood her ground. "Perhaps. But my attire does not seem to be entirely pertinent to the issue at hand. Does it?''

''Nevertheless—''

Matt groaned in obvious irritation. "Just read the damned letter so we can get on with this.''

Nicholas shot him a disgusted glare and accepted the page from her outstretched hand. Sabrina secured the bedclothes more tightly around her and perched on the edge of the berth.

Long moments crept by. Sabrina studied her husband. Anxiety gripped her heart and swirled in her stomach. Once again his face was expressionless, giving no sign, no hint of his thoughts, his reactions. She glanced at Matt. He cocked an eyebrow, as if mildly curious but essentially unconcerned as to Nicholas's opinion.

She could bear the waiting no longer. Nicholas raised his gaze to hers. Her breath caught in her throat.

His voice was cool. "This is without a doubt the most ridiculous missive I have ever encountered.''

Sabrina's heart plunged. "What?''

Matt leapt to his feet and snatched the letter from Nicholas's hand. "I knew it. I knew this would be his reaction. Look at him, Bree—he doesn't have an adventurous or imaginative bone in his entire stuffy, starched body. Besides, it takes a fair amount of courage to do something like this. He just doesn't have it.''

Nicholas rose, anger coloring his face. "I do not take kindly to this type of verbal abuse from anyone, let alone a disreputable, ill-mannered American who confuses courage with stupidity.''

"Jack Winfield would have done it.'' Matt's taunting words snapped like a bolt across the room.

Nicholas clenched his teeth, the muscle in his jaw taut, and fairly spit the words at Matt. "I am not Jack Winfield and I have no desire to be.''

The two shot icy glares at each other. Sabrina stumbled to her feet and staggered to stand between the men, hindered greatly by the coverlet wrapped around her.

"Haven't you both had enough of this bickering? You've nothing to show for the last time you came to blows except aches and pains suffered at the hands of the other. I will not have you at one another's throats again.''

She turned to Matt and cast him a sharp glare. "Nicholas is my husband, whether you like the idea or not. I owe him certain loyalties and considerations. I will not allow you to bait and berate him this way.''

She swiveled to face her husband. "And as for you . . .''

Nicholas raised a haughty brow. "Matt has been a good, true friend to me for more years than I care to count. He helped me when I needed assistance and he is willing to help me now.

"Under the terms of our marriage you agreed to be equal partners in any business venture in which I am engaged. When we reached our agreement you asked what type of business ventures.'' She drew a deep breath. "This pursuit is what I referred to.''

Nicholas's eyes narrowed. "And if I refuse to join you? Or refuse to allow you to continue this ridiculous undertaking? What then?''

Sabrina pulled her gaze from his. Emotions and consequences and fate all jumbled through her mind. She stared at a spot on the floor. A small, discolored blotch. It burned itself into her mind. How odd that, at the moment she would decide her entire life, a tiny mark on the floor should forever imprint itself on her memory.

She lifted her chin and drew up her gaze to meet his. His eyes burned with an intensity that seemed to pierce her soul. Fear, tight and aching, gripped her. Had she found the man she'd searched for her entire life only to lose him now? Could she make him understand that her search for the gold had grown beyond a mere desire to acquire funds? That it now was a quest to return to her the joy and excitement of a life she'd abandoned years ago. A quest she could not give up. Her throat tightened, and she realized she had made her choice long before now.

"I would prefer that you join us. Your participation has become quite important to me. However, if you refuse . . .'' She squared her shoulders and paused, gathering her courage. There would be no turning back. "I shall go on regardless. With you or without you.''

Emotion smoldered in Nicholas's dark eyes, but his words were controlled. ''Do you have any idea how dangerous Egypt is these days? The country is overrun with cutthroats and rabble seeking treasure far more ancient than yours. But to a man they would slit your lovely neck at the slightest hint of French gold.''

''I am prepared to take that risk,'' she said quietly.

''Well, I am not prepared to put you at risk.'' He ran an impatient hand through his dark hair. ''You would continue this foolishness even if I forbid it? You realize your actions, your blatant disregard for my wishes, would destroy any future we have together?''

Tears stung the back of her eyes, but she refused to let them show. She could not keep him at the cost of her soul. ''I do.''

Nicholas turned and strode toward the door. Sabrina's heart stilled, and anguish washed over her. He stopped, one hand poised to grab the knob. ''Bloody hell.''

Nicholas pivoted to face her. A resigned sigh escaped his lips. ''Very well. I shall be a part of this ill-suited venture, if only to keep you alive.''

Sabrina had steeled herself to accept his refusal, and it took a moment for his agreement to register. Jubilation replaced dejection. She threw herself across the room and into his arms in a flurry of bedclothes and the accompanying musky scent of lovemaking.

''Nicholas!'' She laughed with sheer joy and he favored her with a rueful grin.

''I do not believe in this treasure hunt of yours. I have every confidence it will not succeed. However . . .'' He gazed in her eyes and she caught her breath, not daring to believe the passion revealed there.

''It seems traveling halfway around the world is not too great a price to pay to keep you by my side. And if it takes a futile and hazardous search for a treasure that very likely does not exist to make you happy, I imagine I shall simply have to equip myself with a spade, a compass and a dagger.''

"Oh, Nicholas, you won't be sorry."

"Hah. I shall probably be very sorry." He swept her up in his arms and carried her to the berth. His lips nuzzled her neck and shivers coursed through her. He whispered in her ear.

"However, I can think of worse places to get to know my wife than beneath a desert moon."

He placed her on the berth and her gaze met his, the moment abruptly weighted with meaning. Unspoken promises were exchanged, commitments made, agreements forged. If yesterday had been the physical coupling of their marriage, today was the bonding of their spirits. Sabrina realized, regardless of what happened, this man would own her heart forever.

"If the two of you can bear to pull yourselves away from each other, I believe we have some serious talking to do." Matt's dry, sarcastic tones interrupted. He sank into a chair and studied the couple with obvious annoyance.

Reluctantly, Sabrina pulled away from Nicholas. He settled beside her and cast Matt a bored glance. "Proceed."

"First, I want to know why you think this letter of Bree's is so ridiculous."

Sabrina nodded in agreement. "The directions seem perfectly clear and rather clever to me."

Nicholas plucked the letter from Matt's fingers. "Oh, everything written here is indeed concise and easily understandable. The problem is not so much what is written as what is not."

Sabrina drew her brows together in a puzzled frown. "I do not understand."

"It's quite simple, my dear. When Napoleon marched his troops through Egypt he was not exactly the darling of the French government. In point of fact, those in charge were more than content to ignore him altogether. The very idea that the government would send gold to support his efforts is ludicrous." Sympathy shone in Nicholas's black eyes. "I am sorry, my love."

Disappointment stabbed through her. Could it be that after all her efforts she would fail through no fault of her own?

Silence descended over the room, each person lost in his or her own thoughts.

Matt studied his fingernails with an intensity that belied the mundane action. His words came slowly, as if he puzzled each one out in his head before giving them voice.

"Bree?" Her gaze met his. "Isn't there a first page to that letter?"

She nodded. "I believe so."

"And you don't have it?"

She sighed with impatience. "You know full well this is all I have. I don't see what difference another page would make."

Matt leaned toward Nicholas. "Whether or not his own government was behind him, Boney did have supporters in France, didn't he?"

Nicholas nodded thoughtfully. "Indeed. His Egyptian campaign was well before his elevation to emperor, but there were those who saw his potential."

The men locked gazes. Sabrina looked from one to the other. They seemed to have forgotten her presence. Excitement grew in their voices.

"So it is not far-fetched to assume—" Matt said.

"—that the support for Napoleon, and therefore the gold, came not from the government—" Nicholas began.

Matt continued. "—but from private sources, and the first page of Bree's letter could well explain that."

Nicholas concluded with a slow grin, "So, it's possible that this treasure exists after all."

He tossed Matt a look of grudging admiration. "Very good, Madison."

"For an American?" A challenging smirk creased Matt's face.

Nicholas nodded ruefully. "For anyone."

Sabrina studied the two men. Something indefinable had just changed between them. Fascinating to watch, distracting her from—she caught her breath. "Are you saying the gold exists?"

"No. I'm saying there is a chance."

Matt's smile widened. "A chance I'm willing to take."

Nicholas cocked an eyebrow. "A chance we're all willing to take."

Sabrina returned Matt's smile and noted with pleasure that even Nicholas finally appeared excited at the prospect of the quest. Exhilaration spiraled within her. "So, we are agreed then? We will continue? As partners?"

"As partners. If we don't kill each other first." Matt grinned at Nicholas.

Nicholas groaned. "As partners. And God help us all."

Chapter Thirteen

Sabrina rested her elbow on the railing and propped her head in her hand. Her gaze wandered restlessly. Under ordinary circumstances the exotic sights of the bustling Naples docks would have appealed to the adventuress in her. She would have been fascinated by the curious foreign spectacle peopled with odd and intriguing creatures, the lyrical languages of far distant lands, even the powerful and pungent scents of the waterfront.

Instead, a disgruntled sigh blew through her lips. Now that Nicholas not only knew of the purpose of their journey but was, however reluctantly, joining in, frustration stabbed her at any delay. But Matt insisted this stop in Naples was necessary to his shipping interests, and she could scarcely argue with the needs of business. Still, Sabrina feared the remaining hours until they sailed again would stretch to eternity.

They'd docked more than an hour earlier. Nicholas mentioned something about posting a letter and left the ship. Matt was nowhere in sight, attending to the various details of docking and supplies and cargo and a myriad of other maritime particulars. It had been so long since she'd been on a ship, the details of being in port had faded from her memory, along with other useless bits of knowledge. With both men occupied, Sabrina was left to her own devices and, since she had no real desire to go ashore, had to content herself with observing the profusion of activity on the wharf.

"A penny for your thoughts, or should I offer a fortune?" Matt leaned on the railing beside her.

Sabrina's gaze caught on a sailor feeding nuts to a small monkey perched on his shoulder. "I daresay my thoughts aren't worth much of anything right now. Unless you tell me we can be off, I shall continue to stand here chaffing at every second of delay."

Matt laughed. "Bree, your treasure has been hidden for twenty years. It can wait a few more days."

"I'm not at all concerned about the gold."

"Then why the impatience?"

"I don't know exactly. But it's been so terribly long since I did anything even marginally exciting, so long since I've had so much as a meager adventure, I detest having to halt our progress even for the shortest time."

"Can't be helped, Bree."

"I realize that. I simply don't like it."

She pulled her gaze from the sights on the dock and perused the captain. "How are you and Nicholas getting along? In the past few days, ever since he learned of our quest, the two of you have been as thick as thieves. Dare I hope you've put your animosity aside and become friends?"

Matt appeared to choose his words carefully. "Oh, I wouldn't say we're friends. In fact, I don't think I trust him."

"Whyever not?"

"Don't get indignant with me, Bree. You know perfectly well the man's background. He's been active in government, and I suspect his experience goes far beyond missions of diplomacy."

Sabrina's heart skipped a beat. Had Matt learned about Nicholas's previous encounter with them? She still had not decided whether she should tell Matt she'd married the agent they'd beaten a decade ago, or whether wisdom decreed keeping her knowledge to herself.

She threw him a challenging glare. "No doubt, but what difference does that make?"

"He quizzes me, Bree, constantly. He does it extremely well. His questions are so off-hand, so subtle, that it took me a while to catch on."

Apprehension trickled through her. "What kinds of questions?"

"Mainly about my life, my past. He's asked about my parents, my family . . . my sister." He shot her a rueful look. "That's a hard one to deal with. I have no idea how desperate this sister was, what problems she faced, when she—"

"Enough," she said impatiently. "His questions seem relatively innocent."

Matt shook his head. "I don't think so. He's also asked about my ships, how many I have now and how many I had ten years ago. He's tried to find out how I came by the money to build a fleet the way I have. No, he's definitely looking for answers. I just wish I knew what's behind those questions of his. The only thing he hasn't asked me about is you."

"Well, that's something, at any rate," she said under her breath.

He studied her for a long, discomforting moment.

"What's going on, Bree?" he asked softly. "Is there something you're not telling me?"

Sabrina stared, a dozen thoughts flying through her head. Did Matt deserve to know who Nicholas was? Or did she now owe her husband more loyalty than she did her long-time friend and partner? Just because Nicholas asked a few questions didn't mean he was suspicious, merely curious. Still, forewarned was forearmed, and it might well be in her best interest, and Matt's, to tell him what she knew.

She drew a steadying breath. "Perhaps it's—"

"Excuse me, Capt'n, lass." Simon nodded curtly. His voice came as a welcome interruption, and Sabrina breathed a sigh of relief. Time enough to tell Matt about Nicholas later. Besides, he did not trust her husband well enough to betray them.

Matt turned to the first mate. "What is it, Simon?"

"Well, Capt'n," the big man's eyes twinkled, "there's a young gentleman on the dock who says his party's been stranded. They're headed for Egypt and want to book passage."

"How many in his party?" Matt asked, his tone a casual inquiry.

"Himself and two women. The young one looks desperate, like she's about to burst into tears. But the older lady seems right excited. Keeps calling their predicament a crusade of adventure." Simon chuckled. "I'd wager she's damned feisty—got a lot of spirit."

Matt hesitated, and Simon seized the opening. "They're both beauties, Capt'n."

Sabrina groaned to herself. By the look on Matt's face, Simon's assessment finally captured his captain's interest. Simon pushed his point home with the relish of a fencer striking the coup de grace. "And they say they'll pay double the usual rate."

"They're beauties, you say?"

"Aye, sir."

"Do we have any available cabins?"

"Just one that's fit for passengers, Capt'n." Simon wore a look of innocence. "I was thinkin' we could put the young gentleman and his lordship in the empty cabin and let the women all bunk together."

"Now wait just a moment . . ." Sabrina said, her voice rising in irritation.

"That means we'd have to separate the newlyweds." A slow grin spread across Matt's face. "All right, Simon, let them board."

"Matt!" Sabrina adopted her most indignant manner.

"Bree, you wouldn't want us to turn our backs on fellow travelers." He glanced at Simon. "Are they English?"

The sailor nodded. "Aye."

"And fellow countrymen too, Bree. Tsk, tsk." He leveled a mournful glance at her. "I wouldn't have thought you so unfeeling, so . . . I think *selfish* is the right word, don't you think so, Simon?''

Simon appeared appropriately downcast. "Aye, Capt'n. I'd say selfish about covers it.''

Sabrina glared at each man in turn. As if this delay wasn't bad enough, now she would have to share her cabin with two strangers; tourists, no doubt. Quite likely the kind of proper ladies she'd had her fill of in London. Women who would never understand her quest, let alone her traveling sans servants and wearing men's clothes. Worst of all, this would mean no more nights spent wrapped in Nicholas's arms. Disappointment flooded her at the thought.

"Bree?" Matt said gently.

"Very well.'' Sabrina glowered and clenched her teeth. "The more, the merrier.''

Matt grinned at his success. "I knew you'd see it my way. After all, this is business, and passengers are the business of this ship.''

Pointedly, Sabrina turned her back on Matt with a snort of derision and glared at the vessels in the harbor, as if the innocent crafts were responsible for her annoyance. Sabrina would accept this inconvenience, but she positively refused to be gracious about it. And she had no desire to meet these intruders until absolutely necessary.

"Bring them on board, Simon.'' Laughter shaded his voice. "Now, Bree—''

She whirled to face him. "Don't you dare try to justify yourself to me, Matthew Madison. I know exactly what you're up to. You simply can not bear to see Nicholas and me together, and you just want to create problems in whatever way possible.''

"Bree, would I do that to you?''

She shot him a scathing glance. "You would and apparently you are.''

The voices of the new arrivals approaching the ship drew their attention. From this distance their features were not discernable, but there was something vaguely familiar about at least two of the figures.

They stepped up the gangplank and drew closer. The face

of a woman a bit younger than Sabrina came into focus and nagged at her memory. On her heels followed a young blonde—

Sabrina gasped. "Bloody hell."

An appreciative smile creased Matt's face. "Simon was right—they are beauties."

Sabrina's voice rang icy and hard. "Don't even think it, Matt. That's my daughter."

"Your daughter," he said in surprise. "The tall, dark-haired one is your daughter?"

"No, you idiot. The blonde is my daughter. How in the name of all that's holy—"

"What about the other one?" Interest glittered in his eyes.

For a moment Sabrina forgot her shock over seeing Belinda board the ship and wanted to laugh. This would certainly serve Matt right. It was exactly what he deserved.

She grinned. "That, my dear old friend, is Wynne Harrington. Nicholas's sister."

"His sister?" A hint of dismay flickered across Matt's face. "Does he care for her, do you think?"

"Oh, I suspect far more than you care for your sister. Nicholas's sister does, after all, actually exist."

Matt stared at the newcomers' steady approach. Sabrina saw his jaw tense in an attitude of resolve and chuckled to herself. She'd only met Wynne Harrington once, but all she'd heard about the woman indicated that she was far more interested in books than in men. Still, disinterest on the part of a female was one sure way to entice a man like Matt. This new development could, at the very least, provide an interesting diversion.

"Mother?" Belinda's questioning voice interrupted her thoughts. Sabrina steeled herself and turned to her daughter.

Belinda stared in obvious astonishment, as if she were unable to believe her eyes. "Mother!"

Belinda flew the remaining steps between them and threw herself, weeping, into her mother's arms. "Oh, Mother, I didn't know if we'd ever find you. I've been so worried. That loathsome man threw us off his nasty boat. And Erick has been so dreadfully ill. Since the moment we left England everything has just been horrid."

Sabrina was hard pressed to balance concern for her daughter with amusement at her dramatic outburst. She wrapped her arms around her crying child and glanced past Belinda to a sheepish-looking Erick. "What is she talking about?"

He cleared his throat in a nervous gesture. "We have, umm, had a few difficulties."

"Difficulties," Belinda said, and jerked her head off her mother's shoulder. Indignation glittered in her eyes and she glared at her fiancé. "I believe, Erick, 'difficulties' is putting far too mild a face on it. Disaster is a more apt description."

Erick looked like a man caught in a futile struggle to save himself from drowning, or worse. "Belinda, I am certain . . ."

"Erick," Sabrina said, "perhaps it would be best if you let Belinda explain about your problems and, more to the point, what you three are doing here. Darling?"

"Thank you, Mother." Belinda sniffed inelegantly. "When I learned you were heading to Egypt I decided we should go after you." She threw her mother a cautious look. "In your best interest, of course."

Sabrina sighed softly "Of course."

Relief crossed Belinda's face. "At any rate, we decided to follow, and Erick's Aunt Wynne agreed to come along as a chaperone." Belinda cast a quick glance at Wynne, where she stood chatting with Simon, apparently oblivious to Belinda's outburst.

"Come along, Mother." Belinda hooked her arm through Sabrina's and propelled her down the deck and out of earshot. Daughter leaned toward mother in a manner heartfelt yet discreet.

"Wynne is extremely annoying, Mother. She has likely read every book ever written and does not hesitate to share her knowledge and the opinions derived from it. She so upset the captain of the boat we were on, he demanded we leave, virtually abandoning us here.

"And when she is not enlightening us on some obscure point, she is writting in that horrible journal of hers. I feel as if she is noting every little thing I say or do. It is most disconcerting.''

"Indeed.'' It was difficult to keep the smile off her face. Belinda's indignation was obvious, and when Sabrina thought of Matt's interest in Wynne . . . oh, yes, there was indeed promise here for some entertaining moments. Sabrina turned her attention back to her child. "Well, everything has worked out now and we're all together.''

"Oh, no, Mother, that's not all.''

"No?''

"Mother, it's Erick.'' Belinda sighed. "He's been, well, ill. Mal de mer.''

She leaned toward her mother with an air of confidentiality. "I know that when one marries one is suppose to carry on through sickness and all that, but it really is rather unnerving. I realize this is not at all charitable, but seeing him hang over the side of the boat day after day, listening to him groan and watching him turn the most remarkable shade of green . . . well, it's simply not . . .''

"Not romantic? Not heroic? Not quite what you'd imagined?''

"Exactly.'' The tragic exaggeration of youth clouded Belinda's sapphire eyes. "Mother, what shall I do?''

Sabrina once more resisted the urge to smile. She could all too easily remember the heightened emotions of that age. An age at which she herself had already been married and borne a child.

"Do you still love him, sweetheart?

Belinda nodded mournfully.

"Then I would suggest,'' Sabrina said slowly, "that in the future you simply make sure the man never, ever boards a ship again. Keep him on dry land. I'm not certain I should even allow him on beaches or within sight of the ocean.''

Belinda's eyes widened in surprise, and she stared silently, as if digesting her mother's advice.

"But, Mother, what about Brighton? I adore Brighton, and I imagine Erick does—'' Abruptly, she smiled. "Mother, now you're teasing me.''

Sabrina grinned back. "Not entirely, my love.'' Her affectionate tone turned brisk. "Now that we have dispensed with your concerns, I don't believe you've quite explained what you're doing here. I left you in London, and I very much anticipated that you would remain there until my return."

Belinda stepped away from her parent. "Why, Mother, surely it's obvious why we came after you?"

"No, it's not. I require some kind of explanation, and I expect it to be more than adequate. I am not especially pleased to see you here."

"Very well, Mother," Belinda said, in that irritating I-know-far-more-than-you-do voice guaranteed to set Sabrina on edge. "We came because . . ." Belinda's gaze wandered over her mother's figure. "What are you wearing?"

Her face froze in horror. "Do you have on breeches? That's scandalous, Mother, absolutely scandalous. I simply cannot—"

"Wait till you hear her language. It's just as atrocious as her clothing." Nicholas strode toward them, Erick a scant step behind him. "Good day, Belinda. So charming to see you again."

"You!" Belinda's eyes flashed and she whirled to face her mother. "He's why we followed you. We're here to try and salvage your reputation. To save you from him!"

Astonishment swept her breath away and Sabrina could barely choke out the words. "You came to save me? From him? Why on earth would you deem a rescue so necessary you'd follow us halfway around the world?"

"Why indeed?" Nicholas raised an amused brow.

Belinda glared at him. "Mother, perhaps you were unaware of this, but Lord Wyldewood has a rather unsavory reputation with women." Belinda drew herself up in an attitude of imposing propriety. "To put it bluntly, Mother, the man's a rake."

The absurdity of the situation hit Sabrina like a fist. Her gaze caught Nicholas's and his eyes twinkled.

"So you hoped to save me from becoming his next victim? From succumbing to his notorious charms? From sharing his bed?"

Belinda blushed at her mother's blunt words. "Exactly."

"I commend you for your concern about your mother's virtue," Nicholas said. "However, I fear you are too late."

"Nicholas," Sabrina said sharply. This discussion was headed in a direction she was not at all sure she liked.

The color swept from Belinda's face. "Too late?"

"Yes, indeed." Nicholas shook his head sorrowfully. "Had I only known of your concern, I would have restrained myself. As it is . . ."

"Oh, dear." Belinda swayed on her feet.

Nicholas shrugged. "And if I recall, your mother did not seem particularly reluctant to accept my advances."

Sabrina groaned. "Bloody hell."

Belinda gasped. Erick leapt forward and wrapped a steadying arm around his fiancée. "Father, that's not at all the kind of thing you should be saying to her. She's quite delicate, you know."

Nicholas grinned wickedly. "I am sorry. I had no idea. I assumed she was as . . . well . . . sturdy as her mother."

"Nicholas!" Sabrina cast him a scathing glare, and he responded with a look that bespoke a clear conscience. A look designed to fuel her annoyance. "Erick's right. You're leading her to believe something that's not entirely true."

"Oh, Mother." Belinda brightened. "Then he hasn't ruined you?"

Sabrina clenched her teeth. Nicholas was a virtual picture of childlike innocence: hands clasped behind his back, pleasant smile drifting across his lips, she suspected she could even hear him humming. "Oh, he's ruined me all right."

Belinda uttered a pitiful cry and swayed again. Sabrina glared at Nicholas. "He married me."

"Married!" Belinda quickly recovered from her impending swoon. "You're the countess of Wyldewood?" Eyes wide with surprise, she turned to Nicholas. "And that makes you my—"

"Stepfather." In one practiced gesture, Nicholas stepped forward, took her hand and lifted it to his lips.

"Splendid, Father." Erick grinned.

"What an interesting surprise," Belinda said faintly. She

retrieved her hand and cast a chastising look at her mother. "But, Mother, you were a marchioness, and now to be a mere countess . . ."

"Good Lord, Belinda." Anger flared within Sabrina. How could any child of hers turn out to be such a top-lofty snob?

Confusion crossed Belinda's lovely face. "But, Mother, I was simply being honest." She cast an apologetic glance at Nicholas. "And, in point of fact, she did trade a higher title for a lesser one." Belinda explained patiently. "She was a marchioness —"

"And now she's a wife," Nicholas said, a satisfied smile on his lips. "I suspect, if you were to ask her, she'd tell you she's quite pleased with her . . . shall we say, bargain."

An anxious tone underlaid Belinda's words. "Are you, Mother?"

Sabrina's gaze caught her husband's. Surprised, she noted that her daughter's question echoed in his eyes. The bloody man still didn't know how she felt about him. Her heart surged. Perhaps he did care for her after all.

She addressed her daughter but kept her gaze on her husband. "Yes, darling, I am pleased. I am very pleased."

A gleam lit his eyes, and she trembled with the warmth of it. It no longer mattered that this man who had spoken so many words of love to so many women would likely never speak them to her with the meaning she longed for. He simply did not know how. But she suspected that somewhere deep within him a spark for her burned. His eyes told her that. And even if it was not the love she wanted, perhaps it was enough.

"Nicholas! I knew we would catch up to you eventually." A beaming Wynne swept up to them and kissed the air by her brother's cheek. "And in Italy—how exciting. We have already had the most delightful adventures, I can't tell you—"

Nicholas chuckled wryly. "I believe we have already heard quite a bit about these so-called adventures, and it seems delightful may well be a matter of perspective."

"Indeed?" Wynne's brows drew together thoughtfully

above her gold-rimmed glasses. "I can't imagine why anyone would not consider our activities to date thoroughly enjoyable. Of course, poor Erick here has been a bit under the weather. And dear Belinda does not seem to relish new experiences with quite the same enthusiasm one would hope for in someone of her age. Still, I . . ." Wynne's gaze met Sabrina's. "Lady Winfield, I would suspect you of all people would understand the lure of adventure."

"Why on earth would you suspect that?" Sabrina words were cautious.

Wynne shrugged. "Why, it's obvious, my dear. First, you take off on an unexpected and quite mysterious journey to ancient lands. Next, without warning, you marry a man you scarcely know—"

"You've already heard about that, have you?" Nicholas grinned.

Wynne nodded toward Simon. "This gentleman was so kind as to tell me. I must say, I was somewhat amazed."

"Surely you expected I would marry again someday?" Nicholas raised a brow in surprise.

Wynne sighed. "I had hoped, of course. But when the time came I did not expect you to wed . . . well . . . someone like this."

"Forgive my interruption," Sabrina said sarcastically, "but I tend to lose patience when people discuss me as if I were not present. Exactly what do you mean, 'someone like this'?"

"My dear, I do not mean to imply censure of any sort. On the contrary, I quite admire you. I have already mentioned your apparent appreciation of adventure and the unexpected. Your willingness to take on Nicholas as a husband confirms that you comprehend the value of a challenge."

"I hardly view myself as a challenge," Nicholas said with a huff. "I've always been considered something of a catch on the marriage mart."

Sabrina and Wynne stared at him and then traded glances.

"Perhaps I am not making myself entirely clear." Wynne paused, as if carefully choosing her words. "I imagine I had assumed that when Nicholas finally wed again it would be

188

to a woman who was far too proper to ever consider adventure of any type.''

Wynne cocked her head and eyed Sabrina in a considering manner. ''Now that I think about it, I had always supposed you to be that type of creature. At least all I have ever heard about you would indicate that.''

''Things are not always what they would appear,'' Sabrina said dryly.

''So it would seem.'' Wynne smiled. ''I believe we shall get on exceedingly well. Exceedingly well, indeed.'' She cast an appraising glance over Sabrina. ''And if you would lend me a pair of those charming breeches or help me procure a pair of my own—''

Nicholas groaned. ''Wynne.''

''Bree.'' Matt's elbow dug into Sabrina's side. ''It seems everyone is acquainted here but me.'' Matt's gaze met Wynne's, meshed and held. ''What do I have to do to earn an introduction to this lovely lady?''

Sabrina stifled a grin at Matt's blatant display of interest and the forbidding frown that crossed her husband's face. ''Of course. Whatever possessed me to forget myself this way.''

Sabrina fluttered her lashes innocently at Matt and was rewarded by a quick scowl in return. ''Matt, may I present Lady Wynnefred Harrington. Wynne, Matthew Madison, the captain of this ship.''

''Captain, you have a magnificent vessel.'' A slight sultry tone marked Wynne's voice. Sabrina exchanged surprised a glance with her husband.

''Ah, but its magnificence pales in your presence.'' Matt took Wynne's hand and drew it to his lips. His gaze never broke from hers, their mutual attraction readily apparent.

The moment stretched between the two, who were oblivious to the inquisitive stares of those gathered around them. Sabrina glanced at Nicholas. Concern etched his countenance and his dark eyes narrowed. Belinda's features lit with curiosity, and her fiancé sported a man-of-the-world smirk. Even Simon joined the fascinated onlookers, a wide grin stretched across his face.

"I daresay we should get everyone settled." Sabrina's voice shattered the silence and her own growing discomfort. It was as if she and the others somehow had intruded on an intimate liaison, a private moment, a romantic encounter.

Abruptly, everyone burst into animated, nervous chatter. Wynne withdrew her hand from Matt's, but there was a sense of reluctance about the act, as if she and he were unwilling or unable to relinquish the connection between them.

"If you ladies would care to follow me . . ." Simon led the way to Sabrina's cabin, and the women took their leave in a flurry of inane comments.

Sabrina eyed Wynne thoughtfully. Perhaps this would not be as amusing as she had thought, especially if Wynne returned Matt's interest as quickly as it now appeared. As interesting as it would be to see Matt bested by an intelligent and clever woman, she would not want to see his heart broken. And Wynne's reaction to him indicated the possibility of heartbreak could well exist on both sides.

She did not know Wynne well and now wondered if, indeed, anyone knew her at all. Her reputation did not indicate the kind of woman who would be attracted to someone as brash and boisterous as Matt.

Could it be that after all these years of living through her books, Wynne Harrington was now ready to leap into life with a vengeance? Was the well-known bluestocking hiding a spirit just waiting to be released by the touch of adventure and the lure of the unknown? And what would a woman like that become with the excitement of freedom and the promise of passion at long last within reach?

With a start, Sabrina realized that Wynne was not so very different from herself. For years she too had hidden her real self from the condemning eyes of society. Only now had her quest brought out the woman she truly was, the woman she'd always been.

Sabrina smiled to herself and followed her daughter and sister-in-law into her cabin. If Nicholas thought he'd had difficulties with a wife who had a mind of her own, she wouldn't hazard to guess how he would react to a sister enthusiastically embracing an entire new world of experience.

Especially when it appeared that that embrace would very likely include a rakish American sea captain.

Chapter Fourteen

"I daresay you're overreacting, Father. We have only a week or two remaining until we reach Egypt. What can happen in so short a time?"

"More than you can imagine," Nicholas said, brooding. He recalled how little time it had taken for him to fall completely under Sabrina's spell.

Erick sat in the lone chair in the cramped cabin he shared with his father. Nicholas perched uncomfortably on a narrow bunk and surveyed the tiny room with disgust. He thought he'd seen the last of this uncomfortable accommodation when he tossed his valise into Sabrina's cabin.

"Are you certain Captain Madison has designs on Aunt Wynne?"

Nicholas threw his son a disbelieving glance. Surely the boy wasn't that naive. Madison's intentions were obvious to anyone who had witnessed his meeting with Wynne. Nicholas snorted. "As certain as knowing what a rooster's intentions are in a henhouse."

"Perhaps it's just as well."

"What in God's name do you mean, just as well?"

The Perfect Wife

Erick shrugged. "At her age, Aunt Wynne is past praying for. Madison may well be her only chance to wed."

"Bloody hell, Erick." Nicholas leapt to his feet and promptly smacked his head on a low beam. "Yow!" He glowered at the offending timber. He would not put it past Madison to have maneuvered everything up to and including the appearance of his son and sister, simply to place him back in these disgracefully meager quarters.

Nicholas rubbed his head gingerly. "Madison has no intention of marrying your aunt. He has no desire to be leg-shackled. I have seen far too many men just like him to be certain of that. No, marriage is not what he wants."

"Well, surely Aunt Wynne will not disguard her virtue easily."

Abruptly, Nicholas realized his fears might be unfounded after all. His sister was a practical, proper woman. He breathed a sigh of relief. "Of course she won't. I had not thought of that. Wynne will not disregard years of proper behavior, impeccable breeding and her duty to her family simply because a rogue like Madison whispers a few tender words in her ear."

"Still . . ." Erick said thoughtfully.

"Still?"

"Well . . ." Erick's words were measured and evasive. "Aunt Wynne's behavior on this trip has been somewhat . . . different than her manner in the past."

"Different?" Foreboding pulled Nicholas's dark brows together. "Explain yourself."

Erick sighed. "I'm not sure I can." He paused, as if collecting his thoughts. "From the moment I first asked her to accompany us, it has been as if she has had a purpose all her own on this journey. She has always been extremely capable and excessively knowledgeable." He grimaced. "For as long as I can remember she has always had a book in hand.

"But now there is a quiet excitement about her, an odd sort of suppressed energy. . . ." Erick shook his head helplessly. "I daresay I am not expressing this well. It's as if she is waiting, as if she is expecting something. Take my word on it, Father, Aunt Wynne has definitely changed.''

"Surely you are exaggerating differences that could well be attributed to the stimulation of traveling.''

Erick shook his head. "I don't think so, Father.''

Nicholas paced the short length of the cabin in an uncomfortable hunched posture. He could stand upright, but only with care. Walking meant avoiding stout beams lurking in wait to batter his already bruised head.

"If you are right about your aunt, there may well be little we can do to protect her from Madison's advances. However, I think we can at least attempt to intercede in any way possible to ensure that they are never alone together.''

"Father,'' Erick said cautiously, "I suspect that will be extremely awkward, if not impossible. We cannot watch them every minute. Besides . . .'' He breathed a heavy sigh. "I fear I will not be of much assistance. I shall be incapacitated within an hour of hitting open seas.''

"So I hear.'' Nicholas frowned. "I can sympathize, my boy, although I've never felt the ravages of seasickness myself.''

"*Ravage* is the right word for it,'' Erick said under his breath. "But far worse than the illness itself is the effect it seems to have on Belinda.''

"What effect?''

"I feel as if somehow I've let her down. Disappointed her.'' Erick shot to his feet, and Nicholas winced in the anticipation that his son's head would suffer the same fate as his own. Erick was less than an inch shorter than his father, but somehow he managed to stand upright without so much as a hair brushing a beam.

"Damnation, Father, I don't know what to do.'' Erick paced the length of the cabin. Without apparent effort, he avoided contact with the ceiling's lethal projections, and Nicholas watched in admiration. "When we began this voyage I anticipated that it would provide the opportunity for us to see more of each other. To spend time away from the crowded social whirl of London and be with each other without always being under the watchful eyes of chaperones or ton gossips.

"But this annoying problem of mine has destroyed any possibility of our being together. I suspect her feelings for me may even have changed."

"Would that be such a tragedy?" Nicholas's words were matter of fact, but he studied his son intently.

"Bloody hell, Father." Erick glared. "I love her. I want her. And she will be mine." His tone softened and his shoulders sagged. "I am simply no longer certain whether she wants me." His gaze met his father's in mute appeal. "What shall I do?"

For the first time in Nicholas's life his son had turned to him for advice. A small knot clenched in his stomach. He wasn't precisely certain how to give fatherly advice. Lord knew his own father could not be bothered.

Nicholas pulled a deep breath. He was not his father and he would not let his son down.

"Well . . ." His tone surprised him, an effortless mix of sage wisdom and mature authority. "Well," he said again, enjoying the way the word rolled off his tongue with fatherly insight. "It would appear to me that the way to ensnare a young girl's affections would be to appeal to her sense of romance. Plying her with flowers and other sentimental gifts could be extremely effective."

A skeptical expression hung on Erick's face. "I doubt somehow that that would work in this particular situation."

"You know," Nicholas said thoughtfully, "I have noticed women, especially young women, have a peculiar affinity for men of a heroic nature. Lord knows, women of all ages, even the most respectable, seem to throw themselves at Wellington. Perhaps you could be alert to any heroic acts that may present themselves while we are in Egypt. It is a ruthless place these days, and there could well be ample opportunity."

"Do you depend on heroic acts to win women's favors?"

"Me?" Nicholas grinned. "Never. I have rarely had to actively pursue a woman. Quite the reverse. Typically, they seek me out."

"What about my mother? Didn't you court her?"

"No, to my chagrin, I did not." Nicholas shook his head.

"Ours was an arranged match. We met but once before we wed. Your grandfather was convinced he was about to stick his spoon in the wall, and equally certain I would not carry out my responsibility and provide an heir. I had little to say about the match. I was younger than you are now.

"Your mother was a sweet, biddable girl, but I was consumed with work that I perceived as my duty to king and country and was not often with her. I regret to say I never really knew her. So you see, it was not a grand passion. Not at all what you appear to be seeking with Belinda."

"Do you have a grand passion with Lady Sabrina?"

Nicholas paused and considered his son's query. Was this a grand passion? Did he find there was no light in the day if she was not present? Did his heart pound and his pulse race when he held her in his arms? Did he fiercely and jealously want to possess not only her comely body but her very soul?

He grinned again and shrugged, more than a little self-conscious.

"I believe it is, my boy. I do believe it is."

Wynne stood toward the bow of the ship, tangled walnut curls billowing behind her. She leaned slightly into the wind, as if eager for its caress. The breeze molding her man's shirt to her shapely breasts, she resembled nothing so much as a sea nymph basking in the sun.

Lovely indeed, but Matt had seen lovelier. Ports around the world were filled with exotic, intoxicating beauties. No, it was not her striking appearance that drew him like a fish on a line. The woman had an air about her, a promise, perhaps, of excitement. There was a sense of anticipation, as if she were ready to burst into life.

Standing now, proud and tall, facing the winds and the sea, she could well have been the model for a ship's figurehead a hundred years or so ago. Matt grinned at the fanciful notion.

"Is staring an American trait, or is rudeness simply part of your personal nature?"

Her voice was calm and collected, carrying more curiosity

than censure. He hadn't realized she'd seen him watching her. Matt's grin widened.

"A little of both, I expect," he said, and strode the few remaining steps to reach her.

Behind glasses that seemed to highlight rather than detract, her eyes were as black as her brother's. Mesmerizing. Enchanting. Perhaps she was the loveliest creature he'd ever encountered after all.

He flicked his gaze along her supple frame in an impertinent manner designed to incite or possibly challenge. He'd long been used to seeing Bree in men's clothing. He'd seen other women in far more revealing costumes, South Seas islanders with little but a bare scarf wrapped around their waists. But clad in forbidden attire, this vision of the flower of English womanhood stirred his senses. The man's shirt and breeches embraced the curves of her body like a long-lost love. Wynne withstood his assessment without so much as a flinch. "Those clothes suit you."

She stretched her arms wide above her head in a gesture that brought to mind the testing of wings by a rare bird just released from its cage. "They do, do they not? Although," her hands dropped to rest on the flat of her stomach, "I had to locate new laces for the breeches. Sabrina seemed somehow to have misplaced them. How very odd."

"One wonders . . ."

Wynne ignored him. "At any rate, I rather like this apparel. It provides such a marvelous sense of—"

"Freedom?"

"That's it exactly. Freedom." Excitement danced across her face. "I find it glorious."

"I expect you'll be hard pressed to give it up when you return to London."

"Oh, I shan't be returning home."

He cocked his head in surprise. "What do you mean, 'I shan't be returning home'?"

She pinned him with a steady stare. "I daresay the king's English is substantially different than that which you Americans speak, but I never suspected the differences would hinder comprehension. Which word did you fail to understand?''

Abruptly uncomfortable at her cutting response, Matt drew his brows together in annoyance. ''I understood what you said. I just don't understand why you said it. And I'd wager your brother won't either.''

''My brother has little to say on the matter,'' she said loftily.

Matt snorted. ''Your brother will have a great deal to say, and I wouldn't want to be in your shoes when he says it.''

''Captain Madison,'' patience underscored her words, ''I have lived my entire life thus far according to the dictates of my position in society. I have been an exemplary daughter, sister and aunt. My only failure has been an inability to procure a husband who would suit. My only true excitement has been limited to the pages of my books. Books, Captain, have been my life.

''It is past time to see for myself all of which I have read. My father, for all his faults, and Nicholas would no doubt be more than willing to expound on those, has provided me with the means to an independent life. There are no conditions on the fortune he left me, no encumbrances, no trustees. I am, therefore, now the master of my own destiny, the captain of my own ship, as it were. I intend to sail it straight into whatever adventure lies ahead.''

Unease churned in his belly. The woman was an innocent, with no knowledge of the ways of the world. She needed to be set straight, and fast. ''So, it's adventure you seek. Be advised, this world—my world—is as different from your pampered, protected society as night is from day, and a far cry from any book. Here, adventure has its price.''

He grabbed her arm roughly. ''Danger is ofttimes the bedfellow of adventure. Have you considered that? The harm that could befall a woman alone? The men who wouldn't hesitate to take advantage of you?''

She returned his heated glare with a composed smile. ''Have *you* taken advantage of many women, Captain?''

''What?'' He jerked his hand back as if scalded. ''What the hell kind of a question is that?''

She shrugged and sighed. "It seems our language barrier continues. I simply wondered if you are an example of the type of man you are warning me against. If you have had a great number of amorous encounters, romantic liaisons, lovers—"

"Enough!" He ran a shaky hand through his hair. "I understand the question. I'm just not accustomed to having it asked by a well-bred lady."

"Very well. Then—"

"Why don't you ask your brother? From all I've heard he's had a considerable career with the fair sex."

Wynne laughed, rich, mellow tones that lingered on the breeze. "Captain, I could never ask my brother this. He would no doubt choke on the words and end up dead at my feet in a fit of apoplexy."

Matt smiled ruefully at the image. He shook his head in surrender. "Why on earth do you want to know?"

Her dark eyes gleamed. "I rather think I should know what to expect."

Could this female possibly shock him further? "What to expect?"

"Certainly. From those men I will encounter on my adventures. Men eager for my fortune and, no doubt, my . . . virtue." She stepped closer, her scent wafting around him, fresh and vaguely floral, her voice low and intoxicating. "Tell me, Captain, what may I expect?"

He stared into her eyes, flecked with gold, simmering and enticing. Eyes that beckoned and drew him into their bottomless depths. Who was this creature? A siren from beneath the waves? A sorceress from the heavens above? Or was she . . . fate?

"Hell and damnation." He groaned and pulled her into his arms. Her breasts were crushed against his chest, her lips greeted his.

He should be gentle, she was so obviously unused to such treatment, but the eagerness of her response shattered his restraint and spurred his desire. Her lips parted beneath his, and he savored the honey-sweet, sea-salt taste of her. His fingers entwined in the silky tresses at the nape of her neck and his hand splayed across the small of her back.

She wrapped her arms around his neck and molded her body to his. Her books had failed to prepare her for the sheer, unadulterated forces sweeping aside all thoughts beyond touch and taste. It was more than she'd hoped for, more than she'd ever dared dream. The heat of his lips seared her to her very soul, and she strained toward him with the pent-up need of a lifetime. He shifted his hips against hers, and instinctively she responded, pressing closer in rhythm with the throbbing tension winding within her.

Shock shot through him at their embrace, made all the more intimate by the feeble protection of the breeches between them. He pulled away, his breath fast and uneven. Her eyes were glazed with desire, her face flushed with passion. Her breasts heaved beneath her shirt and singed his chest where they met.

"You don't know what you're doing, Wynne." His words rasped from his throat. "I suspect you have never been with a man."

She tilted her face toward his. Her sultry voice belied her words. "If you are questioning my virginity, Captain, it is intact."

He pulled a steadying breath. Deflowering virgins, even those past the first stare of youth and willing to boot, was not a job he relished. In spite of the larceny in his soul, he considered himself an honorable man. There was something distinctly dishonorable about bedding Bree's sister-in-law. But, oh, God, she was lovely, and the passion within her tempted so close to the surface. So ready for the right man to—"Wynne, I don't think—"

"Captain," she feathered kisses on the base of his throat and he swallowed convulsively, "I believe we are far past time for thinking."

"Wynne, I—"

"Let's not think, shall we?" She moved to the sensitive spot behind his ear and nibbled delicately.

He shuddered. "I wouldn't want your brother to say I seduced you."

She laughed softly. "Are you at all certain it is you doing the seducing?"

In one last attempt to dissuade her, he gathered his fraying senses, caught her hands with his and pulled her to face him. "Wynne, this is not one of your books," he said harshly. "There is no love here. This is passion and lust and need. Nothing more."

Her gaze locked with his and slowly she raised his hand, still clasping hers, to her lips. Her manner bewitching and provocative, she rubbed his knuckle along her lower lip, her eyes never breaking with his. His blood pounded in his veins and he groaned aloud, his good intentions melting under her touch.

He jerked her back into his arms and bent his mouth to hers. "You realize I will not marry you."

"No, Captain," she said, scarcely a whisper against his lips. "*I* will not marry *you*."

He stared for a moment, released her and stepped back. "I'll be in my cabin tonight."

She smiled serenely, as if nothing had passed between them but an amusing conversation. Only the stormy fervor in her eyes revealed differently. "I shall no doubt see you later then, Captain." She favored him with a polite bob of her head.

Matt nodded briskly, turned on his heel and strode off. He ached with desire and did not welcome the long hours until evening. Her words echoed in his head. He wondered exactly what she meant, why it nagged at him and why he cared.

No, Captain. I will not marry you.

"Nicholas . . . we cannot . . . we must not . . . not here . . ." Sabrina gasped out the words, her protests sinking beneath a haze of arousal.

Nicholas's lips explored the crook of her neck. "This side of the deck is deserted tonight, my love. There is no one to see us here save the moon and stars." He impatiently brushed the sleeve of her shirt over her shoulder, and chills shivered through her at the touch of his mouth.

"Dear Lord, Nicholas, I have missed you." She slipped her hand into the opening of his shirt and ran her fingers through the rough mat of hair over the hard planes of his chest. His muscles tensed beneath her fingers and he moaned softly.

"Sabrina." He drew her closer, and her palms flattened between them. His mouth possessed hers and her lips opened eagerly in response. Urgency consumed her and she thrust her tongue to meet his, hungry and demanding. Her arms snaked around his neck and she pressed her body tight to his, desperate for his heat. He shifted against her, his manhood insistent behind the layers of clothing that shielded one from another, man from woman, husband from wife.

He pulled open her shirt, freeing her breasts to his plundering mouth. He bent to taste, to savor, first one and then the other. She gasped at the exquisite sensations and strained closer. Desire burned within her and she wanted much, much more.

"Nicholas . . . could we . . . here . . . now?"

"Sabrina . . . how . . . could we not?" He fumbled for the laces at her waist. Blessedly, they released, and he slid his hand under her breeches and down her stomach to cup the moist folds at the juncture of her thighs. She moaned and sagged against him, her breathing ragged with desire.

"Hell bells, Billy, the capt'n ain't gonna like that none."

The voices came from nowhere, nearly upon them, quelling their passion like a bucket of sea water. It would not do to be caught like rutting animals.

Nicholas recovered first, struggling to right Sabrina's clothing. She could do little more than lean against him, drained by unfulfilled need.

The sailors barely glanced at them in passing, too involved were they in their discussion over the captain's displeasure at whatever minor disaster had befallen.

Sabrina smiled weakly and pushed her disheveled hair away from her face. "I fear I am no longer the reserved lady you selected for a wife."

He released a long breath of frustration. "Bloody hell,

Sabrina. I want to be alone with you. I need to be alone with you.''

"It does seem the ship has become rather crowded of late.''

"Erick occupies my cabin, barely conscious and weak as a kitten in the bargain. You share quarters with my sister and your daughter. Only that blasted Madison has a cabin for himself alone.''

"He is the captain. . . .'' A captain who Sabrina suspected no longer spent evenings in his cabin alone. Last night she had spied Wynne sneaking out of their room, apparently under the assumption that all were asleep. Sabrina had noted her return barely before dawn. All day Wynne had wandered the ship with a secret smile on her lips and a faraway look in her eye. As for Matt, each time Sabrina approached his manner was gruff and preoccupied; he was not at all his usual self. She was certain something had passed between the two, and equally certain it would spell disaster to even hint at her suspicions to Nicholas.

"You know him well, do you not?'' His unexpected question jerked her from her thoughts.

"What?''

"Madison,'' Nicholas said impatiently "How well do you know him?''

"Matt? Well . . .'' She chose her words with care. "We were friends long ago. Although I have not seen him for many years, I still hold him in high regard. Somewhat like—''

"I know, I know, a blasted brother. We have been through that before.'' His tone softened and his eyes glowed in the starlight. "He calls you Bree.''

"A childhood name. Americans seem quite fond of informal family names.''

"It suits you.'' He paused for a moment. "But you were involved in some kind of business dealings with him, were you not?'' He tossed the query off indifferently, as if the answer did not matter. Unease shivered down her spine. He was seeking something beyond a simple answer to the outwardly innocent question.

"Oh, la, Nicholas." She winced to herself at the insipid phrase. "That was all so very long ago, I scarce remember any of the details. My solicitor handled much of the endeavor for me." The lie tripped easily off her tongue in as convincing a manner as she could manage. How many more would she have to tell?

He seemed satisfied with her response and nodded thoughtfully. "In your ventures with him, did you ever wonder if he might be involved in something illicit? Did he perhaps mention smuggling?"

"Smuggling?" She forced a carefree laugh from a throat at once dry and tight with tension. "Whyever would you ask that?"

He shrugged and pulled her back into his arms. "Bits and pieces of a puzzle I have fought to unravel for the past decade. A failure, I fear, on my own part that I wish to rectify."

"Failure?" She leaned against his chest and tried to slow her rapid breathing to the beat of his heart.

He sighed. "Surely you do not want to hear—"

"Oh, but I do." She had to learn how much he knew, how much he suspected, for Matt's safety and her own. But it was more than the need to safeguard her secret. Since the moment she'd discovered her past connection with Nicholas, curiosity had gnawed at her. What were his remembrances of that fateful night? Did he dream of her through the years as she had of him? Or did he despise her as a criminal, and possibly a traitor?

"Very well." He paused, as if gathering his memories. "It was during the war. A period when I was charged with the apprehension of a daring band of smugglers. I was unable to complete my mission." He fell silent. "They were led by a woman."

"A woman?" Her breath caught in her throat. "How very odd."

He rested his chin lightly on the top of her head. "She was extraordinary. Clever and courageous. Ultimately, I had to admire her."

"You admired her?" she said faintly.

"Once. She was unlike any woman I had ever encountered. Intriguing and unique." His embrace tightened. "She haunted my dreams now and again. Until I met you."

"Me?" Sabrina held her breath.

"You too are unique." He laughed. "I find I have quite enough to handle with one unusual female on my hands. There is no room left, even in my dreams, for another."

Her heart leapt with joy, then plummeted. His words were pretty enough, but he was a man accomplished in plying women with fine phrases. He was well versed in lust but untouched by love and, very likely, the way he would remain. She'd already accepted that fact; she merely had to remember.

Foolish though it was to pursue his suspicions of Matt, Sabrina pressed forward. "What does all this have to do with Matt?"

"I believe he was involved with her."

"I imagine Matt has been involved with countless women through the years," she said, the lightness of her tone belying the tautness of her nerves. "Why do you believe he has something to do with your mysterious lady?"

Nicholas was silent, and Sabrina stifled the impulse to pull out of his arms and search his gaze with hers. As much as she wanted to see the expression on his beloved face, she did not dare reveal even a hint of the fear his comments aroused. She longed to read his thoughts in his eyes, but she could not permit him to read hers.

Nicholas's words were measured and considering. "It came to me while I was recovering from that blow on the head. The name of the ship, this ship—" fear squeezed her heart "—is that of the woman. *Lady B.* It cannot be a mere coincidence."

Her voice was little more than a whisper. "The ship was named for his sister, was it not?"

"Hah. Madison has no sister. I am certain of it."

"None . . . save me." The words escaped unbidden from her lips, and her breath caught.

Nicholas chuckled softly and pulled her closer. "You are his sister only in the depth of his affection. No, I feel certain the ship is named for the woman. And if I have Madison, I shall soon have her.''

Panic crept into the back of her mind and she struggled to keep it at bay. ''And then?''

Nicholas hesitated. ''And then . . . bring her to justice? Clap her in irons? Toss her into Newgate and throw away the key? I do not know. Yet. I only know her apprehension would set to rest an unresolved question in my life. Close the book, if you will, on a chapter whose ending has been left unwritten for a decade. I will redeem myself.'' He laughed harshly. ''If only in my own eyes. If, of course, I can find her.''

Sabrina swallowed back the terror rising in her throat. What would happen to her—to them—if Nicholas ever learned that he already had?

Chapter Fifteen

Egypt was at once more and less than Wynne had expected. The country was far less civilized than she had anticipated, considering that the land's inhabitants had once ruled the known world. For an Englishwoman unused to travel and accustomed to modern conveniences, Egypt presented unforeseen challenges. They were forced to leave the ship in Abukir Bay in sweltering, dusty Alexandria and board a bargelike boat for a nearly five-day journey through the lush Nile delta, upriver to Cairo.

The Nile flowed at a leisurely pace, as if, having seen man's triumphs and failures for eons, it somehow knew the futility of speed and the inevitability of time itself. Life along the banks of the ancient land existed much the same as it had hundreds, even thousands of years ago. The sluggish pace gave Wynne the chance to observe for herself what she'd only read of, a fascinating, if somewhat relaxed, introduction to her new life of adventure. And each engrossing detail was duely noted in her ever expanding journal.

Cairo itself was much more than even her fertile imagination could conjure. The city rose majestically from the flat of the delta like an improbable vision spun of golden light and magic. Minarets climbed heavenward, rising out of an ever-present blanket of smoke surely cast from the city's cooking fires and not an enchanted mist sent from the gods to remind lowly mortals of the fragility of life and the splendor that had been the pharaohs.

The city was the crossroads of half the world. Caravans headed to Kashmir, Damascus, Timbuktu, and their trade was the lifeblood of the bazaars of Cairo, crowded with goods useless or priceless or both. Nicholas whisked their party through the streets so quickly, Wynne barely caught a glimpse of the kaleidoscope of exotic sights and sounds. She was determined to explore this mystical city in depth before she left.

They were to lodge in the European quarter. It was not substantially nicer than many neighborhoods they had traveled through, although perhaps better kept. It had the additional attraction of huge wooden doors that closed off the homes in times of plague or riot. But the expected accommodations were not available, and the company proceeded to Bulak, Cairo's main port. Here, the wealthy built grand summer palaces complete with oasis gardens offering cool, green sanctuaries from the sun and the stifling heat.

Nicholas had managed to procure a villa for their short stay. They had slept there last night and would begin the trek down the Nile as soon as he and Erick returned from acquiring the permits necessary in this country to so much as turn a spade in the sand, regardless of whether one searched for modern gold or half-forgotten antiquities. In deference to the boy's affliction, it was decided to forgo further water travel and instead follow alongside the path of the river on solid ground. Sabrina and her daughter now busied themselves in their quarters. Wynne stood alone in the garden, enjoying the tropical plantings and the soothing shade.

Matt had told her of Sabrina's quest, delighting Wynne that her first real adventure would indeed live up to her dreams. Matt too fulfilled her fantasies. The American was the bold, brash embodiment of every hero she'd ever encountered in print. Daring and more than a little dangerous, her captain stoked fires of unforeseen fervor and unexplored emotion. Their days were filled with secret, urgent glances, their nights charged with forbidden passion and the glories of touch and taste and soul-searing sensation.

Surely she was in love. Nothing else could explain the leaping of her heart or the unsettled tremors of her body whenever he so much as glanced her way. Still, it would not do to reveal her feelings to him. She'd read enough through the years to know that the way to lose such a hero was to declare herself. Wynne did not dare hope their time together would be lengthy. He had already told her he would not accompany them into the desert. Her practical nature decreed that she accept what they shared for the moment and not anticipate the future. She suspected their parting would be painful, but even agony was a small price to pay for this soaring emotion she had no doubt was love.

His scent, of man and heat and desire, embraced her a scant second before his arms. She relaxed against him with a contented sigh.

He murmured in her ear, "We don't have to go with them, you know. We could stay here in Cairo. Just the two of us. It's an exciting place, Wynne. A place just right for your adventures."

She laughed and twisted to face him. His azure eyes sparkled in the sun, and her stomach fluttered at the need emblazoned there. "But, Captain, even for a city as magnificent as this, I could not sacrifice such a venture. A search for lost treasure among the pyramids of Egypt? It is an opportunity that shall likely never come again."

"Couldn't you give it up," he paused, and his gaze searched hers, "for me?"

Her heart leapt to her throat, and she willed herself to remain calm. "I daresay you cannot wish to shepherd a spinster, a woman no longer in her youth, for very long." The light words belied the yearning within her. "You would surely tire of the connection and then we should part. And I would have missed the exceedingly grand adventure we are about to embark upon."

"Wynne, I—"

"Wynne? Matt?" Sabrina's call shattered the fragile moment, and they broke apart like children caught at mischief. No doubt Sabrina suspected what had passed between them. Wynne had caught her sister-in-law studying her with a considering expression in recent days. Sabrina had apparently not mentioned her observations to Nicholas. Her brother would no doubt not take their affections kindly and would very likely call Matt out. Wynne did not know who would win such an encounter and had no desire to put it to the test.

"There you are." Sabrina rounded a curve in the path and approached. "Wynne, could you help Belinda? She is attempting to pack her bag and failing miserably. I cannot comprehend why she insisted on bringing the vast amount of clothing that she has. If we could convince her to abandon her gowns for the more practical guise of men's apparel as you and I have, life would be much simpler for us all."

"I'll see what assistance I can lend." Wynne cast a last lingering look at Matt and hurried off.

Matt stared after her, his manner moody and intense. Sabrina narrowed her eyes. "I have scarce had a moment alone with you in the past week. We must talk, Matt."

Matt's gaze still focused on his last sight of Wynne. "Talk away, Bree. You have my undivided attention."

"Hardly."

His gaze flicked to hers and he sighed. "What is it?"

"It's Nicholas." Sabrina drew a deep breath. "He knows, Matt."

Matt's eyes hardened, and he shrugged. "I'm not surprised. He was bound to find out sooner or later. I am somewhat amazed I haven't heard any explosions. And so far he hasn't threatened to kill me or worse." His tone softened. "I would hate to do that to her."

Confusion underlaid her words. "To her? To whom? What are you talking about?"

Matt frowned and glared. "What are *you* talking about?"

"I am talking about you and me and the past. I am talking about our previous involvement." Sarcasm mingled with irritation and permeated her tone. "Perhaps you have forgotten our little business dealings? The cliffs? The sea? The midnight meetings? The unquestionable illegality of it all? Bloody hell, Matt, the smuggling. He knows about the smuggling. He does not yet know of my connection, but he knows about you.''

Relief colored Matt's face. ''So he knows. At this late date I doubt if there's much he can do about it. We're not on English soil and I'm not English.''

Was Matt always this obtuse? Why could she not make him understand? She pulled a steadying breath and tried again. ''Perhaps I have not explained this clearly. He knows about you because of the name of the ship.'' She fired an angry glare at him. ''The ship you oh-so-kindly named for me.''

''You've never thanked me for that.'' He grinned insolently.

''And I never will. It has proven to be the root of all his suspicions.''

''I still don't understand—''

''Matt, Nicholas was the agent. The government agent who nearly uncovered my operation.'' She groaned. ''The man I had bashed over the head, twice, and left on the beach.'' Her voice rose. ''The man I kissed in the cave.''

The corners of his eyes crinkled. ''You never told me you kissed him.''

''Well, I did. It was an impulse, regrettable and foolish.'' Sabrina folded her arms over her chest. Odd that Nicholas had not mentioned the kiss in recounting his tale. Why would he omit that one detail? She wrinkled her nose. ''He no doubt thinks Lady B is not merely a criminal but a slut as well. He has spent the last ten years dwelling on his perceived failure to capture me.''

Amazement stamped Matt's face. ''And this is the man you married?''

She nodded miserably.

''Bree, I—'' He laughed, and she stared in disbelief. His laughter swelled and he doubled over, clutching his sides. Her irritation grew in proportion to his mirth. ''You married the one man in all of England, possibly in the entire world,

who would like nothing better than to throw you in prison?"
He wiped a gleeful tear from his eye. "Oh, that's rich, Bree;
that's really rich."

Anger at his cavalier attitude surged through her. "I am
not the only one keeping secrets from Nicholas. How do
you think he'd react to the knowledge of your seducing his
sister?"

Matt stilled. "I love her, Bree."

Sabrina scoffed. "I scarcely believe that, Matt. You are
not the kind of man to fall head over heels for any woman.
Wynne is lovely, but her intelligence outshines her pretty
face. I cannot believe such a woman would suit you."

A poignant smile touched his lips. "It does sound rather
far-fetched, but it's true. She's smart and beautiful and altogether remarkable, and I can't see my life without her in
it." He sighed. "The problem is, I don't think she can see
her life with me in it."

Sabrina pulled her brows together. "I can certainly understand that. Still, most woman so firmly on the shelf would
be delighted by an offer from anyone, even you."

He shook his head. "I haven't asked her, but she's already made it clear she's not interested in marriage. She has
some foolish notions about traveling the world in search of
adventure. I'm afraid I'm not in her plans."

"But you wish to be?" Sabrina said softly.

His gaze met hers. His eyes echoed the blue of the sea,
and Sabrina noted a haunted edge in their depths. "More
than anything, Bree." He laughed again, and this time the
sound rang bitter and harsh. "It's ironic, isn't it? Here in
Cairo, where everything, every product, every experience
and a fair number of human beings as well has its price,
I've recognized the one thing I want most in the world. And
it's not for purchase at any cost."

He pulled his gaze from hers and stared off in the distance. "That's why I've decided not to go with you, Bree.
Gold or no gold, I don't think I could stand watching her
on her first adventure and knowing it's all we'll ever have."

"I've never known you to be a coward, Matt."

"It just seems best, that's all," he said, resignation and

pain in his voice. Matt fell silent, and Sabrina was at a loss for words. He appeared so forlorn, she no longer doubted his sincerity. He shook his head as if to clear his thoughts and turned to her. "Does Nicholas love you, Bree?"

She smiled wistfully. "I wish I knew. Sometimes, when I am in his arms, I think surely he must. But he is so accomplished with women, so experienced, he always knows what to say and precisely how to say it. I cannot trust any words of love he speaks. They fall far too freely from his lips."

"So you don't know what he'd do if he discovered the notorious Lady B and his new wife are one in the same?"

"The very thought terrifies me. I would prefer to live the rest of my life with this secret rather than confront his condemnation." She paused and gathered her thoughts. "I would rather dwell in a fool's world, hoping against hope that love for me would overcome his sense of duty and honor, than know for certain it would not."

"It was a long time ago, Bree," Matt said gently. "Don't you think he's put all this behind him?"

She shook her head sadly. "We spoke of it on board ship. He has not forgotten." Her voice dropped to a whisper. "Or forgiven."

"I'll keep your secret, Bree."

"I know you will, Matt." She smiled through eyes blurred with unbidden tears. "You always have."

It was surely a land forged in hell, that hot, parched, bloody uncomfortable country. Dark-robed heathens swelled the streets of Cairo in an endless stream of what passed for humanity in that God-forsaken land.

Still, there was something to be said for the uncivilized world. A few meager coins bought loyalty and information. He had hirelings watching for Sabrina's party since he first arrived in the city. Now he not only knew of their preparations, he had learned their general direction of travel.

His idiotic companions wanted to confront Wyldewood and Sabrina while they were all still in Cairo. But he argued that it would be far more advantageous to greet her away

213

from the distractions and interruptions of the city. The others agreed to bide their time and trail behind her party, waiting until the right moment for their encounter.

They had come up with a far-fetched scheme to marry her and thereby save her reputation. At first it seemed ludicrous, but after due consideration he realized it fit in nicely with his own plans. If he were to wed Lady Stanford, all she possessed, including the gold, would, of course, be his. And bedding the fair lady would be a delightful bonus. The thought tempted him to laugh aloud with lecherous anticipation.

It appeared even hell had its pleasures.

"I shall not set so much as a foot upon that filthy beast." Belinda glared with disgust at the kneeling camel, which returned her stare with an equally malevolent gaze.

"I daresay it's not your foot that should concern you most." Erick's mild observation earned him the withering look previously reserved for the creature in question.

"Mother!" Belinda's voice rose. "I cannot ride a camel. I simply cannot."

"You can and you shall," Sabrina said in her best no-nonsense voice.

Belinda crinkled her nose in a gesture startlingly similar to Sabrina's own habit. "He's disgusting. Why can't I ride a horse, Mother? Why must I risk life and limb on this brute?"

"Do you see any horses?" Sabrina's patience grew thin. Belinda shook her head. "Very well then. Get your blasted bottom on that animal, now."

Belinda stamped her foot and crossed her arms over her chest. "I don't see why I should. I have absolutely no desire to go traipsing about the desert, chasing after some stupid artifacts."

"Artifacts?" Sabrina said, puzzled.

Belinda nodded. "That's what Erick said this is all about."

"Erick." Sabrina turned to the young man, who appeared as if his fondest desire was to be anywhere except between

214

mother and daughter. "What is this about artifacts?"

Erick shrugged. "That's what Father told the pasha's clerk when he got the permit for us to dig. He told them we were all here on holiday and the ladies had taken it into their heads that they wanted to search for antiquities. He said that in an effort to humor them, or rather you, he was more than willing to go to the trouble of procuring the permit."

"It seemed like a good story at the moment." Nicholas and Wynne joined the group gathered under the baleful gaze of the camel. "Given the vast numbers of Europeans in Egypt right now, it wasn't even questioned."

Belinda sighed. "Really, Mother, I don't know what possessed you to leave home and travel—"

Sabrina grabbed her daughter's arm and pulled her away from the others. "We're not here for artifacts."

"We're not?"

"No." Sabrina's voice was scarcely more than a whisper. "We're looking for gold. The French left it here twenty years ago."

"Gold?" Belinda's blue eyes widened in surprise. "Is it a great deal of gold?"

Sabrina fairly hissed the answer. "Yes."

"Oh, my." Belinda paused for a moment, then squared her shoulders and met her mother's gaze. "Very well, then. Shouldn't we be off?" She pivoted on her fashionably booted heel, gestured to an attendant and allowed herself to be boosted onto the odd arrangement of blankets and leather that comprised what passed for a saddle. The beast's handler urged the animal to a standing position, and Belinda tottered far above them. She paled visibly but managed a weak smile. A surge of parental pride filled Sabrina. Perhaps the child had inherited something from her after all.

"Sabrina." Nicholas steered her away from the forming caravan. "We do not have to go through with this. You have no need of this gold. You are my wife now, and I have all the wealth you shall ever require."

She set her mouth in a stubborn line. "You said you'd come with me."

"Bloody hell, Sabrina, of course I'll come with you."
His dark eyes stormed. "But the closer we get to this fiasco,
the more ridiculous it becomes." She tossed him an accusing gaze, and he rolled his eyes toward the heavens. "Very
well, I give up. I knew it was too much to hope that you
had finally come to your senses."

He grabbed her arms, yanked her to him and glared down
at her. "Why do you want it, Sabrina? Why is this so important to you?"

She raised her chin defiantly. He would never be able to
understand her need for financial independence, even from
him. "It's the quest—nothing more. I started this and I shall
see it through to the end." She returned his gaze without
hesitation. In his eyes she read speculation and conjecture
and knew instinctively that he did not fully believe her.
"Now then, where are the horses?"

His eyes narrowed. "I'll ask you the same thing you
asked Belinda: Do you see any horses?"

"Well, no, not here. But I assumed—"

"I could not get any." He released her and ran a weary
hand through his hair.

"What do you mean, you could not get any? This is an
enormous city. I've seen horses all over. You can't tell me
you couldn't find a few pathetic horses."

"Blast it, Sabrina, I have spent a long, interminable morning dealing with this God-forsaken country's convoluted bu-
reaucracy that makes even the worst ministry in the British
government appear efficient. I then turned my attention to
procuring what is needed for this venture of yours as quickly
as humanly possible because of your insane need to proceed
at once." He clenched his teeth and his eyes flashed fire. "I
have found camels. I have hired attendants and handlers. I
have, in short, done everything you have requested and
more. Right now I am hot, I am irritated and I am bloody
tired."

"But horses, Nicholas," she said meekly. "I really do
believe we need horses."

"Why?"

"Why?" A dozen reasons, none even remotely plausible,

flashed through her mind. "Well, someone—I suggest you and I—needs to be able to forge ahead of the rest. To survey the surroundings, so to speak."

Nicholas glowered. "There will be no surveying and definitely no forging."

"Very well, then . . ." She paused, waiting for inspiration. Surely there was something to persuade him. She tossed him a sly smile. "Nicholas, you have seen the directions in the letter."

"Yes?" His tone was wary.

"It indicates that the gold is buried near the Temple of Isis on a spit of land thrusting into the river. If the river is high, it could be cut off. To get there we shall surely have to ford the river." She gazed up at him with all the sweetness she could muster. "For that we shall need horses. Will we not?"

Nicholas looked like a man at the end of his rope. A rope she suspected he would most probably wish to hang her with.

"Sabrina," he said in a voice obviously barely under control, "your logic makes no sense whatsoever. I seriously doubt there is even the remotest possibility of problems with high water. However, we shall face that obstacle when, and if, we get to it. All I could find willing to take on this trek on short notice were camels." He nodded at the motley-looking collection behind him. "They're damnably expensive too."

"Nicholas," she clutched his arm, "I cannot ride a camel."

Nicholas sighed. "Surely if Belinda—"

"Look at them." Sabrina nodded toward the beasts. "I cannot get on one. It's impossible."

"Sabrina," he said impatiently, "in the name of all that's holy—"

She blurted out the words. "They're just so tall. So bloody high."

Surprise widened Nicholas's eyes. "Are you trying to tell me you're scared of heights? Is that what your reluctance is all about?"

"Yes." She glared, annoyed that he had forced this admission of weakness. "I have a dreadful fear of high places. I simply cannot abide them."

Nicholas visibly relaxed. He smiled and pulled her into his arms. "We could ride together. Share one of the beasts. I would have no problem keeping you securely upon the animal and in my arms." His eyes gleamed suggestively, and she laughed in spite of herself.

"I have the horses." Matt's voice wedged between them, and reluctantly, Sabrina stepped out of Nicholas's embrace.

Matt nodded toward the caravan. Four sleek Arabians stood near the camels, the contrast between the noble beasts and the beasts of burden almost comical.

"Matt, how wonderful." Sabrina's voice rang with delight.

Nicholas glared. "How did you accomplish this, Madison?"

Matt shrugged. "It wasn't hard. You just have to know where to look and who to talk to. And, as you can see, I managed to find fairly good-looking horseflesh."

Nicholas snorted. "Stolen, no doubt."

Matt's eyes narrowed. "Are you calling me a thief, Wyldewood?"

A calculating smile touched Nicholas's lips. "A thief, a rogue, a smuggler. Which suits best, Madison?"

The charge hung in the air like a venomous fog. Panic filled her, and her gaze leapt from one to the other. Surely, Nicholas would not reveal his suspicions now? Surely Matt would not rise to the bait and divulge her secret? After her talk with Matt she had decided to tell Nicholas everything. But not now. At some point in the future, perhaps, when they were old and gray and in their dotage. Possibly when she or he lay on their deathbed. Then she would tell him. Not now.

"Enough." She pushed her way between the scowling duo. "I do not believe we have time for this nonsense. Nicholas," she turned to her husband, "how long do we have before the annual flooding of the Nile?"

"Approximately a month, perhaps longer." His dark,

dangerous gaze still locked with Matt's.

"And it shall take how long to reach the island?" she asked, urging him on.

Nicholas cast a last disgusted glance at Matt and turned to her. "Ten days, two weeks; it's impossible to say for certain."

"Then I suggest we get moving." Matt grinned. "Watch out for the camels, Wyldewood—they spit." He turned to leave and threw Sabrina a wink only she could see. She released a pent-up breath; he would not betray her.

Matt took two strides and Nicholas called after him. "Madison, I did not think you were planning to accompany us. To what do we owe the pleasure of your change of heart?"

Matt stopped and swiveled slowly to face them. A hand gripped Sabrina's stomach at the impudent smile on his lips. "Well, Wyldewood, this trek has been described to me as a grand adventure. I hate to pass on a good adventure. Beyond that," his gaze flicked to Sabrina and back again, "you never know what you're going to find when you go digging about in deserts or . . . other things. I'd wager gold isn't the only secret buried out here."

Sabrina slipped from her tent and cast a casual glance around the compound. Four days out of Cairo and the company had already fallen into a routine, a ritual that changed only in the site chosen and never in the arrangement of animals and people. With a startling efficiency and impressive speed, the attendants threw up the flowing tents that served as overnight shelter. Their competence served as a mild distraction against what proved to be a monotonous excursion.

The trek southward along the Nile moved with the slow, steady beat of a metronome. All concerned grew more and more irritated by the tedious pace, the unrelenting heat and the tiresome, unchanging landscape. Only Wynne among their company apeared to actually enjoy the never-ending journey.

Sabrina did her best to keep Nicholas and Matt as far

apart as possible, although it wasn't easy, given their small numbers. But Matt seemed to cooperate with her attempts; at least he did not go out of his way to incite her husband. She marveled that Nicholas still did not appear to notice Wynne's affection for the American. It was obvious to anyone who cared to look.

Sabrina glanced toward the fire, now burned low and scarcely more than a glow in the night, barely illuminating the tent closest to it. These colorful structures, while airy and passably comfortable, also triggered a fair amount of irritation. Once again the women were quartered together. Nicholas, Erick and Matt shared a tent, although on any given night one or more of them typically rolled up in a blanket and slept under the stars.

The camp had settled for the evening and Sabrina smiled to herself. Nicholas stood on the opposite side of the clearing, a black shadow in the moonlight, tall and dark and compelling. He held out his hand and without words she joined him. Silently, they walked a short distance to a meager outcropping of palms, small but enough to shield them from any prying eyes that had not yet succumbed to sleep. They gazed at each other for but a moment before Sabrina threw herself into his waiting arms.

Locked in his embrace, she lost herself in the still novel sensations fanned to life by his demanding lips. His mouth slanted over hers again and again, as if to make up in intensity what they lacked in time. She twined her fingers in the silken hair at the nape of his neck and greeted him as eagerly as he hungered for her.

His lips traveled the curve of her neck, and she shuddered with need and growing frustration. They could not give into their desire here . . . now. "Nicholas." She gasped. "We must stop."

He groaned and pulled away. "That seems to be the only thing you say to me of late. This marriage of convenience grows more and more inconvenient with every passing moment."

"Tell me again why we do not have a tent of our own."

He released a deep breath. "We do not have a tent of our

own, my love, because you were in such a blasted hurry to begin this journey. Therefore, I had to take what I could get."

"It is an excellent excuse, Nicholas." She sighed and leaned against him. "But it does nothing to subdue this altogether awkward desire you have awakened within me."

He laughed and gazed into her face. She effected a teasing pout and hoped he could see it in the moonlight. "It seems, my dear wife, that we suit after all. I suspected it when we first met, but you have dispelled any lingering doubts. I look forward to a long and happy marriage of convenience."

Her heart stilled. "Do you?" she asked under her breath. The teasing tone left her voice, the moment between them abruptly serious, heavy with a significance she had not intended. Or perhaps she had.

What did he mean? He already had her willingly in his bed, during those rare moments when they had a bed. What more could he want from her? She didn't dare hope his words indicated that he had at last succumbed to the lure of love. Another unrepentant, unreformed rake long ago had loved her. But surely such miracles did not happen twice in the same lifetime.

The swollen desert moon reflected in his eyes and outlined each chiseled feature of his face. He drew her hands to his lips and kissed them with a touch so light, yet so full of promise, that her knees ached from the effort to stand upright.

"Sabrina." His voice was as gentle as his touch and just as weighted. "I feel we—"

A startled shout ripped the desert air.

"What the—" Sabrina whirled toward the camp.

"Bloody hell!" Nicholas grabbed her arm and ran toward the tents. "Come on!"

"What is it, Nicholas? What's happened?" Sabrina struggled to keep up with his long strides. He pulled her behind him, half dragging her in his wake, and she fought to keep her footing.

The camp was in utter chaos. Everywhere, bodies and beasts gyrated in an odd, confusing dance. Firelight and moonlight reflected and shadowed and revealed and hid. It seemed it all moved too fast for her to comprehend, or perhaps she moved too slow.

"Damnation, they're stealing the horses!" Matt's outraged yell cut through her bewilderment and the baffled fog that had enveloped her.

"Nicholas," she clutched his arm, "they're stealing the horses!"

"I can see that!" His voice thundered above the din. "I suppose you want me to go after them?"

Sabrina's eyes widened in surprise. "Of course, Nicholas. Go! Now! Before they get away!" She shoved him in the direction of greatest pandemonium.

"Come on, Wyldewood." Matt sprinted toward them, Erick a step behind. Both men held reins for camels who looked none too eager for this latest venture. "We're going after my horses."

"Your horses?" Nicholas said.

"Yes, they're my horses. Every damned one of them. Bought and paid for. They cost a small fortune too!" Even in the scant light Matt's glare was unmistakable. He tossed her a quick glance. "Not that it mattered, mind you."

"Of course not," she murmured.

"Nicholas! Captain!" Wynne dashed forward, her glasses precariously askew on her nose. "What on earth is going on?" She swiveled her head from side to side to take in all the commotion around her. "Is this some kind of raid?" Her voice rose with excitement. "Bedouins, do you think?"

"No, Wynne, I do not think it's Bedouins." Nicholas's voice was as sharp as possible, given his current attempt to hoist himself upon the camel. "If it were tribesmen, we should very likely be dead by now."

Matt already balanced astride his beast. "I doubt they'd kill us, Wyldewood, at least not right away."

"Oh, that is good news," Wynne said with barely suppressed enthusiasm.

Matt ignored her, obviously chaffing to get underway. Nicholas wheeled his camel about in a surprisingly graceful gesture. "Let's get this farce over with."

"But if it's not Bedouins, then who?" Wynne called after them.

Matt released an impatient breath. "Tomb robbers, my love. It's practically the national profession. No doubt someone's heard about our expedition to recover so-called artifacts, thanks to his royal lordship's little fable, and wants us stopped." In the golden glow of the moon, his lopsided grin was evident. "Sorry it couldn't be Bedouins for your first adventure. Tomb robbers will just have to do." He tossed Wynne a jaunty salute and took off after Nicholas and Erick.

If it wasn't for the gravity of the situation, the scene would have been positively funny. The three men mounted on camels, giving chase to a virtual fleet of handlers and attendants who'd taken off after the stolen horses on foot, black silhouettes against the desert moon. Silence descended upon the camp and they were utterly alone.

"Tomb robbers." Sabrina groaned.

"Tomb robbers," Wynne said, excitement rising in her voice. "This *is* a grand adventure."

Sabrina stared. "My dear, you have an interesting definition of adventure."

"Well, I simply believe that if—"

A scream pierced the now peaceful night.

"Good Lord! Belinda!" Terror surged through her, and Sabrina bolted for her daughter's tent. Wynne followed close at her heels. Her heart pounded in a frenzied rhythm. Fear for Belinda's safety pushed her legs faster and faster, and she seemed to fly above the earth. Something caught at her and she crashed to the ground.

"Wynne, watch out!" Obviously, Wynne had overrun her in their anxious sprint. She rolled to her feet only to be dashed to the ground once more. Sabrina glanced upward to see a rough blanket descend over her head, bundling her in its folds, heavy and suffocating, smelling foully of man and beast. Panic for herself and her child fueled her resistance and she flailed wildly, to no avail. Her arms were pressed flat against her sides, as if a rope was wrapped around the outside of the crude material that imprisoned her.

"Let me go!" Her cries seemed smothered even to her

own ears. Dimly she realized that no doubt the same nefarious devils who had stolen the horses were now abducting her as well. Muffled cries in the distance indicated the same fate had befallen Wynne and Belinda.

Her feet left the ground and she kicked out helplessly. With a soft thud that knocked her breath away, she landed on her stomach across what could only be a horse. Like some felled animal, trussed and ready for a spit, she sprawled crosswise on the beast, feet and head dangling on either side, uncomfortable and terrified. In a moment a solid form wedged itself next to her. She suspected this was her kidnapper and angrily shoved against him. A coarse laugh sounded above her and a sharp slap smacked her buttocks. Even the horse uttered a grunt of protest, and they were off at a gallop. Within moments, Sabrina was too sore and tired to continue any attempt at resistance and gritted her teeth, determined to bear this as best she could.

Fears she'd had no time to consider before now filled her head. What did these marauders want? What had they done with her daughter? With Wynne? What were their plans for them? For her? Would they kill her? Or would death be preferable to whatever fate they intended?

Tears of frustration welled in her eyes. She'd handled herself well back in her smuggling days. She knew how to wield a knife and command the loyalty of men. But never had she faced danger of this sort, unknown and deadly.

The horse pounded on endlessly, and she slipped into a dazed stupor of ache and exhaustion and fear. Nicholas's image shimmered in her mind. Would she ever have the chance to tell him everything? What was he trying to tell her before the raid so abruptly pulled them apart? Did he, as she hoped, love her after all?

Perhaps . . . blackness beckoned and she accepted it with relief . . . it no longer mattered.

Chapter Sixteen

A sharp jolt jarred Sabrina fully to her senses. She lay curled on her side, still wrapped in the coarse, pungent blanket, the ground beneath her strangely yielding, like bread dough not yet risen. Fear kept her motionless and silent. She strained for any noise, any sense of movement, any indication of where she was.

A soft thud and a grunt sounded to her left. A second thunk and a pathetic cry echoed in the air. Cautiously, she stretched aching limbs. The wrap about her was loose. She ripped it off, hurled it away and scrambled to her feet.

Only the stars far above illuminated her prison, some sort of very large hole or trench or pit. A musty scent, dry and unfamiliar, settled around her. A dark shadow lay near by. She stumbled toward it and reached out a tentative hand.

Immediately the shape lunged. "Do not dare touch me, you fiend!" Wynne's muffled voice came from beneath the rough covering.

"Wynne, it's me. Keep still; let me get this off." Sabrina struggled with the tangled cover and the loose ropes holding it in place.

"Where are we?"

"We're in the middle of your bloody adventure," Sabrina said impatiently. "Now, where's Belinda?"

"Mother?" A weak voice called from the dark.

"Belinda?" Sabrina groped toward her daughter and nearly tripped over the huddled form. Belinda too was wrapped in the abrasive, coarse material. Sabrina pulled off the offensive cloth, helped her daughter to her feet and gathered her in her arms.

Belinda sobbed. "Mother, where are we? What has happened?"

"I don't know, sweetheart, but I suspect we're safe." Her eyes strained to adjust in the blackness. "At least for now."

Feet shuffling in the sand and a murmur of deep voices drew her attention upward. Several figures leaned over the pit, dark silhouettes against the starry night. Anger surged through her, dissipating her fear. "Who are you? What do you want with us?"

"We will not harm you, English lady." The coarse voice taunted her, heavily accented but understandable. "You will stay here for a time. Yes?"

"No!"

She could hear the shrug in his voice. "Very well then, leave. Go. Shoo, shoo." His companions echoed his rough laughter.

"What do you want?" she asked again, attempting to quell her growing irritation. "Why have you abducted us?"

There was a pause, as if her captor debated the wisdom of honesty. "We do not permit all those who wish to steal what was left to us by the ancient ones to do so."

"Of course not." Relief flooded her. If she could just get him to understand that they were not here for artifacts left behind by early Egyptians, but for something left far more recently by the French, without revealing that something was gold, then perhaps . . . "I can see where you'd be quite offended at your heritage being stolen. I can assure you—"

His laughter ripped the air above her. "We care nothing for the stones and statues that have littered our land for as long as anyone can remember. But you do. Europeans pay dearly for that which once belonged to our ancestors. For their gods and their temples and their mortal remains."

"Remains?" Belinda asked faintly.

He either didn't hear or simply ignored her and continued without hesitation. "It is extremely profitable to recover and sell the old things. My village has an arrangement with Monsieur Drovetti—"

"Who?" Wynne asked.

Again he ignored the interruption. "We sell only to him and we do not tolerate the intrusion of others on our lands."

"Very well," Sabrina snapped. "You have my word, we shall not search for your damnable artifacts. Now, will you please release us?"

He laughed once more, the caustic sound gnawing on her raw nerves. "Release you? That would be foolish, indeed, English lady. We will trade you back to your kinsmen and turn a tidy profit. And if they do not pay . . ." She sensed his wicked grin. "We will simply sell you to someone else."

A gasp broke from Belinda's lips, and for once mother could agree with daughter. This was not going at all well. The silhouettes disappeared from the rim of the pit. The stars glowed dimmer now. Only a few hours remained until dawn. Sabrina could better make out the figures of Wynne and Belinda. What would happen to them all in the light of day?

"We have to get out of here." Sabrina pushed her hair away from her face and paced. The ground gave with every step, her feet sinking slightly with each footfall. Odd. Already a fine dust covered her. "Whatever is beneath us?" She stamped on the ground, and a choking cloud enveloped them.

"Mother!" Belinda coughed and waved her arms frantically, trying in vain to dissipate the musty, insidious powder. Wynne sputtered and Sabrina spat in an effort to rid herself of the nasty taste that permeated her nose and mouth.

"Sabrina?" Wynne said cautiously. "How much do you know of the customs of ancient Egypt?"

"What everyone knows, I suppose." Surely this was not the time for a history lesson? She gritted her teeth and resolved to be patient with her sister-in-law. The poor creature was probably just as frightened as Belinda. "I know about the pyramids, of course. I know about mummies; something to do with a belief in life after death."

"Very good." Wynne hesitated. "Does anything else come to mind?"

Sabrina sighed in frustration. "What are you getting at, Wynne?"

"Well . . ."

Sabrina's tolerance grew thin with Wynne's obvious reluctance to continue. What was wrong with her? Normally, you could scarce shut the woman up. "Blast it, Wynne, get on with it! What are you trying to say?"

Wynne drew a deep breath. "If you were a great king—not an ordinary monarch, mind you, but a ruler of great wealth and influence—you had a magnificent tomb built. The pyramids are the most well-known example, but there are, of course, countless other royal tombs."

"Go on," Sabrina said. Did Wynne's ramblings have any sort of purpose?

"Entry to the next world was not limited to royalty, however. Every ancient Egyptian believed in a life beyond death." Wynne grew more animated with every word.

Intrigued in spite of herself, Sabrina nodded encouragement.

"But obviously not all could afford a grand or even lowly tomb. Sometimes mummies were buried in shallow graves in the desert, sometimes they were placed in caves and sometimes . . ." Wynne's recitation faded.

Dread churned in Sabrina's stomach. "And sometimes . . . where?"

"Huge, mass graves. Catacombs, if you will. Mummies stacked in rows like firewood." Wynne's voice faltered. She stared at Sabrina for a long, helpless moment; then she blurted the words. "Pits, Sabrina; mummy pits. I fear that very well may be where we are. A mummy pit."

Bile rose in the back of Sabrina's throat and she struggled against it.

"A mummy pit?" Belinda's voice trembled an octave

above normal. "We are in a giant grave? A tomb? With the dead?" She swayed, and Wynne leapt forward to steady her.

"Belinda, you shall not faint," Sabrina said sharply. "I will not permit it."

"But, Mother! Dead bodies?"

"Oh, it's not as if they're at all like real bodies; they've been dead so terribly long, you know," Wynne said in a less than successful effort to allay Belinda's fears. "After all this time there is scarce more left of them than dust."

"Dust?" Belinda held out her grime-covered hands before her. "Dust?" Her voice quavered and her knees buckled. She sank slowly downward in spite of Wynne's support.

"Belinda," Sabrina clutched her daughter's shoulders and shook her firmly, "we have no time for such nonsense."

Belinda's wide, frightened eyes stared into her mother's and she swallowed visibly. "But, Mother, I can not—"

"Of course you can," Sabrina said, a brisk tone coloring her words, as if this was nothing more than a discussion over the acceptance of an invitation to one soiree versus another. "You, my darling, are made of far sterner stuff than you have ever imagined. Your father was nothing if not daring and I suspect he would have been courageous had the need ever arisen. And I, too, have weathered storms with a fair amount of success. Therefore, by the simple matter of parentage, you should be well able to deal with something as paltry as long dead and nearly forgotten ancient Egyptians."

Belinda did not appear at all convinced. "I do not think . . ."

"Belinda, listen to her," Wynne said helpfully. "We are at a far greater risk from those living, breathing desert dwellers who threw us in here than we could ever be—"

"Wynne," Sabrina said harshly.

"Mother!" Belinda threatened to collapse once again.

Sabrina drew a deep breath. "Belinda, my love, let me make one further point. Should you swoon, neither Wynne nor I could keep you supported upright. Therefore, you should sink like a stone onto the ground here." She paused and considered her next words. They were far stronger than she would have liked, but perhaps shock was the best way to get through to her pampered child. Shock, or a firm slap across her lovely face, and Sabrina did not wish to resort to that . . . yet. Her voice rang stern. "And you know what lies beneath this earth."

If the light had been better, Sabrina was certain she would have seen her daughter's face pale. For a few long moments Belinda said nothing. Even Wynne fell silent. Finally, Belinda drew a long, shuddering breath. "Very well, Mother; now what shall we do?" Her voice shook but was at least minimally under control. Sabrina nodded approvingly. Blood would tell after all.

"Yes, indeed, Sabrina," Wynne said. "What shall we do now?"

"Now we have to get out of this blasted pit." Sabrina cast a speculative glance around their prison. "Wynne, if they no longer mummify their dead, what exactly do modern Egyptians do with a mummy pit?"

"No doubt they are exhuming their ancestors. They fetch an extremely good price. Mummies are quite popular in Europe as decorative items and, of course, many people swear by their restorative powers. Medicinal purposes, you know."

"People eat them?" Belinda choked out the words.

Wynne nodded casually. "Oh, my, yes. Ground up, of course. It's been used in certain circles for several hundred years."

"Enough, Wynne. I did not wish for a dissertation on the economic benefits of selling one's forefathers or the healthful properties of consuming them." Wynne's expression fell, and Sabrina immediately chided herself for her abrupt comment. "I am sorry. Your knowledge of all this would be fascinating under other circumstances. However, at this moment all I wish to do is determine some means of escape."

"Forgive me, Sabrina. I fear I tend to get carried away. I am certain to adjust eventually. After all," Wynne grinned, "this is only my first adventure."

Sabrina laughed in spite of herself. "Well, I have had a

fair amount of adventures myself and I'm not sure if one ever adjusts completely." She sighed and shook her head. "However, I have yet to find myself in as difficult a spot as this."

She glanced around thoughtfully. Approximately twice her height, the pit walls loomed over her, not quite straight up but too steeply angled for climbing. In the growing light, the prison did not appear nearly as large as she had first thought. Roughly rectangular in shape, it stretched possibly some twenty by thirty feet. "How do you suppose they get in here to dig the mummies out?"

"Ladders, I would imagine," Wynne said, "or ropes."

Sabrina placed her hand against the earthen wall. "What a shame they did not leave one here." She scraped experimentally with her fingernail. Dirt came away without much difficulty, yet the wall remained fairly firm. "If we had something to dig with . . ."

Wynne's tone was speculative. "Something like, say, a knife."

Sabrina nodded. "A knife would do quite nicely. Unfortunately, since I did not foresee this complication when I left my tent tonight I failed to bring any type of weapon."

"The captain told me you always carried a knife in your boot," Wynne said, admiration in her voice.

Belinda gasped. "A knife? Oh, Mother, surely not!"

Sabrina disregarded her daughter's shock and smiled fondly in remembrance. "I did once, a very long time ago. However, I fear it's a habit I have since lost. I am not as prepared as I was in the past." She laughed shortly "I am no longer accustomed to adventures of any type."

"Well, I should think not," Belinda said indignantly.

Wynne rose to her sister-in-law's defense. "I think forethought is an admirable trait. One to be emulated." She hesitated. "The captain suggested on this journey it would not be amiss if I followed your example."

"My example?" Sabrina asked, puzzled. Her eyes widened with sudden understanding. "Good Lord, Wynne, are you saying you have a knife?"

Wynne nodded and reached down to the oversized boots

she had managed to purchase from a sailor on Matt's ship. "I keep it here, and quite uncomfortable it is too." She slipped her hand into the top of the footwear, pulled out a small but serviceable dagger and brandished it triumphantly. "Although, I must say, just the knowledge of its presence provides me with a certain measure of excitement."

"This is excellent." Sabrina plucked the weapon from Wynne's outstretched hand. "These walls are not perfectly straight. They have a slight angle to them. If we can dig out small footholds to provide a bit of traction, we might be able to climb our way out of here."

Wynne nodded. "Capitol, Sabrina. Really quite good."

"Mother, that's simply impossible." Belinda folded her arms over her chest in an obstinate manner. "There is no conceivable way I can climb out of this hole. Why, I'm not even dressed."

Only now did Sabrina note that her daughter still wore her nightrail. Wynne was as fully dressed as Sabrina herself. Strange; Sabrina thought surely Wynne was asleep when she left the tent. Her apparel made no sense unless . . . it was past time to fully determine the extent of Wynne's involvement with Matt. But in this awkward circumstance it would have to wait . . . for the moment.

She waved a dismissive hand at her daughter. "We will deal with your lack of suitable clothing when and if we escape from here."

Sabrina turned toward the wall and set to work. She outlined a small foothold with the knife and stabbed at the dirt, loosening the soil enough for Wynne to attempt to hollow it out with her fingers. Within minutes the women were hard at work. Sabrina suspected their effort was futile. It would take hours to dig enough holds to enable them to climb to the top. However, as she had no other ideas, the difficult job provided a distraction from their predicament and served to keep her mind off what could happen to them all if they failed to escape.

Wynne and Sabrina worked side by side. Belinda stood a short distance away, assigned to keep an eye on the rim of the pit in the event their captors returned unexpectedly. She watched warily for any desert creature that might decide to pay them a visit, her anxious gaze darting from rim to walls and back again.

"Wynne," Sabrina said casually, "why are you dressed? I thought you were asleep."

"I might ask you the same thing."

"I went to walk with Nicholas." Sabrina raised a brow in emphasis. "My husband."

"I too went for a walk," Wynne said defensively, attacking the foothold on which she worked with renewed enthusiasm.

"Really?" Sabrina considered her answer. "Alone?"

"I . . ." Wynne averted her eyes and sighed. "No, I was not alone."

Sabrina's tone was gentle. "Were you with Matt?" The younger woman nodded. "I thought as much. Wynne, have you given any consideration to the future? To what happens when this journey is ended?"

Wynne's gaze met hers. "I have given it a great deal of thought. When this adventure is over I shall embark on another. I plan to fill my life with exploits and quests and—"

"And . . . what about Matt?"

Wynne turned and concentrated her efforts on a particularly stubborn section of soil. "The captain will continue much as he always has, I suspect. With his ships and his voyages and his . . . life."

"Does that not bother you?" Sabrina said in amazement.

"No . . . yes . . . I do not know." Wynne's eyes blazed with defiance. "What, perchance, am I supposed to do, Sabrina? I finally have the opportunity to experience all I have ever dreamed of. At last I am able to travel and explore and see the world for myself. I feel as if I have spent my entire life in some type of eminently respectable but deadly tedious prison.

"I suspect the captain is the kind of man who should find being tied to just one woman the worst kind of incarceration. Now that I have found my own freedom, I cannot—I shall not—impose such a prison on him." She turned back to the wall and scraped at the earth in a fierce gesture of frustration.

"He might well wish for such a prison." Sabrina's words were soft. "He loves you."

Wynne stilled, frozen in midmotion. "What makes you think so?"

"He told me."

Wynne released a pent-up breath. "I daresay I did not expect that."

Surprised, Sabrina stared. "Whyever not?"

"All that I have read of men such as the captain indicates that love is not an emotion they succumb to easily. Courage, fire, a variety of other passions, yes, but love . . ." her gaze dropped, her voice barely more than a whisper, as if she talked as much to herself as Sabrina, ". . . no, I never expected that."

Sabrina studied her sister-in-law for a moment. "Do you love him?"

Wynne's startled gaze flew to hers. "Do I—yes, of course, without a doubt."

Sabrina smiled. "Very well then; the two of you shall marry and—"

"Oh, no!" Wynne shook her head firmly. "Marriage is out of the question."

"Why?" Sabrina asked, shocked by the refusal of this spinster to even consider wedding the man she admitted she loved.

Wynne's tone rang with impatience. "Surely you realize marriage would never satisfy the captain. He is a man used to adventure and intrigue, even in his personal dealings. Although bound by the vows of matrimony, he would no doubt eventually turn to other women." Wynne's voice softened, clasping her fingers together and staring at her hands. "And that I could not bear." She hesitated for a long moment. Finally her gaze met Sabrina's. "How does one bear it?"

The question pierced Sabrina's heart with an almost physical pain, and her breath caught in her throat. How indeed did one bear such a thing? Wasn't that exactly what she had to look forward to from Nicholas? Oh, certainly he was enamored with her now; only a fool would fail to see that. But what of the future? What happened when they returned to England? When excitement and adventure was far behind them?

Would he expect her to be once more the serene Lady Sabrina she originally had selected for a wife? Could she behave that way again? Her life before now was as much a prison as Wynne's had been, and just like the younger woman, Sabrina suspected she could not return to it. These weeks of reckless freedom were too potent not to have erased years of proper behavior.

And what of Nicholas's behavior? The man was a rake; it was his very nature. She did not expect him to change when they wed, but the marriage of convenience she had agreed to had not worked out quite as she'd foreseen. Love had played no part in her initial plans, especially not this burning passion that ignited whenever the man so much as threw a smoldering glance her way. How long would it be before he turned to others? Before he began anew the liaisons and affairs for which he was notorious?

She thrust the picture of an altogether painful future aside and returned to her work, viciously assaulting the earthen wall as if it were to blame for her fears. Her words were blunt. "Not everyone behaves as characters in a book, Wynne. Perhaps you should give Matt a chance."

Wynne's response was slow and thoughtful. "Perhaps." The sound of the knife scraping at the soil and fingers scratching at the earth filled the silence between them. "And what of you, Sabrina? Will you give Nicholas the same chance?"

"I am married to your brother." The bitter note in her voice surprised her. "I have little choice. I knew the type of man he was when we wed. I shall have to learn to deal with the consequences."

"I fear I do not know my brother well. But I am aware of his reputation. He is well known for his amorous exploits. Still, he is a man of honor. Are you so certain he will betray you?"

Sabrina's answer came short and quick and hard. "Yes."

Her gaze met Wynne's and she shrugged. "It's what I expect. As I said, I shall deal with it. However, I am not completely certain I shall live with it."

"Surely you would not consider divorce?" Wynne asked, her words tinged with horror.

"Of course not. I shall have my gold and therefore no need to depend on your brother financially. I cannot imagine he will not be amenable to living apart, should it come to that. But no, Wynne, I would never divorce him." Sabrina's pride prevented her from saying anything else. She could not tell Wynne that she fervently prayed Nicholas would discover love with her. She could not explain that as long as they were legally bound together, there was hope. And she could not put into words how her very soul would shatter if indeed her fears about her husband proved true.

"Time enough to face that later. We have more pressing problems now." Sabrina tossed the dagger to the floor and eyed the side of the pit speculatively. The footholds were now an arm's reach above her head. "Let's see if this shall work. Boost me up, Wynne."

Wynne locked her fingers together and Sabrina wedged a booted foot in her clasped hands. Bracing herself between the wall and the woman, Sabrina slowly inched upward. Gingerly, she settled one foot into the holds they'd dug and gradually allowed her weight to settle on it. It held. She pulled her other foot from Wynne's grasp and placed it in a second hold. It too supported her. They had not cut footholds more than a few feet above her head, and she could only climb a short distance. But it was enough to show that the plan would indeed lead eventually to escape. Elation and confidence swelled within her.

Sabrina lay plastered against the side of the wall like an insect in a windstorm and grinned down at Wynne, a scant few inches below her. "I believe this will yet work."

Wynne beamed back. "I had no doubts."

Sabrina's optimism restored, she scanned the walls above her. "However, I shall need to cut more holds while clinging like this. It's not that far to the top, so I suspect we shall be—"

"Mother!" Belinda's shriek echoed around the pit. "There's a snake! A snake, Mother, a snake!" She stared wild-eyed at the side of the pit.

Sabrina leapt off the wall, and she and Wynne tumbled to the floor. Her heart pounded in her throat and her gaze frantically searched the earthen walls for the serpent. She snatched the knife off the ground and spied the golden-skinned, undulating creature a bare moment later. Instinctively, she hurled the dagger, praying that her skill with a knife had not dimmed with the years.

A sickening thud reverberated around her. The knife stuck in the earth, neatly skewering the snake to the wall. Sabrina pushed her hair away from her face with a shaky hand and forced a weak smile to her lips. She'd done it. She hadn't lost anything. Not skill, not speed, not courage. A sense of satisfaction surged through her. With or without Nicholas, she would survive.

She turned to the others. Belinda stared speechless. Her gaze traveled from the serpent pinned to the wall to her mother. "Mother," she said in a voice hoarse with shock. "How did you learn to do that?"

She wasn't sure whether it was relief or the stunned expression on her child's face, but Sabrina wanted nothing more than to laugh hysterically. She bit her lip and choked back the mirth. "Darling, it's just one of those handy things one picks up here and there." Belinda blinked in silent astonishment.

"That's an odd-looking snake, Sabrina," Wynne said thoughtfully.

Sabrina studied the creature and cautiously edged closer. A moment later the laughter she'd suppressed burst forth. Belinda and Wynne stared as if she had surely lost her mind.

"It's not a snake," Sabrina gasped through uncontrolled gales. "It's a rope. I've killed a bloody rope."

"Belinda?" The low whisper dropped from above, stilling Sabrina's laughter with the swift surety of a sharpened blade.

"Erick?" Belinda said hopefully.

The silhouette of a familiar head appeared at the rim of

the pit. "Belinda, are you all right?"

Belinda stared upward and excitement rang in her voice. "Oh, yes, yes, Erick, I'm fine. We're all fine. Now, please, please get us out of this nasty place."

"Erick," Wynne called to her nephew. "We greatly appreciate your assistance. However, Sabrina and I were just about to—"

"Wynne," Sabrina said sharply and pulled Wynne away from the wall. "Hold your tongue."

Wynne turned toward her, eyes wide with surprise. "I was merely going to tell him that his rescue, while extremely thoughtful, is also unnecessary." Wynne drew herself up in a gesture of supreme confidence. "We are more than capable of rescuing ourselves and, given a bit more time, would have accomplished that feat quite nicely."

Sabrina sighed. "I know that and you know that, and very likely Belinda realizes it as well. However, your sea voyage and Erick's unfortunate reaction to ocean travel has somewhat paled the glow of young love, at least in Belinda's eyes." Confusion still registered on Wynne's face. "Do you not understand? This rescue of his, this gallant gesture as it were, is just what she needs to forget her distaste for his illness. This allows Erick to be her knight, her savior, her hero."

"Of course." Wynne nodded in agreement. "I had not thought of that." She turned and stepped back to Belinda's side. "Erick, dear, we were so dreadfully afraid. And now that you've come to save us, all will most certainly be well."

Sabrina groaned to herself. Subtlety was not one of Wynne's strong suits. She shook her head and turned to the task at hand. Even while they were well on their way to effecting their own escape, it would be foolish indeed not to take advantage of Erick's presence. Escape was well within reach on their own, but it would surely take more time than she cared to squander. With Erick's help, they should be out of their prison in a matter of minutes.

"Erick." Sabrina tugged at the dagger, pulling it from the wall and allowing the rope to swing free, "I shall wrap this end of the line around Wynne and you may pull her up.'' Sabrina turned to her sister-in-law. ''Wynne, use the footholds to help push yourself up along the wall.''

''Very well, Lady Sabrina.'' Erick's hushed tones sounded above them. ''Let me know when you are ready.''

''Mother.'' Belinda's words rang with indignation. ''I feel I should go first.''

''What?'' Exasperation churned in Sabrina. How much farther could she allow this charming child to push her before she lost control completely?

''Well,'' Belinda said with authority, ''after all, Erick did come primarily to rescue me, and since I am the one among us who is obviously the most delicate, it seems only proper that I should be the first one out of the pit.''

Sabrina clenched her teeth and willed herself to remain patient. ''My darling child, I believe Wynne should go first because she could then assist the rest of us in our ascent.''

''I'm sure I could help just as well,'' Belinda said stoutly.

''What happened to being delicate?'' Wynne asked under her breath.

Belinda ignored her. ''Mother, will you give me the rope or do we continue to debate?'' Challenge sparked in her eyes and she glared at her mother.

Sabrina stared back. How could she have raised a child so remarkably stubborn, spoiled and self-centered? Annoyed, she searched her daughter's eyes. Realization hit her abruptly, and she bit back a caustic retort. Of course. It was so obvious, Sabrina should have noted it sooner. The girl was scared, terrified. With a mother's unerring instinct, Sabrina sensed the fear carefully concealed behind Belinda's obstinate insistence on being the first to escape. Sabrina's ire vanished.

''Very well.'' Sabrina wrapped the line about Belinda's waist. ''Hang on and use the footholds for leverage.'' She trapped her daughter's gaze with her own and her voice softened. ''Are you quite sure you can do this?''

Belinda jutted out her chin and drew a deep breath. ''Yes, Mother, I am sure.''

Sabrina nodded and tugged on the line. "Erick, you may pull her up."

Slowly, Erick pulled Belinda from the pit. She did indeed follow her Mother's directions and used the holds Sabrina and Wynne had dug. In a matter of minutes she was at the top and disappeared from sight. Sabrina heard the murmur of Belinda and Erick's greeting, followed by the silence of what was obviously an embrace. She counted to ten mentally, the limit of her patience. Young lovers or no young lovers, she wanted out of this blasted hole from hell. Sabrina jerked on the rope indignantly, and a scant second later the cord descended once more. Sabrina tied it around Wynne, and then she too was lifted out, leaving Sabrina alone in the pit.

She glanced around the prison, and for an instant abject terror washed over her. This could well have been the beginning of an adventure even Wynne would not have appreciated. Sabrina shivered at the possibilities. They weren't out of danger yet. She gritted her teeth and grabbed the line that now dangled before her. Half climbing, half pulled, she made her way to the top and over the edge, to collapse on the ground, eyes closed, relief turning her legs liquid. A cooling breeze danced across her fevered skin, heated by fear and labor and, finally, elation.

"Mother?"

"Lady Sabrina?" Erick's voice carried a note of concern. "Are you certain you're not injured?"

"Quite." Sabrina shook off her weariness, sat up and extended her hand to Erick. He grasped it and pulled her to her feet. "Erick, you have my undying gratitude for your timely arrival." She swatted at her clothes in a futile attempt to rid herself of the dirt that covered every inch of her, an effort that did little more than release clouds of dust. "Now, I assume you have arranged some form of transportation to carry us away from this beastly spot before those despicable villains return?"

"Indeed, Lady Sabrina." Erick grinned with the justifiable pride of a man who knows he's done well. "I have, shall we say, borrowed two horses. We shall have to double up, and I suggest we leave at once. The sun will soon be up.'' He glanced at Belinda, who gazed at him with unquestioning adoration. ''Belinda can ride with me.''

Sabrina nodded, turned toward the horses and then stopped in her tracks. She swiveled on her heel and studied the young couple intently. Oblivious to the rest of the world, their gazes remained locked, and even the most casual observer could read love and devotion and . . . desire. In the growing light, Belinda's nightrail was transformed from a virginal garment for sleeping to a sheer, provocative veil that tantalized with unspoken promises of seduction and passion.

Sabrina stepped closer. ''I suggest Belinda ride with me. Wynne can share your horse.''

Hot color flushed Erick's face. ''Of course.'' Sabrina smiled to herself. She knew precisely what Erick was thinking; the boy was just like his father.

Erick assisted Sabrina and Belinda onto their mount, then pulled Wynne up behind him. Anxiety gripped Sabrina. The sun would break the horizon at any moment, and surely their captors would return. They must go, and quickly.

The moment Wynne settled on Erick's horse, Sabrina's gaze met the young man's. ''Do you know the course back to camp?''

''I believe so. It's this way.'' He gestured to the left of the glow in the sky that foretold the momentary rise of the sun.

''Let us be off, then.'' She nodded once, and Erick spurred his horse, Sabrina a split second behind. They rode at a fast, even gait until well after the sun broke the horizon and climbed halfway up the sky, then slowed to a less punishing pace. Erick assured her that the camp was not much farther. They rode side by side.

''However did you find us?'' Sabrina asked, curiosity in her voice.

Erick shrugged modestly. ''We had just ridden over the hill when Father decided someone should stay to protect the women. He and Captain Madison had a bit of a row about who should go back and who should go after the horses.

241

They really don't seem to get along at all well.''

Sabrina snorted inelegantly. "That's scarcely a revelation. Each would like nothing better than to see the other dangling by a fraying rope over a pit of vipers.''

"Oh, I daresay it's not . . ." Erick sighed. "You're right, of course. And it shall only get worse when Father . . . well, knows everything.''

Sabrina glanced at Wynne, seated behind her nephew. Obviously, Erick knew about Wynne and Matt. Was Nicholas the only one of their party who didn't know?

"At any rate," Erick said, "I volunteered to go back to camp, and as I came over the rise saw you three plucked off the ground by a virtual horde of heathens in flowing robes. I simply followed on that damnable camel, as discreetly as is possible with a beast of that nature. I suspect I was undetected more because your abductors were confident there would be no pursuit than because of any skill on my part.

"The hole in which I located you is near a small village, and that's where I was able to liberate these excellent steeds." Erick regarded the beasts with admiration. "They are wonderful horseflesh.''

"You're wonderful." Belinda sighed from behind her mother.

Once again a blush colored Erick's cheeks, and he sat a bit taller on his mount. Sabrina ducked her head and grinned. She had no wish to embarrass Erick or her daughter. Still, it was difficult not to feel a certain amount of amusement, not to mention satisfaction. Belinda was once more enamored of her fiancé, and Sabrina had no doubt theirs would be a long and happy marriage. As for her own . . . she would not dwell on that now.

"Mother?" Belinda's tone was cautious.

"Yes, darling?"

"I am sorry if I've been something of a disappointment for you."

Sabrina started and twisted to face her daughter. Belinda's eyes were downcast. "Why on earth would you think such a thing?"

"It's obvious, Mother." Belinda raised her eyes to meet her gaze. "I have come to see you in an entirely new light. You are not the woman I always believed you to be. You have a penchant for adventure I never dreamed possible, as well as a surprisingly expressive vocabulary." Sabrina winced at her daughter's words.

Belinda continued without hesitation. "You are capable and self-reliant, more than able to care for yourself, be it with kidnappers or rakes. Beyond that, you seem to have few qualms about flouting convention and doing precisely as you please." Her voice lowered. "And, Mother, you obviously have had a great deal of experience with exceptionally lethal-appearing daggers."

Belinda sighed. "I am nothing like you. I have found nearly everything since I left London to be irritating and inconvenient. Even Wynne has apparently leapt into this venture with enthusiasm and a great deal of enjoyment. What is wrong with me?"

Sabrina tossed back her head and laughed softly, relieved that her daughter's concerns were not more serious. "My dearest, there is nothing wrong with you. You are exactly what you are expected to be: a properly raised young woman, the daughter of a marquess, who understands her place in society and the world. The fault, my child, is not with you but with me. I am the one who is not as she appears. The one who has never quite lived up to the expectations the world has had of me."

Belinda pulled her brows together in a frown of confusion. "I don't understand. You have always appeared the epitome of propriety."

Sabrina shrugged. "It was an act. For years I pretended to be what the ton thought was appropriate. And I have no regrets about my behavior. However, the freedom I have tasted on this quest has changed me, I fear forever. I feel again as the woman I once was." She shook her head. "I cannot give up that woman again." Her voice softened. "But you, my darling, are exactly as you should be. And I, and Erick, love you."

"Thank you, Mother." Belinda fell silent for a moment.

"Still, I feel as if I have failed you in some way." Her eyes lit. "What if I were to . . . well . . . perhaps . . ." she drew a deep breath, "wear men's clothing too."

Eagerness stamped her face, and Sabrina stifled a smile. "Only if you would feel comfortable doing so."

Belinda squared her shoulders, as if the simple act of changing her garments was a formidable challenge that required courage beyond her years. "I believe I would, Mother. I believe I would."

"Lady Sabrina." Erick's tense tone interrupted them. He reined his horse to a stop, and Sabrina followed. "I do not wish to alarm you, but I fear there are riders heading in our direction." He nodded at a rise that loomed before them.

Sabrina's heart leapt to her throat. A cloud of dust puffed beyond the rise. The faint sound of hooves pounding parched ground sounded in the distance. The din grew nearer and louder.

"Erick, what are we to do?" Belinda's eyes were wide with fright.

Even Wynne appeared anxious. "Surely they're not the same men who kidnapped us?"

"Or worse," Sabrina said under her breath.

Erick leaned across his horse toward her and spoke in a low voice meant for her ears only. "I suspect we have few options. We cannot go back the way we came. Whoever this is will top the rise in a matter of moments, and I do not see any means of escape. Unfortunately, I am also unarmed."

The pressure of Wynne's knife in Sabrina's boot, where she had secured it, was scant comfort. She could only hope those who approached were neither kidnappers nor any other variety of bloodthirsty desert-dweller. A hope she feared was futile. Erick was right; there were few options.

She drew a deep breath and willed the trembling in her hands to cease. Regardless of what happened, she would not give in to fear. After all, she had once been a successful smuggler and leader of men. Sabrina could face whatever came next.

Swift as the desert wind, the riders appeared on the ridge and pounded toward them.

She tightened her grip on the reins and bit her bottom lip. "Bloody hell."

Chapter Seventeen

"Where in the name of all that's holy have you been?" Nicholas's roar sounded above the din of the horses' hooves. Sharply, he reined in his mount so close beside her that the air sizzled with the heat of the beast. "Don't you know better than to take off in the middle of a blasted desert? Have you no sense, woman?" In the back of her mind she noted Matt and a rather motley army of attendants mounted on camels accompanied Nicholas.

"I see you recovered the horses," she said mildly.

"The bloody horses can go straight to hell." His eyes flamed with anger. "You have not answered my question. Well?"

Perhaps it was the already stifling heat of the day. Perhaps it was simply her filthy, exhausted state. Or perhaps it was his self-righteous, outraged manner. Whatever the reason, something snapped within her. She would not put up with even the mere implication of wrongdoing on her part.

Sabrina drew herself rigidly upright on her horse, gazed at him with all the composure amassed from years of practice and smiled coolly. "Well, what?"

Nicholas stared as if he could scarce believe his ears. She met his gaze calmly, coldly, controlling the defiance simmering just beneath the surface, daring him to push her further.

"Nicholas, it was quite awful," Wynne said with a cheerfulness that belied her words. "We were kidnapped, snatched practically from our beds—"

"By the most awful men," Belinda joined in eagerly. "They imprisoned us in this horrible hole with dead bodies."

"Dead bodies?" Confusion diffused the anger on his face.

"A mummy pit," Wynne explained.

"What's a mummy pit?" Matt said curiously.

Wynne drew a deep breath and launched into her by now practiced explanation. "A mummy pit is something of—"

"Quiet!" Nicholas bellowed above the rest. "Erick, is all this true?"

Erick nodded. "Quite true, sir. They have had a considerable adventure."

Belinda cast an adoring glance at the young man. "And Erick saved us. He was magnificent."

Nicholas turned back to Sabrina, his eyes troubled. "Why did you not tell me this at once?"

"Why did you not give me the chance?" She jerked her gaze from his, urged her horse to a trot and headed in the direction from which Nicholas had come, not bothering to see whether the others followed. Vague, excited voices behind her indicated that Wynne and Erick had filled Nicholas and Matt in on the details of their so-called adventure. At the crest of the rise she spotted the camp and headed toward its dubious comforts.

"Mother . . ." Belinda said hesitantly.

Sabrina sighed. "I have little desire for conversation right now."

"But, Mother, Lord Wyldewood was—"

"Belinda." Sabrina's voice cracked in the air. "Please."

Belinda fell silent, and Sabrina dug her heels in the horse's side. The animal seemed to sense her irritation and responded instantly. In no time the beast had covered the short distance to the camp.

Attendants helped Belinda off the horse, and Sabrina gratefully slid to the ground on her own. She leaned against the animal, closed her eyes for a moment and breathed deeply, the air sweet with freedom.

"I believe an apology is in order."

Sabrina snapped her eyes open at Nicholas's words. She laughed, a short, harsh, mirthless sound. "I shall not apologize to you."

Nicholas nodded. "No doubt, but I shall apologize to you. I believe I jumped to some rather hasty conclusions."

"Oh?" Her eyes narrowed. She would not make this confession easy for him. "And what were those conclusions?"

"I believed you and my sister had set out on your own to locate the horses."

She raised a skeptical brow. "That would be exceedingly foolish."

"It would indeed." He ran a weary hand through already disheveled hair.

Only now did she note how very tired he appeared. More than likely, he too had not slept. Still, unreasonable anger, fueled by her own weariness, surged within her at his assumptions. "And you think I am that foolish?"

"Bloody hell, Sabrina." Nicholas's eyes blazed at her goading. "What was I supposed to think? Since the moment I first laid eyes on you, you have been completely unpredictable, not to mention stubborn and, yes, I believe foolish is a fairly apt description for some of your actions."

Fury stormed through her. "And exactly what have I done that was so foolish?"

"What have you done?" Astonishment colored his face. "First you attempt to flee to Egypt without telling anyone where you are going or why. Then you join forces with a man of disreputable background, more than likely a bloody smuggler, and a blasted American at that. Through it all, you disregard even the basic tenants of proper behavior in the manner in which you dress. And you do all of this because of a document of questionable veracity."

Sabrina glared, all the more furious at his words because they struck perilously close to the truth. "It is no doubt difficult to be married to a woman as foolish as I."

"And that's yet another matter." He grabbed her arms and yanked her to him, his eyes stormy, dark and dangerous. "You married a man you scarcely knew simply because he angered you. Because he offended your pride. That was indeed foolish. And yes, Sabrina, sometimes it is difficult. Sometimes it is extremely difficult."

She stared, stunned by his words. Anguish slammed into her chest. His comments confirmed her worst fears. Obviously he regretted his actions. Regretted his marriage to a woman who had turned out to be a far cry from the perfect wife he had expected. The back of her throat tightened, aching with tears she refused to shed. She clenched her fists, her nails digging into her palms. She was bound to this man, no doubt forever. A man who not only did not love her but found her a trial as well. There was little hope here for the future she had dreamed possible in those glorious moments when she was in his arms.

Pain and anger hardened her heart and chilled her words. "I regret you find marriage to me such a distasteful burden. Perhaps it would be preferable if we return to our original bargain. A marriage of convenience, in name only. Preferable . . . for both of us." She turned on her heel and stalked off.

"That's not what I said." His voice rose in frustration and she ignored him. He stared at the tiny, defiant figure striding toward her tent. Gad, she was infuriating. He realized his anger with her was perhaps irrational, and even possibly out of proportion. But damnation, the terror that had settled in his gut when he returned to find her missing still lingered like a poorly prepared meal. On further reflection, it might well have been unwise to assume she would search for the missing horses on her own. Still, if he understood nothing else in these past weeks about the woman he'd married, he had learned she was fiercely independent and more than likely to take matters into her own hands.

Given that, the conclusions to which he'd leapt were not far-fetched at all.

How had her first husband put up with her? His mood darkened at the unbidden thought. She and Stanford were no doubt two of a kind. The bloody man probably would have joined in this misguided quest with joyous abandon and scarcely a second thought for the hazards of the venture. No matter; Stanford was dead and Sabrina was his wife now. And if he did not compare favorably with the notorious marquess in one respect or another, it was bothersome, but so be it.

She disappeared into her tent and his fury ebbed away. Would life with Sabrina always be this frantic, furious and unsettled? Surely when they got out of this blasted desert and returned to London their existence would calm substantially. Abruptly, the thought struck him: He no longer desired a composed, collected woman to share his days. The serene Lady Sabrina he'd selected for a wife was well and good initially, but even in the beginning he'd suspected boredom would be the ultimate consequence. Now he wanted much more. Wanted her. Her passion, her laughter, even her outrageous self-sufficient manner. Life with her would be anything but boring.

For a moment he toyed with the idea of following her into the tent. Of sweeping her into his arms and showing her just how much he wanted her. How much he loved her. No, he would let her calm herself first. Let her ponder her illogical comments, her unreasonable reactions. His resolve was firm: This would never again be a marriage of convenience, never a marriage in name only.

He smiled slowly. He'd let her stew in her own juices for a while. He could wait. He had plenty of time. Whether she believed it and accepted it right now or not, they would indeed spend the rest of their lives together. If, of course, he didn't kill her first.

Sabrina paced before the fire, arms wrapped tightly around her, and glared at the offending flames as if they were somehow responsible for her foul mood. It had been three days since their ordeal. Nicholas said the horses apparently were stolen simply to get the men out of camp so the women could be kidnapped. It all had something to do with the foolish European passion for Egyptian artifacts and the cutthroat competition here among various factions to procure the ancient items. Of course, he did not tell her that directly. She refused to speak to him and avoided his very presence.

He no doubt thought she was still angry. She'd caught him studying her these past days, the hint of a smile on his lips, a glimmer of amusement in his eye. Her ire had vanished long ago, replaced by a deep, abiding pain that throbbed and pulsed with every beat of her heart. A pain she would never allow him to see.

Sabrina kicked at the sand and glanced across the flames. The servants had long since retired. Belinda, Wynne and Erick sat talking quietly. Their voices were low, but even from a distance Sabrina could sense their excitement. None of their party would sleep tonight.

The gold was at long last within reach, a mere few hours' ride from this very spot. Sabrina had wanted to continue on, but Nicholas had insisted they set up camp with nightfall. The others agreed, in an altogether irritating acknowledgment of Nicholas's leadership, and Sabrina reluctantly held her tongue. The thrill of the quest had dissipated with the shattering of her heart. Now all she wanted was the freedom from her husband the treasure would surely bring. How ironic that it was French gold that would bring her liberty. Nicholas hated the French, even more than he disliked Americans.

"Bree, we need to talk." She started at the sound of Matt's voice and turned. Nicholas stood beside Matt, a dark shadow to the American's fair figure.

Irritation washed through her. "What is there to talk about?"

Annoyance crossed Matt's face. "Tomorrow, Bree—we need to talk about tomorrow."

Sabrina shrugged. "Tomorrow we shall recover the gold, then get out of this God-forsaken country as swiftly as possible. It all seems quite straightforward to me.''

Matt nodded toward Nicholas. ''We don't think so.''

''We?'' She raised a brow. ''This is an unholy alliance, is it not?''

Nicholas remained silent. Matt cleared his throat, as if embarrassed by her recognition of the relationship between the two men. ''We are all partners, Bree, more or less. Your idea, I might add.''

She tossed Nicholas a scathing glance. ''I wouldn't trust him, Matt.''

Matt laughed, his natural sense of amusement restored. ''Oh, I still don't trust him. But I've worked with any number of men,'' his eyes twinkled, ''and women too, for that matter, that I didn't particularly trust.'' He grinned. ''I've found a certain lack of trust makes for a better business relationship on both sides.''

''Really?'' Her gaze traveled insultingly over Nicholas's stoic figure until it rested on his eyes. ''You may be right. Trust may not be necessary. In any type of relationship.''

A smile quirked the corners of Nicholas's lips. ''Perhaps trust has to be earned?''

A hot flush swept up her face, she snapped her gaze from his and turned to Matt. ''Very well, Matt; what did you wish to discuss?''

Matt glanced from Sabrina to Nicholas and back. He shook his head slightly, as if exasperated by the continued tension between his old friend and her husband. ''All right, Bree, who's going on your treasure hunt tomorrow?''

''Who?'' The unexpected question caught her unawares. ''I had not given any consideration to the makeup of the party, but I am going, of course, and you—''

''And I,'' Nicholas said firmly.

''No doubt,'' Sabrina said under her breath.

''Well.'' Matt cleared his throat again and darted a quick glance at Nicholas. What on earth was the man so obviously uneasy about? ''Wynne wants to go. Frankly, I don't think you can get away without her.''

''I suspected as much.'' Sabrina nodded in resignation. ''Very well, she may come. I would hate to throw a damper on her enthusiasm for adventure. But I wish to leave as soon as the sun is up.''

''Do you have the letter?'' Nicholas asked.

She stared him straight in the eye. ''I have kept it on my person since we left Cairo.'' She placed her hand on the laces of her breeches, just below her waist. ''I have it here. I did not want it misplaced.'' Sabrina fairly spat the words. ''That would be exceedingly foolish.''

A grin split Nicholas's face. ''It would indeed.'' His gaze trapped hers, and she responded with a withering glare. An odd tension smoldered between them: fury on her part, amusement on his.

Matt rolled his eyes heavenward, planted a look of disgust on his face and ambled off to join the others.

Nicholas crossed his arms over his chest. ''Have you yet reached any conclusions regarding your recent behavior?''

''Indeed I have.'' She narrowed her eyes and softened her voice. ''I should have had you thrown to the sharks when I had the chance.'' Sabrina swiveled on her heel and stalked off. Nicholas's deep laughter trailed after her.

She stopped at the edge of the pool of flickering light cast by the campfire. The dark stretched endlessly into the desert. She dug at the sand with her toe and studied the shifting grains with a focused intensity. How could Nicholas find any humor in their situation? Obviously, the man did not have the merest ounce of sensitivity. He'd stomped on her heart and seemed to find it all laughable. Perhaps he was right about her foolishness in at least one respect: She never should have married him.

''Sabrina.'' A voice hissed from the night.

She snapped up her head and peered into the darkness. Out of the black, three familiar figures slowly took shape.

She gasped. Benjamin Melville, Reginald Chatsworth and Patrick Norcross emerged from the shadows. ''Good Lord! How on earth did you get here?''

''Horses, my dear,'' Norcross said lightly, as if discussing a chance rendezvous in the park instead of a meeting in the middle of a desert halfway across the world. ''We left them, and what passes for servants in this abominable country, a short distance from here. Chatsworth's idea. Thought it would be better if we approached you singly, rather than in what's become a somewhat impressive entourage.''

"Indeed." Melville nodded vigorously. "We all agreed it would be prudent to speak to you privately."

"Privately," Chatsworth said quietly, "seemed best."

Sabrina stared at her former suitors in total confusion. "Best for what? My lords, you have me at a distinct disadvantage. I am completely baffled by your presence. Why are you here?"

"It was the way he spirited you off—" Melville said.

"Wyldewood, that is," Chatsworth added.

Norcross nodded. "Naturally, we were concerned."

"Concerned?" Sabrina shook her head, still failing to grasp the slightest bit of sense in their not quite sensible explanation. "Concerned over what?"

The three exchanged glances. "Wyldewood, of course," Chatsworth said. "His reputation is notorious. He's a rake."

Norcross joined in. "A rogue—"

"A reprobate, Sabrina." Melville paused in the detailing of Nicholas's character flaws. Melville always was a fair-minded man. "Although, to give him his due, he does have an excellent reputation in diplomatic circles—"

"He is expected to make his mark in Parliament," Norcross pointed out.

"Add to that the man's money. Wyldewood is so plump in the pockets, he could likely buy much of England itself," Chatsworth said wryly.

"And his word in affairs of honor has never been questioned." Melville drew himself up in a dignified manner. "Still and all, when it comes to affairs of the heart the man is a scoundrel—"

"A blackguard—" Norcross said.

Chatsworth shrugged. "A cad."

Astonishment coursed through Sabrina. If she were not already stunned by the trio's unlikely appearance, their litany of Nicholas's faults had compounded her amazement. Not that it wasn't true, of course. Nicholas had spent much of his adult life building the kind of reputation with women that brought a grin of admiration and a pang of envy from even the most straitlaced of men.

"Gentlemen, your words flatter me." Nicholas emerged from the shadows with a swagger in his step and a dangerous smile on his lips. Sabrina's heart stilled. Her husband was nearly as well known for his skill with a pistol as his ways with women.

"Nicholas," she said quickly, "I assume you know Lords Melville and Norcross and Sir Reginald Chatsworth."

"We are not bosom bows, but I believe our paths have crossed on occasion." His eyes narrowed. "To what do we owe the unexpected pleasure of your visit here?"

"Well . . ." Melville tugged nervously at his neckcloth. Absently, Sabrina noted that all three were dressed more suitably for an outing in Hyde Park than for a trek through the hinterlands of Egypt. "Well . . ."

"Do get on with it, Benjamin," Norcross said, exasperation in his tone. "The blasted man can't possibly call out all three of us. He can only shoot one of us." He glared at Nicholas and his voice faltered. "At a time, that is."

"Indeed." Chatsworth's gaze met Nicholas's. "He can only shoot one of us at a time."

"Shoot you?" Sabrina's bewilderment increased. "Why would he possibly want to shoot you?"

"It's not at all far-fetched, Sabrina. You see," Melville drew a deep breath, "we have come to rescue you."

"Save you," Chatsworth chimed in.

"From his clutches." Norcross cast a lofty look at Nicholas. "Before he ruins you completely."

"Ruins me?" Sabrina's voice was little more than a squeak.

Melville nodded in agreement. "Destroys your reputation beyond repair."

"Can one ruin a previously married woman, I wonder?" Nicholas asked with an air of casual curiosity. She threw him a cutting glare.

"Sabrina has never been free with her favors," Melville said staunchly. "Not like other widows I could name. Her behavior has always been above reproach."

Nicholas snorted in derision.

Norcross ignored him. "Sabrina, we know you well enough to know you would never go off with this man on your own—voluntarily, that is. Therefore, we assumed—"

"He coerced you in some way," Chatsworth finished.

"But never fear," Melville said. "Few in London know of your ill-advised indiscretion. Wyldewood has turned more than a few heads, and no doubt he swept you off your feet in a moment of weakness."

"One does wonder why he chose this beastly place to spirit her off to," Norcross said under his breath and nudged Chatsworth. "I would have taken her to Paris or Rome. And Venice is lovely this time of year."

Melville continued without pause. "However, we have a solution to your problem. There will be little talk and no hint of scandal if you return to London married—"

Sabrina gasped. "Married!"

"Indeed." Norcross nodded. "To one of us."

A strangled look of smothered amusement crossed Nicholas's face.

"Yes, my dear." Melville took her hand and sank to his knees in the sand. "I have loved you from the moment we first met. I know now I should have pressed my suit harder through the years, but I somehow thought there would always be time. I assumed one day my chance would come. I only hope it is not too late. Marry me, Sabrina."

"Marry you?" Her voice was scarcely more than a shocked whisper.

"Stand aside, Melville." Norcross claimed her hands from his companion. He gazed into her eyes with solemn sincerity. "I shall not get down on my knees, Sabrina. And I am known more for my sharp wit than fine words. But I too have loved you these past years. I should like nothing more than to make you happy and spend the rest of my life doing so. Sabrina, do me the honor of becoming my wife."

"Your wife," she said faintly.

"And what of you, Chatsworth?" Nicholas drawled the words sarcastically. "Do you not have a declaration to add to this outpouring of affection?"

Chatsworth's eyes glittered with an unnamed emotion. He smiled slowly. "Sabrina knows of my feelings. I have offered for her once before. My offer stands." He nodded at Sabrina, his voice quietly intent. "If she will have me."

Sabrina stared, speechless.

"If the object of all this noble concern is to save Sabrina's reputation, I believe you have forgotten one potential husband in your zeal to repair her good name," Nicholas said thoughtfully. "What about me, gentleman? After all, I am the cause of her ruin."

"Nicholas," she said sharply. He smiled innocently.

"Marry you?" Melville sputtered. "Preposterous."

"Completely out of the question," Norcross said.

Chatsworth snorted. "Damned idiotic, if you ask me."

"But, gentlemen," Nicholas said, "I have always heard it said that reformed rakes make the best husbands. And, we are all in agreement here, that is one title I have earned."

"Nicholas!" What was he doing? Was he baiting them? Or her?

Melville shook his head. "No, no, Sabrina will never marry you. It would be a disaster."

"Utter stupidity," Chatsworth said.

"Ridiculous, asinine, absurd," Norcross said.

Nicholas looked thoughtful. "Foolish, would you say? Rising anger strangled the words in her throat. "Foolish?"

Chatsworth nodded. "Extremely foolish."

"Foolish is the least of it," Melville said.

"Indeed." Norcross nodded. "Only a woman who had lost all her wits would even consider such a notion."

"Bloody hell!" The blasphemy exploded from her. "I will not stand here and be insulted. I would not marry any of you to save my life. If I had to choose between you four and the gallows, I'd go to the devil with a smile on my face and a song on my lips, knowing full well I was getting the best of the bargain." She turned on her heel and strode toward the fire, the crimson flames mirroring the fury within her.

"What did we say?" Chatsworth's question lingered in the dark behind her.

"Never mind that. Did you hear what she said?" The shocked tone of Melville's voice was unmistakable.

"Indeed," Norcross said. "Quite appalling for the eminently proper Lady Sabrina. And did you note her attire? Positively scandalous. Although," a note of appreciation rang in his words, "she certainly does wear breeches well."

"Sabrina." Melville and the others hurried after her.

Matt jumped up from his seat beside the fire. "Who in the hell are they?"

"Lord Melville? Norcross? Chatsworth?" Surprise colored Belinda's words, and she stepped toward the newcomers. "Bloody hell."

"Belinda!" Sabrina said in a sharp reprimand.

Belinda blushed. "Sorry, Mother."

"By Jove, Chatsworth, look." Norcross nodded toward Wynne. Her unbound hair gleamed seductively in the glow of the fire, the flames emphasizing her willowy form. Even her glasses winked charmingly above a pert smile. Norcross stared in appreciation. "Yet another beauty in breeches. There are benefits after all to being in this blasted desert." Wynne blinked in surprise and blushed, Matt's eyes narrowed and Sabrina was relieved that Belinda had been unable to find breeches of her own.

Melville's glance swept across the now intermingled gathering and settled on Sabrina. "Sabrina, my dear, I do not know precisely what we've said to overset you so. But we are, one and all, completely serious. Please, grant one of us the honor of your hand."

Matt grinned. "Her hand? You want to marry her? All of you? Oh, this is rich." He laughed. "Thank you, Bree. You always were most amusing, and thank God you haven't lost that gift through the years."

"Captain," Wynne said curiously, "is this always the way with adventure? One never knows what or whom to expect next."

Matt smiled down at her. "Hold your tongue, Wynne, and enjoy it."

She nodded thoughtfully. "I shall have to make note of this."

Melville ignored them both, gripped Sabrina's shoulders and gazed into her eyes. "We all care deeply about you."

"If you have a concern for your own safety," Nicholas said, his words softly ominous, "I would recommend you let go of my wife."

Melville tossed him an annoyed glance. "Come now, Wyldewood. We've been all through this. Sabrina would never marry you. It would be absurd."

Norcross nodded. "Completely unwise."

"Dammed foolish," Chatsworth said.

"As my sainted governess used to say 'Foolish is as foolish does.'" Nicholas's eyes gleamed with an unspoken threat. "Now, once more, Melville, get your hands off my wife."

Sabrina twisted out of Melville's grasp. "I do wish you all would cease discussing me as if I were not here."

"Discussing . . . you?" Melville's eyes widened with astonishment. He glanced from Sabrina to Nicholas and back. "Good Lord, Sabrina, you can't mean—"

"You're not saying—" Norcross said.

"You've married Wyldewood?" Chatsworth finished.

"That's precisely what she's saying." Nicholas smiled smugly. Sabrina's hand itched with the desire to slap the satisfaction off his face.

"I scarcely know what to say. This changes everything." Melville's expression fell, and sympathy twinged Sabrina.

"It does indeed," Chatsworth said slowly.

"I say, Wyldewood." Norcross nervously sidled up to Nicholas. "I rather hope you took no offense at my comment about Sabrina's appearance in those delightful garments."

"Rubbish, old man." Nicholas slapped him on the back as if they were the best of friends, and relief suffused Norcross's face. "I daresay I can't chide you for speaking the truth." His gaze swept Sabrina from head to toe, in a manner that left no doubt in anyone's mind that expressions of appreciation might well be allowed but no more. She clenched her fists and tightened her jaw at his possessive air.

"Now that Sabrina is taken, Wyldewood," Norcross glanced speculatively at Wynne, "could I beg an introduction to this charming creature?"

"My pleasure. I would like nothing better than to introduce her to a man with whom she shares a common background and heritage." Nicholas's eyes twinkled. The man acted as if he were at a ton ball instead of in the middle of the desert. "Norcross, may I present my sister, Lady Wynnefred Harrington."

Norcross grasped Wynne's hand and raised it to his lips. "I am delighted, my dear."

Matt moved protectively to her side and growled, "I'd drop that hand if you value your life."

"Captain . . ." Wynne said with delight.

Nicholas laughed. "Sorry, Norcross. You'd best do as he asks. He is an undisciplined American. They are rather quick-tempered and unpredictable."

Norcross sighed, tossed Wynne one last look of regret and stepped aside. Sabrina stared at her husband in disbelief. The man obviously knew about his sister and Matt, and very likely had known all along. Known and permitted their growing attraction by the simple act of pretending not to notice.

"It does appear our attempt to rescue you was ill advised," Melville said. "My apologies, Wyldewood. I wish you both well."

"Thank you, Benjamin," Sabrina said gratefully. "I am truly touched by your efforts." She nodded at Norcross, standing next to Nicholas, and smiled at Chatsworth, beside Belinda.

"Think nothing of it," Norcross said loftily, as if a trek across the world and a proposal of marriage were as commonplace as an evening at Covent Garden. "Obviously our presence here is no longer necessary. I suggest we take our leave."

"Quite." Melville cast one last longing look at Sabrina. "Although this endeavor has not turned out as I had hoped, it's perhaps all for the best.'' Norcross joined Melville. Chatsworth still lingered on the other side of the fire next to Belinda. ''Chatsworth? I believe our business here is finished.''

Chatsworth shook his head slowly. ''I beg to differ on that point.'' He withdrew a wicked-looking pistol from his waistcoat and aimed it at the assembly. ''My business here is anything but finished.''

Chapter Eighteen

Norcross expelled a deep, exaggerated breath. "Really, Chatsworth, the woman is already married. Do try to be a better sport about all this."

Chatsworth laughed, a short, caustic sound that grated in her soul. Fear shivered along her spine.

"I suspect the man is not overly concerned with Sabrina." The mild tone of Nicholas's words belied the tense line of his jaw and the calculating gleam in his eye.

"You are perceptive, Wyldewood," Chatsworth said. "Although, I must admit, when these two fools came up with the ridiculous idea of wedding Sabrina, it fell in nicely with my plans. As my wife, her possessions would also be mine." He threw Sabrina a look of regret. "We would have got on well together. However, it is not your face I am so interested in as your fortune."

"You are mistaken then, Chatsworth," Sabrina said boldly. "I have no fortune."

"Perhaps not at the moment." Chatsworth's eyes glittered in the firelight. "But you well have the means to what is, in anyone's view, a sizable fortune."

"Do I?" Sabrina stared at him fearlessly, but apprehension settled in her stomach. The only means to a fortune she had was . . . the letter.

"Do not play games with me, Sabrina." Chatsworth's sharp tone cut through the night. "I want the letter."

Confusion washed across Melville's face. "What letter?"

"Yes, Chatsworth, what letter?" Nicholas's voice rang cool and casual.

"You know full well what letter, Wyldewood," Chatsworth snapped. "I have no doubt it is the real purpose of your journey to Egypt." His eyes narrowed. "Although I suspect the story of your marriage is intriguing as well. Ironic, is it not," he waved the pistol at Sabrina, "that your new husband will be made to suffer for the sins of your first?"

Bewilderment drew Sabrina's brows together. "Jack? What does he have to do with any of this?"

"It is a shame, my dear, that Stanford did not keep you better informed as to his activities," Chatsworth said. "The letter should have been mine. I had already paid the idiot who lost it to your husband in that damnable card game. Paid, and paid dearly. But I only received the first page of the letter." He spat the words. "It was worthless.

"Stanford believed the second page was just as worthless. Indeed, he thought it a joke until he learned I wanted it. I was negotiating for it when he was killed." Chatsworth sighed, "I do regret that, my dear."

The import of his words struck her like a physical blow. The blood drained from her face and her voice was little more than a whisper. "What are you saying?"

"I did not intend for him to die. It was nearly as much an accident as everyone believed. However, I did arrange for the tampering with his carriage wheels before his ill-fated race." Chatsworth shrugged. "Stanford was toying with me. He kept raising the price of the letter. I merely wanted to . . . shall we say encourage his cooperation and settle our bargain. It was all quite unfortunate."

Sabrina's head spun. "You killed him."

"In a manner of speaking." Chatsworth shook his head

ruefully. "That was not my intent."

"Mother!" Belinda stepped toward Sabrina. Chatsworth grabbed her arm and yanked her back to his side.

"Belinda!" Erick instinctively leapt forward. Nicholas blocked his movement with a quick sideways step. For a moment their gazes locked; then Erick nodded slightly, clenched his fists and resumed his place by his father's side.

Chatsworth glanced from Erick to Belinda. "Apparently Sabrina and Wyldewood are not alone in forging new attachments in this beastly desert. But for now, my child, you shall remain exactly where you are." His gaze met Sabrina's. "I should have been her stepfather, you know. This would be unnecessary now if you had accepted me when I first offered for you."

"What is the meaning of this, Chatsworth?" Norcross asked. "Are you saying you do not care for her? You have never cared for her?"

"Oh, Sabrina is a fine figure of a woman. She would have made me an excellent wife. Eminently respectable. Unquestionably proper. Perfect, in fact." Chatsworth shook his head. "But no, my foolish companion, I do not care for her as you and Melville do. All I ever wanted was the letter. I courted her with only one purpose in mind until I became convinced she knew nothing of it."

"I only learned of its existence recently," Sabrina said faintly.

Chatsworth nodded. "I assumed as much when you abruptly fled London for Egypt."

Melville's eyes widened in realization. "It was your idea to go after her. What's so bloody important about this letter?"

"Gold, Melville," Nicholas said evenly.

"French gold." Matt's calm tone echoed Nicholas's. Vaguely, in the back of her mind, she noted that in spite of their differences, in this the two men were allied. "A considerable fortune, I might add."

Chatsworth's gaze flicked dismissively over the American and settled on Nicholas. "Excellent, Wyldewood. Perhaps I underestimated you. I wonder as well about this unexpected marriage of yours. The noted rake turned devoted husband. It does not ring true. Did you know of the gold when you married her?''

''I have no need of Sabrina's gold,'' Nicholas said.

Chatsworth laughed contemptuously. ''Come now, Wyldewood. Even with your vast resources you cannot expect me to believe a treasure of this magnitude is not tempting.''

Nicholas shrugged. ''Believe what you wish. I have no interest in the gold.''

''Then perhaps we shall be able to conclude our business here more amicably than I envisioned.'' Chatsworth tightened his grip on Belinda's arm. ''Give me the letter.''

Nicholas nodded at Sabrina. ''Give him the letter.''

She stared at him in disbelief. ''No.''

Nicholas's steely gaze trapped hers. ''Sabrina—''

''I shall not give him the letter,'' she said stubbornly. ''It is mine. Jack left it to me. It is all he left.''

''Not quite all, my dear.'' Chatsworth smiled slowly and turned the gun away from the gathering before him, pointing it mere inches from Belinda. Her eyes grew wide and stark with fear. ''Stanford also left you a daughter. You must choose, Sabrina.'' He pressed the pistol into Belinda's side, and she whimpered in terror. ''One legacy for another.''

There was little choice. Sabrina's gaze locked with Chatsworth's. Here was another arrogant man attempting to control her life, the stakes here higher than any she had ever faced. She might well lose this encounter, but not without a fight.

With slow, deliberate motions she withdrew the letter from beneath the laces of her breeches. She stepped toward him until only the fire danced between her and Chatsworth gripping a terrified Belinda. She held the letter in her hand and stretched it toward him, over the flames, the rising heat fluttering the page. ''Release her, Chatsworth. Now.''

He shook his head. ''Not until I have the letter firmly in hand.''

Sabrina stared with a cold, steady gaze that hid the panic rising within her. ''If you do not release her now, I shall not hesitate to drop this page into the fire. Then the gold will be lost to all of us."

"You are quite amazing, my dear." A note of genuine admiration colored his words. "I fully anticipated, when presented with the imminent demise of your daughter, that you would fold like a losing hand of whist. Could there be more to the serene Lady Sabrina than the picture presented to the world these past years? I am more disappointed than ever. We would indeed have suited well." His voice softened. "I shall kill her, you know."

"I suspect you plan on killing all of us," she said mildly. "However, it will do you no good without the letter. And if you harm so much as a single hair on her head, I shall dash this fragile and no doubt highly flammable paper into the flames without a moment's hesitation."

Annoyance stamped Chatsworth's face. "How do I know you will give me the letter once I release the chit?"

Sabrina lifted a questioning brow. "How? Do not forget, Reginald, you have the pistol." She waved the letter at him. "This is my only weapon." Her voice sounded deep and intent. "You also have my word."

Chatsworth rolled his eyes with exaggerated forbearance. "Very well, my dear." Abruptly, he released Belinda and pushed her forward. "Now, the letter if you will."

Belinda staggered around the fire and stumbled against Sabrina, the impact jarring the letter from her hand. It hung, suspended in midair, for what seemed an eternity. The assembly held a collective breath. Finally, like a feather on the wind, the delicate paper fluttered softly away from the flames to rest gently on the sand.

For a split second no one moved. Then chaos erupted. Chatsworth and Sabrina lunged, their action mirror images. Nicholas leapt toward them, Matt less than a step behind. The four scrabbled on the ground, and Sabrina lost sight of the precious paper.

"I have it!" With a cry of glee, Chatsworth held up the letter.

"No!" Sabrina screamed and threw herself at him, Chatsworth's gun pointing straight for her.

"Bree!" The cry tore from Nicholas's throat and he charged, pushing her out of the way. She tumbled and sprawled on the sand.

Chatsworth's crazed laugh echoed in her head. His weapon gleamed in the firelight. Motion slowed as if in a dream. He raised the pistol toward Nicholas, the barrel no more than an arm's length from his heart. Fear for him squeezed her in a vicelike grip. She could not, would not let him die. Her hands clenched in a spasm of terror, and sand scrapped her palms. In a last futile effort she flung the grains and screamed. "Chatsworth!"

His gaze flicked toward her. The grit and Nicholas struck at the same instant. The two men struggled on the ground in a blur of arms and legs. Sabrina could not tell who was who. Who had the advantage. Who had the pistol.

The shot echoed in the night. Abruptly, all movement ceased. Her breath caught in her throat. Her heart stopped. Her mind screamed a prayer. *Please God, not Nicholas! Please, let him live!*

It was forever, or perhaps less than a moment. The bodies on the ground shifted.

Chatsworth rose to his feet in awkward, jerky movements, like a poorly manipulated marionette. Sabrina froze in horror, her gaze locked on his face. Chatsworth's eyes gleamed red in the firelight, his soul staring naked and evil. He gasped and collapsed in a heap.

Like a valiant warrior from a battlefield of old, Nicholas stood behind him. Blood drenched his shirt. An odd smile quirked the corners of his mouth. He shrugged, a strangely hesitant look in his eye. "I do believe, my love, if you seriously want to do away with me, the sharks may well be more efficient."

A sob of relief burst from her. "Oh, Nicholas!" She flung herself into his arms, laughing and crying and meeting his lips with hers to assure herself he was indeed well and truly unharmed.

"Is he . . . ?" Melville said, unease and apprehension in his voice. Sabrina and Nicholas broke their embrace, but his arm stayed protectively around her shoulders.

267

Matt knelt beside the crumpled body and glanced toward them. "He's dead, all right." He plucked the wrinkled letter from Chatsworth's still clutching hand.

Sabrina gazed at her fallen suitor, shock lingering in her voice. "He killed Jack."

Nicholas's arm tightened around her. "You did not suspect?"

"Never." She shook her head. "Who would have? Jack died while in the pursuit of an idiotic wager. His death came as no surprise to anyone." Her voice dropped to a bare whisper. She spoke more to herself than to him. "Especially not me."

"Sabrina, I hope you understand we knew nothing of this." Norcross's voice jerked her attention away from the bloodied body at her feet and the persistent, unbidden memories crashing through her head. "We would never have gone along with him if we'd had so much as a hint of his true purpose."

"Our intentions were always of the noblest sort," Melville said. "Quite above reproach. Please believe us."

"Of course," she said under her breath, once again mesmerized by the scene before her, the broken body, the blood oozing into the sand.

"Gentlemen, I have no doubt Sabrina holds you blameless in this unfortunate incident. However," Nicholas gazed at Sabrina with a troubled expression, "I am concerned as to leaving Chatsworth's body here for even a short period. If you would be so kind as—"

"Quite," Melville said, anticipating the question. "If we could perhaps get some assistance in moving him to our horses and our camp. It is not far. We shall take care of any difficulties there may be with the local authorities. It seems the least we can do to make up for—" he waved a hand vaguely in the general direction of the body, "—all this."

"Thank you," Nicholas said. "Erick, Madison, if you could accompany them and lend some assistance. Wynne, take Belinda back to your tent."

Wynne nodded, her usual exuberance dampened. She wrapped an arm around a pale, shaking Belinda. "Adventure," Wynne said softly, "does seem to have its trying moments."

Matt cast an appraising look at Sabrina. She smiled absently, then turned an unseeing gaze on the dead man.

Nicholas glanced toward her and frowned. "I shall remain here." He nodded slightly at Matt and drew the American a few steps away. "She has not taken this revelation about Stanford's death well. Did she love him so very much, do you think?" Nicholas fought to keep his voice even.

"Remember, she was very young and inexperienced when she married him." Matt shrugged. "I met Sabrina after Stanford's death. I really have no idea of her feelings."

Nicholas plowed his fingers through his hair in a gesture of futility. "I don't know how to help her." Frustration sharpened his voice. "I don't know how to compete with the memory of a dead husband." His gaze flicked to Sabrina. She stood silently, her stare blank, her arms wrapped tightly around herself, as if to ward off an unexpected blow. "What do I do, Madison?"

Matt's gaze trapped his for a long, steady moment, his expression unreadable. Abruptly, the American nodded, as if he had found whatever he searched for in Nicholas's eyes. "Just take care of her, Wyldewood." He passed Nicholas the letter. "Take care of her."

Nicholas released a breath he was not aware he held. In some odd manner, a bond had been forged between the two men. In spite of their differences, both cared deeply for the same woman. Gratitude surged through Nicholas; whatever else Madison was, or had been in the past, his concern for Sabrina could not be faulted.

Madison took charge of the moving of Chatsworth's body, and within moments Nicholas and Sabrina stood alone by the fire. Helplessness filled him, an unfamiliar emotion. "Sabrina," he chose his words with care, "I believe it would be best if—"

"I want to go," she said quietly. "I want to go now."

Relief coursed through him. "Of course, my love, we can head back to Cairo at sunup and begin the journey home to London."

"London?" Her head jerked up and her gaze met his. Her eyes blazed with . . . what? Pain? Sorrow? Anger? "I cannot return to London yet. Not without the gold. I wish to get it tonight. Now."

"It's out of the question," he said patiently. "You have suffered through quite an ordeal and I—"

"That is precisely why I want to go now. Chatsworth may not be the only one who knows about the gold." Annoyance rang in her voice. "If you will not accompany me, I shall go alone."

"You most certainly shall not," he said, his voice rising. "It would be nothing short of idiotic to go off alone into the desert at night."

She glared at him angrily. "Well, do not hesitate to add it to the list of my foolish acts. With you or without you, I will go. And I shall go tonight."

Fury flared in his blood. All he wanted to do was protect her, take care of her. All she wanted was his assistance in an impetuous, ill-advised, completely ridiculous act. It was not his nature to behave in so reckless a manner. He would not dash off, unthinking, in the middle of the night. Not like . . . his eyes narrowed. "I imagine Stanford would have had no hesitation about falling in with your plan?"

"Jack?" Surprise underlaid her words. "What does he have to do with this?"

"Oh, come now, Sabrina." Impatience fueled his irritation. "I am fully aware of the differences between Stanford and myself. He was well known for his wild behavior. His rash acts."

"Jack is dead and gone," she said slowly.

"Dead perhaps, but is he gone?"

"Yes." She turned away quickly, as if to end the discussion, but he clasped her shoulders and spun her around to face him. He gazed deeply into her eyes, emerald fires of defiance.

"Hear me out. I have had more than my share of what my sister would so charmingly call adventure. And, like tonight, it is very often not pretty. I have risked my own life and that of my companions, but never without cause.

For my country, for my honor. My courage, even daring, has never been questioned.'' He pulled an unsteady breath. ''I am as different from Stanford as night from day. He was your first choice. I cannot fill his shoes. I only hope that you can put him in the past. That you can someday love me as you loved him.''

''No.''

The single syllable struck him like a dagger through the heart. Anguish tightened his hands on her shoulders. She winced, and he released his grip abruptly. ''I see,'' he said softly.

Sabrina sighed. ''No, Nicholas, you do not see. You see nothing at all.

''I was seventeen and straight from the schoolroom when I married Jack. He was gay and dashing and romantic. And I loved him with all the passion of an infatuated child.'' Bitterness and sorrow tinged her words. ''But even children have to grow up. And Jack never did. We lived from one party to the next, with no cares and no worries beyond which invitation to accept and which gown to wear. It was great fun.''

Confusion muddled his mind. ''I do not understand.''

She laughed, a tight, strident sound without mirth. ''Of course not. No one would. It was not the way I wished to live my life. It was a lovely dream, but it was not real. It was never real.'' She paused and stared past him at a distant spot in the night, or perhaps a distant time. ''Still, I did not want him dead. I never wanted him dead.''

''Bree,'' he said gently, ''his death was not your doing.''

''No, I know that.'' She fell silent, and he wanted nothing more than to take her in his arms. Uncertainty held him back. After a moment she gazed up at him and smiled. ''Thank you.'' Her manner turned brisk and bright. ''Let us be off. If we leave now, we shall surely return before sunrise.''

He stared, speechless. How could the woman change an altogether serious discussion so abruptly? And would she ever listen to him? ''Sabrina,'' a warning lingered in his

271

voice, "I believe I have made myself clear on this point. We will not go tonight."

"And I have made my feelings plain as well." She glared at him. "I am going, alone if need be."

"You cannot go by yourself," he said firmly, irritation at her irrational insistence rising once more.

She stepped away from him and planted her fists on her hips. "And why not?"

"Why?" His mind groped for a response. It all seemed so very logical to him, he was nonetheless hard pressed to come up with a reason to sway her stubborn determination. He suspected that her adamant demand to forge ahead after the gold at this moment had more to do with the emotion churned up by Chatsworth's appearance and her own feelings about Stanford than any real desire on her part to conclude her quest. Still, she tried what little patience he had left. "Why? It would be extremely dangerous to go off through the desert alone."

"Hah!" She scoffed. "What is not dangerous here?" She ticked off the points on her fingers. "To date we have been abducted by grave robbers and held at gunpoint by a crazed, rejected suitor. I suspect there is little more that can happen. I am not afraid of what the desert or the night might hold."

He shook his head in frustration. "You're being ridiculous."

"Am I?" she said sharply. "Am I being foolish again as well?"

"Foolish is not the half of it."

"I do not care," she said, her voice rising.

His tone matched hers. "I do."

"Why?"

"I do not want any harm to come to you."

"Why?" She screamed the word.

"Blast it, Sabrina, you are my wife."

"I daresay that will do me a lot of good." Her eyes snapped with rage. "You will no doubt discard me the moment we return to London."

"Discard you?" How on earth did this woman's mind work? "I would never discard you."

"Why?"

"Because I love you!" His voice thundered in the night.

"How would you know?" she said with disdain. "You've said the words so many times to so many women, what could you possibly know of love?"

"What do I know of love?" He grabbed her arms and pulled her tightly to him. She glared, her green eyes dark and stormy and challenging. Anger and urgency powered his words. "I know when I first saw you in Madison's arms I wanted nothing so much as to slice him to ribbons. I know when I returned from recovering the horses and found you missing my heart stopped with the fear of what might have become of you. And I know when Chatsworth aimed his pistol at you I realized my life would not be worth living without you in it."

"And how do you think I felt when that blasted weapon went off and I did not know if you were alive or dead?"

"How?" He shot the word as a marksman aimed at a target.

"As if I too would die if you were killed." Her words rang loud and strong. "Bloody hell, I love you too."

He gave her a quick shake, as if to force the answer he wanted desperately to hear. "What about Stanford?"

She wrenched out of his grasp. "He's dead! He's dead and buried! And I know now, and God help me I've known almost from the first, but I've never said the words aloud and I've never even dared to say them to myself. They were wrong and disloyal and without honor. But I never, ever truly loved him and—" she stopped as if thunderstruck by her own words. Her eyes widened and her voice broke "—I have always loved you."

Her words hung in the air between them. Their gazes locked. Elation flooded him, and he saw his wonder reflected in her eyes. He grinned slowly and held out his hand. She reached hers to his. Electricity sparked between their fingers. In less than a moment she was in his arms.

His lips crushed hers with a ravenous hunger that swelled with the taste of her, the touch of her. He swept her off her feet and strode toward his tent. Her hands clasped around his neck with an intensity that equaled his own.

The silken walls fluttered at their passage and they plunged into darkness, the shelter abruptly shutting out the glow of the fire and the shine of the desert stars. He released her and she slid from his arms, down the long length of his body to stand before him in the night. In a frenzy of urgent need and unrelenting desire, they blindly tore the clothes from one another without heed until the garments lay forgotten at their feet. Her body pressed into his, her breasts crushed against the hard planes of his chest, the rough mat of hair rasping her already taut nipples.

She tunneled her hands through his hair and drew his head down to greet his lips with greed. Her mouth parted beneath his and they joined together in mindless fervor, as if each sought to steal the very life breath from the other, or perhaps the very soul.

He splayed one hand across her back and cupped her buttocks with the other, pulling her tighter against him. His manhood, hard and powerful, throbbed against her stomach, an iron staff shared between them.

They sank to their knees, unwilling, unable to break the bond of flesh to flesh, heat to heat. She dragged her lips from his and along his jaw, rough and firm, to the strong line of his neck. He groaned, and she trailed her tongue to the hollow at the base of his throat, pressing her hands flat against his chest. She reveled in the taste of him, of salt and heat and power. Lost herself in the sheer pleasure of his strength beneath her fingertips.

He pulled away and claimed her lips with his own, a declaration of possession and passion and promise. His impatient hands roamed her sides until they grazed her breasts, his very touch a blaze of scorching, sizzling obsession. She moaned and her head fell back, her neck arched, her chest thrust forward like an offering to a pagan god. He cupped her breasts and bent to taste first one and then the other, until the sweet singe of his lips, his tongue, left her breathless with need.

He laid her back amid the linens and blankets and discarded garments, and she strained upward in relentless yearning for the fusion of his desire with her own. He trailed kisses of fire and chills down the valley between her breasts to the flat of her stomach and lower, ever lower, until his fingers parted the silken curls and his tongue flicked the point of her passion. She gasped and gripped his shoulders, as if to push him away, as if to urge him on. Never had she known such exquisite sensation, such delicious sin that pulsed and throbbed from his touch to fill every part of her. Tension built within her, deep and taut, until she existed only in the skillful caress of his lips, the masterful brush of his hand.

She called his name and he drew back to tower above her, a figure only of shadow and dark. Reaching for him, her hands fell upon the fire of his loins, soft as velvet and hard as rock beneath her fingers. Her own urgency spiraled. He moaned, a sigh of tortured delight. "Bree."

He poised between her legs and plunged into her yielding softness, hot and moist and tight. She surrounded him, engulfed him, welcomed him. He no longer knew where one began and the other left off, and no longer cared. Dimly, in a last coherent moment, he marveled at the potency of this aphrodisiac called love.

She arched upward to met his thrusts with a wanton eagerness that defied mere mortal pleasure. He plunged harder and faster, his fury forging with hers until she thought it would surely tear her asunder and gloried in the sheer power of it all.

Together, they moved in a rhythm ancient and primeval, merged in a dance uncivilized and elemental, fused in an uncompromising frenzy of unbelievable sensation and inconceivable joy. And when each thought they could not survive the unadulterated pleasure of their joining the desert night erupted around them in wave after wave of magnificent, shuddering rapture, and for the barest moment, or perhaps forever, glimpsed eternity. Until finally they clung to each other with an exhaustion born of passion spent and enchantment shared.

The inevitable laughter bubbled up inside her and she wondered through a haze of exhilaration if Wynne had yet discovered: Love was the greatest adventure of them all.

Chapter Nineteen

"Do you expect to laugh each time I make love to you?"

"Oh, Nicholas." Sabrina gasped, struggling to overcome her mirth. "I certainly hope so."

"Very well, then," he growled and nuzzled her neck, "perhaps you will find this humorous?"

Sabrina laughed and snuggled against him, reveling in his warmth, his strength, his scent. The turbulent emotions of the night crept upon her, and she was abruptly too weary to move. A moment's rest would do no harm. Her eyes closed and her mind drifted. Images floated through her head of an impulsive kiss shared in a cave long ago, of a valise tossed into a room and the rogue following close behind, of love . . . and laughter . . . and . . . gold.

"The gold." Sabrina jerked upright. "We must be off, Nicholas. I want to find that gold tonight."

"Very well, my love," he said, his manner resigned and relaxed.

She glared at him suspiciously. "What? No protests? No excuses? No lectures about the dangers of the desert in the night?"

Nicholas grinned. "I believe the night is virtually gone. The sun will be up in less than an hour."

Confusion colored her thoughts. "But how—"

"You slept—quite soundly, I might add." He kissed the tip of her nose. "You were exhausted, and I could not bear to wake you."

"Hah." She scrambled to her feet and cast around her for her clothes. "You just wanted to be certain we would not travel at night. Very well; you have succeeded in delaying us and now we shall—"

"Now we shall do precisely as you wish." Nicholas rose to his feet and pulled her still nude body against his. "Although I would not see the harm in delaying just a little longer." He trailed his lips along the side of her neck. She quivered beneath his touch and melted against him. Perhaps he was right. Would a short delay make even the tiniest difference?

"No." She jerked away regretfully and cast him her most patient glance. "Nicholas, I will not be seduced into putting off this quest."

"Sabrina." He donned an expression of exaggerated injury. "I had no intention of seduction." His eyes twinkled. "I merely wanted to tell you a joke or two."

"I am in no mood for jokes."

"You could be," he said, his voice low and ripe with promise.

He stepped toward her, and she held out her hands, as if to ward him off. "No, Nicholas, I am quite serious. I wish to go now."

He shrugged and stepped around her. "I know you do. I was merely looking for my clothing."

"Of course." She did not believe his words for a moment, but she couldn't very well blame him. As much as she wanted the gold, the idea of losing herself in Nicholas's arms once again was more than tempting.

They dressed quickly and left the tent. The sun peeked over the horizon in a golden glow that forecast the heat to come. Sabrina clenched her teeth in irritation. How could she have slept the night away? "I shall see if I can find some bread and cheese to take with us. You prepare the horses.''

Nicholas raised a brow at her commanding tone. ''I was never in the military, but I do recognize an order when I hear one.'' He swept her a polished bow. ''At your service, my lady.''

She blushed a delightful shade of pink, wrinkled her nose and briskly headed off. He chuckled to himself. She would never cease to amaze him, barking orders as if she were accustomed to controlling and directing armies of men.

He glanced toward the fire. Madison and Erick lay wrapped in blankets, sound asleep. He strode past Madison, and a hand snaked out from beneath layers of wool, catching his ankle, stopping him in midstride.

''Going for the gold, are you?'' Matt said in a sleep-roughened voice.

Nicholas shook off Madison's hand and grinned. ''Sabrina is insisting.''

''That's a surprise,'' Matt muttered.

Nicholas hesitated. ''I do hope you know, even if we find this gold by ourselves, we shall still share it equally with you. Your partnership with Sabrina is not in question.''

Matt squinted up at him. ''I can't say that I actually like you, but I've seen enough to know that you have a certain sense of honor. I have no doubts about getting my share.'' He rolled over and buried himself deeper in his blanket, his voice muffled by the cover. ''I just don't know what I'm going to tell your sister when she discovers she's missed out on this adventure.''

Nicholas's stomach tightened at the reminder of his sister's relationship with this American. He now acknowledged it, at least to himself, but acceptance was a bit harder to come by. Still, he had no choice. Wynne was far past the age of consent and had her own considerable fortune. There was nothing he could do. ''Simply tell Wynne that Sabrina and I chose to savor this moment alone together. She will no doubt find it quite romantic.''

Smothered laughter came from Madison's blanket, and Nicholas couldn't help chuckling in return. He took a step to leave, but Madison's voice checked his movement. "Remember what I said: take care of her, Wyldewood. She is as dear to me as your own sister is to you." A muffled sigh rose from the fabric. "And I am resigned, but not especially pleased, about her choice for a husband. Much as I wager you're not particularly happy about your sister's choice for a—"

"For a what, Madison?" Nicholas asked coldly.

"Husband, if she will have me. Or whatever she wants." The voice from the blanket fell silent. "I love her, Wyldewood."

Nicholas grinned slowly, his concern for his sister mellowed by the considerable satisfaction of just suspecting the merry chase on which Wynne would no doubt lead the American. "Then I fear you are in for as much chaos and turmoil as I have faced." He strode off toward the horses and laughed to himself. "And, with luck, as much delight."

Sabrina slid from her horse with a weary sigh; she had seriously underestimated the distance to the gold. Already the sun was high overhead, and there was no sight yet of the spit of land described in the letter, nor the Temple of Isis.

Nicholas regarded her with a hint of what she feared was sympathy in his eyes. "If we do not find the temple soon, we shall have no choice but to turn back."

She brushed the hair away from her damp forehead. "Not yet. It is barely midday. There are still hours of light left. I cannot give up until all hope is exhausted." She turned away and retrieved the bread and cheese she'd brought along for a hasty meal. Breaking off a hunk of the slightly stale crust, she handed it to him. Her gaze met his. "I have come too far to quit without one final fight."

He stared silently, then pulled a knife from a sheath he had taken to carrying at his waist and gestured for the too warm cheese. She passed it to him, and he carved a piece and handed it back. "I fear I still do not understand. I asked you once before, and your answer was distinctly unsatisfying." He paused, and his steely gaze bored into hers. "I ask you again, my love: why do you want this gold so desperately? You no longer need it. I have vast resources, and now everything I have is yours. Why, Sabrina? Why is this so very important to you?''

She stared into his endless eyes, heavy with questions and concern. A thousand thoughts flew through her mind. She had never told anyone other than Matt and Wills and Simon the sorry state in which Jack's death had left her. But as she had so vehemently told Nicholas, Jack was long dead and in the past. Still, did she not owe him a certain amount of loyalty? Where did an obligation to one husband end and allegiance to another begin? And what of her own personal code of honor? Did she not still have her own sense of duty and morality?

Even if she told him how Jack had left her virtually penniless, that would not completely explain her need to achieve financial stability independent of husband and family. A need she feared Nicholas could never understand. God knows, thoroughly proper women did not act on their own. They did not meddle in the management of their own funds, let alone direct their investment. Beyond that, once Nicholas knew about Jack, how much longer would it be before he connected her to Matt's smuggling and the infamous Lady B?

There was only one answer a man like Nicholas would accept.

''Nicholas,'' she said quietly, ''how important is honor to you?''

''Honor?'' Confusion washed over his face. ''I do not understand. What does honor have to do with this?''

''Bear with me, please, and answer my question.''

He shook his head, obviously puzzled. ''Very well. A man's honor is paramount. Rich as the devil or stricken with poverty, a man's word is all he has. Honor is the one unquestioned principal that rules any man's life.''

She nodded slowly. ''And what of a woman? Should a woman have to live up to those same high standards?''

He grinned. ''Sabrina, women have never been held to

the same ideals as men. Their moral strength is simply not up to it.''

"Oh?" She arched a disdainful brow.

His expression fell and he had the good grace to look chagrined. "Forgive me, my love. For a moment I forgot which woman I was talking to. You are unlike any female I've ever encountered. Perhaps my attitudes need a bit of adjustment, at least so far as you are concerned.''

"Thank you," she said softly.

He stared for a moment, as though realizing she was indeed serious. "I must admit I have never thought about a woman's sense of honor. I have simply never expected a woman to keep to her word. But upon reflection, I can see how honor could be as strong in a woman as in a man. And could mean as much.''

She squared her shoulders and gazed into his eyes. "As trite and ridiculous . . . and perhaps foolish as it may sound to you, I too have principles I live by. My honor means as much to me as yours does to you. My word is just as binding. I consider loyalty—''

"To Jack?" he said mildly.

She nodded. "In spite of his faults, he deserves no less from me. I owe him at least that much. He taught me a great deal." She pulled a calming breath. "It is that sense of loyalty that keeps me silent. I ask only that you respect my wishes in this.''

His eyes narrowed and he studied her for a long, considering moment. At last he nodded sharply, as if he understood, or perhaps simply accepted her reasoning. "I see." His voice was gentle. "I believe I should tell you, I consider you the least foolish woman it has ever been my pleasure to know.''

A weight lifted from her heart and relief flooded her. He could respect honor and loyalty without question and, hopefully, would not quiz her again.

She cast a disdainful glance at the bread in her hand. "I find I have little appetite." She flicked the crust into the river. "Perhaps the fish will make better use of this than I. Shall we be off?"

He shrugged, and his bread and cheese followed hers. "I daresay I would have a difficult time stopping you. We might as well finish this quest of yours," he paused, "and lay to rest any ghosts once and for all."

He helped her mount her horse, climbed on his own and they headed off. Lost in her own thoughts, Sabrina barely noticed their continued progress along the river's edge. She wondered at his words. Would this treasure really lay to rest her fears of poverty? Could mere gold close the door to Jack and her past? If so, this quest was worth far more than simple monetary gain, no matter how vast the fortune. It could well save her soul.

A scarce quarter hour into their ride, Sabrina spotted the Temple of Isis.

"Nicholas, look!" She pointed off to a distant spot. Small and square, the building gleamed in the sun. Excitement surged through her and she urged her horse on.

The crumbling structure did indeed stand on a small finger of land thrusting into the Nile. They dismounted before the edifice, and for a moment the centuries fell away. Sabrina could well imagine the ancient worshipers here. She could envision them bearing tribute for their goddess and offering prayers for health and wealth and long life.

"Now that we're finally here," Nicholas said impatiently, pulling her back to the present, "let's get this bloody job done." He untied two spades hanging from his saddle. "Where exactly does the letter say the gold is?"

Sabrina drew out the paper from her beneath her waist and studied it briefly. There was no real need; she knew it by heart. "It says from the temple face that fronts the river, three trees stand to the left." She glanced from the page to the structure and the point indicated. "There, Nicholas." Excitement rang in her voice. Three palms towered majestically over the sand.

She strode toward them, glancing from letter to trees and back. "The gold is buried at the base of the third tree, farthest from the temple, on the side away from the river." She stepped around the palms and halted. Triumph sounded in her voice. "Here! This must be the place."

Nicholas plucked the letter from her hand, perused it briefly and returned it to her. "Very well, then." He tossed one spade on the ground and pushed the other into the sand beneath the third tree. "Let's get to it."

He dug with a methodical efficiency. Within moments his shirt was soaked and he peeled it off. Sabrina had no such respite from the unrelenting heat. Perspiration trickled along her neck and between her breasts. Her shirt clung to her, wet, sticky and uncomfortable. The sun beat down without mercy.

"You don't seem to be making much progress," she said irritably.

He stopped, leaned on the spade handle and glared. Sweat glossed the muscles of his arms and shined the planes of his chest. "No doubt you can do better?"

Better? She was no match for his physical strength, but when it came to determination . . . "No doubt."

"Excellent." He picked up the second spade from the ground and tossed it at her feet. "Please, do me the great honor of joining me in this little soiree."

"I'd be delighted." She snatched up the spade and dug in furiously. It was far more difficult than he made it look, back breaking, hot and hard. She refused to give up, refused to let him see she could not handle this menial chore. Finally she hit on a steady rhythm, one of her spade turns to three of his, but satisfying nonetheless.

They worked silently, the hole growing deeper, the pile of excavated dirt rising higher.

"Sabrina," Nicholas said thoughtfully, "does it strike you that this is all a little too easy?"

"Easy?" She gasped and straightened upright. A painful stiffness spread through the small of her back and her shoulders ached. "I would scarce call this easy."

"That is not what I meant." He wiped his arm across his forehead. "Aside from digging through twenty years of accumulated sand and soil, and keeping in mind we have not yet found your treasure, getting to this point has been suspiciously easy."

"The directions were clear and explicit," she said

sharply. "What on earth is suspicious about that?"

"They weren't merely explicit—they were really quite simple. Think about it," he said earnestly. "If you were going to hide a fortune in gold, would you make it so uncomplicated even a total idiot could ferret it out? Locate the temple, turn left, find three trees and there you have it." He shook his head. "It's almost as if burying it was incidental. A chore, perhaps. And no one really cared if it were found."

"Of course they cared if it were found." Irritation tinged her words. "I've no doubt those who buried it fully planned to come back for it one day. Although they probably did not intend for it to remain here for twenty years."

"Then why haven't they?"

"I do not know, Nicholas." She shot him an angry glare. "And I do not care. Maybe they didn't have the opportunity to return. Maybe they're all dead. It no longer matters!"

"Still," he said slowly, "I wonder—"

"Well, stop your blasted wondering and start digging." She thrust her spade viciously into the soil. "I cannot see that your speculation makes any—"

The spade struck something solid, the thunk reverberating in the hole.

"Nicholas?" she said cautiously.

"Move." The command came terse and clipped. She scrambled out of the knee-deep pit. With a few deft strokes, Nicholas uncovered what looked to be a modest-sized chest.

Excitement and anticipation spiraled within her and stole her breath. She could not pull her gaze away from the aged cask. "Open it, Nicholas."

"Let me get it out of this blasted hole first." He grunted with strain and heaved out the chest. It thudded solidly on the ground. He clambered out of the trench, knelt before the chest and examined it curiously. "It was not nearly as heavy as I expected," he said under his breath.

"Open it, Nicholas!" Her hands clenched with expectation.

"Odd, it doesn't have a lock on it." Nicholas's brow furrowed in concentration. "There is only a simple latch."

"I don't care if it's held together with spit and string,"

she said, her voice rising, "open the bloody thing."

Nicholas nodded shortly and grasped the lid. It did not budge. "It seems to be stuck."

"Nicholas!"

He tried again. Nothing. He breathed deeply and tried once more, putting his full strength into the effort. Time seemed to stop. Sabrina held her breath. Finally, with an anguished creak, the lid opened.

Golden coins winked and glittered in the blinding sunlight.

Sabrina gasped. "Oh, Nicholas, look!" She sank to her knees beside the chest. Her hand shook and she ran her fingers through the shimmering disks, reveling in the cool touch of the precious metal.

Nicholas selected a coin and studied it closely. "These are unlike any coinage I have seen before."

"They are magnificent." She grasped fistfuls of the coins and let them fall from her hands in a brilliant shower, the clink of coin against coin melodic and musical.

"That does not sound quite right," he said under his breath.

She ignored him, mesmerized by the dazzling display before her and the way the coins captured, then reflected the light, as if each were a magical, miniature version of the sun itself. Their look, their sound, their very touch was more than enough to send her spirit soaring with an undreamed sense of triumph and conquest and victory.

"Sabrina?" An odd note sounded in his voice. "You must see this."

She pulled her attention away from the chest. Nicholas held a coin in one hand and his dagger in the other. "Look."

"What is it?" she said sharply. "I do not see anything."

"Look closer." His voice was ominous. She glanced at his face, his expression unreadable.

"Very well." She peered at the coin. "I see nothing amiss."

He held the coin closer. "Do you see what appears to be a scratch?"

A dull, metallic streak scarred the gold. "Yes, what of it?"

"Watch." He took the dagger and scraped across the coin. The gray scratch widened.

Apprehension gripped her. She met his gaze with hers and struggled to say the words. "What does it mean?"

Sympathy shadowed his dark eyes. "I am very much afraid, my love, it means your fortune is virtually worthless."

"No, Nicholas! Surely not!" Panic surged through her. It could not be true. She had come too far to fail now. "How can you say that?"

"I am sorry." He dropped the coin in his hand back onto the shimmering pile. "It appears this is merely gilded. Perhaps even paint. All this," he gestured toward the chest, "was apparently never more than a hoax."

"But why?" she whispered, her gaze transfixed on the coins, their gleam now tarnished, their promise false.

He shrugged. "Who can say? No doubt it was never more than a sham. A ruse devised to fool Napoleon's supporters and his troops into believing he had solid backing in France." He stood and towered over her. "Perhaps hiding this feigned fortune was all part of the plan. Or it's possible the officers who buried it believed the gold was real and only learned later of its fraudulent nature. That may well be why they never returned. I doubt if we shall ever know."

Sabrina remained kneeling by the open chest. For so very long this treasure had meant so very much. Her daughter's dowry. Her own financial survival. Now, married to Nicholas of course, her material need for it no longer existed. But it had come to represent so much more than mere money. Her quest was at an end and it was worthless.

Slowly, she got to her feet and absently slid the now worthless letter beneath her laces. "Put it back, Nicholas," she said quietly. "Bury it again, if you would."

He groaned. "Bury it? Bloody hell, Sabrina, why can we not simply leave—" Her gaze caught his and he quieted abruptly. She refused to let her chaotic emotions show; instead she fell back on a decade of concealment and adopted the serene face she was accustomed to showing to the world.

Nicholas stared for a long, considering moment. "Very well."

"And do hurry." Her voice, pleasant and calm, belied the disappointment, anger and confusion within her. "I suspect the others may be wondering whatever is keeping us."

"Sabrina, I . . ." He appeared almost helpless, as if he did not quite know what to do. Dimly, in the back of her mind, she appreciated and even welcomed his concern. But she had no wish for comfort yet. She had dealt with worse disasters than this in her lifetime alone, and she preferred to deal with this as well by herself. She wondered if she knew how to do otherwise.

Nicholas closed the chest, tossed it in the hole and quickly covered it with soil and sand. She stared unseeing at his rapid efforts. A heavy silence hung between them.

The journey back to camp was silent as well. Nicholas made valiant attempts at conversation, which she politely rebuffed. She was in no mood for idle chatter, her mind awash with the implications of what she saw as failure, the shattering of a dream.

The long ride back was a blessing. The hours on horseback provided time for reflection, contemplation and thought. It might have been Nicholas's many covert, considering glances. It might have been her own resilience, or her innate ability to adapt, but by the time they arrived back in camp she had reached, if not a sense of peace, then at least acceptance.

Sabrina had not found her gold, her independence, her freedom. But she had found Nicholas, and a love she neither expected nor imagined. And perhaps that was enough.

The sun had long since set when they rode into camp. It appeared the members of their party had already retired for the night. Still, Sabrina's silence continued, and Nicholas's worry increased.

He did not care for this polished act of hers, this facade of placid indifference. He had come to know, and to love, the fiery, spirited creature who, no doubt, considered herself more than a match for any man. The eminently proper woman now by his side was not to his liking at all. He had always been a man who feared little, but her demeanor shivered his spine and chilled his heart.

Nicholas slid off his horse and helped her dismount. His hands lingered at her waist. "Sabrina, we must talk about this."

She refused to meet his gaze. "I see little need. It is over and done with, and I have no wish to discuss it further."

"Sabrina," he said, his voice commanding, sharpened by concern. He cupped her chin in his hand and tilted her head up, forcing her gaze to meet his. Her emerald eyes revealed little. "I do not know why this gold was so important to you—I only know that it was. I am truly sorry it proved worthless. But," his tone softened, "I do not believe this quest has been in vain. I found a treasure far more valuable than mere gold. I found you."

For a long moment he gazed at her, hoping beyond hope to reach through the cool barrier she'd erected around herself to the real woman hidden inside. Then, as if something broke within her, her eyes darkened. Her expression crumpled and she heaved a heartfelt sigh. "Bloody hell, Nicholas. It is just so damned unfair."

He grinned at the obscenities. Relief flooded him, and he pulled her into his arms. "I know, my love. I have never accepted defeat easily.

Her voice was muffled against his chest. "And I do not accept defeat at all."

He chuckled softly at her outspoken words.

"And I do not accept defeat at all."

The laughter froze in his throat.

"And I, my lord—" Her breath, fragrant with an intoxicating promise, caressed his face. *"—do not accept defeat at all."*

Chapter Twenty

Bits and pieces of information, fragments of memory crashed through his mind, at once forming into a picture so clear, he was a fool not to have seen it before now. Madison . . . his sister . . . Lady B—

"Bree!" His voice came hoarse with shock, her name a gasp of anger.

She pulled away, a questioning frown on her lips. "What on earth is the matter?"

"It was you! It was you all along!" His voice hardened with anguish and fury and disdain.

"What do you mean, it was . . ." Her eyes widened with realization. She shook her head vehemently. "Nicholas, I—"

"You what?" His words rang sharp and cold. "You would dare to tell me you are not the woman I searched for for a decade? The infamous Lady B? The treasonous smuggler who left me for dead on a blasted beach ten long years ago?"

"That is ridiculous, Nicholas," she said quickly. "I never wanted you dead."

"A point well taken." His voice dripped with scorn. "I suppose that should provide some comfort. Still, I have been something of an idiot not to have realized who you are before now. It was all so very obvious." He narrowed his eyes, his anger barely under control. "I wonder, have you played me for a fool since we first met? Was our children's betrothal, our hasty marriage, all part of a greater plan?"

"Of course not." She gazed up at him, her expression pleading, her eyes vulnerable. "I did not know who you were until recently."

He laughed, a short, harsh sound. "Really, my dear? And when did this great revelation strike you?"

"When we first made love, on the ship." Her voice came little more than a whisper, the look on her face enough to break his heart. He hardened his feelings toward her, his own sense of betrayal too strong, too demanding, too overwhelming.

He gripped her wrist and yanked her roughly to him. "Why should I believe you? You have lived ten years acting the part of a sedate, proper lady of the ton. I congratulate you. Your skills rival the best I have seen on the London stage." He lowered his face to within inches of hers. "How much was an act, Sabrina? How much of this was a performance?" He pulled her tight against him, grasped her hair in his free hand and brought his lips to hers in a kiss hard and savage, wanting her to know the pain, the anguish that surged through his veins and filled his heart.

He drew back abruptly and she gasped, her hair disheveled, her lips reddened. Triumph shot through him at the shock and hurt in her eyes, and he knew a flash of regret and shame. He shoved it aside viciously. "Do you recall the first time we kissed?"

She nodded mutely.

"I wondered then what kind of woman kissed so boldly. Tell me, Sabrina, when you said you had not lain with a man for thirteen years," his voice lowered, his tone cruel and exacting, "was that an act as well?"

"I have never lied to you about us, Nicholas." Her voice rang quiet, intense and sincere.

"Never?" He laughed bitterly. "Forgive me for not accepting your declaration with wholehearted certainty. One does tend to wonder how a woman who could so easily deceive her own country could hesitate to lie, to betray, her husband. The man she claims to love. For such a woman it would be so very tempting, I should think, to use him for her own purposes. To satisfy her own—" he raked his gaze contemptuously over her, "—desires." He glared with disdain. "Or was it for my wealth?"

She wrenched out of his grasp with a quick, unexpected jerk and slapped her palm across his face in a stinging retort that caught him by surprise. The echo of her blow seemed to reverberate in the night air. The pain in her eyes now tempered with fury. "Again, I have never lied to you about us."

He rubbed his hand ruefully against the smart sting on his cheek. "That is scant solace for my wretched soul." She winced at the scorn in his voice. "Although it is pleasant to hope that at least one thing between us was not a fabrication."

She stood before him, fists clenched at her side. "What do you intend to do now?"

What did he intend to do? For so many years he had considered what he would do if he ever caught the elusive Lady B. There was no one in the world who cared any longer about her capture. No one but him. He would be fully justified in hauling her back to England and throwing her in Newgate. He would be fully justified in exposing her publicly, shattering her prim-and-proper image with society. He would be fully justified in any number of options.

"I do not know," he said coldly.

She squared her shoulders and drew a deep breath. "Will you at least listen to my explanation?"

"What do you wish to explain?" He spat the words. "The past? Or the present?"

She stared at him with eyes wide with grief. Then, as if a door closed, a shadow crossed her face. A face now composed and controlled and expressionless. The face of the serene Lady Sabrina. "Perhaps . . ." her voice was cool, unemotional, ". . . it no longer matters."

She'd fallen back on a habit of deception, on years of hiding her true feelings, on a disguise perfected through much of her lifetime. The realization triggered another surge of anger, swamping any temptation toward sentiment and compassion. He hardened his gaze and his voice. "Perhaps."

She nodded sharply. "I shall be in my tent when you have decided what steps you wish to take now." She turned away.

"Sabrina." His words cracked in the night and she stopped. He struggled to keep his agony in check, to match her calm demeanor with his own. Still, he could not fully keep the torment from his voice, fraught with anguish and disbelief. "You spoke to me of honor."

She did not turn toward him and her voice seemed to float in the desert air like a chill breeze. "And you, my lord, spoke to me of love." She walked off and disappeared in the dark.

A few steps more and she would be out of his sight, hidden by the black cloak of the night. A few steps more and she could allow herself to react to his discovery and his disdain. A few steps more and she could crumple into a heap of sobbing misery. If she could but continue a few steps more.

She reached the shelter of her tent and stumbled inside.

"Sabrina?" Wynne's sleep-filled voice greeted her. "We tried to stay awake until you returned. Did you find the gold?"

The gold. She had all but forgotten about it. She sighed deeply. "It was a hoax, Wynne. It was all a horrible joke."

"But what? How?"

"Go back to sleep, Wynne," Sabrina said wearily. "I shall tell you everything in the morning."

"Very well." Wynne yawned, her voice drifting off. "Gold or no gold, I still expect it was quite a marvelous adventure."

Sabrina couldn't contain a quiet, bitter laugh. It was indeed an adventure, and very likely her last. Or was it merely the final moments of an adventure that had begun long ago?

What would Nicholas do now? His revelation obviously triggered feelings of betrayal and anger. No doubt the man assumed she had used him for her own purposes. But he had claimed to love her. Nicholas's love. That was indeed a laugh. She had suspected from the start that this rake could never know love. Now that the moment of truth had come, her worst fears were confirmed.

How fitting that Nicholas thought he was the fool in all of this, while her foolishness was far greater. She had truly believed he had finally come to love her. Or perhaps she had simply wanted to believe so badly that she had ignored the reality of his nature.

She sank down amid her bedclothes and cradled her head in her hands. She wanted nothing more than to give in to the pain surging within her. She wished to weep uncontrollably until she could no longer see or feel or hurt. There was no question now that she had lost him, had no doubt never really had him. What would he do now? Her fate, her very life, lay in his hands.

Abruptly, her anguish faded, to be replaced by a burgeoning panic. She would not go to prison. Would not spend the rest of her days in a dank, grim cell, or worse, face transportation. Not for events that had taken place a decade ago. Even when Jack had died and left her with nothing she had not experienced panic so intense, so overwhelming, all rational thought flew in the face of it.

She had to get out. Now. To run as fast and as far as possible. She willed herself to remain calm, to attempt to act with composure. Escape was impossible otherwise.

Quickly and quietly, she lurched to her feet. Wynne's still form told her the woman was already fast asleep. Sabrina stumbled toward her portmanteau and blindly pawed through its contents, finding the money from her jewels by touch alone. Her funds were still intact; Nicholas had paid for virtually all her expenses. She closed the case regretfully. It had to be left behind; baggage would only hinder her progress. Silently, she moved to open the flaps of the tent, glancing back once at Belinda's huddled form. How could she leave her child without some explanation?

She crept to where Wynne lay and cast about for her journal and the stub of a pencil Sabrina knew Wynne kept tucked inside the book. She found it easily but hesitated at ripping out a page of her sister-in-law's precious diary. Instead, she pulled the rumpled letter from her breeches and nearly laughed aloud at the irony of using the ill-fated missive for her message. With the light of the desert moon for illumination, she quickly scribbled a brief note. Her eyes blurred with panic and pain and tears.

She strode the few steps to her daughter's side and knelt next to her. Sabrina brushed the hair away from the sleeping girl's forehead and kissed her lightly, much as she had done when Belinda was a mere child. She set the note beside her and stood gazing down for just a moment. Belinda would never understand. Sabrina was not sure she completely understood herself. All she knew was that the need to flee was overpowering and could not be denied.

She crept from the tent and glanced toward Nicholas's shelter. A light glowed inside and she heard the low murmur of male voices. No doubt he was now confronting Matt. Fear for her friend flickered through her and she resolutely pushed it aside. Matt had nothing to fear from Nicholas. He was not English, and Nicholas had no power over him. Matt could take care of himself.

The horses were hobbled on the farthest side of the encampment from Nicholas's tent. Stealthily, she made her way to them, selected one and quietly led the beast away. She did not know where she would go from here, or what Nicholas would do when he found his quarry had escaped him once again. But she had no doubt of one thing.

She too could take care of herself. She always had.

Nicholas strode into his tent, his anger a palpable, throbbing haze about him. He noted the lone lantern still burning and his son's sleeping figure. Madison did not appear to be present. Nicholas clenched his teeth. If the American was with his sister, he would have to kill him. At this moment the thought of slicing Madison's throat struck a satisfying chord of anticipation.

"I heard you and Bree ride up." Matt strolled through the silken entry. "Where's the gold?"

"Where have you been?" Nicholas cracked the words.

Matt's fair brows drew together in a frown of annoyance. "Not that it's any of your business, but I've been sitting out by the river. Everyone else went to bed. I couldn't sleep until you and Bree came back. So, where's the gold?"

"There was no bloody gold."

"No gold?" Matt's frown deepened. "I'd wager Bree isn't too happy about that."

"You know her so well," Nicholas said evenly.

"I've known her for a long time." Matt nodded. "I really do think of her as a sister."

Nicholas narrowed his gaze. "No doubt that's why you named your ship for her."

Matt's eyes widened slightly. Silence stretched for a long moment between them. "You know, don't you?"

"I do." Nicholas's words rang hard as steel.

Matt crossed his arms insolently. "What do you plan to do about it?"

"What I should do is hang you from the nearest tree." Nicholas fought to contain his simmering fury.

Matt snorted. "That's a laugh. You and I both know you have no authority here." He studied Nicholas thoughtfully. His voice softened. "What do you plan to do about Bree?"

Nicholas tunneled his fingers through his hair and rubbed the back of his neck. Outrage mingled with despair. "I do not know."

"You don't know?" Matt stared incredulously. "That's hard to swallow. Bree tells me you've spent all these years dwelling on your failure to catch her. I can't believe you haven't considered what you'd do if that glorious day ever arrived."

"I have considered it," Nicholas snapped. "I have thought of it often this past decade. But everything has changed." His tone grew bitter. "I did not expect to find that Lady B was my wife. I have been a fool."

295

"Have you?" Matt asked quietly. "Why?"

Nicholas cast him a contemptuous glance. "It's obvious, Madison. I have searched for this woman for ten years. And when I have her right under my nose, not only do I not recognize her but I end up wedded to her as well. My honor, my duty, my responsibility to my country demand that I finish what was started a decade ago. That I complete a mission that was a miserable failure. That I turn her in."

"And why don't you?" Matt tossed off the question with a casual air. "From what you're saying it seems you've already made your decision."

"Bloody hell, Madison!" Anger exploded in his words. "It's a decision no man should have to make. I love her. I cannot envision life without her. But I must choose between what I've always believed in and this stubborn, clever, enchanting creature who has captured my heart." He laughed sardonically. "I have to choose between my honor and my soul."

Matt studied him curiously. "Did she tell you why she did it?"

"No," Nicholas said sharply. "I did not wish to hear her explanation."

"You should. It might make a difference."

"Very well," contempt underlined his words, "tell me why a lady, a marchioness no less, smuggles goods, betraying her own country in the process."

Matt's gaze hardened. "I doubt that she ever considered it a betrayal of her country. Times were extremely difficult, and Bree was not alone in choosing this particular pursuit—"

Nicholas snorted. "As I well know."

Matt ignored the interruption. "She molded a group of fishermen and farmers, desperate men in those days, into an efficient operation." He chuckled. "I'm still not exactly sure how she did it, but, even among my own men, I've rarely seen the kind of loyalty and fierce allegiance they accorded her."

"I remember," Nicholas murmured.

"At any rate, they adored her and worked hard both for her and with her. She was fair with them and honest—"

"Honest?" Sarcasm dripped off the word.

Matt cast him a cutting glance. "Honest. They did well, and when you came along, far too close for comfort, they closed down and went on with their lives, substantially better off than before."

"That's all well and good, Madison, but you've still failed to tell me why. Why did she do it?"

Matt hesitated, as if considering his words. He blew a long breath through his lips, apparently coming to some sort of decision. "I feel as if I'm betraying a confidence. Telling you things Bree has never wanted anyone to know."

"I am her husband," Nicholas said through clenched teeth. "Do I not have a right to know?"

Matt shrugged. "Probably. But Bree should be telling you this, not me—"

"Blast it, Madison," Nicholas said sharply, "spit it out. Tell me what you have to say."

"All right." Matt paused, as if choosing his words with care. "How much do you know about her first husband?"

"About Stanford?" The question took him by surprise. Matt nodded. "What everyone knows, I suppose. He was a well-known rake when he married her, with a reputation for wild living and gambling. Together, they cut quite a scandalous path through society."

"Did you know he was penniless when he died?"

The query struck Nicholas like a physical blow. "No, I did not."

"It's true." Matt's gaze burned with intensity. "He left her with nothing but a small child and a lot of very large debts. She never told anyone but me and Simon and one of the men who worked with her." He shook his head. "I never did understand why she was so determined not to let the rest of the world know what a bastard her husband really was. Bree just said she owed him a measure of loyalty even in death."

"I see," Nicholas said slowly, so much of Sabrina's behavior abruptly clear to him. "But what of her family?"

"She had little family—an elderly great-aunt who apparently had enough money for her own household and not much else.''

''Still,'' Nicholas said stoutly, ''there are other ways to earn one's keep.''

''Are there, Wyldewood?'' A sarcastic smile quirked Matt's lips. ''What? Think about it. She could become a governess. Take care of someone else's children until the life and the spirit was wrung out of her. Or let's see . . . she could marry for money—''

''She did,'' Nicholas said under his breath. Matt threw him a cutting glance, and a twinge of shame flickered through him at his comment.

''Or . . .'' Matt's gaze narrowed, his voice cool, controlled, without inflection, ''she could have let a man take care of her, provide for her and her daughter. She could have become someone's well-kept mistress, doxy, whore—''

''That's enough, Madison!'' Rage colored Nicholas's words, and he clenched his fists to keep from striking the insulting American.

Matt stared silently, his expression considering, challenging. ''The truth can be quite painful, can't it? What would you have had her do?''

''I do not know.''

''You don't seem to know much of anything tonight, do you?'' Matt's question went unanswered. ''Do you know why this gold was so important to her?''

''She refused to tell me.''

''No surprise there. She wanted it for a dowry, for Belinda.'' Nicholas opened his mouth, but Matt waved his words aside. ''I know she didn't need it now that she was married to you. She knew that as well. But it was important to her to provide for her daughter, to pay her own way.'' He shrugged. ''You and I probably can't understand why a woman would be so fiercely determined to have her own resources. But then, you and I have never been abandoned with nothing left and no one to turn to.

''I'll tell you something else, Wyldewood: Bree is an extraordinary woman. Her brains match her beauty. She has no lack of courage and strength and tenacity. I doubt that any man deserves such a prize.'' He laughed shortly. ''Especially not you.''

Nicholas's mind spun with the revelation of Matt's words. So much of Sabrina's nature, her actions, made sense now. All his questions were answered. Save one.

''Were you and she lovers, Madison?'' he said quietly.

''Never.'' Matt heaved a sigh of regret. ''Not that I didn't try, mind you. But the affection we shared was far too much like family for anything more to develop. And I'm convinced, while many men pursued her in London, her amorous activities never went beyond an occasional embrace, a stolen kiss. It seems only one man ever had a lasting effect on her. Apparently, the thought of him haunted her for years.'' Matt pinned him with a gaze hard and intense. ''She kissed him in a cave and never even saw his face.''

Nicholas's heart stilled. A knot settled in his gut. Matt's words throbbed through his head. Silently, he turned toward the tent opening. He needed to be alone, to think, to make a decision that, for good or ill, would impact the rest of his days.

Matt grabbed his arm. His stern gaze locked with Nicholas's. ''Be careful, Wyldewood; be very careful. She was terrified of what would happen when you learned of her past. Bree truly loves you. I suspect she always has. If you lose her,'' he shook his head, his manner almost pitying, ''then you are indeed a fool.''

Nicholas shook off Matt's hand and stalked out of the tent toward the river. Sand whispered across the desert floor. Horses nickered in the distance. The muted sounds of the night registered dimly in a distant corner of his mind, his head too full of Sabrina, of the past and the future, to pay more than a glancing thought.

He sank down upon an outcropping of rock at the river's edge and gazed at the slow-moving Nile. The moon's reflection ebbed and swelled in a rhythmic heartbeat, torpid, measured . . . mesmerizing. The white-gold image shimmered and winked, and for a moment he let his mind drift with the water . . . peaceful and serene.

Serene. That was how he had thought of her when they

met. As placid as the Nile and just as boring. An insistent memory tugged at the back of his mind. Hadn't she seemed anything but boring in their first moments together? Wasn't there right at the beginning a spark between them? A beckoning of desire? An odd sense of destiny? Of fate? Of recognition?

He thought back to the days of his ill-fated mission. How she and her men had let him get so close but no more. He remembered his shock at learning that his adversary was a woman and his grudging admiration at her skill and intelligence. His thoughts lingered on the inexplicable desire that grew within him, even as he searched for her until the fateful night when she kissed him and disappeared from his life.

Until now.

Were her crimes really that heinous?

A traitorous voice whispered in his mind. He had always believed so. But he had never before been able to place a face and a form to the image of his opponent. Never before had he stopped to consider the reasons for her behavior, the desperation that could drive even an honorable person to acts that, although illegal, could under certain circumstances be considered acceptable, even heroic. He had never given a thought to the strength and courage it must take for anyone, let alone a woman, to refuse to bow to circumstance and instead take control of her life.

Until now.

He shook his head in the hope of clearing the confusion of his thoughts. For so long he had held to his frustration and anger at his failure to capture her. Through the years his fury remained fresh, his determination unwavering, his goal clear.

Until now.

He stared blindly at the river, examining the past weeks spent in her company. He recounted every word, every gesture, every touch. Aside from her prevarication as to the exact nature of her business dealings with Madison ten years ago, he realized she had never lied to him. Not about them.

Still, he argued, what of honor? Did not his own sense of honor insist—no, demand—that he turn her in?

But was it honor or was it pride?

He bolted upright at the startling idea. Did honor compel him to atone for his failure, or was it simply foolish pride? His mission was a botched mess in his eyes alone. A failure because he was outsmarted by a mere woman. At the time his perceived inadequacy stung and threatened his self-respect. But here and now, did it still matter? Was pride so very important?

Through the endless night Nicholas sat beside the ancient waterway until the sun glowed on the horizon. With dawn he rose to his feet, stiff muscles aching in protest. He ignored the discomfort. He had not slept, and did not feel the need for rest through the lonely hours, his mind too busy wrestling with his own unresolved conflicts.

Now, at last, renewed spirit surged in his soul. The warmth of the sun washed over him, the new day bringing a sense of peace and resolve. It was as if a weight lifted from his shoulders and, with it, years of anger and disappointment.

There was no decision to be made; he had made his choice when he admitted to himself, and finally to her, that he loved her. The past was over and done with. He could face the future with Sabrina by his side.

He chuckled and turned toward the camp. Who would have believed that he would spend the rest of his life with the very woman who had bested him so long ago? A woman who, he had to acknowledge, was his equal in so many things and, in at least one instance, more than his match. It was an odd way to think of a woman. Any woman. His woman.

He headed toward her tent. He would take her in his arms and tell her that the past was behind them. There would be no recriminations. He would be magnanimous yet gentle. Firm but kind. He would graciously forgive her.

But would she forgive him?

The unbidden thought struck him in midstride, and his step faltered. His mind raced over what he had said to her. Words fired by anger, spouted in unthinking haste. What accusations had he thrown at her in his blind need to hurt her as much as he was hurt? Unease settled in the pit of his stomach. Surely she would understand that his charges came from the shock of discovery, nothing more. He picked up his pace.

A cry rang from Sabrina's tent and Wynne burst into the clearing, a weeping Belinda two steps behind.

"Nicholas!" Wynne raced to him. "She's gone, Nicholas. She's left."

"Whose gone?" Matt asked, instantly at his side. Erick joined Belinda.

Wynne gasped for breath, her eyes wide with dismay. "Sabrina. She's gone."

Fear squeezed his heart and he grasped Wynne's shoulders. "What do you mean, she's gone? Where did she go?"

"I do not know." Wynne shook her head. "When we awoke Belinda found this." She waved the letter under his nose. Matt snatched the note from her hand. "On the back."

Matt scanned the page and turned an accusing gaze on Nicholas. "She's gone, all right. This says she's doing what she feels she must. It says—" his tone hardened—"she believes she has no choice. She doesn't explain why. It also turns over ownership of her town house to Belinda, as a dowry."

He glanced at the page again. "She sends Belinda her love and tells her not to worry." Belinda broke into fresh sobs. Matt crumpled the note in his hand.

Shock rooted Nicholas to the spot. His chest tightened and he could not seem to breathe. "Does . . . does she mention me?"

"No." The single word was an indictment.

Panic surged within him. He would not let her go. He could not let her go. "We have to find her. Erick, get the horses. Madison—"

"Hold on, Wyldewood." Matt grabbed his arm. "Let her be."

Nicholas stared in disbelief. "Are you insane? This is not a country for a woman alone."

"I said let her be." The American's grasp was firm, his

voice commanding. "Bree can take care of herself."

Nicholas wrenched out of his hold. "That's ridiculous. Not even Sabrina can handle this. I cannot—" His eyes narrowed in sudden suspicion. "If you know where she's headed, where I can find her, you'd bloody well better tell me."

Matt hesitated.

"Now," Nicholas grabbed the front of Matt's shirt. "Or so help me, I will kill you where you stand."

Wynne gasped. "Nicholas!"

His gaze locked with Matt's. "Make no mistake, Madison, this is not an idle threat." For a moment neither man moved, neither backed down, neither gave an inch.

Matt expelled a long, pent-up breath. "I don't know where in the hell she went." Nicholas released his shirt and stepped back, running a weary hand through his hair. "But look, Wyldewood, she's not stupid. She's bound to head back to the coast, where she can find a ship."

"Let's go then." Nicholas turned to leave, but once more Matt barred his way.

"I'd wager she left hours ago. There is no possible way to find her out here. Our best bet is to turn back toward Alexandria. We might well find her on the way. Or we could find her in the city." Matt pinned him with a straightforward gaze. "There's nothing you can do here."

"Very well," Nicholas said reluctantly. "As much as I hate to admit it, you are no doubt right."

Matt nodded sharply. "Good. We'll have the camp packed up and be off as soon as possible."

Nicholas clenched his fists and struggled to stay calm, to control unfamiliar emotions that threatened to tear him apart. Never had anguish and fear and sheer panic faced him like this. He could not lose her. He would not lose her. Not again.

Matt stared at him with something akin to compassion or sympathy but said nothing. They both cared for the same woman, each in his own way. There was little left to say.

"I will find her, Madison." Nicholas pulled his gaze from

303

Matt's and stared out over the desert, his voice quiet and intense.

"I found her once and I shall find her again. If it takes another ten years, if it takes the rest of my days, I vow, I will find her."

Chapter Twenty-one

Sabrina stood on the cliff and stared unseeing at the angry sea battling the rocky coast far below. The brisk wind blew her fair hair away from her face, occasionally whipping an errant strand across her eyes. Absently, she brushed it aside. She drew a deep breath and reveled in the fresh, sharp salt air. Crisp and clear and invigorating, it replenished her spirit. A spirit deeply in need of nourishment.

It had been four months since her escape from Egypt. Even now the panic that had spurred her flight still rose like bile just below the surface of her every thought, her every move. A panic that had haunted her days and threatened her nights.

And when, too exhausted to fight on, she slept, dreaming of loss, of pain, of him. Dreamt of the pleasure of Nicholas's touch, the caress of his gaze and the laughing timbre of his voice. A voice she vowed, and feared, she would not hear again.

It had been remarkably easy to flee. Within a few hours after she left camp, she had crossed paths with a party of English tourists. They had accepted her somewhat garbled fabrication of how she happened to be wandering around Egypt alone in men's garments with few questions and quite a lot of sympathy. Together, they traveled to Cairo and on to Alexandria.

Her luck held. She managed to avoid Matt's ship and crew and find a seaworthy craft preparing to sail for England that very day. A portion of the money from her jewels bought her passage and paid her expenses until she could reach her haven, the tiny coastal village she'd always considered home.

Once the people here had been her playmates. Later they worked side by side with her in the smuggling operation that had put food on their tables and money in their pockets and hers. And now they offered her a sanctuary, a refuge, a safe harbor from the tortured seas her life had become.

She'd been too afraid to travel to London, too afraid to stop at her own home and speak to her butler and longtime friend. But she did send word to Wills, to assure him of her safe return and to warn him about Nicholas.

Sabrina tried not to dwell on her husband. Tried not to wonder what he'd done when he found her gone. Tried not to speculate on what he'd decided to do now that he'd found his nemesis and the answers to decade-old questions. Tried not to hope.

It wasn't so much the fear of what he would do with knowledge of her past that worried her now in the sane moments of hindsight. No doubt even the most zealous government would have little interest in a long-forgotten smuggling case. Still, the threat remained. But the possibility of his distaste for her actions, his disgust, chilled her bones. She was neither proud nor ashamed of those long-ago days and could not live with a man she had somehow, even inadvertently, disappointed. No matter how much she loved him.

But as much as she tried to cast him from her mind, his presence lingered with her always. She closed her eyes against thoughts of him. Sometimes she could almost sense him beside her. She could almost breathe the spice of his scent. She could almost hear his voice. . . .

"Sabrina."

Her name drifted on the wind. Her heart stilled.

"Bree?"

She was not mistaken. She could never be mistaken. It was his voice. She did not turn to face him and was not sure if she could.

"How did you find me?" she asked quietly, struggling to control the urge to throw herself in his arms, the irrational desire to beg his forgiveness.

"I managed to get it out of Wills." Nicholas chuckled. "It was not easy. The man is devoted to you."

"You did not hurt him, I hope."

"No. However, there was some question as to who might hurt whom." His voice drew nearer.

Sabrina clenched her hands by her side. She feared to ask the questions uppermost in her mind. She groped for words to keep him at bay, to divert him from his purpose. A purpose that would surely spell her doom or break her heart.

"How is Belinda?" she asked abruptly.

"Belinda and Erick married in Italy and left the ship to travel slowly on a wedding journey back to England. My poor son could take no more of ocean voyages."

"That's lovely," she said softly, choking back tears. She had missed her daughter's wedding, but at least her child was safe and happy. "And what of Wynne and Matt?"

"When last I saw them they were sailing to America. Matt insisting on a wedding," she could hear the grin in his voice, "Wynne refusing on the grounds that her days of adventure were not yet over."

"I see." Silence stretched between them. A knot formed in her throat. "Why are you here?"

"I have come for my wife." His voice sounded beside her ear, and she jumped with the closeness of it. Still, she feared to face him.

"Why?" she asked, the question little more than a heart-felt sigh.

"Why?" Anger underscored his words. He grabbed her shoulders and spun her around to face him. His black eyes flashed, his dark brows drew together and his lips compressed in an unyielding line. "How can you ask me that? I have been beside myself with fear for your safety. Every day a torture of searching to no avail. I did not know whether you were alive or dead. If you'd been lost or slaughtered in the desert."

He tightened his hands on her shoulders. "Imagine my relief when I learned you had sailed safely from Egypt. I tried to come after you. But that bloody American, Madison, came up with one delay after another to slow me down. We must have stopped in every blasted port between Alexandria and London on one pretext or another. Even when I finally arrived back in England I could get no cooperation. At first your steadfast Wills refused to even admit he had heard from you."

"You have not yet answered my question." She stared into his stormy eyes. "Why?"

"Bloody hell, Sabrina." Nicholas groaned. "This is why." He pulled her to him roughly. His lips crushed hers with a desperation she recognized and shared.

His tongue invaded her mouth, his breath fused with hers, his desire conquering her resistance. Sheer joy trembled through her and she melted against him. Her heart thundered in her chest and life soared within her.

For a moment she could believe the false promise of his touch. But only for a moment.

"No!" Her cry rent the air. She pushed hard against him and stumbled away from the cliff's edge. Once again flight from him beckoned and, for a moment, tempted. But she would not run this time. She stopped short and whirled to face him.

"I will not go to some damnable prison, Nicholas, just to satisfy your sense of honor. And I will not allow anyone to ship me off to some God-forsaken wilderness for an indiscretion committed a lifetime ago."

"Indiscretion?" He stared incredulously. "You smuggled goods. You consorted with men the Crown considered traitors. Consorted—hell, you led them. It was hardly an indiscretion."

"Nonetheless," her voice rose in fear and anger, "I will not let you turn me in."

"Then we are in agreement." The rising timbre of his voice matched hers. "I do not plan to turn you in."

"Oh?" Sarcasm rang in her words. "How do you expect me to believe that? You have done nothing but dwell on how I beat you for ten long, bloody years. Why on earth would you swerve from your dedicated mission of vengeance now?"

"Because," his voice roared across the cliffs, "you're dead. I killed you off."

"What?" Confusion and annoyance swept through her. "I am bloody well not dead."

"No, you're too damned stubborn and clever and infuriating to be dead." His eyes smoldered, dark and stormy. "But she's dead."

The man made absolutely no sense. "Who's she?"

"Lady B!"

She gasped. "But that is me."

"Not anymore." Nicholas grabbed her and pulled her into his arms. "I made a full report." He smiled wickedly. "With a few minor changes."

"What do you mean?" A small flicker of hope flamed in her heart.

"I mean," he leaned forward and kissed the tip of her nose, "I informed my former superiors that, while in Egypt with my wife, I learned that the infamous Lady B had immigrated to that parched land and succumbed to desert fever."

"Desert fever? Very clever." Thoughts and questions and implications crowded her mind. "I do hope it wasn't too painful?"

"She scarcely felt a thing, my love." He winked. "While it is a fatal disease, it is also a mere figment of my imagination. I made it up."

"Nicholas." She laughed in spite of herself, then sobered and pulled away. "I appreciate what you've done. Still, you do not want me. You want that calm, serene Lady Sabrina you selected for a wife. You want a proper, perfect wife."

She shrugged. "I fear I can never be what you want."

"I do not want a perfect wife. I want you."

Surely he didn't mean that the way it sounded? "Thank you, I think."

He rolled his eyes heavenward and sighed. "Sabrina, for a woman who is obviously far too intelligent for her own good you cannot seem to see what is directly in front of your charming little nose. I love you."

"Hah." She crossed her arms over her chest. "And how many times have you said that to unsuspecting women? Dozens? Hundreds?"

"Perhaps thousands." A seductive glint sparked in his eyes. "But I never meant it before you."

"No doubt," she said, her tone skeptical.

"Bree." He sighed and pulled her back into his arms. "Listen to me. I followed you from the ends of the earth because I love you. I lied to my government because I love you. I do not care if you are the most improper, imperfect wife in the civilized world, I love you."

She gazed at him for a long, considering moment. How could she believe him? How could she not? She stared into his deep, ebony eyes and at once knew that, for good or ill, she was his.

Elation surged through her. "Well," she said breathlessly, throwing her arms around him, "I love you too."

He bent to kiss her but stopped short. "Just a moment," he said abruptly and released her. "I nearly forgot something." He drew a note from his waistcoat and handed it to her. "Wills asked me to deliver this. He said it was important."

Sabrina unfolded the message, skimmed the contents and smiled slowly. Before she'd left for Egypt she'd sent some of the funds from her jewels to her idiot solicitor, with instructions to invest in a highly speculative scheme to recover treasure from a sunken Spanish galleon in the West Indies. Wills wrote that the impulsive gamble had paid off quite nicely, and she was financially solvent once again.

"Is it important?" Nicholas quirked a questioning brow.

She stared at him for a moment, then glanced at the letter

in her hand. Her need for money had started all this in the first place. Now she had all she could ever want. Her gaze traveled back to Nicholas. And so much more.

"No." She crushed the letter in her hand and allowed the wind to whisk it away. "It was not important at all."

"In that case," he wrapped her in his embrace once again, his words rough with desire, "I suggest we find somewhere a bit more private and oh, say," he grinned in an altogether wicked way that sent delicious shivers of anticipation coursing through her veins, "tell a few jokes."

"Jokes?" At once she grasped his meaning, and her breath caught in her throat. "I could certainly use a good laugh right now."

His lips descended on hers and swept away any vestige of doubt and uncertainty. And in the last instant before she lost herself in the magic of his touch she marveled at the irony and the miracle that in the eyes of this one proper lord, this arrogant rake, she was indeed the perfect wife.

Lord of The Keep

Ann Lawrence

He has but to raise a brow and all accede to his wishes; Gilles d'Argent alone rules Hawkwatch Castle. The formidable baron considers love to be a jongleur's game—till he meets the beguiling Emma. With hair spun of gold and eyes filled with intelligence, she binds him to her. Her innocence stolen away in the blush of youth, Emma Aethelwin no longer believes in love. Reconciled to her life as a penniless weaver, she little expects to snare the attention of Gilles d'Argent. At first Emma denies the tenderness of the warrior's words and the passion he stirs within her. But as desire weaves a tangible web around them, the resulting pattern tells a tale of love, and she dares to dream that she can be the lady of his heart as he is the master of hers.

___52351-5 $5.99 US/$6.99 CAN

THE HOLDING

CLAUDIA DAIN

It is done. She is his wife. Wife of a knight so silent and stealthy, they call him "The Fog." Everything Lady Cathryn of Greneforde owns—castle, lands and people—is now safe in his hands. But there is one barrier yet to be breached. . . . There is a secret at Greneforde Castle, a secret embodied in its seemingly obedient mistress and silent servants. Betrayal, William fears, awaits him on his wedding night. But he has vowed to take possession of the holding his king has granted him. To do so he must know his wife completely, take her in the most elemental and intimate holding of all.

__4858-2 $5.50 US/$6.50 CAN

BLACKHEART
TAMARA LEIGH

Desperate to put an end to the humiliating rumors surrounding his lack of an heir, Lord Bernart Kinthorpe orders his virgin wife to the bed of his sworn enemy, Lord Gabriel de Vere. Though Juliana expects to feel revulsion and pain in the arms of the blackheart responsible for her husband's impotence, she discovers a man of passion and honor.

When Gabriel de Vere learns that the sensual lover who had come to him in darkness is the wife of his enemy, he vows to take back the child stolen from him. Yet something about the woman he abducts turns him from vengeance. But the flower of their love will have to be carefully nurtured if they are to triumph over Lord Bernart and raise the child of their love as fate has intended.

___4855-8 $5.99 US/$6.99 CAN

Dorchester Publishing Co., Inc.
P.O. Box 6640
Wayne, PA 19087-8640

Please add $2.50 for shipping and handling for the first book and $.75 for each book thereafter. NY, NYC, and PA residents, please add appropriate sales tax. No cash, stamps, or C.O.D.s. All orders shipped within 6 weeks via postal service book rate. Canadian orders require $2.50 extra postage and must be paid in U.S. dollars through a U.S. banking facility.

Name_____
Address_____
City_____ State_____ Zip _____
I have enclosed $ _____ in payment for the checked book(s).
Payment <u>must</u> accompany all orders. ❑ Please send a free catalog.
CHECK OUT OUR WEBSITE! www.dorchesterpub.com

SAVAGE SPIRIT

CASSIE EDWARDS

Winner of the *Romantic Times* Lifetime Achievement Award for Best Indian Series!

Life in the Arizona Territory has prepared Alicia Cline to expect the unexpected. Brash and reckless, she dares to take on renegades and bandidos. But the warm caresses and soft words of an Apache chieftain threaten her vulnerable heart more than any burning lance.

Chief Cloud Eagle has tamed the wild beasts of his land, yet one glimpse of Alicia makes him a slave to desire. Her snow-white skin makes him tremble with longing; her flame-red hair sets his senses ablaze. Cloud Eagle wants nothing more than to lie with her in his tepee, nothing less than to lose himself in her unending beauty. But to claim Alicia, the mighty warrior will first have to capture her bold savage spirit.

_3639-8 $4.99 US/$5.99 CAN

APACHE CONQUEST

THERESA SCOTT

Bestselling Author of *Forbidden Passion*

Sent to the New World to wed a stranger, beautiful young Carmen is prepared to love the man her uncle has chosen. But on the trail to Sante Fe, a recklessly virile half-breed Indian sets her blood afire, tempting her to forget her betrothed. And though Puma has suffered greatly at the hands of the Spanish, he vows to do anything, to defy anyone to make the fiery senorita his own.

_3471-9 $4.99 US/$5.99 CAN

LOVE A REBEL...
LOVE A ROGUE
SHIRL HENKE

"A fascinating slice of history and equally fascinating characters! Enjoy!"
—Catherine Coulter

Quintin Blackthorne will bow before no man. He dares to despise his father and defy his king, but a mutinous beauty overwhelms the American patriot with a rapturous desire he cannot deny.

Part Indian, part white, and all trouble, Devon Blackthorne will belong to no woman—until a silky seductress tempts him with a passion both reckless and irresistible.

The Blackthorne men—one highborn, one half-caste—are bound by blood, but torn apart by choice. Caught between them, two sensuous women long for more than stolen moments of wondrous splendor. But as the lovers are swept from Savannah's ballrooms to Revolutionary War battlefields, they learn that the faithful heart can overcome even the fortunes of war.

3673-8 $4.99 US/$5.99 CAN

Dorchester Publishing Co., Inc.
65 Commerce Road
Stamford, CT 06902

Please add $1.75 for shipping and handling for the first book and $.50 for each book thereafter. NY, NYC, PA and CT residents, please add appropriate sales tax. No cash, stamps, or C.O.D.s. All orders shipped within 6 weeks via postal service book rate. Canadian orders require $2.00 extra postage and must be paid in U.S. dollars through a U.S. banking facility.

Name _____
Address _____
City _____ State _____ Zip _____
I have enclosed $_____ in payment for the checked book(s).
Payment <u>must</u> accompany all orders. □ Please send a free catalog.

A lady does not attempt to come out in London society disguised as her deceased half-sister. A lady does not become enamored of her guardian, even though his masterful kisses and whispered words of affection tempt her beyond all endurance. A lady may not climb barefoot from her bedroom on a rose trellis, nor engage in fisticuffs with riffraff in order to rescue street urchins. No matter how impossible the odds, a lady always gives her hand and her heart—though not necessarily in that order—to the one man who sees her as she truly is and loves her despite her flagrant disobedience of every one of the rules for a lady.

___4818-3 $4.99 US/$5.99 CAN

Dorchester Publishing Co., Inc.
P.O. Box 6640
Wayne, PA 19087-8640

Please add $2.50 for shipping and handling for the first book and $.75 for each book thereafter. NY, NYC, and PA residents, please add appropriate sales tax. No cash, stamps, or C.O.D.s. All orders shipped within 6 weeks via postal service book rate. Canadian orders require $2.00 extra postage and must be paid in U.S. dollars through a U.S. banking facility.

Name_____
Address_____
City_____ State_____ Zip_____
I have enclosed $ _____in payment for the checked book(s).
Payment <u>must</u> accompany all orders.☐Please send a free catalog.
CHECK OUT OUR WEBSITE! www.dorchesterpub.com

"Each new Connie Mason book is a prize!"
—Heather Graham

Spirits can be so bloody unpredictable, and the specter of Lady Amelia is the worst of all. Just when one of her ne'er-do-well descendents thought he could go astray in peace, the phantom lady always appears to change his wicked ways.

A rogue without peer, Jackson Graystoke wants to make gaming and carousing in London society his life's work. And the penniless baronet would gladly curse himself with wine and women—if Lady Amelia would give him a ghost of a chance.

Fresh off the boat from Ireland, Moira O'Toole isn't fool enough to believe in legends or naive enough to trust a rake. Yet after an accident lands her in Graystoke Manor, she finds herself haunted, harried, and hopelessly charmed by Black Jack Graystoke and his exquisite promise of pure temptation.

_4041-7 $5.99 US/$6.99 CAN